FATE'S HAND

T0243971

DARREN PEARCE

Published by Outland Entertainment LLC
3119 Gillham Road, Kansas City, MO 64109

CEO & Publisher: Jeremy D. Mohler
Editor-in-Chief: Alana Joli Abbott
COO & Games Director: Anton Kromoff

Paperback ISBN: 978-1-954255-88-3
Ebook ISBN: 978-1-954255-90-6

Worldwide Rights
Created in the United States of America

Editor: Scott Colby
Copy Editor: Alana Joli Abbott
Cover Illustration: Ann Marie Cochran
Cover Design: Jeremy D. Mohler
Interior Layout: Jeremy D. Mohler

Printed and bound in the United States of America.

Visit outlandentertainment.com to see more, or follow us on our facebook Page facebook.com/outlandentertainment/

PROLOGUE

AN UNUSUAL BIRTHDAY GIFT

A white bird cascaded down through the air, wings pulled tightly in, and eyes firmly fixed on the prize below: fat, juicy, fish. A sudden explosion of super-heated air and the whine of a turbine engine knocked the seagull away from its flight path, sending it squawking off into the nearby rocky crevice to sulk and sit moodily. The bird had no desire to share the same airspace with the metallic behemoth that broke cloud cover over the port.

The vessel bore the mark and insignia of the Church of Progression—the One-Eyed Cog of the Infinite Machine—and the tell-tale red and gold of the Cardinal herself. To the seagull, it was just another metal interloper in a speckled blue and white sky, with clouds hanging pensively over the western edges of jagged, sharp rocks.

To the people below, the vessel marked the arrival of saviors and the protectors of their little town, Sullavale Port, a minor fishing locale perched on the western shoreline of the Raven's Claw Reef. As the sleek ship's pleasing lines and curves tilted over the edge of the land, it cast a deep shadow across the ground below and startled a flock of wild sheep.

Upon the observation deck of this magnificent, dart-like wonder stood two figures, one clad in the purple raiment of a senior Inquisitor and instructor of the church. The other was a Scribe, her subordinate, dressed in flat grey.

The woman in purple pulled her long, black hair into a braid and expertly piled it atop her head. She cast her gaze to the man at her side.

"Are you sure Seaborne is here?"

"Our spies reported he arrived only a few hours before we did. He has no idea we are tracking him, and he certainly has no idea he's been sold out by someone he implicitly trusted." The man tugged at his beard and tapped a finger idly on the metallic rail before him.

"Excellent, Scribe Prentiss." The woman nodded and allowed him to see a thin line of a smile before it vanished behind her habitually flat expression. "Verity once again proves her usefulness."

"Inquisitor Lin." Prentiss looked nervously behind him, as though a snake were about to sink its fangs into his neck. "Do you think the lad will be up for it?"

"Kalon?" She shrugged. "Knowing what you do of the young man in my care—what do you think?"

Scribe Prentiss chewed on his bottom lip, appearing to be mentally checking off a list of things in his mind's eye. Inquisitor Lin watched him, hawk-like, for a moment and waited to see if he'd answer her.

"Well..." Prentiss began.

"Deep, usually full of water."

"Droll."

"I try," Lin chuckled softly, the mirth almost breaking the surface of her voice—but not quite. She was always more stoic when on official business. "Do you have an answer?"

"The variables are so complex; one could take months putting the right equations together in one's head to sufficiently calculate the outcome," Prentiss continued, caught up on the minutiae of the question. "A simple yes seems it might suffice."

"There, it wasn't that hard now, was it?"

"For a man like me, who is ruled by tiny numbers and equations—all factors must be considered, otherwise I cannot give a full and detailed answer." He tapped his fingers together as if counting off items with his right hand.

Inquisitor Lin took pity on the man for a moment. She watched him center himself and take a few deep breaths. "I am sorry, Scribe Prentiss; I did not mean to cause you discomfort."

"I have a compulsion to focus on the tiny things, Inquisitor. It can be overwhelming at times." Prentiss barely smiled as he looked out of the window. "There are exactly thirty-seven seagulls in the air, three on the roof on the right, and two more on the roof on the left. Six seagulls are circling that boat near the shore. There is one on the reef, somewhat disturbed by our arrival."

"Impressive. Your observational skills are second to none." Lin nodded and then answered Prentiss's previous question. "Yes, Kalon will do well. He is special—one of the only recruits I have ever seen embrace the Dogma of Progression from day one. He almost seems born to it, and he has the attention of our Cardinal."

"So much in such a short time. How old was he when the fire claimed his parents? Eight?"

"Yes, just eight. It was his birthday."

"Happy Birthday to him, saved by the Church of Progression." Prentiss smiled.

Lin's expression was more predatory. "Yes, saved by the church."

"He's, what, fifteen now?"

"Yes," Lin pondered and nodded. "Today would have been his fifteenth birthday, if the church celebrated such archaic concepts."

Prentiss nodded. To him, it always seemed sad that such things were put aside by the Church of Progression, but as a pragmatist and someone who valued his own survival over poking a hornet's nest, he declined to ask the reason why.

As the ship nosed down to the ground and settled above the gate to the port, tufts of grass were charred by the engine exhaust. The vessel was a wonder of tech-magis, the combination of magic and technology purely owned and operated by the Church of Progression and those who held a writ of operation signed by Vincent Daroni—the chief inventor of the church and master of the art.

"We've arrived," Lin said and turned to the door. "Let us collect our charge and see if we can't seal Seaborne's fate."

"Must he die?"

"Yes," Inquisitor Lin confirmed with a final snap of her head, lifting her gaze to meet Prentiss's own. "He has been using magic without the permission of the church, spreading heresy and putting everyone in danger."

"Even simple hedge magic must be dealt with?"

"Yes," she snapped harshly, followed by a dogmatic nod fueled by the rote learning of an Inquisitor and the purity of someone loyal to the church. "A small spell could allow one of the demon-kind in, and this town would be infested before we could stop it."

"By the One-Eyed Cog-God...I had no idea."

"This is why you are a Scribe, and I am an Inquisitor."

"True, the hierarchy must be maintained as they say." Prentiss's head bobbed in assent, his expression and demeanour those of a scolded child as he shuffled his feet from side to side.

"Come. The longer we delay here, the further our quarry slips from our fingers." With a flick of her purple long-coat she strode away from the rail and into the corridor. Prentiss followed behind her, admonished and silent for the moment.

The port was crowded as usual. Waifs, strays, vagabonds, and all kinds of travelers came to Sullavale Port, some by boat, some by carriage, and some—those who could afford the luxury—by such conveyances as the airships that often dotted the sky throughout Hestonia. The port was a melting pot for all kinds of people, and a mix of every skin color and creed flitted through the streets. Men strode arm in arm, women kissed under the sunshade of a nearby café doorway, and children laughed as they played with animals under the watchful eye of their parents.

Lord Ryan Seaborne tried his best to blend in. He'd sold off his clothes earlier and adopted the dowdier garb of the common folk. He muddied up his face a little and reeked of Sul bass, a local delicacy that made his stomach churn. He was not a well man; nights of little to no sleep as he played cat and mouse with the church's spies and hunters had taken their toll.

The arrival of an airship that belonged to the church sent him into a panic, so he weaved and bobbed through the market. He stopped to examine a juicy apple and took a moment to look around, suspiciously eyeing every single person as though they all carried a hidden knife. He narrowly avoided a man and a woman kissing in the shadow of a nearby stall.

"Bloody Amadis," he muttered. "I was drunk. How was I to know she'd tell the sodding church that I could cast magic? It was a blasted single flicker, a point of light," he growled under his breath as he pulled his cloak about him and popped a coin into a tray. "Keep the change," he snarled. "Oh wait, you can't because there won't be any. Daylight robbery for an apple—a silver—bloody cheek."

The swarthy faced shopkeeper narrowed his eyes, took the money, and snorted. "You'll want to keep your voice down. Talking to yourself, especially about magic, could get you killed."

"Not as though it is any of your business, but I thank you for the unsolicited advice and warning—good day, sir!" Seaborne stormed off. He was having a hard time adjusting to life on the run, without his hangers-on, his lackeys, servants, and trappings. His former life afforded him certain leeway that the common folk simply did not have.

The shopkeeper made a rude gesture involving a pair of upwardly v-turned fingers at the ex-nobleman's back. Then he went about his business as Seaborne melted off into the throngs of people.

"Cheek of the man," Seaborne mumbled. "Me, a lord no less, and him a petty apple-peddler."

He shoved his way forward, elbowed a pair of women out of the way, knocked their basket of eggs to the floor, and raged on past. They stared after him open-mouthed and aghast, then one by one they put the eggs back into the basket—all save for those ruined on the cobbles at their feet.

"Hey!" one of them called. "You should pay for the eggs you broke, you tramp!"

Seaborne stopped and furiously turned around, only to see a purple gloved hand land on the speaker's shoulder. A soft voice followed with: "Take this silver. The church is only too happy to reimburse you for the loss of your goods."

Scribe Prentiss stepped to one side and gestured the women over. "How many eggs, and what kind were they?"

"Just give the ladies their money, Prentiss. The details do not matter."

"Well, while you argue with women about eggs, I have a ship to catch!" Ryan Seaborne quipped and turned to run. He stopped dead in his tracks as his path was blocked by a tall, fresh-faced youth. The young man was attired in a simple black tunic, coat, breeches, and belt, all only slightly darker than his hair. Notably, he wore a pendant bearing the cog and eye of the church.

"Hello, young man," Seaborne said hesitantly. "Please get out of the way."

A gloved hand raised a pistol in his direction. "Stay," commanded the youth, in a voice like cold iron with no hint of fear. "We have not finished with you yet, Lord Seaborne."

"Tell the whelp to move, Inquisitor, or I'll cut him down where he stands," Seaborne warned, edging his hand toward his sword as he addressed Lin.

The egg-carrying women took their silver and rushed off as Prentiss fretted about the actual cost. He looked at Kalon in the distance and shuddered as the lord made his ultimatum. "This is bad."

Inquisitor Lin watched her charge but did not interfere. She adopted a bystander pose, folded her arms, and said to Prentiss, "Now we see if the lad can do what he has to."

"He will," the Scribe muttered softly. "I can sense it in his voice."

Lord Seaborne looked at the boy before him, sized his opponent up, and thought better of the sword-ploy. After all, the youth had a tech-magis pistol, and those guns were fast. They did not obey the rules of regular, flint-based firearms. He'd be dead before he even got an inch closer to strike.

"You will come with us, or you will die on the spot, here and now," Kalon said with a finality that impressed Inquisitor Lin. "There is no discussion, there is no chance for escape. I ask you to surrender. Failure to comply with this request means death."

"Can he do that?" Prentiss sidled up to Lin.

"I told you, my charge has the attention of the Cardinal. She has a vested interest in him. Not even I know the full extent and means of his training. I was asked to take him with us on the hunt, so here I am. I am here to evaluate him, yes—but for both of us, this is new ground. My orders were clear, though: do not interfere." Lin sounded put out by this last part.

"Oh dear."

"Pardon me for asking," Seaborne said and smiled a little. "But, as much as I know about Inquisitors and the whole church hierarchy—you aren't a Justicar, so you can't shoot me in cold blood before all these witnesses."

The boy answered flatly. "I can."

"Pardon?"

"I can. You are a heretic; you have cast magic and endangered the people of this world. Demons claw at the walls of our dimension, and you dare to even spin a single thread of the Tapestry with your childish weaves." Kalon Rhadon fixed the gun on the man, his finger tightening gently on the trigger. "Magic is heresy unless permitted by the church under the clause three-hundred and thirty-one, sub-section two, paragraph eight."

Prentiss quickly worked that out. "He's right."

"I know." Lin snorted.

"He's quoting the Imper Vatica Doctrine perfectly, as it pertains to Church-sponsored magic, for the benefit of all, protected by seals and equations ratified by Vincent Daroni himself. Who is this boy we've been given?" Prentiss's fear was overridden by his excitement at all this new information.

"I told you, he is special."

Kalon studied the man before him once more. He watched him for any motion at all. The pendant around the young Inquisitor's neck tingled slightly, and he tilted his head to the right, as if listening.

From afar the Cardinal's sugar-smooth tones purred in his ear. *This is your moment, young man—your moment to prove to us and the church how loyal you are. Your opportunity to cast aside childish things and truly become the right hand I know you can be. He will try and bargain, then he will threaten, and then he will hurt you and others with magic—his magic that is not ours, not the church's, not SAFE. He can be given no quarter, no chance, no redemption. In my name, you must kill him for the good of all.*

Ryan Seaborne mistook this for hesitation, for some kind of signal that he might yet escape capture. "Look, boy, I don't know who you are."

"Kalon Rhadon," Kalon said flatly.

"OK. Yes, now I know who you are." Seaborne's tone flickered with irritation for a moment. "I repeat, you are NOT a Justicar. I demand capture. I can offer you names, others like me who use magic to further their own ends." The Cardinal's first words echoed in Kalon's ear as Seaborne spoke.

He will bargain.

"No." Kalon replied, the Cardinal's order firm in his mind.

"No? What do you mean no, you little shit? Do you know who I am? Lord Ryan Seaborne, of the Seabornes...my father will hear of this! He lays the laws that your church beds down with. When word reaches him, you'll be lucky if you don't end up locked in a dungeon and stripped of your rank!"

He will threaten.

"I do not care," Kalon replied and tilted his head again. "You are a heretic."

On the side-lines Lin and Prentiss remained steadfastly silent, observant and impressed. The rest of the port town stood a respectful distance away and watched this scene play out. They had love for the church, and the mere fact that Seaborne had been outed as a spell-flinger wizard sent a wave of revulsion through them.

Ryan Seaborne looked like a land-locked fish. His jaw hung open and then closed as his mouth moved but no words came out. "YOU... DO...NOT...CARE?" he growled finally. "Oh, you'll care when my family puts yours in the gutter, you little dog shit."

Kalon remained quiet.

"No answer. Cat got your tongue, boy? With your dogma and your endless rhetoric of church-spewed bile."

Still no answer. Kalon could not be riled. He would not make a mistake.

"What kind of protectors send a boy out to die in a man's world, eh?" he asked, addressing the crowd. "Are none of your eyes open enough to see the church for what it is? Magic is not heresy; magic should be freely used to better all around it. Not controlled and locked away like a case of explosive chemicals."

The crowd jeered; this did not go as Seaborne expected it to.

Kalon's gun remained level. He locked eyes on the man and kept an unblinking stare fixed on Seaborne until the older lord could not take it any longer.

"Say something!"

Kalon tilted his head.

"If magic is so dangerous...let me go, or these people will suffer." A last-ditch effort by a man driven to extremes by fear. Ryan Seaborne made a huge mistake. He moved his fingers in the first attempt to pull the dancing threads of magic into his presence: part of the Tapestry, part of the spell. "If I finish the final thread of this, you don't know what will happen with the spell. It's chaos—I pulled all the threads at different times. I didn't even care what colors they are. Let me go, or I finish it."

He will hurt you, and others, with magic.

At these threats many in the crowd fled, putting as much distance between them and the errant mage-lord as they could possibly manage in a few short moments. But there were also those who saw the teenager as their protector, and they remained. They had faith that Kalon Rhadon would stop this wizard in his tracks before the foul sorcery could be completed.

They were not wrong.

"Magic is heresy," the teenager said flatly, and then pulled the trigger. One shot rang out, the Tech-magis pistol barking like a murderous hound. The lord rocked backward, and the spell died on his fingertips. A single hole smoked in his forehead, and the back of his skull decorated the cobbles in a pattern of blood and viscera.

The sound of the gun caused the remainder of the crowd to jump, even Prentiss, for in truth he was a far gentler soul than Inquisitor Lin. She looked on impassively, impressed to no end by the boy's first kill at age fifteen. Now she understood why the Cardinal had picked him, why she was so secretive. Something truly interesting had transpired within the boy, and the leader of the Church of Progression was at the forefront of it.

As if detecting her thoughts, the Cardinal's voice echoed in her head now. The amulet that all Inquisitors wore, the cog and eye, vibrated slightly around Lin's slender neck.

See, my dear Lin. He is my right hand, Fate's Hand, the loyal servant and enforcer of the church. The son I never had; the child we wish we could be. His loyalty is unquestioned, his training unparalleled by even the Justicars. A true warrior of the order, a youth now, but a man who will bring balance to the chaos these wizards peddle. I have shaped his path since he came to us, honed him, and ensured his training is like no other's. His bond to us—to me—is, one could say, magical. The Cardinal's soft voice sounded deep in Lin's mind and coiled around her like a lover's embrace. *Bring him back. It is time I told you the destiny of this young man.*

"Yes, my Cardinal," Lin answered and turned her gaze onto Kalon, who she now regarded with more respect than she had in the past. She looked at Prentiss and the dead lord, then back at the crowd. With the air of a practiced diplomat, she fixed her stare onto one of the onlookers, by chance the storekeeper Seaborne had belittled earlier.

"Excuse me," she said to the man. "Might I have a moment of your time sir?"

Not used to being addressed in such a manner, the merchant in question looked behind himself for a moment and then back at her. "Yes, Inquisitor, how can I help?"

"Fetch the port guard for me and see they deal with this body. Here is a token of our appreciation, and remember that the church always looks after their own." She dropped a silver coin into the man's hand—it was a gesture designed to placate the masses and create the right impression in the minds of those who observed it.

It rarely failed.

The storekeeper pocketed the silver, then turned on his heel quickly and vanished into the direction of the port guard house. Meanwhile, Inquisitor Lin walked slowly to the side of her charge and nearly laid a hand upon his shoulder. She thought better of such a familiar gesture and instead settled for a pensive nod.

"Well done, young Inquisitor," she said to Kalon and looked down at the dead man. "He could have doomed us all, even with a simple spell. To pull at the threads with no direction, no thought...it shows you just how dangerous wizards are."

"Yes." Kalon's answer was flat, and he put the gun back in its holster. "This weapon needs adjusting," he said. "The sight is off by two millimeters, and the trigger mechanism is too slow. He nearly completed that spell."

Prentiss appeared at that point. He sought safety at the side of the two people who could protect him. "I can inform Master Daroni of the fault, Inquisitor."

"Yes," Lin nodded. "Kalon's note of this imperfection will ensure future models of the weapon perform better. One small ripple might change the lives of hundreds. Just as his one shot saved the lives of *thousands*."

Kalon shifted his gaze from one speaker to the other as he stood impassively, watchful, alert for any further signs of heresy. His attention was drawn to a hooded girl who watched him from the shadows for a moment, then vanished into the crowd. Kalon knew her: Verity, a fellow trainee at the Imper Vatica and an accomplished student. She spent a lot of time with him and the other youth, Rand. Many of their instructors often called the trio inseparable.

Verity's training always seemed to focus on the shadow-arts, rather than direct confrontation. It was rumored that she would enter the Shadow Knife, the Church Sponsored Assassins, a branch of the Imper Vatica that did its very best to remain hidden.

Kalon's thoughts of Rand seemed to have summoned his friend, because he was sure he saw the youth at the hooded girl's heels as she departed. If Kalon cared at all about such things, he might have wondered if Rand being her shadow alluded to more than the pair being allies in the church—but he didn't bother to think past his initial observation.

Inquisitor Lin followed his look and nodded; she saw Verity depart as well. "Your friend is watching out for you. Good. Bonds like this make our people stronger."

"Verity and Rand. They did not need to do so," he noted.

"Rand as well?"

"Yes."

"I see."

Lin looked around. "We are done here; our orders are to return to the Holy City of Messania at once. Our task is complete, and the Cardinal has expressed a wish to see you." She paused and added, "Rand, you say. He is usually at Verity's side—not unusual to see with young men and women, Kalon."

"As you say. I believe this concludes our task here, and crowds gather thicker than storm clouds," Kalon mused softly and looked in the direction of the vessel outside the port.

"Yes," Lin answered and followed his gaze. "Shall we go?"

Taking this as a sign their talk had ended, Kalon set his path toward the waiting vessel and his meeting with the Cardinal—the heart and soul of the church, and the woman who firmly had the strings of his destiny and fate wrapped around her slender fingers. Inquisitor Lin waited a few moments before following the impassive young man. Prentiss—as always full of worry and concern, and processing too many variables in his head—was the last to fall in line. They left the market with the body of Ryan Seaborne just as the port guard came thundering in from the opposite direction.

The last thing the captain of the guard, Anna Kora, saw as she reached the body was the flash of purple in the distance.

"Bloody hell," she muttered. "We're always the ones left to clean up. All right, you have your orders. Secure the area! Get rid of this corpse, and hop to it!"

She shielded her eyes with her hand, brushed a lock of auburn hair out of the way, and sighed. Wizards. No good ever came of wizards. She'd have to fill in all that paperwork and write a report. Oh, to be an Inquisitor, free of all those drudges—now that was the life.

As she left the market, life in the port carried on. People went about their daily business as though nothing had really happened. The port returned to normal, and while Seaborne's death had shaken some of the folk, they were more disturbed that they had almost perished at the hands of a rogue wizard.

The crowd of humans, kelanari, jakatra, and the snake-like

humanoids known as the sylthen, moved slowly away as the guard captain's men dealt with the aftermath of the church's work.

The Church of Progression had once again proven why it was sorely needed.

Which was exactly what the Cardinal wanted.

CHAPTER 1

THE FATE OF YOUNG KALON

The purr of aetheric engines sounded throughout the church windship. The magnificent vessel bore Inquisitor Lin, Prentiss, and Kalon toward the Holy City of Messania across a sky studded with stars and thin whispers of cloud. The journey from Sullavale to the city took a couple of days. Kalon filled those moments with meditation and study.

He was not quite a fully-fledged Inquisitor yet, but he was on the right path. He knew deep in his soul that his actions a few days ago, monitored by Lin and recorded by Scribe Prentiss, would be judged by Cardinal Terusa, and this would determine his fate in the church.

Kalon was under the supervision of Lin; she shared a cabin with the young man. Her watchful gaze never left him for more than a moment. She took great delight in studying the fledgling's reactions to the world around him and mused on the apparent lack of emotion he had to many things. His behavior was akin to an itch in the back of her head, a mystery she could not let go.

Many would have called it an obsession, but to a woman like Lin, who thrived on riddles and enigmas of the mind, it was just one puzzle more to crack.

"Do you have a moment, young Kalon?" Lin asked, peering over the edge of her book, her glasses tipped downward at the bridge of her nose as she fixed him with a long stare.

Kalon's thin fingers flexed, and he put down his pen to face the woman. "Of course, Inquisitor. What do you wish to discuss?"

"I would like to test some image recognition, play a kind of game."

"I do not have time for games," Kalon said flatly and looked back at the scripture before him.

"It is a training game," Lin countered with a honeyed smile.

"Ah. If this is truly the case, then I will use it to speed the passage of time," Kalon replied, standing. He moved across the cabin and sat next to the woman. "Logically, I presume you wish me to sit here, so that I can see your images more clearly."

Lin blinked and nodded. "Logically, you are correct."

"Begin," he instructed.

Lin took out a thin leather wallet and set down the rectangular cards on the table before her. "Each one of these cards is designed to elicit a response. The game is simple: you tell me what the cards mean to you and the feeling associated with each."

Kalon wrinkled his nose subconsciously. He did not blink. "Go on."

Lin picked up the first card and smiled a little. She placed it face up before the young man and waited. The picture was that of a house, a lovely little cottage surrounded by trees, in many ways similar to where they had found the young boy before he joined the church.

Kalon studied the image. He dissected it with his mind, drew out detail after detail, and made notes where the art failed in some subtle area of architecture. A brick out of place, a reflection from the glass that was unrealistic, and a tree that grew in the wrong direction based on several visual factors. None of these were answers to Lin's question, but he told her of the imperfections regardless.

"The glass is wrong; the light falls in the wrong place. The tree is growing in the wrong direction based on numerous factors found in nature, the branches are too short, the bricks are wrong for that style of building. The picture is good, but it is not perfect." Kalon rattled off these elements as if they were the most important things in the world to him.

"I see." Lin bit her lip slightly. "But how does this house make you feel?"

Kalon studied that word, his mind attempting to pull the definition of feelings from the depths of his brutal, dogmatic, and unusual training at the hands of the church. It was almost there, and then, as if something just ate it from his soul, it flitted away. "It does not," he said finally.

"Moving on." Lin was oddly unsettled by this, flustered even. "Another?"

"If you desire."

She rolled the cards around and selected another one, this time a fire, burning brightly around the same building. In any normal person this might have elicited a response regarding the cottage's destruction.

"Now, how about this one? Anything?"

Kalon looked at it and shook his head. "A waste of resources. The building could have been repurposed, or even torn down and the materials used elsewhere. The trees that surround the house would have been burned down as well. The fire does not touch them." There was a brief tinge of sadness that he did not comment on. It was too fleeting to capture, and again it was gone in seconds. The air between the young man and Inquisitor Lin grew a little colder, and she could see their breath for a moment.

"I must speak to the captain; I think the thermal controls for the cabin are slightly misaligned." Lin said, rationalising what she'd just seen. "So, you feel nothing?"

"I feel as though this is a waste of my time, but perhaps it provides you with useful insight."

"I...well...yes it does." Lin bit her lip again. "Your training at the church was very specialised, wasn't it?"

"I cannot speak to you about this. You know the rule." Kalon replied with a curt nod. "Cardinal's orders."

Inquisitor Lin was about to reply when the internal speaker on the ship buzzed to life. It broke the moment and she sighed with relief.

The voice of an older man crackled across the communication array. "People aboard the ship, this is your captain speaking: we are about to enter the Imper Vatica's airspace. Secure all belongings and prepare to depart."

"Good, a timely arrival—and a punctual one at that," Kalon said and returned to his desk with a swift motion. He gathered all his things, packed every bit of his writing equipment away into a leather satchel, and left nothing at all behind.

As the ship settled down on the ironwood landing pad deep within the confines of the Holy City, the Imper Vatica, a vast and city-like complex at the center of Messania, gouts of steam and heat emanated from the cooling vents and made the vessel appear as if it were alive. The ramp lowered, and Prentiss, Lin, and Kalon disembarked.

A couple of dock workers sat nearby. They chatted idly, sharing a flask full of a dark tea, and looked up as the three church agents alighted on the platform. The men shared a quick kiss, and the taller of the two, dressed in the uniform of a mechanic, made his way past the trio and to the side of the ship. His practiced eye roved the hull for signs of wear and tear.

"Kalon Rhadon, come with me to the Cardinal. She is eager to meet you," Inquisitor Lin said to the young man and looked then to Prentiss. "Scribe," she said gently, "report to the Hall of Records and ensure the mission is logged to the best of your ability."

Prentiss offered a solemn smile and bowed to both before he headed off deeper into the sanctum, toward the safety of books and parchment where he could be at peace among literature and numeracy to his heart's content.

Kalon and Lin took a different door out of the docking bay. This fed into a long corridor, where people milled about on missions of their own. One of them, a short-haired young woman with glasses, moved to one side, expertly piloting her wheelchair with a swift flick of her hands. She smiled at Lin when she saw the Inquisitor, then studied the woman's charge for a moment.

"Inquisitor Lin!" she said with an impish smile, adjusting her glasses. "How're you?"

"I'm good, Sara." Lin paused, thought for a moment, and nodded to herself. "This is Kalon Rhadon, soon to be *Inquisitor* Kalon

Rhadon." She gestured to the figure by her side. "He's just returned from his first mission."

Sara stuck out her hand and offered a cheerful greeting, "Hey, I'm pleased to meet you, Kalon."

Kalon's flint-colored eyes regarded Sara as he replied in a formal manner. "I am pleased as well." Then, as protocol dictated, he shook the young woman's hand. "What is it you do at the church?"

Sara let Kalon's hand go and returned her own to rest on her chair. She looked up at the pair and pondered, answering absently. "A bit of this and that, mostly assisting Master Daroni in his workshop. I'm an inventor, a mechanic, and a designer—I planned and built this chair, for example. It's a mark one version, but it's brilliant and handles different terrain better than the civilian standard models. Later I'm going to make one for combat, but that'll need a lot of testing and...I'm not boring you, am I?"

Kalon shook his head. "Inventor and mechanic to Master Vincent Daroni is an impressive station indeed."

"Thank you." The young woman beamed a little.

"Might I ask you to look at something of mine?" Kalon withdrew his field agent issue tech-magis pistol, adjudicator model, and offered it to the young woman. "I believe the trigger can be improved, and the sight might be off by a small margin."

Inquisitor Lin watched this exchange impassively. They were ahead of schedule, and regardless of the time this took, she could use the opportunity to study Kalon in a social situation she had never seen him in.

Sara took the gun and turned it over and over in her hands. She felt the metal, sensing the magic intrinsic in the weapon, and popped her glasses into her pocket. She took out a monocle and set that in place over her right eye. Then she began to examine the gun more closely, humming and making tiny comments softly as she studied the features of the weapon.

"I think I can see the problem. May I fix it?"

"Be my guest." Kalon folded his arms—not to show impatience, but because he found the position comfortable.

Sara took out her tools, everything from micro-measuring

equipment to tiny screwdrivers. She folded a tray out from the side of the chair and laid it across her lap, then opened an ornate wooden case that contained her beloved tools. In seconds, she began to work on the intricate and deadly weapon. The pair observed her in the corridor as she worked, and Lin noted the young woman's concentration was unbreakable.

After half an hour, she stowed her tools into the box, each in its correct place, and set the gun down on her table. "Done."

Kalon inclined his head. "May I?"

"Of course," she smiled. "It's yours, and I think I managed to fix the issue."

"Excellent." He reached down and scooped the weapon up in his black gloved hands, turned it over and over, lifted it to sight along the empty corridor, and nodded. "You have improved the sight; I will take it to the range later to test the efficacy of your trigger modifications. All in all, impressive." Kalon stowed the gun and then returned to his cross-armed pose. "You have my thanks, Sara."

"Forgive us. We must leave you now, my dear," Lin said with a half-smile and looked down the corridor. "By now Cardinal Terusa will have learned of our arrival, and we need to meet with her."

Sara, still blushing a little from Kalon's praise, nodded. "Oh, don't let me keep you. It was nice meeting you, Kalon."

Nice was a word that Kalon knew but did not fully understand. In truth, there were bigger reasons, but the young man had no idea why the word made sense, even though he could not feel the meaning. "Yes, it was," he said with a curt nod. "Inquisitor, lead on."

Sara closed the tool case, listened to the click, and slipped the tray back into the holding position. She put her glasses back on and wheeled off in another direction, down a second corridor deeper into the Imper Vatica. Her hands tingled from the feel of the tech-magis weapon, and her mind whirled with ideas on how to improve the gun. She was determined to talk to Master Daroni about this. With a last turn of her head to watch Kalon and Lin leave her sight, she rolled on, quite pleased with the encounter.

The Cardinal waited in one of her many chambers—not her private quarters this time. A less ostentatious meeting place served as Terusa's first proper encounter with the young man she had a vested interest in.

It was a simple room, still lavish by commoner standards, and the roaring log fire warmed the muted tones of brown and gold quite nicely. She adjusted her hood in the mirror before her and set a choker around her neck—engraved with the cog and eye of her order—then looped another necklace, set with a gorgeous, faceted ruby, at her collar bones. She studied the reflection of her naked body, taking in all the beauty and blemishes of her soft, golden-toned skin. Her corn-colored locks tumbled about her like a gilded waterfall. A tall woman, she stood just shy of six feet. She turned a few times to regard her form.

Her body told a story through several scars from her past. Hard won battles, nicks from her brother's less-than-playful sword instruction, and muscles gained from her own training at the Church of Progression. Her striking blue eyes held mischief, set in an impish face that shone with intelligence and cunning.

The sibilant voice of the One God of the Infinite Machine filled the room and wrapped her in seductive, honey-drenched tones.

"I am pleased with you, my Cardinal. You alone understand the task set before us. You alone know the danger that the unshackled wizards pose to this world. You alone can fix the damage done to Hestonia by these Anshada renegades over a thousand years ago. You are my weapon in the war to control magic and bring these creatures to heel."

The Cardinal nodded solemnly. "Our task is great, One Eye; I fear I am not up to it."

"You have aid," the voice soothed. "Kalon Rhadon is your right hand in this—or will be. He is marked by Fate."

"Fate's Hand," mused the Cardinal. "I like this, the name, the idea. Tell me more of what I must do?"

"I guide; I do not command," the voice assured her. "I am unlike the Demon King. I only ask that you turn your eyes to me and listen.

Kalon is a child of two bloods. His mother, the Anshada witch; his father, such a diligent soul of the church."

"What must I do?"

"Let me show you in your mind's eye the plan I suggest, the plan that will save this world and create for us the perfect servant who will be your Right Hand of Fate and Justice." The soft voice whispered into every corner of Terusa's mind as she began to put on her gold and red robes. "Behold."

What she saw as she dressed pleased her—it pleased her to the core. The voice of her god laid out a plan so clear, so perfect, and so flawless it could only come from the One God of the Infinite Machine. As she tightened the belt over her robes, she heard a knock in the other room, and a slow smile spread onto her thin crimson lips.

"Thank you, my lord."

The voice was silent, but she sensed the One-Eyed Cog God approved.

Terusa left the mirror and swept into the main chamber. She picked up a pair of rings and set them on her fingers before she reached the door. She paused halfway, smoothed down the hem of her skirt, and said, "Enter."

The door opened, and in walked Inquisitor Lin, followed by Kalon Rhadon, who offered a formal bow and then remained at a respectful distance from the Cardinal. He folded his hands behind his back and set his weight onto his heels. From that point on he remained like a statue, stock still.

Lin approached Terusa and bowed before her. The Inquisitor paused and looked over her shoulder. "We came as quickly as we were able."

The Cardinal looked at the young man and back at the Inquisitor. "Welcome. At long last, Kalon Rhadon in the flesh. I have been watching you, young man. Your rise to power in the church has been—well, one could say meteoric."

Kalon did not correct her; meteors did not rise, they fell. "A pleasure, Cardinal Terusa," he said flatly.

"Oh my, he is formal, isn't he?" She chuckled softly and smiled at Lin. "Did he do well?"

"Better than I expected, in all elements. Prentiss has the full report, but here's mine, simple as it is: Kalon is one of our most talented students, next to the older Inquisitor candidates, Rand and Verity. I foresee a great Inquisitor in this one."

Cardinal Terusa shook her head and pursed her lips. "Oh, no, Kalon is more than a mere Inquisitor. It is time that I discuss with you a new position, Lin, something that we must talk about in my office—privately."

Kalon listened impassively. His eyes never left the women, and he continued to stand regimentally still.

Inquisitor Lin nodded, hoping this was related to her earlier mind-talk with Terusa. She looked at Kalon. "You are released, Kalon. Go about your duties until the Cardinal has need of you once more."

"Goodbye, Kalon Rhadon. We shall speak again soon." Terusa offered the young man a bow and gestured that Lin should follow her.

Kalon returned the bow politely, and then addressed Lin. "If you need me, I will be in the test range. I am going to test Sara's adjustments to my gun."

Lin nodded and watched the door close behind the youth. She blinked a couple of times; his formality at such a young age, with none of the fire of a teenager, always took her aback. She locked the door behind the young man, then swiftly followed the Cardinal into the other room.

"An intense young man," Terusa noted, chuckling softly. "How much do you know of him, or his parents?"

"There was a fire," Lin recalled. "An accident. Something caused by the parents?"

"The common knowledge." Terusa poured herself wine and held the glass to the light. "This is what we had to tell the people, and even our closest allies. In truth, his father and mother were very good friends of ours until their son was born. He was born with demon blood—he's half Anshada, that one."

Lin's face fell, and she took a deep breath, more to steady herself rather than convey any kind of surprise. "Why is he still alive?"

"The One-Eyed Cog God desires it." Terusa took a sip of wine and moved to the window. She closed the curtains with the pulley mechanism. "Kalon's mother was Anshada, and his father was a loyal servant of the church. Their deaths came as a shock, but we rescued Kalon before the flames could consume him. Disturbing events I will not recount; suffice it to say that we were right to do so."

"A half-Anshada is like having a bomb among us," Lin said, panic in her voice. "Do not the teachings of the church warn of such folly?"

"I *am* the church," Terusa replied coolly. "Kalon is important to me. I made sure his Anshada blood could not harm us. The One God of the Infinite Machine ensured this was possible, for he gave me the means to do so." She tapped the medallion around her neck with a slender finger.

Lin sat down on a small chair and wrapped her fingers together. "Terusa…what? How? You speak as though the god directs your actions."

"Does he not direct us all every day?"

"I don't know. I have prayed many times, and he is yet to answer." Lin sighed and looked at the sign around the Cardinal's neck.

"Do you trust him?"

"It goes without question, my Cardinal."

"Good, do you trust me?"

"Yes."

"Do you serve me?" Terusa swirled her wine and canted her head slightly to the right.

"Of course, I serve you and the god. You have my trust and faith." Lin knew better than to question the church; she'd heard the stories of those who did and those who fell out of Terusa's favor. "Nothing gives me greater pleasure."

Terusa nodded, pleased, and she set the glass down on her desk. "Return to Kalon. Train him. Push him harder than anyone you have ever pushed before in your life. I want him honed, I want him coldly logical, and I want him to be our instrument of punishment for all wizards who oppose the church. I want my Fate's Hand to be uncompromising and ready to act at a moment's notice against demon or mortal."

Lin blinked, just the once. "Fate's Hand. It's fitting."

"I think so." Terusa moved back to the window. "Go, then, and enact our will with the boy."

Lin stood up and bowed. "Of course, it will be so, Cardinal." She left the chamber quickly, ignoring the questions flying around her skull.

Terusa watched her go and nodded to herself. "I hope I did well, my lord."

"You did…perfectly," the voice answered, and a soft chuckle snuck behind the reply. "The die is cast; the Hand of Fate will soon move all before him to sweep aside our enemies."

The Cardinal smiled softly and sat down in her chair. Everything was going to plan as ordained by her god, the One-Eyed Cog God of the Infinite Machine and Master of the Eternal Engine. She picked up her glass, drank the contents down, and settled back to plan some more.

Kalon Rhadon would be like no other in her church. His power would be next to hers, and she would make the wizards tremble at the mere utterance of the name Fate's Hand.

CHAPTER 2

LESSONS

Within the Church of Progression, there were just as many trials for its agents as there were branches. The church was like a giant tree in the center of the Holy City, and the Inquisitors were just one of its many boughs.

Fate had turned her eyes on several people in the order that day, casting a long and lingering glance over Kalon, Verity, and the slightly older Rand, three youths separated by their roles within the organization. Kalon, earmarked for a brutal and comprehensive regimen unlike any to enter the church. Verity, given over to the church by her scheming brothel-owning Aunt Doria at an early age. And Rand, the closest person that Kalon could potentially call a friend, and perhaps a boy with a deeper relationship to Verity than either dared admit. The son of a farmer and a seamstress, Rand entered the church at an early age and excelled at marksmanship, enigmas, and oratory. He had a good heart, and often attempted to find the good in most people and situations.

Out of the three of them, Kalon's reputation would quickly grow above the others. Even though he was trained in the Imper Vatica, he would often embark on missions in the Holy City, directed by the Cardinal and overseen by a senior Inquisitor, or even a Seeker, such as the incomparable Winter. The people would refer to him as

Fate's Hand, his title, making him the talk of the city, and as wagging tongues whispered in shady alleys, the youth's uncompromising manner would become firmer.

People spoke in hushed tones about the youth who took no prisoners. These stories began to grow in stature, and they also took flight elsewhere. From the lips of a talkative gossip, to the ears of a passing air-ship trader, to the next port of call. So it was, in a game of Hestonian Whispers, that Fate's Hand became better known across the land, even as far as Wyrden itself.

This was how legends grew, and it suited the Cardinal perfectly.

Kalon, Fate's Hand. Verity, a Shadow Knife, otherwise known as a Church Sponsored Assassin. And finally, Rand, who was either to become an Inquisitor or a Justicar.

There were many years before this would happen, many lessons to learn in the meantime, and that day was no different. It began with Kalon's meeting with the Cardinal and his return to the training halls deep inside the Imper Vatica.

Kalon could soon be found at the shooting range, a place he liked to retreat to and hone his skill with the firearms provided to him by Quartermaster Sati. The older woman watched the fledgling Inquisitor as he took up his place. He let off a few shots, and she tutted at the back of her throat. There were things wrong with how he held the gun, for a start.

Kalon cocked his head and fired the tech-magis pistol. Sara's adjustments to the weapon were impressive—especially since she had not been afforded time to use her fully-equipped workshop. The shots hit the target in the right place, and the young man wrinkled his nose. "I still have to compensate for some drift."

The quartermaster adjusted her sari and made her way elegantly down to the podium, just as Verity and Rand both came in from opposite side of the room.

"It looks like we have a full house," the woman said, and her kohl-rimmed eyes sparkled with amusement when she saw Verity and Rand quickly unlink hands. "You three seem to be inseparable, and one wonders if anything at all could break your bond."

Both Verity and Rand blushed. Rand's dark mahogany skin made it harder to detect subtle changes in tone, but his expression told the quartermaster all she needed to know. "We do not frown on such entanglements here at the church," Sati said gently. "Be young. Be careful though."

Kalon fired three more times before the quartermaster's soft hand landed atop the gun. "You are holding the firearm too tightly. These pistols are not prone to so much recoil. One thing that Master Daroni eliminated early on in this design was the kick from a regular propelled round. This is tech-magis; it requires a lover's touch, lad—not a stranglehold."

Verity and Rand moved over to stand close by and observed Sati as she adjusted Kalon's posture, his grip, and his sight line. She took a lot of time to explain her reasoning for the changes, and then nodded once the young man had been posed.

"Now try."

Kalon wrinkled his nose again and nodded. He kept the exact sight line and fired three more shots. They landed one after the other dead-center of the target, and the hole grew progressively bigger. He made a mental note of this impromptu lesson and turned to look at the woman.

"Impressive. Your lesson is a valuable one."

"Thank you, Kalon Rhadon." She almost chuckled at this. "I always say that anything you learn, good or bad, is valuable in some way."

"Those are wise words, quartermaster. Maybe one day Kalon will actually listen." Rand grinned from ear to ear, his friendly jibe totally lost on his stoic friend. "Right, Kalon?" he added, grinning again.

"I am listening," Kalon replied with a quirk of his brow. He studied the gun again and took aim once more.

Rand's face fell a little, but Verity gave his hand a little squeeze and spoke. "You know how Kalon is. You'd think he was married to the church."

Sati shook her head. "Have you come for any reason, young agents?"

"Oh, yes," Verity nodded swiftly. "I wanted to show Rand how to shoot, and he claimed he was a better shot than I was."

"Ah, a competition."

"Yeah."

"Kalon, you going to join us?" Rand asked softly.

"No." Kalon shook his head. "Such frivolity is a waste of time. Only training can hone the skill. Competition breeds resentment."

Verity and Rand were about to offer a reply, but the door to the chamber snapped open suddenly. Two figures entered, one in purple, and the other in a voluminous grey-colored long coat. White hair flowed down from under the brim of an expansive wide-brimmed hat. Her eyes were hidden behind round-rimmed spectacles balanced on a snow-white nose.

"I will return after I have attended to this matter, Miss Flynn," Inquisitor Lin said to the woman in the hat. "Please excuse me for a while."

"Of course," Reva Flynn answered with a nasal reply. "I will be right here."

Lin nodded and breezed straight over to Sati. She gave the quartermaster a small, polite bow and fixed her eyes on Fate's Hand. "Kalon," she addressed him. "Come with me. Your lessons have changed. Orders from the Cardinal. You are going to be pushed to special training."

Rand and Verity exchanged glances, and then Verity spoke up. "Inquisitor Lin, what does special training mean?"

Sati shook her head and smiled at the girl. "I am not sure my colleague can answer your question right now."

Reva watched all this from her position just to the right of another gun range. Her nose wrinkled at the smell of gunpowder and oil.

Lin pursed her lips and replied, "It means that Kalon will see less of you both for the weeks to come, but when you meet him again, he will have become something far more than he ever was. He will be more than a mere Inquisitor," she bragged, and her lips turned upward in a wicked smile. "The Cardinal has instructed me to oversee his training in this regard, personally."

Kalon stood there impassively, then put the gun away and turned to face Lin with a flat expression. "I will see you and Rand at some point, Verity." He looked at the woman, made a mental note of her and her albinism, and filed the name Reva Flynn away in his mind.

"See you later then, Kalon. We'll miss you," Rand said and sighed softly. "Ok, Verity, let's do this!"

Lin turned on her heel. Her cloak swished, and she beckoned Kalon to follow. He bowed to all and left in the wake of the senior Inquisitor.

"She enjoyed that far too much," Sati sighed softly and turned to watch the young pair. "Now, I want a fair competition, and no putting the other contestant off!"

"I would never do that," Verity pouted mischeviously in Rand's direction. "Would I?"

"I often think of this place in regard to the saying my dad used to tell me, which I adopted." Rand's eyes narrowed a little at a memory. "'Never take your coat off here, young man,' he'd say. 'Why, dad?' I'd ask. 'Because it's impossible due to all the knives in your back.'"

Verity put her hands on her hips. "So rude." Then she snapped a quick shot off before anyone could stop her. "One to me!"

"Hey!"

Reva chuckled at Rand's saying, watching the rest of the gunplay from where she stood, but only after she'd also kept an eye on the youth leaving in the company of Inquisitor Lin.

After catching Rand's words, Kalon closed the door behind him and caught up with Lin. He had no desire to ask questions. He had been ordered, and as a dutiful son of the church, he obeyed without question.

In the days, weeks, months, and years that followed, Kalon was trained. His lessons were harsh, brutal, and unforgiving. His body, mind, and spirit were subjected to incredible hardships, and he only saw his friends once or twice a month during designated breaks. As Verity and Rand grew closer, Kalon grew more and more distant. He became like a logical machine, doing the church's bidding with a pin-point focus.

He learned the innermost workings of the Church of Progression; he drank in information on Hestonia's past and how the order came to be. He was taught to fight with specialized weapons, given lessons on the operation of supernatural equipment. His arsenal was provided by Master Vincent Daroni and the newly appointed Master Artificer, Sara, with the aid of the aforementioned Reva Flynn, an artificer and inventor herself, and an apothecary. He came to know the pale woman more in passing than any deeper bond of friendship.

From a youth of fifteen summers, he grew to a man of over forty, stoic, ruthless, and a perfect servant of the church. His training removed all joyous pursuit, snuffed out by the regimen and the dogma he endured. He matured into a man with a level head and a brilliant mind honed razor-sharp by the now aging Inquisitor Lin.

As Kalon matured, the world around him changed. Hestonia grew ever darker. Demonic influence grew across the globe, and demons were sighted in regions they had not been seen in before. Rumors and whispers of the Anshada cult's resurgence flew in and out of the church like birds.

The Cardinal consolidated her power and provided a solution, and the people grew to praise the One God of the Infinite Machine over all others. They needed the church more and more each day, turning from the old ways toward a new future promised by technology and magic combined. With this mix, church agents managed to push the demons back out of the cities, for the most part. The tech-magis weapons of old were replaced with new models, and new methods to combat the rise of magic followed in their wake.

This did not sit well with the Young Gods, who brooded in their own dimension and eyed the machinations of the church with jaundiced eyes.

In this changed world, Kalon's final lesson was at hand.

Within the Imper Vatica were many rooms, and all of them served a purpose. This one was a hexagonal chamber fitted with tech-magis lamps that ensured the lighting levels remained comfortable and subdued at all times. The soft tinkle of crystalline wind-chimes filtered into the chamber, alongside the sound of water from the many small fountains that flowed into receptacles around the room.

Kalon sat on the floor of this meditation chamber in his shirt and breeches, barefoot and cross-legged. He reached out with his mind and touched the center of his being. This was the place where he felt most at home. Some of the mystics in the church, those wizards who had been converted to the Church of Progression's dogma by the Cardinal, had been instrumental in these final stages of the man's understanding.

He heard soft footsteps. A slight smell of jasmine and an odd herb wafted into his nostrils. His eyes remained firmly shut, and he inclined his head.

"Kalon," a soft whisper came into his mind. "Magic is a force neither for good nor evil. Unchecked magic is dangerous, as all magic is more dangerous in the hands of those outside the church. Here we can make it safe, turn it into a tool to help the common people, and prevent the destruction of the church by those who would unleash it without oversight."

He nodded. "I hear you."

"Do you understand?"

"I do."

"Open your eyes."

He did so, and before him was the Cardinal, clad in a meditation robe of gold and red, her long golden hair pulled into a single plait and looped over her shoulder. She had not aged a day since they last met; it seemed like she had been granted eternal life by the power of the god she served.

"Cardinal." Kalon bowed his head once more.

She sat before him and put her hands on his shoulders. "This is the final lesson, Kalon. My spirit form here is going to share with you the underlying secret of our universe."

"An impressive feat, Cardinal, to appear so solid as a spirit."

"One of my many talents." The woman bowed her head. "Open your mind, Fate's Hand."

He did so.

Into Kalon's psyche was poured a fundamental understanding: magic, the chaotic force of the universe, was opposed by the cold logic and progression of numbers. For every spell, there was an opposing mathematical formula. This revelation burned itself into Kalon's mind and flooded every fiber of his being. He saw the Tapestry of magic overlaid with the string of numbers and ever-changing colors locked in an eternal war, the force of science and numeracy against the tricks and illusions of sorcery and the Anshada.

He realized fire was countered by the chemical formula for water; the mental construct of such a model could undo the magical threads that bound the flame to the material plane. With the right equation and correct inscription, it was possible to break down this sorcery and undo it.

"Do you understand now, Fate's Hand?"

"Yes." Kalon inclined his head to the woman's spirit before him.

"We use logic, science, and understanding to disrupt the flow of magic. We inscribe those equations onto our bullets, into our technology. We will put those equations into the raiment of your office. You will be my right hand, with no equal save for me. Others will attempt to control you, but you are the faithful enforcer and arbitrator of my will," the Cardinal said softly, her words dripping like honey.

"I will be worthy of this office."

"I know you will, my enforcer."

The Cardinal faded from view and left the man alone with his thoughts. Kalon's mind had been expanded. He understood now just how the church functioned to battle magic and demons. He had always thought their advantage had been the technology they were given by Sara and Vincent, but now he saw the math behind the constructs, the equations carved into every bullet by the mechanism to make this possible.

This was the final mystery of the church, and it was now open to him.

Fate's Hand…what did that mean? More than an Inquisitor, more than an Arch-Inquisitor—a servant of Terusa alone?

He closed his eyes once again and meditated on all of these revelations.

CHAPTER 2B

BREAKING BONDS

The lives of Kalon's two friends diverged from his, and even each other's. Verity followed the path of a Shadow Knife, a Church Sponsored Assassin, and enjoyed the freedom to come and go as she pleased. Her work took her all across Hestonia, and she was instrumental in removing many a troublesome opponent to the church before they could even begin to act. Killing came easily to her. It was just a job—the target often did not matter.

Her hair had fallen out years ago due to an underlying condition, and she used this to her advantage. She cultivated persona after persona and amassed an impressive array of wigs and disguises that kept her opponents off her scent. She could get close to the church's enemies in a variety of guises and end them before they became a problem.

One of her many personas was the Lady Amadis: a wealthy merchant woman with a string of broken lovers, a vast fortune (provided by the church), and a lavish manor house in the upper-class ward of Sullavale Port. She was far enough away from the church to pretend that this was who she really was, and at least Amadis's hands were not stained with the blood of so many. As Amadis, she brushed lips and shoulders with the wealthy, powerful, and magnificent of the port. This also meant she was able to overhear rumors, listen carefully to those who might wish the church ill, and inform local law enforcement of dissidents.

She indulged herself as a little bit of a hedonist, broke rules to save lives, and set Sullavale Port afire with rumor after rumor. Over time she became associated with the criminal elements of the port, people who could move in the shadows and do things Lady Amadis could not. People who cultivated a select menagerie of talented movers and shakers, those who called themselves by the name of Stealers, and those who were just as skilled as her with poison and knives—fellow assassins.

Life was good as the years rolled by and the young woman's talents grew and grew. Her skill with a sword was unmatched by her peers, and her passion for music and theatre allowed Verity to open a playhouse in the port under the guise of a talented playwright: the reclusive and much sought-after Carnival.

But what of her friend, Inquisitor Rand? Often, she would think on the fate that had pulled them apart, their nights together and their classes. Her task for the church that had taken her back to the port where she'd first seen Kalon shoot down Seaborne left little time for pleasure with her companion. Yet she knew he would eventually come and find her, once his own tasks had been completed—she was sure of it.

When he finally arrived, she did not expect how or why he'd sought her out.

Those answers would shake her world to the core.

It was the third week of summer, and the port was as lively as ever. Verity sat on her balcony overlooking Gala Square where the players and the jugglers entertained the public. It was a colorful cacophony of sound and spectacle. Her spies had ensured that the people knew Amadis was away on business, involved in a new trade venture at the Holy City of Messania no less. This meant she could focus on being Carnival for a short while, enjoying a carefree life away from the maddening crowds of nobles and fake hangers-on.

She sketched a small bird that had alighted on a nearby ledge, a beautiful golden thing with tiny specks of silver. It was tricky to capture the creature as it peered at her from behind the stained glass of her window that led to a balcony.

A knock sounded on door to her private chamber. She put the canvas book down, grabbed her bright red wig, and popped it on in seconds. Then, with a bright "Come in!" she directed her voice toward the solid oak door.

It was Handrik, a short, mousy-haired fellow, an actor and a percussionist. He also served as Carnival's assistant and did mostly everything she asked of him. "Beg your pardon, lass, but there's an Inquisitor here to see you," he said in his thick accent that flowed like treacle. "Shall I send him up?"

"Please do," Verity answered and flopped back in a chez lounge, chuckling softly. "Perhaps he's come to bring me flowers, or a rave review of my latest bawdy play!"

Handrik shrugged. "Not sure. Be right up, though." He stomped off and shut the door behind him.

A few minutes later the door opened once more. The handsome and ruggedly scarred Inquisitor Rand stood there. He was dressed in the formal coat of a ranking member of the church; the black trimmed with silver looked good on him. Handrik looked past him to Carnival and waggled his hand.

"You can go, lovely," she said to her assistant. "You, though—you can stay."

Rand chuckled softly as the door behind him closed with a click. "When they told me that Carnival was here in town, I had a suspicion it might be you."

"Oh?" Verity placed a hand to her forehead, as though she might faint. "You saw right through my disguise? How perceptive! I'm all over with the vapors."

"I wish I could be as frivolous and as carefree," Rand said and sighed. His time at the church had pulled him away from all that. "I had to come and see you. There's a problem."

Verity's face changed. Her eyes went flint-like, and she sat bolt upright. "What, who, and where?"

Rand moved further into the room. "To explain this, I need to tell you what happened to me at the church. I changed in the last couple of years; something awoke inside me. It has only ever happened to a few Inquisitors who train under Seeker Winter, and apparently it's very rare." He continued after a short pause. "I began to see things, lines of magic, strange shapes, and even spirits. Seeker Winter told me I had awakened my third eye, and that I was like her, potentially a powerful psychic whose skill could be honed with further specialized training. It's not perfect, though, and it happens randomly."

"Go on?" Verity sat enrapt for a moment. She'd known there was something special about Rand when she met him, something that bubbled just under the surface and set the young man apart from his peers. "Isn't that marvelous?"

"Yes." Rand nodded, and then he sighed. "It would be. It means I could train as a seeker and be like Winter."

"But?"

"I saw something, and I fled from the church…a monster next to Terusa!"

"Slow down."

"I cannot!" Rand looked furtively around the room. "I needed to confide in my oldest friend, someone I trust will be able to keep this secret locked up."

Verity blinked several times and quirked a brow. "I'm flattered you came to me, friend. What did you see?"

"When I was sent to meet with the Cardinal, my third-eye showed me a great many things. I saw her…I saw something in the room with her!" Rand said quickly. "I couldn't make it out, but I could feel it, a dark and palpable evil in the room with us. It was wrapped around her, tendrils of black energy passed in and through her skin. I told her what I saw, and she dismissed it as if it were a child's ravings."

This revelation caused Verity to clutch her pendant to her chest tightly and she felt a tingle at the back of her mind. She blinked a couple of times and tried to block out the images she conjured from Rand's words. "Horrible." It was the only word she could manage after what seemed like a pure eternity.

"Yes."

"Could you be mistaken? Perhaps it was your mind's eye playing tricks, perhaps you didn't see what you think you did?"

"I wish it was that. I really do."

"What happened next?"

"I went about my business, and I was shaken to the core. I went to tell Winter, but she was on an assignment—or so I was told. So, I took some time to meditate and try and clear my head. That's when he came for me."

"Who, love? Who?" Verity's face betrayed her true feelings for the man.

"An assassin, the church's own, one of your mentors."

"Who?" Verity snapped.

Footsteps sounded outside the door and paused just at the very edge; the doorknob turned very slowly.

"Damnit Rand, who?"

"I should not have come here." Rand stiffened under Verity's gaze and then turned to face the doorway as if he sensed impending doom. "I've killed us both."

The door opened slowly, and in stepped a man with green eyes, handsome and fierce. He sported simple attire with just a little flair to the jacket. Verity looked at him, and her heart sank; she recognized the gentleman as Drako Mallori—the head of the Shadow Knife.

"Him," the Inquisitor said with a sigh.

"Hello, Carnival—or should I say Verity? Conspiring with Rand, I see." Mallori chuckled softly and patted his hip where a knife lay in a beautiful crimson scabbard. "What to do with you?"

Rand moved quickly and slammed himself against Mallori. He grabbed for the knife and shouted, "Go, run! I'll buy you time." His other hand pulled a cylinder from his belt and depressed the icon at the top. It turned a soft red.

Verity wanted to stay, wanted to help her friend, but she felt the push of his mind against hers. It was a rotten trick, but no psychic under the employ of the church was against using it to get what they wanted. Winter was right: he would have made a great Seeker.

In the confusion Verity made her escape and smashed through the window, sending glass outward with a crash, just as Mallori's gun barked and Rand stiffened as the shots pierced his body. He knocked the knife out of Drako's hand and headbutted the assassin in the face twice. Sensing Verity was safe at last, he smiled through bloody lips. Mallori pulled the cog and eye pendant from around Rand's neck.

"You don't deserve to wear this!"

Rand spat on him and headbutted him one last time as he felt his strength leave him. The gun had torn his insides and organs to shreds. "I think we both lose this one, old chum."

The cylinder slipped from the dying man's hand, and he chuckled softly.

"See you!"

Drako looked down in horror as the realization of what Rand had done gripped him. He had just enough time to pull the threads of the spell together, pushing a protective Tapestry out with his mind to save himself as the explosion that claimed the whole top floor nearly shook the theatre off its foundations and sent clouds of smoke and fire into the air. It could be seen from miles away, but for one observer it marked the end of her career as a playwright and the death of her best friend.

As Verity fled into a nearby alley, the smoke on the top floor cleared and Mallori stood unharmed. His quarry had been obliterated by the blast, and the whole top floor was covered in rubble and debris. He snarled at the back of his throat and kicked part of Rand's body across the room.

He collected his thoughts and dusted himself off, then as calmly as possible he made his way out of the room and down the stairs. He caught Handrik coming the other way and stumbled before the man.

"Who the bloody hell are you?" the fellow demanded and levelled a short stub-nosed firearm at the intruder.

"Drako Mallori, Arch-Inquisitor of the Church of Progression," he lied swiftly. "Carnival is not who she claims she is; she is a dangerous assassin, one the church has been hunting for years. She killed the man who tried to arrest her, my brother in arms. She's fled, and I must go quickly to try and find her before she escapes. Stay here, my good man, give the captain of the guard this, and tell him of the work that I have to do." He pressed Rand's pendant into the other man's hands, covered in blood. "The top floor is too dangerous, get everyone out!"

"Her," Handrik corrected and took the pendant. He closed his fist around it. "The captain is a she."

Drako Mallori ignored him, and before Handrik could prevent it, he pushed past and staggered out of the door, breaking into a run. The guard were not far behind.

Before they could halt the fleeing assassin, Drako Mallori was gone. Captain Anna Kora snorted softly, blinked, and heard a noise. She turned her attention to the door of the theatre just as Handrik appeared, looking crestfallen.

"Han?" She was older now, the same guard captain who had seen Kalon's handiwork with Ryan Seaborne all those years ago. Her left arm had been replaced with a prosthetic limb which functioned as her meat arm and had been made to exacting standards by the finest artificers of the port. It was a work of art. Her hair was whiter now, but her eyes had lost none of their brightness. Her armor, dented and repaired in several places, showed the marks of a woman who'd led an interesting life.

"She's a killer, Captain. Carnival was an assassin. An Inquisitor showed up, a bloke called Rand, and she killed him before she ran off. Nearly killed an Arch-Inquisitor with a bomb or something." He looked up at the ruined top floor. "I'm to get everyone out. It's not safe."

"You go and get a cup of hot sweet tea, Han. Faron, take him to get one. We'll handle it from here." Once again, Captain Anna Kora had to clean up after the Inquisitors and their handiwork. Though she supposed this time it was their quarry who had caused this ruckus, but still, she knew that the church would not let this lie.

Anna pondered all of this; they would send someone here to investigate, especially if an Arch-Inquisitor was involved. It was about to get messier, and she really needed to be paid more.

With those thoughts behind her, Anna walked into the building and began to round up stragglers.

"All right," she bellowed. "Everyone out!"

That was better, something she could handle and didn't require the church.

Faron Grey, the young bright girl at the captain's side, did as her superior ordered and led Handrik off in the direction of one of the port cafes at the sea front.

CHAPTER 3

FIRST ASSIGNMENT

F ar from Sullavale Port, several days after the explosion, the news from the port reached the ears of the church. In the hallowed corridors of the Imper Vatica a man paced nervously, his hands fixed in a faux prayer. Dumpy, short, and nervous, with beady little eyes, he perspired a lot, his brow always seeming to generate an inordinate amount of sweat. He mopped his hairline furiously as he waited outside one of the many meeting rooms of the church agents.

Arch-Inquisitor Roland was worried as he was about to meet for the first time with Kalon Rhadon. Everything he knew about the man frightened him from the tip of his bulbous red nose to the bottom of his flat-soled shoes. He had reread the account of Kalon's first mission in Sullavale Port when the lad was fifteen.

Kalon had offered the lord a chance to surrender, but then he shot Seaborne dead in the street. It weighed heavily on the Arch-Inquisitor's mind.

It was not the only thing that did so. He had been told Kalon was second to the Cardinal in power, his rank above those who had served her faithfully for years. Roland could not help his irritation in being passed aside for a mere thug and a foundling at that! It was preposterous and unfair, and he could do absolutely nothing about it. So, he paced outside the door and checked his appearance in the nearby reflection of a mirror-polished statue.

Roland's back stiffened when he heard the sound of precise steps on the marble floor. He smelled the leather before he saw the man. Kalon had arrived. No longer the boy he had first set eyes on all those years ago, this Kalon was tall, imposing, and utterly infuriating in just how perfect he seemed to Roland's irritated gaze. Kalon's long, dark hair had been secured with a simple hair-clip at the back of his neck and trailed down his long coat to the mid-point of his shoulders. His split-coat was black leather, trimmed with gold, and unlike any of the church agents' garments that came before it—it was the raiment of Kalon's rank and put the Arch-Inquisitor's red and black garments to shame.

Roland loathed the outfit and Kalon immediately.

"Rhadon," he said and waved his hand in the man's direction. "You are late."

Kalon studied Roland. Raven-like in manner, he inclined his head and raised a slender brow. He saw the beads of sweat, each glistening on Roland's forehead like a tell-tale crystal ball. A mark of worry, fear, concern—and to the practiced eyes of the Cardinal's top enforcer, they told a story of a man weighed down by too many secrets.

"No time was agreed on for this meeting," Kalon replied honestly, as he continued to study Roland, detecting the twitch of irritation at the edge of the Arch-Inquisitor's eyes. Where his laughter-lines should have been, there were signs of stress.

"Nonsense! I clearly indicated a time in my missive," Roland lied. It came naturally to him, as he came from a long line of skilled liars. He looked down at the floor, then continued. "Or are you insinuating that I am growing senile in my years?"

"Incorrect," Kalon once more replied. "You are lying. Your breath is shorter, your brow has more perspiration than is normal, and your body tells me more than you want it to. You glanced at the floor. If you had looked inside your own head to remember, you would have shown this clearly."

He looked at the nervous motion of the Arch-Inquisitor's fingers and shook his head. "Your fingers dance as if you are trying to reassure yourself, you lie as easily as I breathe. It serves you well, but in this instant, Arch-Inquisitor, I am not fooled."

"I... I..." Roland clenched his hands into fists and laughed nervously. "Very good, very good. You are a perceptive one, eh?" He changed tack and tried to appear friendly, but his words collided against Kalon's impassive exterior like a tumbling stone. "All a test, all a test. You passed."

"Now that you have finished embarrassing yourself, good morning, Arch-Inquisitor," Fate's Hand said and then stood against the far wall. Waiting. Now silent.

The stony silence was broken at length by the whisper of a blue robe and the shuffle of soft feet against the floor. A tall, thin woman with soft, ice-blue eyes rounded the corner, entering the corridor with a swish of motion. This was Seeker Winter, a powerful spy, psychic, and investigator of the church.

"Your meeting is cancelled, Arch-Inquisitor Roland. I have need of Kalon Rhadon for urgent matters, and you are assigned elsewhere. Go now, and keep the wheels of innovation ever-turning." Winter brushed a lock of pure-white hair from her shoulder as she spoke.

Roland opened and closed his mouth slowly, but knew better than to argue with her. "Of course, Seeker, I will endeavor to do just that." He did not acknowledge Kalon at all as he beat a hasty retreat down the corridors.

Winter opened the door to the meeting room and walked in. "Kalon, join me."

Fate's Hand did so. He followed and wordlessly closed the door behind him. The room was small, functional, and served as a meeting point for two to six people. A table and chairs provided the only comfort in the dimly lit chamber.

"Forgive my interruption, Kalon, but I am sure you would rather spend time with a Seeker than the Arch-Inquisitor. His meeting was a ruse to attempt to leverage some sort of power over you. I am sure of that." Winter set a folder onto the table and took a seat. "Come, sit."

Kalon sat beside her. "I am unsure as to Roland's motives in this case. I assumed it regarded some important information, but his missive was unclear and written as if a child had penned it."

"That, my friend, is Roland." Winter chuckled softly and smiled a little. "He is always trying to climb the ladder, although I am not sure where he thinks he can go. He is an Arch-Inquisitor. Before you came along, they were second only to the Justicars. Now, you are above them all and the Cardinal's right hand."

"The One-Eyed Cog God wills it so," Kalon said and spread his hands atop the table.

"He does indeed, and honestly, it will do the lower ranks good to see people like Roland put in their place."

Kalon remained impassive. He studied the black folder and then regarded Winter narrowly.

"Something wrong?" Winter quirked her brow and opened the folder.

"No," Kalon sat back in the chair. "I await the urgent matters you mentioned."

"Ah, yes." She smiled thinly and shook her head. "You will probably not like this, since it concerns one of our own. But the Cardinal was adamant you were shown this. She—and I—value your insight and your talents for investigation."

Kalon knew about Seeker Winter. Like him, she had come to the church as a foundling, taken from parents who did not understand her, who she really was, and who feared her mind, body, and spirit. Winter was a powerful psychic; many thought it akin to magic. However, Kalon knew it did not act like magic, or work like magic. He knew that it was far harder to control psychic powers than it was to hold the threads of the Tapestry.

Psychic powers worked on the mind, allowing the wielder to move objects and influence others. Magic bent the rules of reality, and in many cases often broke them—punching vast gaps between the real world and the demon world, allowing demonic beings through.

"My talent for uncovering the truth comes from years of training. Your hand in this has been the most valuable teaching tool in my arsenal." Kalon thought on this. "I owe all I am to the sum of many lessons, not to myself."

"Thank you, but no," Winter corrected. "You owe who you are now to you. Never forget that. The church shapes us all, shaped me more than most. But I always knew who I was, even if my body didn't yet. I always knew I was a woman. Your training mirrors my own journey—mine was one of self-discovery, even if that self is who you see now, and yours is the same, Kalon—even if it is church mandated doctrine and combat arts."

Kalon nodded in understanding. "The news?"

"Ah, yes, I forget that you have little time for discussion or pleasantries." In truth, to Winter, as her psychic powers ebbed and flowed around her, Kalon was a dark smudge on a bright star. There was something there, but it eluded her, and when she tried to focus on it, she got the most thundering headache. So, she gave up trying to pierce that veil.

"Inquisitor Rand is dead. We know an assassin known as Carnival killed him. She masqueraded as a playwright in Sullavale Port. Rand was sent on an assignment by the Cardinal, and one of our agents, Drako Mallori, caught up with him just as the assassin activated her bomb. Rand perished in the explosion, and Drako was wounded by flying debris." Winter studied Kalon's reaction to all this. She knew that he and Rand had been close as children.

Kalon put his right hand under his chin and rested his arm on the table. He took the folder and stared at the images of the building captured by the church's photogram technology. The scene was rough, black and white, but even without details, the images showed utter devastation.

"I will need to see this for myself," Kalon said at long last. "I presume this is what you wish me to investigate?"

Seeker Winter took a soft breath and nodded. Her eyes settled on the man before her as she studied him for any reaction to Rand's demise. There was none, nothing, not even a ping on her mental probe. She shuddered a little and sighed. "Rand was a good agent; he will be missed."

"Yes." Kalon nodded. "His skills and knowledge are a great loss, and what he could teach others—whoever did this will be brought to justice once I uncover the truth."

A few moments more passed in a silence that lingered like smoke, then drifted away with Winter's next words. "Investigate this, Kalon, and turn over every single stone. Find out who killed Rand and why, and do not take anything at face value." Her words and tone lowered for a moment. "Drako Mallori is the head of the Shadow Knife. He should not have been sent there to follow Rand. It should have been another Inquisitor's job."

Kalon's brow tilted ever so slightly, and he pursed his lips. "This is indeed odd."

"Odd is one way of putting it, irregular another, and, I'd hasten to add suspicious."

"I will leave forthwith." Kalon nodded and stood up.

"Be discrete." Winter looked him in the eye, adjusting her gaze. "Watch out for Roland and others. Your rise to power has put their noses out of joint."

"I am always discreet. I also never take my coat off here. It is impossible."

"I don't understand?" Seeker Winter's face betrayed her confusion.

"It was something that Rand said. I believe it happens to be humor." Kalon moved toward the door and rested a gloved hand on the handle. "The end of the saying goes, 'because of all the knives in my back.'"

"Ah." Winter nodded. "Accurate. Go with speed, Kalon, and report back if you hear anything. I've prepped the *Ori* to take you to the port. She's fast and small, good for a mission like this."

"I shall. And thank you, Seeker. You are, as always, an exemplar of your order and ours."

With that, Kalon opened the door, let himself out, and left the snow-haired Winter to her thoughts in the room. Kalon scanned the corridor for a moment and then proceeded with purpose to his next destination: the hangar and a waiting church windship that would return him to Sullavale Port for the first time in over twenty-five years.

The hangar bay was a hive of activity, stocked with smaller tactical ships and merchant vessels as they flew in and out of the Imper Vatica. It was more like a commercial port than a secret hangar bay deep in the heart of the most powerful order in all Hestonia. The lift stopped with a sharp click, and Kalon stepped from the platform, his long coat swishing behind him as he made his way down the gantry stairs, polished boots clicking against the metal.

He looked across the lit bay, his sharp eyes picking out different vessels. One stood out from all the others, dark and dart-like with sleek lines and a low profile.

"Inquisitor—is that the correct form of address?" A young sailor with a shock of short red hair greeted Kalon as he stepped from the bottom stair. "I know you are Fate's Hand, but I'm not sure of the formalities."

"Inquisitor will do. Is that the Ori?"

"She is, yes sir, all ready to fly for you. Fastest and quietest. The captain is waiting for you to embark so they can get underway."

"Who is the captain, so that I may know the correct form of address and so forth?" Kalon began to walk slowly toward the vessel.

"Captain Imani. They are one of the best." The dockhand answered, following behind.

"And you?"

"Harker, sir. A pleasure." Harker smiled and hustled to match Kalon's pace.

"Imani—you use 'they' for the captain?" Kalon was a man of detail, and when he wrote reports, he required the correct form of address in every way. He was that precise.

"Yes, sir. That's their pronoun."

"Thank you, Harker." He paused. "And you?"

"He, sir. Thank you for asking." The grey-clad captain of the Ori waited for Kalon at the bottom of the ship's loading ramp. They were dressed in the formal flight uniform of the church, which sported a fetching beret and a slim but elegant jacket. They stretched out their hand to the Inquisitor in a formal greeting.

Kalon shook their hand and nodded formally as Harker peeled off to check one of the skid-like landing gears of the vessel as it sat on the iron-wood pad. "You have an impressive ship and an eager crew, Captain." Kalon said as he looked the Ori over.

"Thank you, Inquisitor. I must admit I am honored that I am the first to transport Fate's Hand on their maiden voyage." Imani's dark skin creased around their eyes, and they turned to enter the ship. "If you will follow me, we will get underway. Harker, make sure all is in order, and then inform Dock Master Ryss that the ship is ready to fly."

"Yes, Captain." Harker offered a smile to Kalon and then rushed off to do as he had been asked.

With one last look at the dock, Kalon stepped aboard the ship and followed Imani down the subtly lantern-lit inner corridor. He took in every detail of the exquisitely crafted vessel and made a mental note of the route inside the ship. While it wasn't as large as some of the vessels he'd traveled on as a boy, it was no less impressive and no less grand.

"Only a short way now to your cabin, Inquisitor," Imani said as they walked side by side down the ancillary corridor. The path turned and went past several doors and up a flight of well-lit stairs. "I took the liberty of placing you in one of the officer's rooms on the top deck of the ship. I hope this was not too forward of me?"

Kalon shook his head. "Not at all. It will be just fine, thank you."

Imani smiled. "We should be at the port in just over a day. We are going to take a more direct route and avoid the air lanes of commercial vessels. The *Ori* has been outfitted with atmospheric enhancement; she flies higher than any of the civilian ships are allowed. If you need anything at all, the intercom is just there, and you are welcome on the bridge of the ship any time." They stopped just outside the door and opened it with the tap of a lever. "Here you are, Inquisitor."

"The *Ori* sounds like an impressive vessel, and I expect great things from you and the crew. It is always a pleasure to meet someone who is as dedicated to precision as I am," Kalon said, stepping inside the room. "I will be fine; I require very little save for food and drink. However, as a student of tech-magis myself, I may well come by the bridge at some point to see the controls." These words rang hollow for Fate's Hand, but he knew this was the correct polite way to converse.

"Very well. I will see us in the air shortly. Rest well, sir."

"Thank you, Captain." Kalon closed the door with click and listened as Imani's footfalls indicated they'd headed off toward the front of the ship. He took the cabin in. It was lavish but comfortable, and a stocked bookshelf meant he would not be devoid of literature on his trip to the port.

"This will do." He selected a book on history at random, sat down, and opened the tome.

Imani was true to their word, and the *Ori* soon left the hangar to ascend into the cold sky above the city. Messania was lost to sight in seconds, and the dart-like ship pierced the clouds and roared upward to crest the edge of the horizon. At full throttle she gracefully put distance between Kalon and the Holy City. The journey passed swiftly, and the travel time was indeed just over a day. Kalon kept to himself, feeling no need to socialize or explore the wondrous ship. He ate and drank the fare provided for him and read many more of the books. Some of them were of the history of old, and several talked about the Old and New Gods at great length.

Only near the end of their trip did he leave and walk onto the bridge.

Kalon stepped into a beam of sunlight as it cast an angular ray through the curved window of the *Ori*, his boots ringing out on the deck. Captain Imani turned in their chair toward him. The triangular setup of the bridge had the captain seated at the back and the array of machines—flight and engine controls—at the front. The view port was constructed from a crystal shard and provided a beautiful view of the glory outside the window.

Many of the vessel's inner workings and machines were hidden from the eye, carefully concealed behind ornate panels. Those controls on display were state-of-the art and impressive. Reactive liquids, illusionary displays, and touch-crystals were just a few of the tech-magis delights on offer.

"Ah, Inquisitor." Imani waved Kalon over. "Come and see the wonder of the *Ori*'s vision for yourself."

With a few more footfalls Kalon stood at the captain's side. He looked out across the bridge and the intricate machines. This was not his first such vessel, but the *Ori* was an impressive testament to the arcanists and mechanists who worked on these windships for the church.

"We are on time?" he asked the captain.

"Absolutely. As we drop height you should see the port."

As Imani said this, the ship dove. Kalon could hear the whirr of engines and the click of the deck plates as the tech-magis devices countered the pull of gravity that by all rights should have sent him into the back wall. He was impressed from a technical point of view and watched their descent approvingly.

"Our technicians and crafters have done us proud," Kalon said finally and rested his hand on the captain's chair. "Your crew handled the drop with precision. This will all be in my report."

There was a glow of pride about Imani now, and the captain brightened considerably. "It was our pleasure, sir, and you have been a model passenger." Imani laughed a little.

Kalon did not laugh. He took the comment at face value and replied, "I always strive to be."

"Not quite what I meant, but yes." Imani took a little gulp of air and waggled a finger into their right ear. Then they returned their gaze to the gull-strewn sky of the Sullavale Port approach.

The *Ori* bore down on the port like a sharp shard of obsidian against the gorgeous sky, clouds torn into shreds as the ship curved through the air and pivoted to change flight path suddenly, her engines whispering where other ships of her class roared. The ship's voice rose and fell as the thrusters brought her softly down atop the pad at the far edge of the dock.

"My instructions are to commandeer this pad, close it off to civilian traffic, and assist you in your return to Messania or any other location you need to visit as part of your assignment, Inquisitor." Imani settled back in their chair and relaxed.

"Thank you, Captain." Kalon turned and walked from the bridge. "I will inform the dock master that this pad is now under church control, and they are to assist you in every way. I will communicate with you if I require anything. I have the Far-Speaker's Shard; ensure our stones are attuned."

"Very well." Imani looked across the bridge deck and eyed one of their officers. "Do as the Inquisitor requests."

"Aye, Captain," the officer tapped a few buttons, turned a dial, and threw a lever. "Attuning now."

As the officer did this, Kalon took an oval shaped shard of stone from his pocket, set it into the palm of his gloved hand, and turned it over. The metallic lines on the surface of the object began to emit a faint blue light, then the shard grew warm against the leather.

"Attuning done."

Fate's Hand nodded. "Excellent."

"It saves us from shouting all the way to wherever you are," Imani said with a little chuckle. "This way we are connected to the Magis Ley Relays across Hestonia—facilitating perfect communication with our key agents everywhere."

Kalon put the shard away. It was now part of the Magis Ley Relays, another weapon of the church hidden from the eyes of the general public, a network of tech-magis communication devices that allowed the order to talk to their agents across distances that would otherwise be impossible for other methods—such as the outdated wire communication devices.

"Good luck, Inquisitor," Imani offered.

"Luck is not required for this investigation, Captain. Until we meet again."

Kalon made his way from the bridge through the corridors of the ship. He paused at the ramp and lowered it, letting his eyes grow accustomed to the bright light of the sun outside the vessel before he stepped purposefully down the ramp and onto the floor of the landing pad. That early in the morning, the smells of fresh baked bread and the bitterness of coffee all mixed with salt filled the port's air.

A small entourage was already waiting for him, and he took note of every person there. As he approached them, the ramp of the *Ori* closed behind him with a satisfied whisper.

There was a woman, her arm replaced by a fine prosthetic limb. The tech-magis design was not one from the church, but there were other artificers who plied their trade here. She had both of her arms folded before her and wore the regalia of the port guard. A short and buff man stood to her right, another guard. Finally, a gentleman with a puffy collar, his face covered in far too much white makeup, was on her left. His medallion marked him as the governor of the town.

"Keys Leyland," the governor said as the Inquisitor approached. "You are?"

"Kalon Rhadon." Kalon replied formally. "Fate's Hand, here on an investigation. I presume you have been informed about this and it is why you are here?"

"Yes, yes." Leyland nodded and shielded his eyes from the sun. "This is my guard captain. She's a fine woman, and a worthy one at that."

Kalon quirked a brow at this and regarded Captain Anna Kora with a nod. "We've met. She was younger back then. So was I."

"I wager we are both different people now, Inquisitor," Anna said and chuckled softly. "You have grown to be a fine man, if I may say so. Anna Kora at your service, and this is Balik, my grumpy right hand."

The buff, short man scowled and shrugged his shoulders. "We should be investigating this, Anna. Not the church—it's our port."

With a flint-like gaze, Kalon made a note of the man and his response. He studied the guard intensely, and before anyone could say anything else, he replied, "Balik, you may assist me in the investigation if your captain permits it. I value other eyes on the scene as well as my own. In fact," he continued, looking at Anna Kora now, "I would be open to the guard captain lending her wisdom to this search as well."

Anna shot Balik a dirty look and mouthed something rude, then she smiled sweetly at the Inquisitor and spoke. "I'd be honored."

Keys Leyland watched this exchange with a little bit of mirth. He was amused at Kalon's sharp use of local resources and his swift request. *Keep people where you can see them*, he thought. He was not far wrong either.

"Very well, I shall leave you in the captain's masterful hands and retire to my manor. This whole business has upset my humours, and I feel somewhat sick. I hope I'm not coming down with something. Good day." Keys walked briskly off before anyone could rope him into anything. He was a sly old fox of a man.

Balik wasn't sure how to respond to this; he'd expected the Inquisitor to breeze in, take charge, and run his mouth like the other ones he'd met. He was taken by surprise, and Kalon sensed it. Anna Kora, on the other hand, knew exactly what Balik felt like. She had previous dealings with the church from Inquisitors to Arch-Inquisitors over the years since Kalon shot a man dead in the market. She pondered something, and then looked across at a small café outside of the dock.

"Inquisitor Rhadon, perhaps I can buy you a coffee or a tea, something wet—you must have had a long trip?" She looked at the ship and reconsidered that assumption. "If not for you, for me. I've been on my feet all morning dealing with this, and honestly, I really could use a sit down."

"This is acceptable. We can talk strategy and how you might assist me in this investigation. We can also discuss why Balik has a sour attitude toward the church and what I might be able to do to remedy this without the need for a formal report to the Imper Vatica," Kalon said, following the woman's gaze to the café. "Does that work for you both?"

Balik looked as if he might faint. As much as he disliked the church poking their nose in, the thought of an inquiry from the Imper Vatica chilled his blood to ice. "I think that would be excellent. Perhaps I can tell the Inquisitor why I was terse and may have spoken out of order."

Kalon nodded. "I would very much like to hear your reason for this, yes."

"It's settled then." Anna walked swiftly to the café to break their tension. "Gents, if you will. Coffee's not going to drink itself."

Kalon followed. He watched every person for their reaction and was pleased to see they treated him with wary respect. His official garb and pendant of the church stood out, the black and gold stark against the classical pillars and curved fluted grey and white marble of the dock.

Fate's Hand cut an impressive figure indeed.

CHAPTER 4

THE GUNSLINGER INVESTIGATION

As the cries of gulls echoed overhead, rising and falling with the sweep of their wings, the Inquisitor, Anna Kora, and Balik settled at their table outside the café. They were protected from the sun by the shade of a large and colorful canopy. An olive-skinned man poured out three drinks: two dark coffees and one amber colored tea with just a splash of milk. Kalon regarded the scene with the air of a man who was pressed for time.

The young waiter hesitated. Nervously, he put down several cubes of sugar as he looked at Kalon.

"Yes?" The Inquisitor lifted his gaze to regard the waiter.

"He's waiting for a tip, Inquisitor. Here—let me." Anna quickly passed the young man a couple of coins and shooed him off. "He's new, and obviously awe-struck by your august personage."

With a deft flick of black-gloved fingers, Kalon moved the sugar away, selected just one lump out of the lot, and placed it in his drink. He then took a spoon and in silence stirred the liquid exactly thirty-five times clockwise, and then the same counterclockwise.

Balik bit his bottom lip and considered his next reply. "So, about my earlier terseness, Inquisitor?"

With a soft tink, Kalon's spoon ceased its final anti-clockwise rotation, and the man returned it to the edge of the saucer. "Go on?"

"I want to apologize again. We've all been shaken by the events of late. To find out a beloved figure of ours, Miss Carnival, was really a heretic responsible for the death of Inquisitor Rand...it's been a shock. The Arch-Inquisitor Drako Mallori is not exactly a man who—how can I delicately put this—engenders cooperation and fosters a good working relationship?"

Anna waited quietly for the Inquisitor's answer.

Kalon's cup rose, he drank, then he lowered it again. In silence.

"Did I offend?" Balik asked nervously.

"No," Kalon finally answered. "I was collating your statement. I must ask one thing of this hearsay: do we have evidence that Carnival was indeed a heretic?"

"Arch-Inquistor Mallori's word, only," Anna interrupted softly.

"He is not an Arch-Inquisitor."

"Not an Arch-Inquisitor?" Anna and Balik said at the same time.

"Drako Mallori is a Shadow Knife. I am sure you have heard of them—perhaps by their other name, Church Sponsored Assassins. They are not trained to the full extent of an Inquisitor, and are not able to speak for us. By masquerading as an Arch-Inquisitor, Mallori has sullied this investigation and hoodwinked the people of Sulla-vale Port. I intend to find out why." Kalon calmly picked up his cup, drank deeply, and set it back down. "Then I will decide what to do with him."

Anna and Balik exchanged glances. They had forgotten their own drinks in the wake of Kalon's revelation, and now they sat quietly. Each wondered just what to say next.

"I will need to see the site of this supposed assassination, and I will need to know who saw Carnival, Rand, and Mallori that day." Kalon placed his hand onto the cup once more and lifted it to examine the design on its edge: a set of keys, gaudily embellished and crossed over each other, that marked Keys Leyland's vanity.

He observed this symbol in a few more places visible from where he sat outside the café. It was displayed on the guards' own uniforms and fluttered on several pennants, banners, and flags.

Anna pondered for a moment and caught sight of one of her people as he was crossing through to the other side of the port's market, a little way from the café. She made a snap judgement and called out. "Hey, Andreas. Over here a moment!"

This sudden outburst, and a new arrival to the scene, drew Kalon's gaze. Regarding the newcomer with a raised brow, he put the cup back down and rested his gloved hand on the edge of the table.

Anna's shout carried over the milling crowds gathering around the market, haggling, walking, discussing, and pawing the various goods on offer at the stalls. Her voice cut right into the ears of a dark-eyed, short-haired man, and he stopped dead in his tracks. He was dressed in a simple leather tunic and breeches. The guards' symbol emblazoned on his right shoulder, the crossed keys of the governor, glinted in the sun.

He didn't waste time approaching the trio's table, ducking past a pair of jakats, the humanoid panther-jackal people of Hestonia, as he did so. One look at Kalon told him all he needed to know. He sensed the man's importance and nodded in Kalon's before bowing formally.

"Gunslinger, I mean…Investigator Andreas at your service." His bass-voice was a soft growl directed at Anna. "Captain."

Kalon quirked a brow at the word "gunslinger."

"Sit down, Andreas. This is someone I'd like you to meet." Anna kicked out a stool and inclined her head to the investigator. "Gunslinger indeed."

"It's my own moniker. I like it." With a crackle of leather, Andreas sat and folded his arms onto the tabletop with a grin. "So who's this guy?"

"Kalon Rhadon, Fate's Hand," Anna Kora said by way of introduction. "Right Hand of the Cardinal of the Church of Progression."

"Fate's Hand." Andreas nodded. "Now that's a title I can appreciate. Like an Inquisitor, only more powerful?"

Balik looked nervous again and coughed politely. "I must away. Captain, Fate's Hand, Investigator." He stood up abruptly, almost knocking his half-finished drink flying, then backed away to avoid further embarrassment. "I fear I've neglected my duties for too long. Inquisitor, it has been a pleasure to meet you, and I hope the investigation is concluded swiftly. Captain, I will see you later. But you know me—work is my life, and I cannot tarry any longer. Until next we meet." He offered a curt bow and left Kalon, Andreas, and Anna Kora to their own company as he hurried off into the thronging masses of the port.

"That's the fastest I've ever seen him move. You'd think there was a limpet crab in his breeches." Andreas took the man's half-drunk cup and downed the contents. "Hmm, not bad. Bit too thick for me."

Anna Kora sighed. "Forgive Balik please, Kalon. He's young, and he's driven."

"Nothing to forgive." Kalon said flatly. "His drive will see him succeed; I appreciate he has more to do than waste time on idle banter."

"That's our Balik, always balls to the wall busy." Andreas leaned back. "So, Captain Anna, what's the job? It's a job, right?"

"Inquisitor Rhadon needs to investigate the scene of Rand's murder. I want you to assist the Inquisitor while he's here in Sullavale Port. I, like Balik, have a job to do, and I am sure Kalon understands my first duty is to the people of the port and my own guard. Especially in light of what you said about that bastard Mallori."

"Bastard Mallori?" Andreas caught a waiter by the arm, asked them something in a whisper, and then leaned forward.

"Drako Mallori, so-called Arch-Inquisitor," Anna replied. "Remember him?"

"How can I forget? He was rude, belligerent, and totally without regard for crime scene decorum." Andreas shook his head three times. "So...demanding. You're not like that, are you, Kalon?"

"Inquisitor," Kalon wiped his mouth with the corner of a small serviette. "That is my title. However, if it makes our working relationship better, you may address me informally."

"Nice. Kalon it is, then. Call me Andreas—none of this *Investigator* crap." As the waiter returned, the investigator whipped the cake off the plate and scooped the small slice into his mouth in one bite. He pulled out a coin and put it on the plate in the same smooth motion. "Thanks," he said with a grin. "No breakfast. Needed a quick boost."

"I can see we are going to be an interesting combination," Kalon said without a trace of amusement. Then he put an additional coin atop the one on the plate for the young waiter. "A tip."

The young man smiled and swung by another table on his way away from theirs.

"Well." Anna rolled her eyes, and her prosthetic clicked as she lifted her arm. "I'm going to sit here a moment, finish my drink, and then get back to the station. Kalon, it was a pleasure to meet you again more formally this time."

"Thank you, Captain, I will endeavor to make my trip here a short one and ensure that your woes are not compounded a moment longer. I apologize on the church's behalf for the deception of Mallori. Rest assured I will bring this to the Cardinal as soon as I am able." Kalon stood up and looked at Andreas. "If you are to assist me, do you need anything before we depart to the scene of the crime?"

Andreas finished his cake and wiped his mouth with the back of his hand. "I need the tools of my trade, just in case. Not as though I'm expecting I need to use them, but I feel naked, you know, without them."

"Where are they?"

"The station."

"Very well, lead on."

The men left Anna on her own, and she sat back, rolling her eyes once more. "If I live through today, I need a break." She drank more. "Oh, great...cold."

———————————

Far from the market, Kalon and Andreas made good time to the watch station. Like many of the watchhouses in the world, it was a functional building. It processed criminals, held them, and had an area out back for execution, a device designed to immolate the accused and leave nothing but bones and ash. One of the cleaner methods, compared to beheading, hanging, or shooting.

"I won't be long, Kalon." Andreas ran toward the door. "Just getting my friends, and we'll be right back."

"Friends?" Kalon quirked his brow again and stood by one of the gate posts—settling into his usual routine of observing everything with a scrutiny that bordered on obsessive. The slightest factor out of place caught his attention, and he made a mental note of it.

Andreas left the watchhouse and walked over. As he did so, he buckled his gun belt tightly around his waist and set a pair of pistols at his hip. "My friends and I are ready, just in case. You never know with an investigation like this."

"A pair of three-shot deadlock revolvers. Port-made artifice, I presume?" Kalon regarded the guns and nodded. "Satisfactory."

"Silver inlaid, pearl and walnut, with an inscription that reads 'Unguided but true.'" Andreas flipped a short leather coat over the shirt he now wore, his tunic replaced by a layered set of interlocked armor pieces. "Yours are tech-magis. Daroni, right?"

Kalon nodded just once.

Andreas let out a whistle. "Now, what I wouldn't give to get my hands on a pair of those! Best technology that exists in all Hestonia. Maybe one day I'll get to meet Sara too—I heard she has made mods to the guns, even better than they were before."

"As much as I would like to continue this," Kalon said, looking at the sun as it moved across the sky, "time is wasting."

"Sure. We can walk and talk. So, Sara, I'm right, yeah?" Andreas swept his arms wide and beckoned Fate's Hand to follow him.

"You are correct." Kalon fell into step and followed the man into the wider streets of the port. "I have known Sara for many years. She is talented and extremely capable. She has an eye for detail, exquisite design sense, and a technical acumen equal to the Master Artificer himself."

"Damn, that is some praise." Andreas nodded and patted his guns. "Maybe one day I'll get Sara to take a look at these and see what she can do."

"One day, perhaps."

Dogs ran barking to and fro. Children played with spinning tops and hoops in the streets. Some stood back from their peers, their toys more advanced, flying devices that hummed softly. Powered with tech-magis, these floated around their front gardens, making soft whooshing noises. Tech-magis touched the lives of all, the perfect bond of magic and science, created by the Church of Progression, with the Master Artificer Vincent Daroni at the forefront of the art. Even the lowliest household had some form of device within, even if it was merely a light or a form of heating. Small crystal lamps sat atop metal poles, ready to cast light when the sun went down.

Fires lit themselves if the temperature dropped beyond a certain threshold.

People's limbs could be replaced with a mix of magic and technology. It was a wonder—and yet another reason the church was adored.

At length the pair reached their destination. It did not take a skilled Inquisitor or investigator to spot the top floor where Rand died. The building had been shored up by workmen in the intervening time. Scaffolding and braces made a haphazard spider's web of metal and wood. Even now, tradesmen worked to correct the structural defects and faults caused by the bomb.

"It was a forceful blast." Kalon stopped and looked up at the buckled stonework as it pushed against the metal girders. "Concentrated on the inner side of the room, but the compression wave did not litter the street with the window opposite. Nor did it buckle the stonework around it."

"You want to go in?"

"Let me look around a little first," Kalon replied and moved to the front of the building, the street where the balcony had a grand overview—and where Verity made her escape, unknown to the two men investigating.

"Ok. I'll go tell Handrik we're here." Andreas jogged to the back door and let himself in.

Kalon ignored the sound of the workers. He focused on the area around the street and walked it for a good ten minutes. He took carefully measured steps back and forth, studying the pavement and the cobbles. What the cleaners had missed, he found. Shards of window glass that matched the one above him. Shards of glass that were caught between the cracks of the cobbles but not bent, twisted, or otherwise deformed by the heat of an explosion. He put two of them in a small bag.

Even a compression wave would have had some effect on the glass—at least that's what Daroni would have said had he been here. There were also traces of blood on the shards, slight but unmistakable.

That was not the only clue either; the unmistakable scent of a woman's perfume, one he knew well, lingered on another shard of glass he picked up. It had not been attenuated by the smells of the port's constant foot traffic, nor animals. It was a shard that had nestled just on the edge of the pavement itself, preserved from damage by luck more than fate.

The glass had been broken by a tumble; it had not been thrown outwards in the blast.

"Verity, what did you do?" he asked the shard as it reflected part of his face back at him, a tiny streak of dried blood upon its pale green surface. "What did Rand do?"

"Kalon, we're good!" Andreas shouted from above him as he appeared on the edge of the balcony. "Come in the back—ignore Handrik. You have got to see this room. It's a wreck."

Kalon put the glass in another bag. He had a few ideas for further investigation. "I will be there in a moment," he said and began to make his way to the back of the building. He ignored workers, who wisely got out of his way, as he went into the back gate and through the open back door.

Handrik gestured up the stairs and went off to wrangle his workforce.

When Kalon entered the room, he paused, needing just a moment to take all the details in. The damage to the walls was concentrated near the door. The blast had been forced backward rather than forward, and the damage to the door itself was considerable. The second wave, more an explosive wave of force, had gone outward after the first, but completely ignored a circle on the floor that was slightly stained with dark blood.

Words had been scrawled on the walls, and a lot of the tertiary damage was done by hand rather than by explosive device. "Heretic, witch, wizard, and kill the sorcerers!" These slogans had been painted in red over the crime scene, and much of Carnival's—Verity's—furniture had been smashed with what appeared to be a blunt object, likely a hammer. Rubble and stonework were ruined, dislodged by the force of something more powerful than mere hands.

"Andreas, what do you make of this?" It was a good test. Kalon wanted to see what the investigator would find.

The man stopped picking through the rubble by the window; his demeanor changed, and he chewed his lip slightly. "Letting me take the lead for now? Ok, I'm game."

"I am."

Kalon watched Andreas's whole body language shift. The investigator gained confidence as he stalked that room in a way that would make another Inquisitor proud. He stopped at the door and knelt.

"Something?" Kalon asked.

"Yeah, this is odd."

"In what way?" Kalon folded his arms and stood at the side of the room, away from the prime evidence.

"Blast wasn't a regular explosive. No damage ahead of this point here." He stood, walked past the circle, and drew a line with his foot at the exact point where the explosion began. "Only a short distance here for the blast to begin, then it goes backward and hits the door. That's the true force right there—shredded it." Andreas bent down now and ran his finger around part of the strange circular mark in the floor. "This is the odd shit. Not a mark, not a single bit of damage. Floor here should be just as bad as the rest of it at ground zero."

"Go on."

"If I guessed, Rand used something like a breach charge to do this. I've studied explosives, and it's consistent with the blast pattern of one of those. Only thing is, it should have blown in the direction of the doorway—not back toward the window. So why...?"

"An error on Rand's part?"

"Oh." Andreas pursed his lips. "Maybe?"

"No, Rand was far too precise for such a mistake," Kalon admitted. "So, what else in the scene tells you about what happened here?"

"Ok. Blast doesn't make it to the door...it bounces back somehow and goes right toward the window. Tears Rand apart, at least. Doesn't make sense. Breach charges blast to the front like we said."

Kalon walked over and knelt by the circle. He looked at it. "How?"

"Magic, only way. Not heard of a psychic outside of the church who could lay down that kind of protection at all." The investigator answered plainly. "So, it's got to be magic."

Kalon stood and walked the room, speaking as he did so. He

paused at the window to scent something with his nose. "Correct. There were three people, at least, here that day. One by the window, a woman. Unique perfume, one I know. One at the circle, and the other, Rand, torn apart by the explosion." Kalon looked around; to him, it was clear. His analytical mind stripped bare the scene of any superfluous evidence, and he almost saw it play out. Perhaps it was a trick of his Anshada blood, of which he was yet unaware—but he could see the event in his mind's eye.

"There was a struggle—the foot patterns are there in the flooring. Blood splats indicate that some violent action happened prior to the explosion. Someone took something from here as well—there was a knife in the corner that had been dropped. See the pattern in the ash by the charred stone?"

"Yeah. Think a worker, or...?"

"I do not yet know."

"Ok. Need me to do some asking around?" Andreas offered. "Leave you to piece all of this together?"

"A good idea." Kalon pursed his lips thoughtfully. "Ask Handrik—perhaps he knows." He knelt again by the circle.

Andreas put his right thumb up and left the room carefully to allow Kalon to further concentrate on the crime scene.

"Gunshots, Mallori. The bomb, Rand. The assassin, not Verity, as much as the rumors would want me to believe it," the Inquisitor said to himself as he stood up.

Kalon's quick eye roved the scene once more, deconstructing it into component parts as he focused all his training. He cleared the rubble mentally and began to gain a much clearer picture—then it happened. He saw it as it was. A ghost of an image overlaid the scene of the crime.

The struggle, the gunshots, the broken window as Verity fled, and the blossoming explosion of a breach cylinder triggered by Inquisitor Rand. Their assailant, none other than Drako Mallori.

For a moment, for the first time in his life, Kalon felt a sense of wonder as the Anshada power in his blood flooded his body. He put it down to his training at the church, a potential psychic awakening as happened to Winter and, he'd heard, Rand before he left. That wonder vanished as quickly as it came. It was replaced with a logic that he had gained another tool in his kit, one that would come in handy in other investigations, no doubt.

Andreas returned just as Kalon was about to look for him. "Hey, Kalon. Here's the culprit. Handrik picked it up—thought someone might steal it—then forgot until I asked him about it. I'm inclined to believe the guy; do you need to question him?"

"No. His will be an immaterial account. We have all we need, and I have the crime scene figured out. I know what happened here." Kalon looked at the knife and nodded. "Mallori's. A special one given to the leader of the Church's Shadow Knives."

"Damn, that is odd." Andreas looked down. "Shit, that means… he's a mage."

"I was about to say so, yes. Mallori has magical training, and unless approved by the Cardinal, this is suspect to say the least." Kalon mused for a moment. "You should take the knife, Andreas. Put it safely in the watchhouse under lock and key, and do not let Mallori reclaim it. If he tries, tell him to seek out Fate's Hand."

"Yeah, badass. What is a Fate's Hand exactly?"

"The right hand of the Cardinal, an enforcer and investigator of the church. Above the Justicars, and the Inquisitors, Arch-Inquisitors—I am her will made manifest," Kalon replied as he repeated the words burned into his subconscious by the years of rigorous training and rote mastery.

"Impressive man, impressive." Andreas put his thumb up again and looked around the room. "So, what now?"

"For now, I have some evidence I want to test and a few things I want to follow up on," Kalon replied with a tilt of his head. "This scene is of no more use to us. Allow Handrik's men to clear this room up for a new purpose or repair it. Whatever he decides."

"Will do. Meet you outside?"

"If you wish."

Kalon left the room with a swish of his black leather coat. He walked down the stairs, ignoring Handrik and the workers, and returned to the street outside of the building, looking up once again at the balcony. It had a clear route to the ground floor, with some need to jump from one place to the next. Verity was athletic, lithe, and capable of doing this even if injured.

Muffled voices echoed inside the building, filtered through an open skylight: Andreas and Handrik discussing the top room.

Kalon paced along the axis of the street. He looked for more evidence, then noticed a shadow flit across an alleyway. It was the briefest of shapes, and it looked human-like—only something felt off about it. Years of Inquisitorial training had given Kalon that intuition, and coupled with his Anshada blood, it made a potent combination.

Andreas came out at the same time. "Done. Handrik thanks you for your aid and…what's wrong, Kalon?"

"Alley, shadow, figure," Kalon said and made a direct line toward where he'd seen the motion. "Come with me, or not. Your choice."

"Oh, I'm with you!" The investigator broke into a run to catch up and grinned. "Might even get to use my friends after all. Good old Thought and Memory!"

"I will not ask why you name your weapons."

"Don't you?"

"No."

"Oh, man, you are missing out on a connection with some tech there!" Andreas followed Kalon as they both entered the alley. Before he could do anything, the Inquisitor shot his arm across the investigator's chest and shoved him right to the back.

The spell burst forth down the alley, gathered by quick fingers and a quicker mind. Threads of gleaming red and orange, wrapped around with motive force, were sent hurtling in a ball of ever-expanding super-heated gas and fire as the magic fought to superimpose itself upon the world.

Kalon whispered the equations that he had been taught, feeling the air grow warmer around him as the ball of flame splatted like a rotten egg against the anti-magic woven into his impressive attire. Against the equation of undoing, against the written symbols that tore magic asunder, the spell might as well have been made of tissue paper.

The scholars called the Church of Progression's study of anti-magic numeromancy, an offshoot of numerology and a far more powerful divine science.

"Shit, that was seriously close." Andreas moved from behind Kalon and whipped out one of his guns. He took a quick shot at the sorcerer, and it impacted against some kind of mystic barrier. "Oh, come on. That's just unfair," he growled.

"Good thing you did not discharge that by my head," Kalon said. "I'm a little more professional than that. We don't deafen our allies."

"We need this one alive, if possible. I have questions." Kalon shook his head and charged down the alley toward the bewildered mage.

"I'm going up. We'll catch them yet!" Andreas stowed his gun and leapt up onto a low roof.

The chase was on!

The mage turned tail and ran, clothing flapping as they took flight down alley after alley. They tried to lose Kalon and would have been able to, having prior knowledge of the area, if it hadn't been for Andreas. The investigator became Kalon's eyes and ears above, moving across higher and higher roofs, clearing gaps with immense ease, and freerunning as though his life depended on it. The Inquisitor had saved him from that spell—saved them both—and Andreas was the kind of man who did not forget such things.

"Left! Straight! Hiding in that hay cart over there!" he called from the rooftops as he pursued the sorcerer alongside Fate's Hand.

The populace pointed the mage out as well. Their responses aided the hunters as they tracked across Sullavale Port to a blind alley. It was here that the trail went dead as Andreas dropped down by Kalon's side just as the man reached the alley entry.

"Magic again, eh?" he asked and took a deep breath.

Kalon showed no signs of fatigue as he replied, "It would appear our sorcerer has vanished into thin air, or at least walked through stone. Not impossible—the church teaches us about their magic and what it can do."

"What now?"

"We follow."

Kalon stalked down the alley to the far wall where he could almost smell the after-stench of the magic lingering there. He stopped and put his hand against the stone.

"I thought so."

"Spell?"

"Concealed door. Stand back."

"Breach charge?"

"Of course."

Kalon unhooked a cylinder off his belt and placed it against the rough stone. He pressed the red crystal atop it and stepped back six paces. Andreas followed him and looked over his shoulder.

"Same thing that killed Rand."

"Yes."

The explosion was impressive, focused toward the hidden door. Debris flew backward with an impressive force. All that was left now was to take a step into the unknown and enter the corridor that wove through the rock.

"Keep your wits about you, Andreas. This is Anshada trickery. It won't be easy. This wizard wants us to follow them, I am sure of it."

"Right." The investigator drew his twin guns. "I wish you hadn't said that. I was happy when I felt we were the hunter and not the prey."

"We are still the hunters." Kalon moved forward into the darkness.

CHAPTER 5

DARKNESS AND REVELATION

B eyond the ruin of the door, there lay an ever-encompassing, almost-palpable darkness. As the pair moved into the shadows, their steps grew quieter. The air felt as though it might reach out and strangle them at any moment. If not for Kalon's training, he might well have turned tail and run. The only thing that kept Andreas from doing the same was his determination to prove to Kalon he could handle whatever was thrown at him.

"This corridor just goes on for damn ever," Andreas muttered softly under his breath, his fingers tightening against Thought and Memory. "Do you not think so?"

Kalon stopped for a moment and canted his head to the side. "We have crossed an imperceptible threshold, moved from one place to another."

"What do you mean, like a magic portal?"

"Not quite, but close enough."

"Shit."

"We're farther underground than we were before. The air is different, colder, and there is more magic here than the port. I cannot guess as to where we might be, but I can tell you this is a dangerous place—be on your guard, investigator." Kalon motioned the other man to continue and moved with soft footfalls down the corridor of dark stone.

A soft radiance lit the walls. Kalon presumed it was again magic, designed to do away with gas driven lamps or glowstone lights. Perhaps it was also scientific, using a natural bioluminescence of some kind.

The corridor led into a larger chamber, decorated in a manner that brought to mind a heady mix of torture chamber and alchemical lab. The kind of place, Kalon mused, where the likes of Reva Flynn would feel at home amongst the alembics and other apparatus of the alchemist's profession. There was no sign of the mage that had ambushed them and then fled, but the chamber held many side passages and potential places to scurry or hide.

"This will not be an easy search," Kalon concluded from the nearby archway. "Nor am I predisposed to just entering without caution."

Andreas nodded and looked around. Dim light remained in long, spear-like shafts, cutting the air in rods and picking up the dust of ages that floated around the room. A tenuous low hum set his teeth on edge as he continued to look around, his eyesight aided by the thirteen small glowstone lamps set at intervals around the walls.

"Circular chamber, thirteen lamps, lots of low vibrations. You feel all that?" he asked the Inquisitor.

"Yes."

"Magic?"

"I expect so. After all, this is an important chamber, and a mage led us here."

"A mage," concluded the investigator, "who we can't find."

"Yes."

"Bugger." Andreas put one foot forward and winced, half expecting it to be blown off at the ankle. "What do we do?"

Kalon examined the floor, looked at the walls, and sought out any clues or patterns that might reveal the use of magic to track, entangle, or even harm anyone who dared to venture into that ominous chamber. Curiously, there was nothing visible in the architecture. "It appears safe, but we both know that might not be the case. I am protected from magic for the most part, but you are not."

"Yeah." Andreas frowned at that.

"My knowledge of numeromancy will keep us safe, as long as you remain behind me when I command you to."

"Ok. Whatever you said, I'll just do as you ask," Andreas grumbled softly.

Safety check done, Kalon entered the room and stopped suddenly as their quarry stepped from an alcove, almost gliding across the stonework, carefree. What fear had been in the man's mind at the time of his flight gone. Something felt off to Kalon; something else slithered along with the man's movements—his shadow did not look right.

"Stop!" Kalon ordered. Andreas moved off to his right and trained his guns on the hooded figure.

"Inquisitor...and a lap dog." A soft tone sneered at Andreas from under the shadows of the low-pulled cowl. "How lovely."

Kalon paced a few steps closer. "You will come with us for questioning."

"I cannot, even if I wished to." The mage chuckled softly.

"What do you mean, you cannot?" Andreas snorted. "You put one foot before the other and follow us...or Kalon here shoots you full of holes you'll never be able to magic away."

"The die is cast, I'm afraid. My race is run. My body is spent." The mage grinned from under the hood. A flicker of one eye opened, then another, and another, and slowly in the dark of that cowl grew a multitude of eyes within eyes.

"Fortune protect us!" Andreas stepped back. "What the hell is that?"

"I am the end of the regime; I am the undoing of the Inquisitor and the Cardinal's lapdogs." The mage sneered. "Waste your time destroying this body, and it will only bring about your death all the quicker."

In all his time in the church, Kalon had not seen a single thing like this manifest. He had read and studied the ancient histories of Hestonia, and he knew of the Anshada and their terrible rituals, which opened doors that should not be opened. A passage of one book rolled into the back of his mind, sneaking in unbidden, like a cat hunting for a mouse.

Some doors lead to fame, some doors lead to riches, some doors lead to power, some doors should never be opened.

Every single fiber of Kalon's being wanted to blast the heretic into cinders. He wanted to pull the triggers of both his pistols. He knew, however, that it would be futile, like trying to sew using a needle made of mist.

"So, you understand, then..." The mage's neck snapped sharply under the hood, and something dark blossomed from behind him. He screamed. More cracks and whip-like snaps echoed around the chamber as what had once been a man was replaced by something else entirely.

"The final heresy, the worst that a mage can commit, and the ultimate pledge to those who lurk beyond," Kalon said softly under his breath. "A conduit, a blood door, and..."

He didn't finish the rest as the creature ripped itself from within the sorcerer's dangling form, as if it used the mage as part of a puppet-show made of grisly red strings. Tendrils of magical energy bound up in a visceral spray of fluids marked the monster's arrival into the world and the mage's ascension to demon-hood.

"Fuck..." was all Andreas could say. He was not prepared for this.

The demon snuffed out the light in the room as ever-tangible shadows grew. It lashed out suddenly, nearly taking the gunslinger's head clean off. Andreas ducked sideways and threw himself to the floor. As he rolled, he peppered the demon with crack after crack of gunfire.

The bullets exploded against the unearthly hide and blew holes right through the demon, trails of acrid smoke curling upward into the air. Kalon seized his chance and raised a gun to fire. As he did so, a black, oily tendril slapped toward him with inhuman speed, catching the Inquisitor off guard and smacking the weapon from his left hand, numbing Kalon's fingers.

Kalon, knocked to the side by the sheer force of the blow, felt his bones rattle. He hit a hard wooden table with a bone-jarring crack. He groaned in pain and righted himself, only to find that he was once more under assault. The beast was fast, pulsing with magical energy and flickering with whispers of demonic power.

It hoisted the Inquisitor from the ground and wrapped a clawed hand around his throat. A multitude of eyes opened across its body, and it stared at Kalon through all of them.

Then slowly, inevitably, it opened a massive maw lined with sharp, hook-like teeth in what remained of the mage's upper torso and neck. Andreas watched the transformation and dropped his guns back into their holsters. Casting about for something to lend Kalon aid, he threw random bottles from the shelves against the creature's back. The liquids mixed with unexpected results, as part of the demon caught fire with a blue flame, and it howled in sudden pain.

The gunslinger became its focus now. It dropped Kalon, who sagged like a rag doll and took a long, deep breath to force air into his lungs. One pistol down and his left hand numb, he drew a cylinder from his belt and pressed the activation crystal into his right thumb. A tiny prick of pain and a drop of blood later, his reward snaked out from the hilt of the weapon.

Liquid metal flowed like silk and coalesced into a fully formed blade, carved with anti-magic equations and layered from metals that its maker, Daroni, knew sundered the weave of magic that wrapped all creatures, including demons.

Kalon was far less concerned with the artifice of the sword than effect it had on demonic entities.

Andreas kept hurling bottles at the monster until he had nothing left to throw. He moved out of the way as it surged toward him and started to throw books from the nearest shelf. The demon howled— the remaining part of the mage's mind was angered by the treatment of the tomes. The Inquisitor steeled himself, pushed aside his pain and, calling on his training, gripped the hilt of the sword, not too tightly, but with enough conviction to ram it in into the demon's back. The monster did not see his strike, nor his approach. Andreas' impromptu alchemical mixtures had blinded its eyes-within-eyes, stripping it of a vital sense.

The sword hit home, equations tearing through layers of hide and magic as if they were smoke. As Kalon turned the blade and sliced left, then right, gouts of magic-tainted blood burst forth, igniting as they mixed with the alchemical reagents on its back.

The demon thrashed, howling in agony and rage. Kalon was lifted into the air, hanging on as the monster thrashed around like a beached whale. It tried in vain to shake the Inquisitor off, but Kalon held on with fierce determination, sword buried deep as the equations took their toll and the creature began to phase out of existence.

It was almost impossible to kill a demon. They were incredibly resilient against most forms of damage and mundane weapons. But the church had an arsenal developed by the finest minds, artificers, and crafters in the land. The sword might not have killed the monster...but it ripped it from this world and sent it howling to another plane entirely.

Kalon dropped down a good eight feet and landed as nimbly as he could on the ground, his whole body one big ache. He shut the sword down and put it back onto his belt.

"Thank you," he said to the investigator. "Your distraction saved my life."

Andreas smiled a little. "Fifty-fifty. No one's counting, Inquisitor. We did what we had to, and it was all I could think of while I was busy trying not to lose my mind. I don't know how you can handle this kind of thing day in and out. But, nifty sword, tech-magic—got to love it."

"Training," Kalon replied and retrieved his gun from where it had fallen, then stowed it. As he reached back down, his hand brushed the side of a mysterious, dark-hued book, and he stopped. He felt a tingle run down his arm, and the feeling of pins and needles vanished from his numb hand.

"Curious," he spoke quietly in reply.

"What is?"

"This book." Kalon lifted it up and put it on a table. "I am drawn to it, and I do not know why. Yet."

"Be careful—though I don't need to tell you that." Andreas moved to Kalon's side and leaned on the table. "How's the hand?"

"Better..." Fate's Hand wrinkled his nose and placed his recovered left hand on the top of it. "I find that curious. I do not know why...I should be protected from magical effects by my clothing and gloves."

"Fortune's smile, eh?"

"The One-God of the Infinite Machine might have permitted her aid." Kalon mused on this and shook his head. "No, there is but One God according to the church, and all others are merely shadows of his power."

"That's going to start a few wars." Andreas shook his head. "People don't like it when you take away their right to believe."

Kalon flipped the book open with his gloved fingers. "Immaterial at this time, inconsequential to the investigation at hand." He pored over the pages, then closed the book with a look of concern on his face.

"What is it, magic?"

"Yes." He knew it was more, but he could not yet confide in the investigator. "There are secrets in this book. It is old, speaks of history, and of things I shall not utter, for fear of inviting calamity. Books like this need special care and attention, that much I can tell you."

"Oh?" Andreas took a few steps back out of concern for his well-being.

Fate's Hand lifted the book up off the table and placed it into his coat. A long, wide pocket inside provided the perfect place to stow extra equipment or sudden discoveries. He turned a half-step and looked around the room until he met Andreas's gaze once more.

"We have found out all we can, dispatched a demon, and discovered a whole sanctum of heretical knowledge. You will, of course, be commended for your role in all this, but for now, we should return to Sullavale Port proper before any door we might have passed through is closed," Kalon said, retracing his steps toward the way they came in.

"I'm happy to follow you on this, Inquisitor. I don't want anything to do with odd books, magic rooms, demons, or damn wizards any longer than I have to. I like proper criminals, you know? Give me a heist or even a murder. I'd take a good murder investigation right now."

"That's what began all of this."

"Oh, point to you. Maybe a robbery, then, or something like that. Yes." Andreas chuckled to himself nervously. "Something simple."

"Wizards are rarely simple. Even the most basic of sorcerers can cause great issues," Kalon replied and pointed to the way out. "Come."

Andreas nodded and moved swiftly toward the way they'd entered the chamber.

They finally stepped out into the sunlight of the port—blinking to adjust to the sudden brightness and taking a few soft breaths to pull in the fresh, salty air.

"So good to be out of that place, right?" the gunslinger breathed. "All that magic and stale air, dust, and goddess knows what else."

"I am pleased we were able to leave," Kalon replied as he continued to head toward the center of town, his long coat flapping against the strong breeze. "It would have been a long trip to return from wherever that was. I'm glad the mage's death did not seal the way."

"Ah, yeah, I didn't think of that bit."

"I did."

"Right, well, it's been fun, but you don't need me to get under your coattails any longer. I can't say I enjoyed my time as an assistant to Fate's Hand, but I can't say I didn't learn a thing or two. Kalon, Fate's Hand, Inquisitor, or whatever you prefer—catch you around!" Andreas pivoted, tilted his head in Kalon's direction, and beat a hasty retreat toward another alley. "I'm off to find lovely ladies and get drunk!"

Kalon never broke his stride as he continued along his way, the man's words barely reaching his ears as the Inquisitor sought to find a quiet space and muse over what had transpired. As usual, the port was full of people living their lives.

He passed an arched door, disturbing a pair of young men who kissed fiercely in its shadow, away from the heat of the sun. They stopped, a look of fear in their eyes as they saw Kalon. It was natural to eye any agent of the church with a mix of fear and awe. They were enforcers and protectors—but that protection came with a cost if they discovered you hiding magic from them.

They embraced again as the Inquisitor did not stop to engage them.

Kalon ended up near the edge of the pier, where he leaned against the rail, his course diverted at the last few steps from the center of town. He took in the air, but the beauty of the place, the cry of the gulls, only touched him on a superficial level.

Only a young man and woman, hand in hand, strolling down the edge of the pier toward the lower dock disturbed him. He waited, and after they passed, he took a moment to collect his thoughts and process all he had seen.

Once he was sure he was away from prying eyes, he took out the book and found a quiet place to sit. A few seagulls scattered as he eased himself down on a long bench. Now, without distraction, he opened the battered tome and flicked through it.

The more he read, the more he knew what he had to do. Someone had written in the book, leaving a series of notes and a partially drawn map. One name stood out from among all the tell-tale words upon the page. It was circled, and next to it, someone had written a label: *Stealer*. Next to this was a picture of an ornate mirror and the word *Key* that had been hastily underlined several times.

"Spry Genris." Kalon mouthed the name once and looked at the skyline beyond the port. "Here in Sullavale, and marked in this book." With a flick of his gloved fingers, he snapped the book shut, stowed it once more, and stood.

"Who are you, Spry, and what do the Anshada want with you?"

CHAPTER 6

THE STEALER

Elsewhere in Sullavale Port, someone was asking that very same question as he dug his hands into his pockets, picked out a small crust of bread, and dropped it on the ground next to his feet. A small creature with a long body and a perfectly furred dark mask looked up at him with beady little eyes and chirped a polite thank you—or at least that's what Spry thought he said.

Spry Genris was lithe, short, whip-cord thin, and dressed in a manner that only those who know the streets could pull off. Tatty clothes, with just that hint of respectability—nothing about his outfit drew attention to him. The nobility of the port looked vaguely in his direction and then pretended he wasn't there—like they did to so many others.

It was important in his line of work to remain as invisible and inconspicuous as possible, since the best Stealers didn't wander around in dark, hooded cloaks packing a bandolier of throwing knives or tools. His accomplice, a ferret by the name of Charlie, was his only true friend—the rest of the people around him used him, and he in turn used and got what he wanted from them.

That was life in the slums and alleys of the port.

"Oi, Spry!" He half-turned to see the bustling figure of a curvy chimney sweep approaching fast. "I want a word with you on behalf of Mister Packet."

"I'm done, May. Bastard still hasn't paid me for the last job." Spry punted Charlie up the backside with his boot. "Off you go lad, out of sight."

With a snort the ferret shot under a table, dragging his bread with him, and glowered in the shadows at both Spry and May.

May was ragged, covered in the dust from a chimney, and held Spry's eye like any lass might. He kind of liked her, but he was painfully shy and completely out of his depth.

"I could pay you?" May winked.

"Tempting, but no. I need money to live, and while the sex would be fun and full of frolics, I can't live on sex alone," he said, dodging her question.

"One day I'll get you to come to bed with me." May wagged a finger, heaved her soot-covered bosom, and mock-pouted at him. "Is it 'cause I'm not one of them Kharnates?"

"N-no," Spry stammered a little. "Of course not. That would probably seal the deal."

"I bet it would. You'd be like one of them stallions or a rutting dog if I was. Fancy a bit of wolfwoman do you? Oh, the things I could do to you if I had that goddess's gift flowing through my body."

"That's an image I'm going to spend most of the day removing from my mind."

She laughed; it was like a dozen small crystal bells combined with a wind chime. Oddly soothing, yet somewhat off-putting at the same time. "I saw one once, she was all legs…goddess, so much leg. Ripped a bloke in half who thought to slap her, the change was quick like, fast… never forget it lovely – not as long as I live."

Spry shuddered and sat on a small wall in the dilapidated alley. "So, what does Packet want exactly?" The shadows of a pair of pointed-eared, lithe kelanari passed close by, followed by a jakarta with her tail swishing softly behind her.

May sauntered over and put herself right before the teenager. "He wants you." She winked again. "He's got a powerful need, like me, for a Stealer to nick something."

Spry was about to say something when he stopped cold. His dark, sorrowful blue eyes, framed under thin brows, locked onto

May. Her own hazel eyes met his, and she tousled his shaggy, short, corn-colored hair, moving her lips close to his.

Just before she could kiss him a voice rang out into the alley.

"Spry Genris?" Sibilant tones were molded into that question. They came with a ring of power about them, and Spry blinked a little. May stepped back in frustration. "Bugger," she blurted out in irritation. "What do you want with Spry, eh?"

The question died on her lips. Spry hopped off the wall and stood right in front of her, following her gaze. He narrowed his eyes at the figure who sauntered down the alley like a dancer, long fingers playing against the stonework, a whisper of sound following behind them.

Charlie squeaked an "eep" and curled away out of sight.

The figure in the robe and hood made no move to hide, nothing to assuage Spry and May of the feeling of terror they both experienced. Their robe, as green as emerald, marked the figure as Anshada, and without needing to see a spell, both sweep and Stealer knew this was trouble.

"I have come to take you with us," the hooded mage said, extending their left hand. "We need your talents, young man. You will be rewarded with anything your heart desires. We can elevate you beyond these murky streets and whores."

"I ain't no whore!" May snarled and looked for something to throw.

"Nothing wrong with whores, either," Spry said, keeping himself between May and the Anshada. "Better than wizards." He spat onto the floor.

The shadows in the alley moved, shifting into a pattern that should not be, especially at the time of day. The air seemed to thicken, and Spry blinked as his eyes started to itch, as though he had been chopping onions.

"Magic, May...RUN!" Thinking only of her, he pushed the young woman and did something stupid.

Out from his belt he pulled his little fruit knife, set it into his right hand, and charged the hooded wizard. May screamed at him, called him all sorts of words she only reserved for good friends, and took to her heels down the alley—only to look back the once.

What she saw scared her half to death.

As Spry came at the wizard with murder in his eyes, Charlie followed suit. Both youth and ferret struck at once, Charlie with his tiny dagger-like teeth and Spry with his knife. They met nothing except shadow, and that shadow became a mass of writhing, whip-like tentacles populated by bloodshot eyes. Both were wrapped in darkness and swallowed whole, pulled inside this morass of demonic energy in a blink.

While May stood stunned at the end of the alley, her mouth moved absently, and she hugged herself. "Spry?" she asked the wind.

Spry, Charlie, and the wizard were gone.

"Spry?" she yelled.

Only a small mote of dust replied, swept off by the uncaring wind into the rest of the now silent alley.

May sank to her knees as her ragged dress folded about her—and cried.

Tapper Sizemore worked for Mister Packet. He did the things Packet was too lazy or cowardly to do. He was a big man, good with his fists, and wore the kind of clothing associated with the gentry. He was very proud of his top hat, stolen from a nobleman after he beat the man senseless, and he was very pleased with his colorful attire that belied his true rotten nature, hidden beneath the peacock-like sham.

He walked the alleys of the port as the sun dragged on. It would be a few more hours until the night crowd rolled out. May should have had the Stealer by now. He passed a man in black who sat at a small table, concentrating on a book, and paid him no mind.

Tapper paused, licked his lips, and waved a denizen over—another one of Sullavale Port's resident charmers, a man by the name of Dandy. He was neither dandy nor very pleasant.

"Wot?" He picked his nose as he walked over to Tapper. "I got things to be doing."

"Pardon?" Tapper's faux-cultured reply punctuated the sudden right-snap jab that he threw into Dandy's belly.

Dandy went down on the ground, and people close by stepped back, startled.

"That's 'Excuse me Mister Tapper sir, what can I do for your august personage today?'" Tapper said.

Dandy looked up from the ground and groaned. "Bastard."

"My legitimacy has nothing to do with the present enquiry, peasant." Tapper lifted his right foot and placed his muddy boot under Dandy's chin. "I have a question. Then you can go back to violating pigs."

"That's no way to talk about your sister." Dandy just didn't know when to keep his trap shut.

Tapper hauled him off the ground and growled into his left ear. "One more crack like that, and I'll ask Mister Packet if I can introduce you to my fish-filleting knife I got for my last job."

"All right, all right." Dandy smoothed himself down. "What do you want?" he groaned.

"Better."

"Yeah, come on."

"Spry, the Stealer. Did he come this way with May?" Tapper's impatience was wearing thin, sort of like his hair.

"Probably shagging in a back alley. You know May." Dandy mimed something graphic and drew gasps of amusement and disgust from some onlookers.

"I don't care. Packet wants them both, and what Mister Packet wants, Mister Packet…" Tapper left this part hanging in the air.

Dandy chewed his bloody bottom lip and thought about this. "Gets?"

"Right, good lad. So, seen May at all?"

"Not since she waltzed past earlier this morning, doing whatever it was she was doing." Dandy answered and rubbed his gut where an ache remained from Tapper's blow.

"Which way?"

Dandy stepped a little way back from Tapper, out of punch range, and replied, "Down Finkle Street and up Backend Lane."

"Charming. Her usual haunt, then?" Tapper noted the man's movement and smiled a little. Intimidation always seemed to work for him. "See, life is far less painful if you cut the gob, play nice, and stop being a smart-little-arse."

Dandy snorted but kept otherwise silent.

"You can go, then. Bugger off, my good man." Tapper raised his top hat and looked at the crowd, who also gave him a wide berth. He winked at a couple of women on the edge of his sight and bowed. "Ladies."

Dandy watched him go and envisaged a knife sinking into the other man's side, just between the third and fourth ribs. He smiled widely and sighed. Such small pleasures, he thought.

The book held Kalon's interest at the small street-side café for a while, until he heard the name: Spry. Without giving himself away, and shrouded by the disturbed crowd, Fate's Hand had his eye on the bully. He studied the interaction, concluded that Tapper was more afraid of people than he let on, and marked Dandy as a fool.

But that wasn't what caught his ear. Spry was the name in the Anshada journal, a name Kalon had no idea where to find or how to follow up on. Until now.

Now he had a person, a target, and a handful of questions—he sincerely hoped that Tapper was intelligent enough to recognize the trappings of his role. May was immaterial for now, but he filed her name away as a potential lead should Tapper fail to provide what he needed to know.

As the man in the hat left on his search, Kalon closed the book, put it into his wide pocket, and rose like a shadow from the table. His coat spread like raven's wings as it brushed over the iron and wood chairs. He passed a coin to a jakarta waitress; the panther-jackal woman swished her tail and tucked the offering into her tunic, beaming a bright but toothy smile as he left.

An Inquisitor did not blend in, and Kalon's outfit marked him as more than a mere Inquisitor. Many stepped out of the way. Some offered a deferential nod. A few nearly fell over their own feet to put as much distance between themselves and the Inquisitor as was humanly possible. Dandy cleared off quickly so he could observe the other man from behind a stack of boxes piled high with fish.

Those non-humans present there in the port kept a respectful distance as well. The jakarta panther-jackal people from across the sea—traders, and seafarers—their jade eyes ever watchful. The long-limbed kelanari, who folk often mistook for elves from the old stories. The brutish-looking hadul, hardworking and full of fire for righteous causes. Kalon ignored all this, his eyes on the man in the hat.

Tapper realized someone was on his tail. He stiffened his shoulders, felt in his jacket for a knife, and slipped it into his left hand, where it lay against a scar quite comfortably. Then, with another elegant doff of his top hat to a young boy, he swerved right into his favorite hunting ground: Bell Alley.

If the walls of the alley could speak, they would tell a tale of misery, blood, and murder so long it would take dozens of tomes to capture the details. Bell Alley was a forbidding place, described by many in the port as a place where life came to an end, where mortar was made from bone. Hundreds of ghosts lurked out of sight and mind, just on the edges of reality. They poked and tore with fingers made of vapor at the people who dared venture there, night or day. Those who died in the alley were often caught by these specters, hungry for any morsel of soul energy they could garner.

Tapper knew it well, and often after a few ales he'd regale crowds with his grisly exploits down that alley. He could recite where he murdered each and every unlucky sod for Packet, right down to how and when, even what they were wearing and what they said as they met their end.

Kalon would be no different if Tapper had his way, the killer was sure of that. He just needed to use his usual trap, and his usual killing ground. The knife would do the rest. The sweet feel of that blade going into the man's flesh would add to his stories around the tankards.

Kalon observed the change in the man's demeanor, the tip of the hat, the sudden shift into the nearest alley. He paused at the edge of the turn, looked at the urchin, and then back at the gap in the stonework. The child smiled at him in the way that children who grow up on streets appear to be pleasant enough but hide a lifetime of suffering under their dirty and matted hair.

The Inquisitor emotionlessly dug out a coin and tossed it to the boy. "Tell me of that man."

A means to an end, the currency of information. Need, want, ignorance, and greed.

The child looked down at the coin with the cog and eye and the woman on the other side. He looked back at the tall stranger, and his mind drew a picture of someone larger than life. The cog and eye around the Inquisitor's neck seemed to stare back at him, and he blinked.

"Tapper, sir?" He held the coin close and bit it, just to test. "He's a bad one. He'll kill you if you go into the alley. Seen him do it before. Takes all his victims in there, he does. Men, women, children, others."

"Go on."

"Seen him cut a man so bad that they had to sew him back up when the Baggers came to take him."

"Baggers?"

"Yes, sir. The people from the mortuary."

"Ah."

"I can keep this?" The boy held the coin carefully, as though it might vanish from his fingers at any moment.

"I gave it to you," Kalon replied and looked down the alley again. He read the sign out loud "Bell Alley."

"Yeah, s'right murder place."

Kalon nodded and started forward. A thought flickered in the back of his mind, and he stopped, his coat settling once more at his ankles. To the child, it seemed almost alive.

"Spry. Do you know him?"

The child nodded. "Yeah, Spry is the best—always looks after us kids. May has it bad for him. I saw her once doing things with her fingers and moaning his name over and over."

Kalon put up his black-gloved right finger. "There is no need to tell me more. Where is he?"

"I don't know. But why do you want him?" The urchin shifted uncomfortably from one foot to the other.

"I have more of these coins to give him for a job I need him to do," Kalon answered flatly. "Perhaps he will share those with you when he's done."

"Oh, that would be nice, sir, nice indeed."

"So, do you know where he is?"

"About this time, if May has anything to do with it…he'll be with her in the Ramshackle House."

"Ramshackle House? Where?"

"Off Little Lane, cross the east side, and into Packet's territory. A whorehouse, sir, for everyone. She's a sweep, but she's got a hidey-way in there. Takes all the special people to it, she does."

"Ah, Packet." Kalon nodded sharply. "Thank you, young man."

"Taylor, sir."

"Thank you then, Taylor. I would probably leave now if I were you. What is the quickest way to get to the east side?" Kalon never took his eyes off the alley where Tapper had gone.

Taylor raised his small, grubby left hand and pointed past the Inquisitor. "Bell Alley, sir, where Tapper went."

"Excellent," Kalon said smoothly, and he stepped into the gap between the stonework, leaving Taylor with a few final words. "Speak of this to no one, and if I see you again, you will gain one more coin as a reward."

Taylor's eyes lit up.

As the Inquisitor moved further into the alley, he was aware of eyes on him. People perched like scavenger-birds upon the rooftops, a hungry yet apprehensive look in their eyes. Many knew better than to attempt to mug an agent of the church, and those who had observed him from the start knew even better.

Especially Scarlet—or Verity, as she was truly known. Her life was something else now, and she remained clad in dark colors, masked, hooded, and far from anyone's eyes atop the roofs of the port town. Her friend was stalking in that alley below her.

"Are you here for me, old friend?" she whispered to the oncoming night. "Or is another your target?"

She shadowed Kalon for a while, leaping nimbly across from gap to gap as he followed the maze-like corridors of Bell Alley. Then she saw Tapper around a corner; the glint of metal in his hand gave his plan away. He lurked out of sight, a shard of polished glass positioned to give him a full view of Kalon as he approached, waiting to get the first and hopefully last strike in.

Verity had a choice to make once again, and this time there was no bomb to stop her.

CHAPTER 7

KNIVES AND PERFUME

B ell Alley waited, and so too did the hungry, ravenous, and starved ghosts who had escaped or eluded the notice of the ever-present God of Death—the Shroud. Truth be told, the Shroud had little time for the souls of the dead; they had no meaning to him. He only picked the best, the most soul-ripe apples from the tree of life.

His faithful companion, the beast at his heels, Fathriir, was less choosy, and he could smell death from centuries away.

The Shroud's domain sat at the end of all things, all life, where only he and Fathriir remained, and the souls of the dead were sport for the greedy wolf. Those who entered the god's domain found quickly that their promised afterlife was nothing but a wicked lie designed to fill endless pews and provide power to people who desired control.

He sat on a wrecked throne at the center of what was once the Imper Vatica and observed the ages of Hestonia with his mind's eye, just like the creature at his heel. He would let the canine off his leash, let him devour the dead, and that was their fate—their eternal reward.

The Shroud reached a pale hand down and ruffled the wolf's neck. "Patience," he whispered. "What will be, will be."

Bell Alley hungered in the land of the living. The rooftop night-lurkers made bets on the stranger's survival. It was their entertainment, the best that their perches could provide. Riffraff, scoundrels, ruffians, killers, the scorned, and more called the upper parts of the port their home, and they had many secret routes above the town.

Verity knew them all; she had come to the roof-ways early on. A natural at slipping into social circles, be they lower, higher, or downright rotten. Her penchant for disguise carried her even further, and her role as a Shadow Knife meant she knew how to deal with overly amorous would-be suitors in any lifestyle she chose to mimic.

So as Kalon drew closer to Tapper, Verity flitted like a bat from roof to roof in utter silence against the dying light of the sun.

Tapper angled the knife and pulled it back, watching the mirrored glass carefully, licked his lips, and tensed. Closer, closer, closer... AND...

As he shot forth to strike, he felt the bones in his wrist shatter as a weight landed on them with such force he heard the crack echo in the alley. The knife dropped with a clatter. He was aware, through the pain, of a metal ball on the end of a length of rope above him before it snapped like a whip and coiled around his throat.

He went up, and Verity came down to land catlike on the cobbles, just as Kalon rounded the corner into the last turn of the alley.

She picked up the knife slowly, then she wrapped the ball around an exposed pipe and folded her arms. She shoved the knife into the stonework and tilted her head.

"Kalon," she said and then put her hands up defensively.

"Verity," Kalon replied but made no move. He observed the dangling Tapper as he kicked, tried to scream, choked, and scrabbled against the rope with his fingers to try and save himself.

"Shoot him down if you want," Verity said. "He was going to kill you."

"I know."

"You didn't look like you knew at all." Verity bristled, then remembered who she stood before. Now a man, Kalon was as cold and formal as he'd ever been as a boy. The only thing that had changed were his skills. "Or perhaps you were the hunter."

"I was," Kalon answered and observed the dangling man as he slowly choked to death. Broken curses flew from Tapper's lips as he expended his oxygen doing the last thing he should have been doing. "He was to help me with my investigations."

"I can help, if you let me." Verity announced.

"You are part of it."

"I know." She echoed his earlier reply, almost perfectly.

Tapper's kicks slowed. Verity sidestepped, and a pool appeared at her feet.

"He'll be dead soon," she said quietly.

"He is no longer part of my investigation," Kalon replied, dismissing the man dangling from the weighted rope. "Taylor told me he was a gentleman with deaths under his belt. Perhaps the alley is the best place for him to retire."

"I thought so." Verity grinned a little, predatory in the gathering dark.

The watchers above were displeased. Most of their bets had been wrong. The few who were right rolled in their newfound wealth and knew better than to stick around for an encore. With the promise of many drinks to share in victory, they left into the oncoming night before they had an accident with gravity or a sharp knife.

"Did you kill Rand?" Kalon asked flatly.

Verity hid her anger well, under her mask, under her hood, but her shoulders fell a little. Some of the defiance vanished before it struck back, and she straightened her shoulders. The woman walked right up to Kalon and put her face before him, took down her mask, and spoke. "I fucking well did not. I loved Rand."

Kalon judged her words, heard the emotion in her voice, sliced the sincerity and anger out of her reply. A single nod confirmed it.

"Mallori, then?"

"That fucking snake. If I find him Kalon, I'll…"

"He is protected. Be careful."

"Rand was someone I could have married; I could have had a life with him beyond all this shit." Verity snapped her gaze up. Tapper was dead, so she let the rope loose, slamming his body to the ground with a satisfying crack.

"Our life is the church," Kalon said flatly, making note of the body. "I need to find a young man, Spry Genris. You know him?"

"I know May, and she knows Spry. I can help you find May." Verity coiled the rope around her arm and then stowed it into her bag. "Is that all you want?"

"Yes." Kalon nodded and looked at Tapper again. "Meet me at the Ramshackle. The perfume you wore as the Duchess...do you still have it?"

"The fancy strawberry one?"

"Yes. It is distinctive. Wear it, and I will know you beyond any face you create."

"Ok. Give me an hour?" Verity kicked the body over and rifled the pockets. "Once a thief, always a thief, eh luv?" Her voice took on a crude and unpolished tone.

Kalon offered one last parting reply as he left for Sullavale Port's safer areas. "Thank you, my friend." It sounded flat, hollow. But it was something.

Verity pushed back tears from her memory of the day Rand died: Mallori's smirking face, the explosion, and her escape. She kicked Tapper's body in frustration twice before she left him to the rats and, with a defiant face, pulled her mask back over her chin and nose. She took to the rooftops once more and left the body to lay in a pool of blood and urine. Anna Kora could deal with it—she'd love that.

Dark mist pulled over Tapper's body as he became aware of chanting—or was it laughter, singing maybe? A mix of them all. He stood. The walls of Bell Alley looked old, broken. Bits were missing, and bones lay all around him. He kicked a pile of them away with a disgusted snort and muttered, "What the fuck?"

He stumbled out into the street beyond the alley. No one waited to greet him. The landscape was different, the sky pocked with holes, and there was no sun. The wreck of a windship, smashed into the side of a tavern, drew his attention; it was one he'd seen time and time again at the port. The once golden, eagle-like shape was broken and battered, twisted and mangled.

"Hah, serves you fucking right, kelanari scum. Hope they chopped them points off your ears!"

A figure coalesced from the air, tall and pale, dressed from head to foot in a robe over clothes made from black leather. At the figure's left heel sat a dark-furred, ember-eyed wolf lolling its tongue in a manner that made Tapper nervous.

"Who the fuck are you, and where's everyone?"

"Hazard a guess." The Shroud chuckled softly and swept his bone-white arm out to encompass the street. "All life ends; all things come to a stop. Mist Reavers fall from the sky, hearts cease to beat, empires collapse into rubble. Even gods can perish."

"Make some fucking sense, my head's ringing..."

"Here at the end of all things, only we remain."

"Who the fuck are we?"

"Fathriir..."

The wolf looked up expectantly.

"Fetch."

The howl that followed shook the ground, and Tapper's spirit felt more fear than he ever had while alive—not even his own death at the hands of the assassin had made him truly afraid. In fact, he was angry he'd been killed by a slip of a thing. But the beast that shot forth and grew by leaps and bounds frightened his soul more than anything he'd ever known.

First as large as a wolf, then a horse, then a house...and then the creature's maw engulfed the man, darkness on teeth and slavering tongue.

The Shroud smiled thinly.

"Account settled."

The body in Bell Alley bucked up into the air suddenly as a pair of greedy men rifled the pockets. Teeth marks appeared upon it, blood fountained forth, and bones snapped. It kicked more, rocked, and shook from side to side.

The men ran screaming into the night, piles of assorted loot left to witness the final chapter of a murderer's life.

Anyone who saw felt a deep chill in their bones as they witnessed Tapper's body devoured by an invisible hunger.

In the Shroud's realm, the wolf came back to his master's side, sat down, and licked a paw covered in whispers of grey and blue energy.

"Sated?" The Shroud ruffled the creature's neck.

Fathriir whined a little.

"Of course not. He was merely a morsel compared to the eventual banquet you will have." The Shroud snapped his fingers. "Come, let us tour my kingdom for a while. Pay homage to those who have yet to reach this point and are yet to understand my realm."

The smell of strawberries punctuated the air with a blossom-like scent, mixed with something else, raw and vital. Kharnate slid out from behind a pillar of stone, lithe, with blood-red hair and clad in a thin, red garment that flowed like a crimson tide washed on the shores.

"Red sister, what brings you to the end of all?"

"I sensed the soul of a murderous bastard and wanted to see who it was, but your beast ate him before I could even get a peek." Bloody lips cracked into a curved smile; her own golden wolf's eyes looked on from under that frizzy mane. "You could have waited, lovely, just for a little."

Fathriir slipped to the side of his master...and slightly behind him.

"Oh, I don't bite, little wolf, unless you ask me to, very nicely." She gently bared her pointed teeth.

"Don't tease him," the Shroud sighed with a wave of his left hand. "Walk with me. You must have another reason for being here."

Kharnate pouted and slipped to the other side of the Shroud, brushed against him a little, and chuckled. "Lovely, pale, such skin. If only you didn't think of me as your sister."

"All the gods are siblings of mine."

"We were human once."

"That doesn't matter. Does a flightless bird who gains wings want to be the same again?"

"Ooh, birdy!" Kharnate laughed softly, licked her lips, and made a catlike purr.

"My question remains the same." The Shroud put a little more distance between him and the goddess at his side.

"Spoilsport. I guess your manhood is as dead as you are." She walked off and looked across the endless wreck of a ruined world. "How do you even exist here?"

"Easily," the Shroud replied with a smile. "I am the only one here, me and my wolf."

"I thought so. Well, visit over. I'm off to find life and lust and all that good stuff." With a mock bow, a little wave, and a flash of her teeth at the wolf again, the goddess stepped from one world into the next.

Fathriir whined.

"She's gone."

He whined some more.

"Really?"

One more whine.

"I despair of you, sometimes."

An hour later, far away from godly dealings, night had come to embrace the port with soft, salty winds, cool breezes, and a layer of mist held briefly on the air. Small halos danced around the streetlamps where the gas churned away to create bright light in the older districts. The night crowd donned their finery and stepped out into the port to while away the hours till dawn.

Oh, what a "while" it was, too.

Humans and non-humans mixed in these streets, more so after hours, as the workday wound down and the evening jobs began.

The Ramshackle House functioned as a tavern, a place to find companionship if you were looking for it—more if you knew the right questions to ask. From the outside it appeared to be an ordinary looking old building, once a port office, and marked with some of the town's earlier, more revolutionary history. Gunshot holes still peppered the exterior brickwork and created tiny marks all over the wall nearest the latrines.

Now it was full of people from all walks of life. None of the nobility set foot here, but the others—including workers and entertainers—were thick as molasses throughout every room and bar inside the building. Sex work was good work, and plenty could be found for the right person in the house.

Kalon sat outside. The cacophony within the tavern was enough to keep the Inquisitor far away. That, and he could easily keep an eye out for people bearing him ill will and knives—especially knives. A woman with a dark, curly mop of hair slapped his table with a washcloth. Her blouse was open just enough to enthrall boozy patrons, a trick learnt by all pub servers since the dawn of time. It was a trick, too, that had no effect on Kalon.

Verity knew this; it's why she did it.

"Ello, love," she said with a soft sniff. "Like what you smell, like what you see? Only a crown for some information."

Kalon's nose wrinkled, and he caught the strawberry scent he knew from his youth. "Verity," he said softly. "Or who are we today?"

"Lucy at your service, fine gent." She dropped an awkward curtsey. "Not often we have a guest of such high social standing right in our little establishment."

"Lucy, hmm."

"Mind if I take the weight off these feet? Not in that way, either." Verity laughed lewdly and sat down with a heavy sigh. "Oh, my arse is better for that."

Kalon titled his head, bird-like, and wrinkled his nose again. "Lucy, what news do you have for my investigation?"

"So." She leaned in close, as though she were offering a good display of treats on offer, then her voice dropped into a low whisper. "May is at her hideout, guarded by one of Packet's men. Rumor has it she's terrified out of her wits, Packet's angry with her, and she's going to be punished for losing the Stealer."

Kalon tapped on the table with the fingers of his left hand. He rested his right hand across Verity's wrist for a moment, and she felt the weight of a coin. Quickly she snapped it up as though it were the last coin on the planet.

"Ooh, thank you, love. You can definitely come again." She winked. "May's hideout isn't far. Want me to come with you?"

"Like that?"

"If you like, love, or I can dress for my other job?"

Kalon raised a brow. "Which one is that? I lose track."

"Humor?"

"No, I am being serious," Kalon replied and folded his arms. "You have so many faces, accents, and looks that I am impressed you can keep all of it straight."

"I have a little book I write it all down in."

"Really?"

"No, I was making a joke."

"Ah."

"It's years of practice, lovely, living many lives, many faces, many people, and many jobs." Verity sighed and joined Kalon on that question. *Just how do you keep track of an ever-expanding collection of identities, and which one is the real you?* she mused as she idly wiped the table down.

"I would appreciate your assistance," Kalon finally said as he watched her.

Verity smiled a little. "I'm glad you're not trying to kill me over Rand."

"I am convinced and satisfied that you had nothing to do with his death, that your feelings are genuine, and that your role was as much a victim as Rand's," Kalon replied without even a second thought. "Mallori will pay eventually, but for now he is beyond your reach. Even mine, since the Cardinal favors him greatly. Her personal assassin, her own Shadow Knife, and one she has hand-picked to do her bidding and lead the organization."

"Fucker."

Kalon ignored this and continued. "How long will you need?"

"I've got to serve a few more customers, then—oh, my back!" She mimed being in agony. "I'll meet you at that corner over there, just at the intersection of Crook's Avenue. Lovely, eh?"

"Understood. Signal me, and I will rise to meet you."

Verity chuckled in a ribald manner.

"Something wrong?"

"N-no," she stifled a laugh. "All is good. Just getting into character."

Kalon observed the woman as she left his table. He watched everyone constantly; his mind latched onto every single aspect about them, and his memory served to imprint that data into his brain to recall at any moment with perfect clarity. Years of rote training, his Anshada blood, and innate connection to magic gave him an edge that many others were incapable of achieving.

He noted the bonds of friendship, those who were enemies, lovers, jealous—and more—as he sat. He credited his training, but the Cardinal, safe in her velvet and silk palace, knew better. It excited her and scared her in equal measure. If he'd known this, his opinion of Terusa would've been vastly different.

He waited and lost sight of his friend as she passed inside the tavern.

Forty minutes later he caught a flicker of light from the assigned place. Verity waved him over as she snapped her compact shut with a soft click.

The hunt for Spry continued.

CHAPTER 8

HUNTING A STEALER

With a snap of motion, Kalon joined Verity in the alley. She narrowed her eyes at him and sighed. His departure from the table had caused quite a stir, and his attire always meant he stood out. The Inquisitor's outfit was very distinctive, finely made, crafted by Vincent Daroni, and enhanced by the church with equations and crystals. It was one of a kind for his role as Fate's Hand.

"Could you seriously have made any more noise? Perhaps next time you could jump up and down and yell 'FATE'S HAND is here!'" Verity chided and canted her head slightly, looking past Kalon and rolling her eyes. "You've set all the eyes in the street on you now. I had wanted to slip away quietly."

"Time is of the essence, for reasons I cannot divulge." Kalon shook his head. "Expediency is the best option. Is May not in danger?"

"Well, yes, but what good will it do if someone runs off and tells Packet's men we're coming?"

Kalon mused on this and replied. "I prefer the straightforward approach, Verity. Sneaking around these people only gives them more time."

"If they kill May, I'm blaming you."

"They won't."

"Oh, are you psychic now as well as a strait-laced pain in the buttock?"

Verity's jibe bounced off Kalon like rain from a tin roof. He gestured with his left hand that the Shadow Knife should move on. "Lead the way."

"Fine, but we're doing this my way. I have an idea."

"Very well, if it gets us there with less digression...we shall do it your way."

"See, you can be reasonable." Verity grinned and melted into the shadows of the alley, beckoning Kalon onward as they both moved further into the slums of Sullavale Port.

"Why does everyone want Spry?" the Shadow Knife asked Kalon as they traveled the maze-like alleys. "It seems he's popular all of a sudden."

"In Packet's case, it's because he's a talented thief," Kalon said quietly. "Or at least that is why it appears so."

"Stealer," Verity corrected. "Thieves are common-all garden thugs and robbers; Stealers are more refined. Their thievery is like an art form in most cases."

"Packet does not sound like he cares for refinement."

"He doesn't, but the people who Packet often works for do. I don't expect you to understand, Kalon. You deal with magic, wizards, witches, heresy, and all that."

"Your explanation makes sense."

"Hush now. We're almost there!" Verity moved across a wide street. She kept to the shadows and waved a hand for Kalon to move.

He did so, as quietly and carefully as she had.

May's day had started out well. She was sure she could have broken down Spry's resistance and shown the lad a thing or two about how to tumble properly. Then Packet's orders came in: bring the lad to him for a "job." She was about to do that, and then the wizard turned up, and...

May shuddered as she sat on her small cot, flanked by two of

Packet's thugs, Gallows and Facker—who were less than cordial. They knew better than to lay a hand on her without Packet's approval, but their definition of a light touch needed some redefining.

Gallows was as pale as death, thin as a rake, and as gangly as a whip-cord rope. Facker was much bigger, but showed signs of a bad diet, with yellowed eyes and infected teeth that marked the man as someone who dined a little too much on sweet things. Gallows sported a shock of messy blond hair; Facker had a crewcut which had dug into his scalp, an obvious "do it yourself" style.

"What happens now, eh?" May looked from one to the other.

Gallows rifled through her things while Facker busied himself stuffing the last of her cheese and bread down his throat from a now empty cupboard.

"Packet's going to decide what to do with you, having failed him so badly," Gallows said and tossed a pair of knickers to one side. "Expensive. Fetch a pretty penny at Juno's Pawn."

"Fuck off, they're mine." May spat.

Gallows and Facker both laughed in unison.

"Listen, May, the only reason we haven't carved a new mouth into that pretty face of yours is that Packet still has some use for you." Gallows snorted and shook his head. "We're waiting for the knock—it's the knock that decides your fate. One of Packet's runners will be here soon, with a message from the boss. So, when we open that door, you'll either end up dead in a gutter and stuffed in the harbor—or the Peddler will have a new girl." Gallows grinned like a shark. "No matter how you slice it, though, this house will be Packet's soon enough."

"Don't you gots more grub?" Facker licked his lips. "That cheese was rancid."

"You stuffed enough of it down your gob, you damn greedy sod." Gallows picked up another garment and tried it on. "Hey look, I'm May." He pranced around a bit in the frilly garment and then threw it in a pile. "Another one for Juno's!"

May was scared; she had every right to be. She'd heard the stories of Packet's vacancy program. Whichever runner delivered that message, it would end in the same way. Her home would be gone, and she'd be dead or sold to the Peddler.

Gallows caught her look and smiled thinly. "Cheer up May, Peddler's good to girls like you, especially if you give 'em what they want."

"I bet." Facker poked around the cupboard some more. "Empty."

"Ain't gone to market yet, but if you let me go, I'll get you some nice sausage to shove down your throat." May narrowed her eyes and looked at the door, counting the minutes.

"One of us could go with her." Facker looked expectantly at Gallows, rather like a puppy at an empty food dish. "She'd not get away then, and we could still watch her."

"You berk!" Gallows threw a soggy cloth at the other man. "Market's closed now."

"Oh yeah, shit." *Thwap*, the cloth hit Facker in the face. "Oh, that stinks of...what is that?"

Before anyone could answer, someone knocked quietly thrice and then once more with one loud bang. Three pairs of eyes turned to the door; three voices fell silent until Gallows moved across the room. "Well, May." He grinned wickedly. "Time's up. Your fate lies on the other side of that door. Boss's message is here—I'm hoping, honestly, it's a kill order."

"But you said the Peddler," May replied in fear. "Girls like me, you said."

"What we say, and what Packet decides to do..." Gallows winked. "Pray for the Peddler, Maysie." He paused before the door. "Me, I want some time with you and the knife."

"If we have to do it, how we gonna do it?" Facker looked at May. "Break her arms and legs so she can't struggle?"

"Like we did with Giselle," Gallows nodded. "Easier to tie them up and throw them in the drink that way too."

"I was thinking...quick...so we could stop for food just after we does it, and then I won't be hungry no more."

"You and that bloody stomach of yours." Gallows opened the door and looked into the dim street beyond.

The first punch caught him square in the face, his nose shattering like an eggshell. Blood sprayed the doorjamb as he yelped in agony.

Verity kicked him square in his crotch for her next trick, and as he doubled over, she dropped her elbow into the small of his back. The thug crumpled, yowling like a scalded child until one more kick from Verity took all the breath from his body.

Facker lunged over the table to try and get to May, but she kicked backward on her cot, and he missed. She rolled to the side and scrambled out of the way.

Two knives swirled from the shadow of the door, spun end over end in the air, and sunk deeply into Facker's flesh. As he tried to recover from his lunge, his left arse cheek felt the sting of one blade and the second slammed into his outstretched left hand.

Facker repeated "Fuck!" several times, and then as May smashed a metal bedpan over his head twice, he slumped to the floor. Fearful of the intruders in the doorway, May brandished her dripping pan at them, intent to take on all comers.

Verity stepped in and over Gallows's writhing body, lowered her hood and mask, and looked first at Facker, then May. "It's all right, May. We're friends."

May took in Verity and then the man who followed her in, ducking under the door lintel as he entered and standing like some regal bird of prey surveying its new perch. "An interesting plan, not dissimilar to my own," Kalon finally said as he regarded Verity with a newfound respect. "You have improved—not a single movement wasted and not a single mistake. Very impressive indeed."

In her work attire and with her untouched face, Verity did not look like anyone May knew. "Fuck you are! You don't look like anyone I bloody well know."

"I'm Cassie, and this is Kalon Rhadon, Inquisitor of the Church of Progression and Fate's Hand. Lofty titles, but you can trust him. He's good people." Verity smiled disarmingly—hiding her name for now. "Are you ok? Did they harm you?"

"No, they didn't," May stammered softly. "They were going to tie me up after breaking my legs and arms, though, just like they did to poor Giselle. I knew it was them—off to her aunt's for extended leave my arse!" She thwacked Facker on the head again with the bedpan and snarled. "I should cut your throats, you bastards!"

Kalon pondered both men and then decided to leave them to Verity, looking at her directly as his voice took on the authority of the church. "I need May for my investigation. You can deal with Packet's men."

The church-sponsored assassin looked back at him, and a gleam entered her eyes. "You heard what May said about Giselle, right, and what they were going to do?"

"You do what you feel is an adequate response for this. I will support you," Kalon answered. His flinty grey eyes turned to the other woman. "May, I need your help. I wish you to take me to where you last saw Spry."

No compassion, this one. No use trying to woo him, May thought as she looked Kalon over. She couldn't help it; he was easy on the eye. She pouted a little and then threw on a shawl. "Anything to get me out of my hovel for a bit. Hope your Cassie here guts these two like wild hogs."

"She might well do so," Kalon said flatly and held the door open for the woman. "Time is of the essence. Take me to the location now."

"All heart, your friend," May said and stepped over Gallows, kicking him in the balls and smiling as he yelped loudly and thrashed a little more. "Better follow me, then, Inquisitor Rhadon."

"They are all yours, my friend," Kalon said to Verity as he shut the door and followed May into the night, his footsteps echoing against the stones beneath his feet. Verity turned to regard both men, her eyes narrowing as another of her knives slipped easily into her hand.

The twists and turns of the port's streets and alleys were like old friends to May. She had grown up here as a child and knew the safest places to run and the paths to avoid. But right now, even though her ordeal had shaken her up, she was in the company of an Inquisitor of the Church. One of the heroes of old, the protectors against the wizards and mages who dared to endanger them all with reckless use of magic. She proudly used that to her advantage, knowing full well that the eyes of her friends, acquaintances, and enemies were on them both as they made their way to where Spry vanished.

"Not far now, Inquisitor," May said as she stepped quietly down another alley. "I didn't get to properly say thanks for the rescue."

"Cassie was concerned."

"What about you?" she asked coyly.

"You are a valuable asset in my investigation. Professional concern is part of that. How far now?"

"Only professional?"

"Yes."

Tough nut, this one, thought May. *Unless he's not...oh...he might be.* "One more alley, straight as an arrow, like yourself?"

Kalon quirked a brow. "I am tall, yes, but I am not sure what you mean?"

"No matter sir, no matter." *Bugger,* thought May, *won't get anything out of him.*

Finally, they reached the alley. May paused as the memory of the event crept back into her mind. She shuddered and shook her head. "This is it, but I'm not going in. I'll just wait here under this lamp if that's all the same with you, sir." She stood directly under the gleam of the only light attempting to shove the darkness far away.

"As you wish." Kalon nodded and made his way into the alley. He looked left and right and then stopped level with the place where May had tried to kiss Spry. From here he began to investigate the alley for any kind of clues, his trained eyes spotting numerous signs that anyone else might have missed.

A slight discoloration of the paving slabs caught his attention.

"What did you see here in this alley, May, that made you so afraid?" Kalon asked, running his gloved fingers against the stonework. "It could help me to find Spry—alive."

May looked back down the alley into the shadow, toward the Inquisitor. She was torn. Fear gripped her heart like a vice, but her desire to see Spry safe overrode her caution. She left the safety of the light and moved to Kalon's side.

"I saw a wizard-witch. A woman, I think—sounded female anyway. They wanted Spry for a task, just like Packet. Popular lad, but I can see why." May sighed a little and closed her eyes. "He defended me, drew his knife. Him and Charlie attacked her."

"Charlie?" Kalon queried.

"His ferret. Loves that little fella as much as I love him," May explained. "There was magic, I think. I'm not sure. I was scared, and I just don't know." She clamped her hand over her mouth and stifled a sob. "It were terrible, Inquisitor. I ran."

"Magic." Kalon put his right hand against the wall and tapped his fingers. "Thank you, May, this location will help greatly."

"It will?"

"Yes."

"How?"

"Just like an animal leaves a trail for another animal's nose to follow, magic leaves a mark on the world that the church agents like myself can track." Kalon ran his fingers down the wall where the mage had done the same. "The stronger the wizard, the more of a trail—and the more their antics disrupt the Warp and Weft."

May listened. The words didn't make much sense, but she hoped it could save Spry.

"You can see magic?" she asked finally.

"Not quite," Kalon paced, his long coat flickering at his heels. "Not without help. Fortunately there are traveling companions of mine here who will allow me to follow this trail."

"You must have a lot of resources," May said quietly. "Never met an Inquisitor before, let alone Fate's Hand."

"I am the product of much investment from the church—an agent, a tool, and a stalwart servant of the Cardinal." Kalon examined the stonework one last time and nodded. "There is enough here to latch onto." He stepped away from the site.

May had no idea what Kalon meant, only that she felt the man was dangerous and she wanted to be out of his sight as soon as possible— these events and dealings were beyond her. "Can I go home now, sir?" May asked, hugging herself tightly, her voice barely a whisper.

Kalon nodded. "Come, let me take you back to Cassie. I have much work to do, and the quicker I deliver you back, the quicker I can follow the trail of this wizard."

With that, he gestured to May and led her out of the alley, back onto the street. They traveled the rest of the way in silence. Expediency was on the Inquisitor's mind, and May was no longer in the mood to talk. Eventually they reached the slum street where May's hovel was, and she smiled a little upon seeing the familiar broken-down old shack with a single light just barely illuminating the front door.

Kalon knocked, and Verity opened the door cautiously, until she saw it was him.

"Any luck?" She gestured to May to come inside. "Come in, lovely, got a pot of tea on and a little bit of stew."

"Where are they?" May asked as she looked around.

"Oh, they're no longer your concern, May. Don't worry about it. I've tidied up a bit and set things right." Verity's eyes were warm, but inside they held a shard of cold. "Kalon, are you stopping for tea?"

"No." The Inquisitor shook his head. "Time is of the essence. I have a trail. I can catch up to Spry, but I shall need the talents of the *Ori* and her captain."

"Well, be seeing you?"

"Our paths will cross again, I am sure. Be safe and well, Cassie. You too, May." Kalon did not do long goodbyes, or even consider that someone might truly miss him. He waited for May to go back into her home, shut the door, and then stalked off into the night in the direction of where the *Ori* was resting on her freshly commandeered landing pad.

He left Verity to look after May and wonder if she would indeed see him again, and when.

Kalon walked back in the direction of the windship port. He cleaned his gloves with a grey cloth and put it into a small bag he kept inside his coat. *There should be enough residue from the magical interaction with the fabric of the real world to use,* he thought as he paced under the lamplight glare toward the *Ori*.

The light scattered in splintered shadows as the sky grew thick with clouds. It felt like a storm was on its way, and by the time Kalon reached the dock, the first tell-tale whispers of rain heralded dancing flickers of lightning across the bay, leaping from cloud to cloud.

He made his way to the sleek vessel; its slender ramp lowered as if it sensed the man's approach. A sliver of radiance grew and cast an oblong path onto the metal floor under the ship. Rain dribbled down the hull, pinging from every surface as Hestonia's heavens threw down great squalls of wind and water.

"The weather does not seem to like us," Imani said, sheltered in the safety of the lower deck. "You need a towel?"

"The heated air of the ship will suffice. There is no time. I need to speak to the Weaver aboard."

"Shall I take you to her?" Imani closed the ramp off as the wind howled through the hatch.

"Immediately."

"Follow me." Imani turned on their heel, walking back into the *Ori* proper.

The pair stopped at an ornate door. Before the captain could knock, a cold blue light flickered on and the door opened wide. "Come in." The occupant's voice had soft mellow tones that flowed like rich honey wine.

"After you." Imani waited.

Kalon stepped inside, looking around the decadent room. Silk, satin, and many fine furnishings adorned it. A double bed with red linen and a wide canopy lay against the eastern wall, and smoke drifted casually through the air.

The occupant sat cross-legged in the very center of the room, clad only in a chiffon-like robe of red and gold. Her long hair was red as blood, and her eyes held a small fragment of fire in the depths of their beaten-gold sheen.

"Crimson," Imani said with a formal tone. "This is Inquisitor Kalon Rhadon, Fate's Hand."

The woman did not rise. She inclined her head, and a slight smile danced on her red-tinted lips. "An honor."

"Well met, Weaver."

"Inquisitor. Or should I say, Fate's Hand?"

Weavers were indentured servants of the Church of Progression— or, as the commonfolk snidely said, pet mages, shackled and leashed to do the will of the church, a blemish on the otherwise spotless concept of tech-magis, science and magic combined. A Weaver's concern was with magic in its purest form, not magic in thrall to technology. They knew how to grasp the threads that crisscrossed reality and wove their way through it. They created the Tapestry, the combination of magical threads known as the Warp and the Weft.

Kalon knew they were favored by the Cardinal, and a necessary evil—otherwise, like the mages who chose to resist, they would be eliminated quickly. "I thank you for using my title."

"It is only fitting, Inquisitor."

Kalon nodded just the once and respectfully sat down before her, dropping into a cross-legged pose that mirrored her own.

"Crimson, we have work to do."

"We do." It was not a question.

"I am eager to begin."

"You are." Again, not a question.

Kalon dropped the cloth on the floor and placed a finger on it. "A powerful Anshada has taken a youth known as Spry. He is key to an ongoing investigation of mine, one that could change everything. You are familiar with the *Book of the Anshada*, yes?"

Crimson nodded once, a wry smile on her lips.

"I believe they seek it, and this boy is the way to get it," Kalon continued. "Understand, what I have said and continue to say does not leave this room."

Imani nodded. "Absolutely."

"Of course," Crimson's voice purred softly. "Inquisitor."

"I found a journal; it mentions Spry. The youth has been kidnapped from this port with the help of a powerful practitioner of magic. Demon or demon-aided, I do not know. But I know that a Weaver can follow a powerful thread to its source."

Crimson brushed Kalon's hand away gently and lifted the cloth. She sniffed the fabric delicately, her eyes flickered, and she nodded. "We can."

"Find this Anshada, and find me the one they call Spry."

"Yes, Inquisitor."

CHAPTER 9

GHOSTS OF TERRALION

Imani watched Crimson carefully. The captain was an observant sort. When it came to the practice of heresy—namely magic—only Weavers were permitted, by law and order of the church, to do so without any restriction. Imani always wondered how the Cardinal kept the mages on such a tight leash, and why they didn't turn their destructive sorcery upon others.

Only Cardinal Terusa knew that answer, and she kept her silence.

Crimson put the cloth back on the floor and moved her hands as though she were making a cat's cradle from several lengths of string. She plucked at the Tapestry carefully, her eyes picking out the threads and the colors she needed for this spell. Reality, disturbed by this like a lazy dog might be bothered, did not take kindly to the laws of mundane life being flouted so. It bucked and pushed against Crimson to make the magical connections harder to solidify.

However, the Weaver was adept at such trivial sorceries. She pulled the threads down and wrapped them in a complex pattern before Kalon could even blink.

He was quietly impressed by her skill. Even a man who had been trained to oppose magic knew the value of Weavers as tools.

"Your talent is impressive," he said as the first flickers of magic battled against the mundane. "I can see why the church recruited you."

A low, sonorous chuckle trickled from Crimson's lips. "Recruited, yes." Her fingers flew through the secondary and tertiary threads, binding them all together in a final shimmer of gold and purple. "I am ready," she said after a few minutes had passed.

A vague heat-haze settled between her hands, and small flickers, like sparks from a tinder box, danced from finger to finger. "Seek," she said to the air, and a small blue fire danced out of nothing in response.

"I've never seen you do this before," Imani broke into the conversation. "How does it work?"

"Watch," Crimson whispered, her eyes set on the fire. "Find me that which I desire, little soul."

At first, the fire flitted over Kalon's head, and Crimson let out a barely audible chuckle before it danced back to her, finally flickering down to gently touch the fabric, swirling for a few seconds, and growing brighter. A trail of embers formed in its wake, and slowly it drew a picture in the charred parts of the material. The smell of burning fibers followed tiny whorls of smoke into the air.

The Weaver studied the image and smiled a little. The flame winked out as she clicked her fingers.

Kalon furrowed his brow and looked directly at the chiffon-clad woman. "Do we know where Spry and this Anshada are?"

"The picture my little soul drew is perfect; the canvas less so." Crimson picked up the cloth and examined it. "Terralion, Inquisitor. They have gone to the ruined city of the past. The building depicted here is Prescott's Asylum, so I presume you will find the answers you seek there, or at least a further trail."

"Thank you, Crimson." Kalon stood from his position before the sorceress. "You have assisted me greatly. This will not be forgotten."

Her golden, fire-lit eyes settled on the man before her, and she nodded. "Thank you, Inquisitor. It was a pleasure to put you back on the trail."

"Captain, set the *Ori* on course for Terralion and get us over this storm," Kalon ordered and made his way toward the door. "I will be in my cabin. Summon me if you require my aid."

Imani offered a half-smile to Crimson, then turned to leave. "At once, Fate's Hand." They followed the Inquisitor out of the room and caught up with him.

"Is there anyone we should be bringing with us, Inquisitor?" Imani asked.

Kalon stopped for a moment and thought on this. *Verity could be useful, but she might well be needed here in the port if Packet or his men decide to turn their attention to May.* He had a feeling the Shadow Knife would turn him down, due to the incident with Rand. Kalon being Kalon, therefore, decided to skip asking and just leave her for now.

"No. We should be gone as soon as possible."

"Aye, Inquisitor."

The captain went toward the bridge, Kalon toward the cabin he had been assigned, and Crimson sat in silence, playing with the residual flickers of magic as they popped from one hand to the other—before they finally vanished with a faint sigh.

As the storm cascaded overhead, the *Ori* lifted from the pad on a shimmer of anti-gravity energy, then rose majestically, pivoting toward the sky and cleaving the storm clouds like an arrow. Lightning rippled across her hull, drawn into specially deployed collectors across her surface. As the church ship skipped toward the heavens, she passed another vessel on the way down.

This other vessel was much bigger, gilded, and its shape akin to that of a bird of prey—an eagle, albeit somewhat stylized. Imani paid no attention to the other ship; their eyes were firmly on their destination, a location hundreds of miles away in the center of an old, decaying forest.

Across the vast sky, beyond the gulls of Sullavale Port and the banks of cloud through which the *Ori* gathered speed and flew on, lay the ancient City of Terralion, a former capital of the world until its ruler invited calamity and demons in all at once. Ancient history recorded this city as the birthplace of an empire, one reduced to ashes and almost as dead as the old gods.

Yet, for some, Terralion was home, and many who weathered the injustices in their own lands had come to the place to escape the long reach of the church or their own personal troubles.

Towers and spires littered the skyline of the city, the old forest that cradled it showing its age and suffering the effects of magic unleashed without control. Many of the trees had been turned to calcified wood by magical effects; others had been warped, and those trees that were lucky to survive were few and far between.

Prescott's Asylum had been the center of this magical upheaval. It was set in vast, overgrown grounds, thick with thorn and ivy. It lurked like a brooding giant. Keep-like watchtowers on the walls were originally designed to keep intruders out and inmates within. Now, like the old guard, they leaned against the stonework and drunkenly slouched with cracked and pitted bricks.

Below the asylum, two figures walked, one of them the Stealer known as Spry. The other, Bala Mora, the woman who had abducted him. Spry cradled Charlie in his arms, and his steps were sad and sullen.

"Did you know it would kill him?" Spry asked the witch-woman.

"Do you still brood upon that creature?" she shook her head. "How can such a one as you, with all that latent power, just whine about the death of a candle-flame life?"

"Charlie! Charlie was his name, and I knew him years, you callous cow." Spry's eyes fixed the woman in the hood with a vile gaze, and he rubbed his feet along the floor in the dust just to kick a cloud up. "Not as though you care. You probably never cared about anything in your life—stupid wizard."

She stopped, dark eyes gleaming in the dark, and with a sudden motion snatched the ferret's body from the young man's arms.

"No!"

Before he could stop her, she held Charlie aloft and burned the creature to a crisp with a flash of white-hot flame. Ashes dripped from her fingers, and she smiled, relishing the look of anguish that appeared on her captive's face.

"There," Bala Mora said with a sneer. "No more distractions."

"I'll kill you," Spry hissed and then felt a vice-like grip on his throat as the woman's magic snapped out from her without pomp or circumstance. An invisible hand closed about his flesh and bruised it.

"Not in this life, little Stealer," she promised him. "Now, come, you can always get another Charlie. Or we can make you one, even though it won't quite be the same as the old." Her voice took on the tone of a warning, or perhaps a threat.

Spry felt the invisible pull of magic, and he was forced to follow. The grip lessened as the mage relaxed her spell, but it was still enough to ensure he had to work very hard on breathing to keep from dropping into the shadow of unconsciousness.

The lower corridors were maze-like, confusing at first, but the woman seemed to know where she was going. At length, they came to a room where a door hung off its hinges and splinters of old wood were scattered upon the floor, curiously only on the outside of the room. She walked inside, dragging Spry with her.

The walls of this chamber were covered in scrawled, rune-like carvings, and a picture of what appeared to be some kind of doorway with darkness around it. A great wolf was pictured eating the souls of the dead, and around the rest of the walls were thousands of tiny scribbled eyes of all shapes and sizes.

Eyes within eyes was written in barely legible text.

"Witness his ascension," Bala Mora said, voice filled with longing. "His rise, and his release."

Spry felt the grip on his windpipe drop away, and he gasped for several good lungfuls of air, bending over as he coughed violently. "You're mad."

"They said that about him," Bala Mora replied, and her eyes gleamed in the shadow. "They locked him here and claimed that demons weren't real. That he was just an evil man."

"Who, what?"

"Your bloodline, Spry Genris: the catalyst, Rogart the Third."

"What now? Are you off your bloody rocker?" Spry shook his head. "I'm not related to that genocidal maniac! No fucking way!"

"Like it or not, you are. Why do you think you are needed, wanted, respected?" The wizard walked around him. "I did not want to be so harsh, but you forced my hand."

"That's right, blame me. It's always the victim and never the criminal."

"You are one to talk."

"I steal things to help the kids of the port, not to do whatever it is you're going to do to me in this room, or whatever wicked ritual you're planning," Spry replied in a stream of sudden indignance. "I will never forgive you for Charlie, ever."

"He needed to go. The body was done. No distractions meant we could focus on the here and now." Bala Mora ran her hands over the walls. "He escaped from here, but look, he left clues for us all to find him again."

"What, who?" Spry blinked. "The Regent? He's dead, gone, like Charlie."

Bala Mora turned to fix Spry with her gaze, eyes within eyes that whirled at the core, and he shut his own in fear. "Akas the Bloodless," the Anshada intoned. "Our master, the wicked one, the lewd one, the rod and the iron that bends all to his will."

Spry suppressed a shudder, not sure if it came from the woman's sudden reverence, eyes, or a combination of both. "What do you need me for?"

"You are the key, Spry. Without you, there is no book, and without the book, our place in this world will be lost. He can never rise again, and we can never enter his kingdom."

"Sounds like a bunch of religious zealotry to me."

"No, this is *not* religion. This is *not* a system of control—it is *freedom!*" she snarled, and her fingers swiped at his face. He felt her long nails whisper across his skin.

"Ok, ok." He put up his hands to ward her off. "Fine, not religion, then." He made a mental note to never say that again, or at least, never where she could hear.

"Idiot."

"So, how does my being here…" He paused and took a deep breath. "Help you find Akas, whoever, or whatever he is?"

"He is the Demon King, the master." Bala Mora bowed her head. "The wellspring of our power."

"Ok, wellspring, *how* does *my* being *here* help?" Spry's patience for riddles was wearing thin.

Bala Mora traced the symbols on the wall and waited a moment before she replied. "In two days, the red moon comes, and the shadow ring devours the sun. Here, the answer will be found—for it is the only time during that special eclipse that the power of this room is strong enough. It will resonate with your body, and your blood will provide me a map to the book."

"My blood?"

"Yes. Do you think I need you as some sort of child of prophecy?" Bala Mora tapped her teeth with an elongated nail. "Oh, goddess, you are I."

"Shit."

"Child fated to…that's rich, to think a man would be fated to do anything in Akas's Kingdom, that he would allow a mere Stealer to be the spear of his return." The Anshada laughed harshly. "Spry, your death is all I need to lead me to the book."

The youth looked around carefully. Spotting a sharp piece of wood, he made a lunge for it. Bala Mora was faster, though; she whispered to the air, and an invisible weight crashed onto the Stealer, knocking the oxygen from his lungs. As he crumpled to the floor, she wove her hands in a complex pattern.

Spry was shackled in invisible magical chains.

"Sleep." She spoke another old word, *"Kazkata,"* after the first. Spry tumbled into a dreamless haze. "Two days will pass quickly. Then, the map." Bala Mora smiled slowly, and the eyes within her own whirled away in silent agreement.

Sorcerer and Stealer were observed by silent, restless, hungry ghosts as time moved forward.

The *Ori* cleaved above the storm clouds and left the roiling mass of thunder and lightning far behind. The church vessel shot across the sky and left a trail of ionised particles in its wake, the only tell-tale sign that the ship had passed. Imani stood on the bridge for the last leg of the journey. It had taken them just under one full day at maximum speed to reach their goal.

The Inquisitor had expressed a desire for expediency when Imani had first met him, and as a loyal captain of the fleet, they had no desire to upset Fate's Hand. Kalon seemed to them like a man who did not tolerate failure, no matter how composed and polite he appeared.

The swish of the bridge door alerted Imani to the arrival of the very man who occupied the captain's thoughts.

"You are just in time, Inquisitor, to see the ruin of the once mighty Terralion," Imani addressed him as he stepped to the side. "How are you feeling?"

"Rested," Kalon replied shortly as he fixed his eyes on the distant spires that sliced the grey cloud. "A once-mighty kingdom—and this is the result of magic unbridled. No wonder our church seeks to bring an end to such heresy."

The captain turned their head to regard him. "How can you tolerate magic at all, if magic is heresy, Inquisitor?"

"Simple." He let a superficial half-smile form. "The Cardinal's will is our will, and she has decreed that Weavers are to be given our protection. They serve the One God; they understand that the Infinite Machine is the prime force of all things, and sensible, controlled, directed magic is a benefit, not a dangerous weapon that could backfire and kill thousands in the blink of an eye."

"Uncontrolled magic is heresy, but directed, church-ordained magic is fine?"

"A tool, yes, like Crimson's seeking spell. It helped me attain Spry's location." Kalon folded his hands behind his back.

Imani's brow furrowed. The captain wrinkled their nose, but remained silent.

"What do you believe?" Kalon asked without looking in the captain's direction.

Imani wrestled their fingers together, tapped their thumbs against each other a couple of times, and sighed. "Magic is dangerous, and I am not sure trusting sorcerers, even those bound to the church's will, is the right course of action."

"You would have made a good Inquisitor," Kalon replied without a single shred of humour in his tone. "Many of them think as you do."

"Yet they are still loyal."

"Yes."

"So, there is room in the church for opposing viewpoints?"

"It would seem so."

"Would you kill them all if you had to? The mages I mean?" Imani asked and then turned away, slightly embarrassed.

"Wanton slaughter achieves nothing, and tools are better used than broken." Kalon lowered his voice slightly. "Or at least this is what Cardinal Terusa says in her manifesto."

"I see."

"Think no more on this. It is the will of the One God of the Infinite Machine that we combine our technology with their magic. Without tech-magis, this marvel of yours—the *Ori*—would not be able to take wing and fly." Kalon settled his gaze once more on the vast oncoming skyline of broken towers that comprised the ruined city and fell silent.

The *Ori* skipped down through a cloudbank. One of the wings clipped a small fluff of white into two and scattered it into whispers of mist. As the ship threaded her way in and out of the old towers and the once magnificent spires, the lower hub of the city appeared from the mist.

"Here it is, ancient and decrepit," Imani stated. "Law here is lax—be on your guard. The church is far enough away for some to think they can make a name with the death of an agent."

"Truly?"

"Yes, truly," Imani promised. "One Inquisitor lost his life here only a few months ago—Inquisitor Ketter."

"I remember Ketter's name, but not much else," Kalon replied. He fixed a point on the city's rambling structures with his right finger, then followed the line of sight to the tip. "Prescott's Asylum should be in that old ward there."

"You know it?"

"Only stories from my time in the Imper Vatica. Part of the history of our order more than anything. Dark tales, experiments, old ghosts, demons, and the blood of many innocents have seeped into that aged stone."

"I see. Thank you for that, Inquisitor." Imani nodded formally. "Do you want me to get you as close as possible?"

"As close as you feel is safe enough for the *Ori*." Kalon turned from the bridge window and made his way back to the door. "Then remain on station. If all goes well, I will need you to extract Spry to a safe location."

"Very well."

Kalon left the bridge and made his way to the exterior airlock of the ship, where he waited patiently for the *Ori* to make her landing. He felt the vessel dip down and watched the horizon change from one of the sleek side windows.

The *Ori* circled a graveyard before the ship settled on a flat piece of ground not far from the ward where the asylum lay. Jets of steam and flickers of energy issued from the vessel as her landing gear folded out and cushioned the ship from the impact.

Kalon waited again. The ramp opened, and wan sunlight illuminated the metal floor as he stepped out into Terralion on the trail of both Stealer and sorceress.

CHAPTER 10

DARK IN THE ASYLUM

What majesty remained of Terralion from the air was completely lost on the ground as Kalon stepped from the *Ori*. He squared his shoulders and adjusted his coat before he dug into his left pocket and produced a hard leather case from within. He flicked it open with one hand and drew out a pair of lenses, thin and delicate, like a dragonfly's wing.

In one smooth motion, he affixed them over his eyes and closed them, listening to the sounds around him. The *Ori*'s idling engine whispered as Imani put her into low-power mode. A dog barked several streets away, then yelped as a thud sounded and a harsh voice scolded it into silence. Birds twittered among themselves, sharing stories of flicker-fast adventures and in a gabble of high-pitched tweets.

When Kalon opened his eyes once more, the street was tinged with bright spots and slight flickers. A quick snap-blink three times in rapid succession cleared the effect from his vision.

Inside his coat were many pockets, and in those recesses, more cases that contained the Inquisitor's arsenal of tools against the many supernatural threats lurking across Hestonia. The lenses were just one; he had his book of equations, his pen, and several phials of a liquid that would produce a high-intensity heat reaction when applied to bodies and the like. Reva Flynn would likely describe his coat as a "Regular Cave of Wonders, only shaped like a coat." Sometimes an Inquisitor needed to leave no trace of demon or monster for others to find.

"Daroni's work," Kalon mused to himself as he slipped the case back into his long coat, "once again proves useful—it's no small wonder the man holds such a high position in both the church and the crafter's academy. Then again, perhaps these are Sara's. I will have to inquire when I return."

It did not take the Inquisitor long to make his way from the *Ori* to the edge of the city where Prescott's Asylum lay. On his way, he walked past the broken-down remnants of a once-beautiful garden, a gathering square, and a statue that depicted the goddess Fortune— *wrapped in moss-covered finery and clutching a bag of coins to her bosom.*

In its hay day, Terralion had been a huge city, sprawling, full of life and packed with colorful markets and gigantic noble houses. The Anshada, before their corruption, had worked to weave magic into every facet of their society and used it as a tool or beast of burden, just as a farmer would use a donkey to pull a plough. They had everything perfected for a while, until these wizards of old decided that into their arsenal of tools, they would add demonic thralls, summoning these beings, binding them to each other, to objects, to weapons. Just as they turned magic into a tool, they did the same with demon-kind. This slavery did not sit well with the rulers of the demon world, and they began to corrupt the ancient wizards.

Books told of the disaster that rocked the world over two hundred years before; the books might have been wrong, but they were the only histories that had survived. Demons almost overran Hestonia, and then a final battle was fought. Just as the world was about to lose, the final tier of the City of Wyrden was constructed, acting like a weapon. It blew part of the landmass into pieces, sundered it, and left places like Terralion a shadow of their former selves.

It was through this shadow, filled with so many old specters, that Kalon made his way.

Children dressed in rags loitered on every street corner, beggars with cold, numb hands, and sallow-eyed waifs who watched the tall, dark figure cleave his way through their lives. Many shrank back, fearful of the sudden appearance of this agent of the church. Others shadowed him slowly to see what he might do or whom he might be hunting.

Kalon drew ever closer to the asylum. One last stretch of street remained between him and the rusted iron gates. He knew he was being followed; his alert eyes and sharp ears caught the sound of three sets of feet matching his own as he walked slowly to his goal. He stopped, they stopped. He walked a few paces, they waited and then followed him.

One to the left, one to the right, and one above and behind him, which used the cracked pillars nearby as a handy perch to keep pace.

He altered his path slightly to ensure that he passed between two of the pillars on the way to the outer courtyard. A calculated move, and one he used as the scene played out as expected.

Church Combat Doctrine, the art of predicting a battlefield with almost mathematical precision, was taught to Inquisitors and Justiciars. Kalon took to it better than most, and excelled in the mental side of their teachings. He also trained in the physical combat arts, the use of the sword and hand-to-hand. Lastly, he'd taken to firearms extremely well thanks to Sati's expert teaching.

Though he remained unaware of it, his Anshada blood gave him another edge entirely—he was able to touch a small thread of magic without awakening his power. This, coupled with small shifts of probability and luck, combined into an almost supernatural ability to predict the flow and outcome of a fight.

It was not as useful against demons, who obeyed their own rules— but humans were not so fortunate.

One of the men came at Kalon subtly. He hoped to use his momentum from a downward fall to knock his prey to the ground. Kalon heard him kick off the pillar and saw the other two men come in rapidly from both sides.

First, the tech-magis pistol barked in the silence of Terralion, scattering a murder of crows nearby; the sky blackened with their wings. Their cawing almost drowned out the report from the Inquisitor's firearm. The sneaky man's face mulched with the close impact of the shot, and as Kalon stepped to the side, his body rolled away with only the lower jaw left, the rest of his face a mass of mangled bone and tissue.

As quickly as it was drawn, the gun vanished into Kalon's holster under his coat.

Second, he dealt with the other two men quickly, cleanly, and without prolonging anyone's suffering. As they flanked him, knives drawn, Kalon adjusted his posture and turned to the side. What was once a target was now thin air, and the first knife glanced harmlessly off the specially treated fabric of the Inquisitor's coat with a trail of sparks. The second man's knife never got that far, as the Inquisitor stepped to the thug, shifted his weight slightly, changed position, and caught the knifeman's arm.

A single upward strike to the elbow numbed the whole arm. The knife fell. Kalon caught it and stabbed the man three times in his vitals. Quick, efficient; in seconds he was dead. Fate's Hand stepped back and let the body hit the floor.

Before the third could recover, Kalon hurled the knife into the thug's throat and followed with a vicious spinning-kick that connected with a bone-jarring crunch.

Only a few seconds had passed, and three men were already dead. Fate's Hand stood a moment, spoke a soft prayer to the One God, then moved on as if nothing had happened.

Bala Mora hated to wait for things, but knew that power often came over a longer period of time. It didn't matter, since the boy would soon allow her to gain more than she ever imagined when the master returned and rewarded her.

"Soon," she whispered to Spry's unconscious form, "he will come. He will take me and raise me up to serve as his right hand. Akas, the demon king. I will be his queen. He whispers to me, boy; he calls my name and speaks such words as a lover never did."

She paced the cell and looked at the scrawl on the stonework. "You squander your blood, blood that you do not deserve. A key you are, nothing more, nothing less. Once the path to the book is open, once the book is mine, ahhh—ours—the demon king will step through the door that should never be opened."

Bala Mora's voice took on a whisper, and behind it, almost as though another echoed her words—a second voice joined in her ranting. "Some doors lead to fame, some doors lead to power, some doors lead to riches, some doors should never be opened." Her fingers traced the contours of the scrawl, and she steadied herself as the energy from the oncoming eclipse started to gather.

"Think not of rescue, Spry Genris. No one comes for you. Even if they did, they would be destroyed by my hand. My sorcery is nothing like the other Anshada. I have the power of Akas behind me. Your blood will unlock my true potential, and then I will rip the heart of the church from its still beating breast."

Her words were lost on Spry; he was trapped in a dreamless, magical sleep.

What she did not see were the eyes on the wall. They took on a red-hued gleam, hundreds of them depicting the eyes-within-eyes motif central to the Anshada. Had she seen them, her conviction might have doubled.

"Sleep soundly, Stealer," she whispered into Spry's ear and smiled. "Soon, you sleep for good, and I reign eternal.

Kalon noted the position of the sun and the other stellar body that had moved since he began his journey to Terralion. He stopped and shielded his eyes, wrinkled his nose in thought, and calculated the arc of the moon to the sun. "Eclipse," he said finally. "Not just any. I can feel the magic cloying the air as the energy of that moon gathers."

He stepped through the wrought-iron gate and beyond into the grounds of the asylum. The hairs on the back of his neck prickled, and he made his way toward the yawning portal, once a door, that was now only an arch of stone, supported by interconnected vines and undergrowth that snaked through the stonework like veins.

The farther he moved in, the more he felt the shift between light and shadow. Anshada magic hung over this ruined building like a pall of smoke. He took a deep breath and blinked rapidly three times. The interior's dim light was replaced by washed-out colors—and a perfect clarity of vision even in pitch black darkness.

These tech-magis lenses were indeed a marvel, he thought as he picked his way through the detritus and sought a way into the cells below.

Under the broken frame of a once-grand picture lurked a staircase, inviting him to traverse the old wood and iron. He tested the steps with his feet, and, once satisfied they would bear his weight, he made the slow descent into the unknown.

Many Inquisitors would be disturbed by this, perhaps even fear it, but Kalon did not. Why was a mystery, even to himself, and he did not question it. He credited his training at the hands of the finest the Imper Vatica had to offer and left it at that.

He did not need light, not with the lenses. They peeled back the layers of darkness as if removing an onion's skin. The pastel-like color was a small price to pay to avoid lanterns and the tell-tale light sources that could give him away to the Anshada he knew lurked here.

At an intersection he stopped and did not move. He listened for ten full minutes and picked out every sound in the dark. He perceived the ghosts of inmates long past, still bound there, still caught in the very moment they died, unable to move on to the Shroud's domain, chained by the deeds they'd done in life and shackled by so much pain and guilt in death. Each of them had a demonic jailor who held the chains. Some were unlucky to have more than one, but Kalon did not have the time or inclination to set them free from these multi-eyed, long-limbed grotesques. He had one goal: Spry and the elimination of the Anshada sorceress who had taken the youth from Sullavale Port. The ghosts were distractions, no more, no less. He adjusted his perception to filter them out, a trick that he had been taught by Winter at the church's lessons in the supernatural, and pushed on in the dark.

Ghostly hands reached for him, and he walked through them as if they were mist. The wail of the dead ended, and in the following quiet, Kalon once again picked out sounds in the lower chambers: movement, pacing, and a soft whisper-voice that flirted with heresy. The woman and the youth must be there.

He timed his steps carefully now, drew his pistols, and walked toward the speaker. He felt the energy that the woman held—the shift in reality that her very presence caused on the corridors—and he narrowed his eyes. To allow such magic to exist, to remain unchecked, was dangerous indeed. One like this could not be brought to serve the church; she would only drown the world in blood and destruction.

By the time he reached Rogart's old cell and stood in the darkened doorway, he had made his choice.

Bala Mora bent over Spry. Her cloaked form in the robes of the Anshada made her look like a vulture about to peck his eye from its socket. Her back stiffened, and Kalon realized his mistake; focused on the hunt, he forgot about the door that led into the room. A simple hex, but easily missed in the overall flood of magical resonance.

"I know you are there in the dark, black raven, shadow hunter—not who you are, but I smell the stink of the church on you." Bala Mora chuckled and tapped her finger on the hilt of her black-handled knife.

Kalon remained impassive. He looked at the room, and his mind flew rapidly as he calculated. The scrawl on the walls would amplify the woman's power; they were ancient and as old as the regent who once broke free in here. She had already absorbed a great deal of power from the room.

"So silent, so strong?" she mocked softly and turned to face him. "Oh, and so handsome a church-soldier that the Kharnate herself would fuck-gobble you up."

Kalon's emotionless face did not reflect anything as he listened. Bala Mora was unnerved, and her Anshada eyes-within-eyes saw a darkness surrounding Kalon, a cloud of something she couldn't quite pierce with her vision.

"What is this? What manner of church-minion are you?"

Kalon did not reply, the insult ignored.

"Darkness, I see darkness and…what have you done?"

Again, Kalon did not reply. He was ready, pistols at his side.

Tired of his indifference, Bala Mora launched her magical assault without warning. Her sorcery bubbled and spilled over into the real world, callously pushing its way from a rip in reality as it asserted itself like a truth in the air before them both. A wall of hate-fuelled demonic energy spat like a geyser and threw itself at Fate's Hand. With the aid of Akas's fury, she was able to conjure this sorcery without the rules of the Warp and Weft. She did not need to pull a Tapestry. Where it passed it scorched the stone, froze the air in chunks of ice, and left splats of red ichor in its wake. No threads were woven, no weave was made. This was the power of the Anshada unleashed without compromise—one spell designed to kill and do it quickly.

Chaos itself! Without threads to guide it, it was her will made manifest, to kill the Inquisitor. The effects it brought onto the world were the pains of reality as it tried to make some sense of the magical energy she had thrown at her foe.

Thankfully, regardless of Warp and Weft, the magic itself—the energy brought into being via the Tapestry—still obeyed the fundamental laws. Reality had some say; science was still required to allow ice to form and fire to burn. Spell or not.

It was this rote-mastery of the counter-arts that saved Kalon's life and allowed him to speak the mathematical formulae that undid spells at a thread level. In a few whispered breaths, he pulled apart the magic by countering it with equations held most secret by the Church of Progression.

What of a spell that was purely driven by the witch-woman's malice, conjured with the direct aid of the Demon King's power? Even though there were no actual threads woven, the spell buckled and flickered—changed by the numeromancy, fire became warmth, ice flashed into cold white flakes, and the red ichor melted away. Swirls of snow encrusted Kalon's long coat and dripped from the hem slowly as they melted into nothing. The fabric of Daroni's fibers and the runes written inside and across every surface crushed the remains of Bala Mora's magic, and the Inquisitor stood unharmed.

In a sharp-snap motion, he trained both pistols on the woman and pulled the triggers. The tech-magis weapons came alive as their mechanisms activated. Shards of metal sliced from the internal magazine were fed through a complex series of components to form a bullet carved with symbols and runes of undoing. The template-firearm contained the written form of the equations wrapped around each round, bullets made from magically resonant metals and pushed out with explosive force.

Rapidly.

Bala Mora threw up a demonic shield, an interlocking hexagonal blackness made from the hides of servitor demons, bound together with dark strings of sorcery.

Kalon's bullets found their mark. They passed like a hot knife through butter, vaporizing the demonic energies. The equations ripped their demon forms asunder and blew massive holes in the shield. Other rounds followed, and the Anshada witch's life was cut short in a hail of gunfire.

She staggered backward. Blood sprayed the wall behind. Pockmarks marred parts of the scrawl vanished as the bullets blew into the stonework.

One final shot smashed into her forehead and exited at the back with a gaping hole.

Kalon returned his guns to their holsters and observed his handiwork.

The woman crashed to the floor, a lifeless mass of spent flesh. A small whorl of smoke curled upward from a bloody hole. Yet the dark powers were still not done with her; life tried to return to her form. She kicked a few times, and her mouth opened and closed like a fish caught in the air.

Kalon acted without thought. He pulled out a small red book, tore a page from it, and slapped it down on the woman's face. He spoke one word: "Rest." The lettering on the page, a mix of runes and formulas, smoldered, and the parchment turned to ash.

She stopped moving, and her body went limp. The Inquisitor nodded, put the book back, and drew out a bottle. He opened the stopper and tilted the glazed green glass at an angle. A mixture of chemicals poured onto the dead wizard. It didn't take long for the reaction to begin, and her body went up in a sudden, green-tinged flash of smoke and fire.

"A useful concoction, Miss Flynn," Kalon said to the air. "Once again, alchemy and science triumph over demons and magic."

Spry did not stir. He remained asleep, trapped in a dreamless world of the woman's creation.

Kalon left the corpse to smolder into incandescent ash and turned his attention to the unconscious Stealer. He exchanged the green bottle for one of smelling salts, waved it under the youth's nose, and quirked a brow when it had no effect.

"Sorcery, then," he concluded, stepping away from Spry. "Fear not, Spry, I will break this magic without harm to you."

Once more he took the red book out, flipped a few pages, and withdrew an elegant stylus. Upon the paper he wrote an equation, then turned the page again, repeated the process three more times, and turned the stylus to the other end. He pricked his finger and placed another symbol on the four pages with a mix of ink and his blood.

"Now." Kalon tore out the four pages and bent down. He placed one at Spry's head, one at his feet, and the other two exactly level with the Stealer's left and right hands. "Let us see what she used to keep you so deep in sleep, young thief."

With four carefully taken steps backward, Kalon took six breaths: three in through his nose, held for four seconds each time, and three out through his mouth, the exact timing for all breaths measured perfectly.

The reality of the room fell away, the corners of his vision darkened a little, and the periphery of his sight flickered with unseen things. Some were small, some were large, some held a shape that the Inquisitor dared not look at—but one caught his eye in particular.

It hovered over the Stealer, wrapping him in tendrils of energy.

"There you are."

It was hard to explain exactly what the creature was, but Kalon knew from the church's books on demons and servants of the Old—as well as New—Gods, what kind of entity he was now dealing with. A servant of Kresha, mistress of the dream realm and bringer of nightmares. A dream demon, no doubt summoned by the Anshada to keep Spry locked in this sleep until she brought him out.

Bala Mora's death would not break the spell; it was pre-cast, so

Spry would not have seen it coming. It was likely triggered by a command word agreed in advance with this multi-limbed, foetus-like abomination of heretical magic.

The dream demon turned spider-like eyes to the Inquisitor, and a thin mouth with rows of shark-like teeth opened wide.

"Your pact with the wizard is at an end," Fate's Hand whispered, throwing his stylus like a dart. It embedded into the monstrosity's center and pierced it with a sudden flare of light. "Your magic is thin, and your master is no more." The pen was truly mightier than the sword in this case, and the drop of Kalon's blood mixed with the four pieces of paper, each marked with the ancient text of the church, acted like a ritual and a catalyst.

In the old days, there would have been a bell, a book, and a candle.

Not in these enlightened times.

The creature burst into blue flame and black oily smoke. It vanished at the same time the four pieces of paper ignited and swirled into the air before they, too, became as ash. The Inquisitor scuffled the ash with his boot and looked down at Spry.

The youth moaned softly, rolled to the side, and drooled on the floor. His eyes opened, seeing nothing in the pitch black.

"Welcome back to the land of the awake, Master Spry."

Kalon watch the youth come out of his enforced slumber. Spry opened his eyes, and, panic in his voice, cried, "I'm blind, I can't see!"

"You are not blind; the room is pitch black. I can see for us both," Kalon replied and knelt down close to Spry.

"Who are you?" Spry asked of the velvet-toned voice with a core of iron command.

"Fate's Hand. Inquisitor of the Church of Progression."

"Oh, shit. Does that mean the witch is dead?"

"Yes."

"Good!"

"She had you trapped in enforced sleep. How do you feel now?" Kalon studied him in the dark.

"Hungry, thirsty, and I still can't see."

"I can help with one of those. The others I can assist with once we get out of this place."

"Help me up, then, Fate's Hand, because unless you have a light source, you're now my eyes."

Kalon nodded in the darkness. Spry couldn't see it. "Come, then, take my hand."

When the youth clasped his hand, Kalon hauled the Stealer to his feet. He waited a few moments for Spry to get his balance and then started to leave the chamber.

CHAPTER 11

CARDINAL DIRECTIONS

Without another word, Kalon urged the young man to the doorway. Spry followed obediently, glad to be in somewhat safer hands, even though he'd heard stories of the man who the church named Fate's Hand—not all of them good. Sullavale Port remembered Ryan Seaborne.

The ghosts of past inmates clung to the asylum corridors, observing both Kalon and Spry as the Inquisitor led the thief from the depths. They lamented on soft, sighing winds as the pair stepped into the light, unaware of the spectral fingers that reached for them and then shrank back into the depths.

Spry held onto Kalon as if he were a lifeline, his fingers wrapped almost childishly against the man's gloved hand. To the casual observer, they might as well have been father and son.

Spry blinked a couple of times, took a breath, and cleared his lungs of the fetid air when they emerged into the courtyard of the asylum. The city lay before them; he'd never seen it, and as his eyes grew accustomed to the light, his gaze took in the magnificent yet crumbling ruin around them.

"Where are we?"

"A city of ghosts, lost in the past, barely clinging on," Kalon answered as he too observed the fallen splendor around him. He let go of Spry's hand and folded both of his behind his back, interlocking the fingers. "My ship is close by. Come."

"Can we wait a moment? Need to catch my breath."

"Yes."

"Thanks."

"You are no use to me broken," Kalon said. He turned his gaze onto the streets beyond, where he knew trouble still lurked. Just like in the ocean, where the water might seem calm and still, under the surface sharks waited for the slightest drop of blood.

"Yeah, I thought you didn't come for me out of the goodness of your heart," Spry said with a snort and rubbed his hands together. "Be nice if someone did."

"You have no parents, no guardians?"

"None."

Kalon mused on this. "Then I make you a ward of the church."

"What?"

"Article six, paragraph ten of the Vagrant Act of Messania," Kalon replied almost automatically. "A person, or persons found with no parents nor legal guardian, may be brought into the care of the church by a senior member."

"Why?"

"It is so."

"But, why?"

"I have my reasons. You are more use to me as a ward of the church than you are as a vagrant thief and vagabond."

"Really?" Spry narrowed his eyes.

"It is the law, and as a ward of the church, you become our responsibility. Your talents are bent to our will. You are our son, and we provide room, board, food, and so forth." Kalon gestured in the direction of the *Ori*. "I ask this once: follow me. I will not ask again."

"Not even a second to mourn a friend," Spry sighed and began to walk in the direction Kalon pointed out. "See ya, Charlie."

Kalon followed, then quickened his pace on the short walk back to the *Ori*. He picked up his tech-magis Communication Shard from his pocket and contacted the ship.

"I am on my way back with the Stealer. Prepare for departure not long after. Have food and drink ready for when we return. The boy is malnourished and in need of hydration."

The voice on the other end answered softly, "Yes, Inquisitor."

It was that simple.

"Kalon."

"What now?" the Inquisitor studied the youth.

"The wizard, she said something about a book to me while she had me in that place, and I heard her while I was dreaming." Spry twisted his hands nervously.

"Go on."

"A book that belongs to the Anshada. Do you know it?"

"What?" Kalon's whole frame stiffened, and he almost stopped in his tracks.

"That's what she said. I was the key—my blood—to the book, and then the Demon King would..." Spry blurted out through gritted teeth.

"Speak no more of this in the open," Kalon cut him off, and his eyes betrayed his reaction to the mere mention of such things, even behind the contacts. "We speak on this later, on the ship. Quickly."

Spry followed Kalon more rapidly now.

Thanks to mentioning the book, it was about to get more complicated than either of them could imagine, as Kalon retraced his steps to the *Ori*, with Spry just behind him. No one dared stop the straight-backed figure who stalked their streets—they had seen the fate of the last people who had tried to engage him.

Their efforts had not worked out well.

They boarded the *Ori*, and Kalon greeted Imani with a nod. "Captain, this is Spry."

"Hello, young man." Imani smiled a little. "Do you want me to take it from here? We can get him some food and drink, make him comfortable in a cabin."

Kalon nodded. "That is acceptable. I have a report to make."

"Very well, then." Imani indicated for the dejected youth to follow and pressed the control to raise the ramp. "I will see you in the stateroom, then, Inquisitor."

"Very well."

They parted ways. Imani took Spry off to the galley, and Kalon made his way to his assigned room, private enough for his report. Out of his long coat he drew a series of objects and assembled them quickly. The result looked like he had crafted a gyroscope set with a couple of mirrors, one silver, one black. He gave the contraption a flick with a gloved finger and set it spinning.

A shimmer formed above, and slowly the image of Terusa hazed into view.

"You have something to report, Fate's Hand?"

Kalon bowed . "My investigation into Rand's death has taken a turn, Cardinal, into uncharted alleys and waters."

"Go on?"

"I set about investigating Rand's death, to discover the truth. Verity was not the assassin who killed my former colleague—it was Drako Mallori."

"What?" Terusa's voice dripped coldly.

"Mallori killed Rand. I have proof, and I have more than this."

"Tell me?" A faint tone of interest piqued into the Cardinal's poker-face expression.

"Mallori wove a spell when Rand triggered one of his explosives. Did you know he could summon magic?"

Terusa's face remained impassive as the connection wavered a little, and she replied, "No, I had no idea. Tell me more?"

"Rand died. Mallori is a wizard—and there is something else. I teamed up with a gunslinger, an investigator from the port. Andreas, a talented man who could be of some use," Kalon continued and remained still. He did not pace one step.

"You cooperating with another on an investigation...this is a first, my dear Fate's Hand." Terusa seemed almost amused. "It bore fruit?"

"In more ways than one. I will be brief: our investigation led to a lair of the Anshada, hidden from the eyes of all. We found a book which spoke of a key and a Stealer, a thief known as Spry."

"Fitting for a thief, a name like Spry." The Cardinal of the Church of Progression lowered her gaze, and her eyes took on a slight gleam against the foggy image. "What of this book, then?"

"It seemed to be notes, with Spry Genris as the forefront of the matter."

"Curious."

"Yes. I could have destroyed it there and then, but I felt it should be studied."

"You did the correct thing, Kalon. Who knows what heresy this will uncover and what secrets could have been lost had you acted in haste?"

Kalon mused on this. "I agree. If the book leads me to a greater den of wizards or heresy, then all the better to follow that trail."

"Absolutely." The Cardinal smiled a little. "I have decided what to do, but I will not speak of it here. Return to the Imper Vatica at once and bring with you the investigator, Andreas. Then you may explain in full everything you have learned and tell me more about this key and boy."

"Yes, Cardinal. Any reason for Andreas's involvement?"

"He has seen things that most mortals should not, and so he might be useful in the long run. I also desire to meet a man of his calibre; he might join the church."

"Very well."

"Spry as well—bring him."

"Of course. He is central to the investigation now."

"Marvellous. My faith in you has not been misplaced. Is there aught else?"

"Just one matter: what of Rand?"

"I will assign Maxis Kane to investigate with Winter as his second." Terusa waved a hand in the foggy image. "They will leave no stone unturned in regards to his death."

"The Justicar—a good choice, perhaps a little overzealous when it comes to law and order."

"That is what Justicars do, my friend. They are judge, jury, executioner. Can you think of anyone else to bring Mallori to justice?"

"I cannot."

"Good. Then bring Spry and Andreas to me. Make sure you do this soon, Fate's Hand."

"Very well, Cardinal." Kalon nodded just the once. "Spry is now a ward of the church."

"Oh? Excellent!"

"That is all then?"

"For now, I think you have more than enough to deal with. I want you to recover the book personally, Kalon. This must be your task now. Forget Rand and focus." Terusa inclined her head. "I wait here for your return forthwith."

The connection cut; the machine slowed and stopped spinning. Kalon stood impassively, processing all this in an eye-blink, and turned on his heel. His destination: the *Ori*'s bridge. He had a feeling he would find both Spry and Imani there by now.

He was correct. Kalon stepped onto the ship's bridge to discover Spry peering out the front, gawking at the sky around him. "How does it fly?" the young thief asked the captain, waving his arms like a bird.

"Tech-magis," Imani answered with a slight chuckle. "Far too complicated to explain, and far too detailed for such a time as this." Imani heard Kalon's footfalls as the bridge door slid open and closed behind him. "Also, your benefactor is here."

"Spry."

"Kalon," Spry said and turned around. He frowned.

"We return to Sullavale Port," Kalon told Imani. "We have another guest to bring with us as we return to the Imper Vatica."

"Oh?"

"Andreas, the investigator."

"I don't know him, but if that is your wish."

"This comes from the Cardinal."

Imani blinked and snapped an order to the helm. "Sullavale Port, with haste."

Spry chuckled and said, "That lit a fire suddenly. The Cardinal has to be a man of power, right?"

"Woman," Imani corrected the youth.

"Forgive me." Spry shook his head. "Us lowlifes don't get the luxury of knowing who's who in the big codex of famous people with more than what've we got."

The *Ori* adjusted course and shot across the sky with a sudden burst of speed, the occupants protected by the ship's internal acceleration dampening field, yet another marvel of tech-magis—and one more secret of the church.

It seemed like no time at all to the passengers as the dart-shaped vessel clove the sky like a knife, whipping the clouds apart with a silent whisper of engines, as she made good time to the port city. Imani's helm crew brought the ship down on one of the public landing pads, right next to the massive, golden, bird-shaped vessel Kalon had seen many times in the skies around Hestonia. Without further ado he alighted on the ground, leaving Spry aboard the *Ori* in the care of Captain Imani.

"So that is the *Mist Reaver*," he commented as he walked past it toward the dock proper, taking in every graceful line, curve, and intricate gleaming feather under the hazy sun of the day. "Impressive design."

"I'm sure the captain will be most happy to hear that, good sir," said a voice in his direction. It held a slight tinge of ice, wrapped around a whisper of satin.

Kalon observed the speaker, a woman with long, flowing, argent hair and bright blue eyes. Tips of slender, pointed ears poked out from the long waterfall. She was dressed elegantly, caught in a symphony of velvet, lace, and silk. Not a single peep of flesh was on display, all covered by sensible tooled leather armor. A red cloak that hung from her left shoulder completed the picture, along with a pair of dagger-drop earrings. Her face bore the long, thin features of the kelanari, which made them appear fae-like and hauntingly beautiful.

"Please pass on my regards to Captain Talon Mane, then," Kalon answered. He paused in his stalk toward the port center. "You are?"

"Busy," the woman chuckled with a wink, then tucked a dagger back into the top of a knee-high turn-top boot. "Lady Danae Silvercrest. You can call me Silver, if you prefer. First Mate of the *Mist Reaver*."

"Kalon Rhadon, Fate's Hand." He offered a hand.

The kelanari woman wiped her fingers on a cloth, removing some oil, and took it. "Almost as impressive as the ship you arrived in. Not seen her like afore." She shook Kalon's hand, noting his grip. Strong, polite, but not commanding. "You know how to shake hands, too. Many men don't."

Kalon tilted his head. "No?"

She shrugged. "They use too much pressure, try to dominate the other. It's an animal thing, and they run with a lot of those instincts."

"Ah, I was taught the ways of proper etiquette by our most learned souls."

Silver nodded at this and smiled a little. "Well, please don't let me keep you, Kalon. We both have work to do."

"Of course." Kalon nodded again and began his journey to find Andreas. "Fair skies, Silver."

"You, too." She waved, tucked a lock of her hair behind her ear, and busied herself with the task at hand. "Don't work too hard!"

Fate was kind to Kalon that day, or perhaps she simply felt a little more inclined to throw him a bone. He stepped out into the busy street and observed Andreas enter a nearby alley. He caught sight of the investigator and followed swiftly.

The Inquisitor was in time to see the man meet up with a good-looking woman, her hair the polar opposite of Silver's—tousled and jet-black. Her shapely figure was poured into a mix of black leather and corsetry. A few exposed areas of skin hinted at a plethora of body art. She turned her green eyes on both men and blew a low, sultry whistle.

"Well now, if it isn't my lucky, lucky day. Stalked by the men in the dark coats. Are you a double-act, boys? Or are you twins separated at tailor?"

"Kaitlinel, don't be rude to me, or to..." Andreas turned around as he walked toward the woman, and then he blinked. "Kalon!" He almost fell over, but the woman caught him by the shoulders, spun him back round, and planted a kiss on his lips.

"Er, ok, that's new," Andreas said and blushed.

"Sorry." Kaitlinel grinned, catlike. "It's a Kharnate thing."

Kalon stopped and folded his arms. "What is this?"

"She's trouble," Andreas stepped back a little. "But yeah, she's also one of my informants. Allow me to present the lewd, rude, and definitely-no-prude darling of the back streets of Sullavale Port: Kaitlinel."

"Quite an introduction," Kalon answered. "I need you."

"Ooh, that sounds inviting." Kaitlinel's eyes gleamed as her mind sank below the level of the gutter.

"Not like that, you." Andreas ducked out of range of the woman, and he sighed. "What do you need, Kalon? Is it about that Anshada lair we found or something else?"

Kalon's expression remained impassive. He shook his head, looked at the dark-haired woman, and mused, "Kharnate, you said?"

"You don't miss a trick. Yes," Kaitlinel replied and did a little half-turn one direction, and then another. "Like what you see?"

Kalon's logical mind ignored the obvious display of Kaitlinel's assets, and he pondered. A Kharnate would be a good tool in the search for the book; they had incredible senses and a connection to their goddess that allowed them to transform into a creature equal parts wolf and human. Not much could put them down; they shrugged off wounds that would kill him. They were not bound to the cycles of the moon, the books said, and they shifted form as easily as breathing.

"Waiting?"

"I have a use for you," Kalon said to the werewolf.

Andreas blinked a couple of times. "Ok, this went weird really quick. What use could you put her to?"

"Oh," Kaitlinel chuckled softly. "Baby, I can think of quite a few."

"I bet you can." The gunslinger laughed. "What are you thinking, Kalon?"

He was thinking, and quickly. "Do you know much of the lands outside the cities?" he asked the Kharnate.

"I was born out there, raised out there, and on the streets of lots of different places. I've fucked around all the major woods and forests of Hestonia."

"Then you could act as a guide." Kalon rubbed his chin thoughtfully.

There was another reason: a connection between gunslinger and werewolf. He could potentially leverage one by involving the other. Perfect.

Andreas looked from one to the other and folded his arms. "Hey now, I thought you needed me. Now you need her?"

"Yes," Kalon answered.

"To what?"

"Both."

"Ok. Good. I can work with this. Going on an adventure with the church Inquisitor and a badass murder-wolf lady. I like it." Andreas nodded a couple of times. "Three people, one common goal."

"I have lots of goals, and some of them are very common." Kaitlinel winked lewdly.

Kalon shook his head and looked at Kaitlinel. "Are you with us?"

"Try to get rid of me. You got my attention at being handsome... and stuffy." She almost purred. "My kind of man, like a delicious orange, ready to peel."

"Ew!" Andreas shook his head to clear that image. "I've seen your claws, and the idea of you peeling anything scares the shit out of me."

The woman winked; her chuckle held the vaguest hint of a growl.

"Good." Kalon ignored the statement regarding being peeled.

"On one condition," Kaitlinel said.

"Ah, there it is." Andreas rubbed his chin. "What wicked condition is this?"

"Let him ask me." The werewolf's face took on a sly expression.

"What condition?" Kalon folded his arms.

"You owe me a favor, church-man–a big one. A massive one. If I'm going into the jaws of whatever, you're going to pay me back."

Kalon thought on this. Again, diplomacy and the teachings of his peers at the church came to mind. "Agreed. As long as you do your part and never call me church-man again."

Kaitlinel grinned at Andreas and whispered, "There are some parts I'd definitely hold up. Ok, no more of that then...promise."

"I...I bet you would," the gunslinger replied with a cough. "Lots of parts."

"I'll show you later."

"Really?"

"Yes, really. I get bored, and you're available."

"Kharnates."

"Yep, we're like that." Kaitlinel growled again and kicked a stone with her boot. It skittered off into the street with a soft *tink.*

The Inquisitor watched the interplay. He knew that this level of social interaction was important for people who were not servants of the church like him. "It is decided, then: you and Andreas will come with me to Messania and the Imper Vatica."

"Ooh, do I have to wear a robe, or a gown, or some kind of uniform?" Kaitlinel walked over to Kalon and peered up at him. "V-necked, right? I've seen some of the Cardinal's outfits, and WOOF, those things should come with a warning."

Kalon inclined his head and looked down at the grinning were-wolf. "No."

"Aw."

"Pencil that in for later," Andreas whispered to her. "I can hook you up."

"Hook...me...up?" Kaitlinel mock-swooned and fell back into the man's arms. "Promises, promises!"

Kalon had a feeling that this journey was going to require chap-eroning, and he would be the one to do it. "Enough frivolity. Come with me. The *Ori* awaits."

Andreas snapped to attention, dropped into a slow walk, and flicked his head to indicate to Kaitlinel. "He's serious."

"Yeah." She smirked a little. "I can see."

"Kalon, if you owe her a favor, and I'm coming along because well...I don't want to let her out of my sight, and I reckon it's going to be good for my career—can I have a favor too?" Andreas loved to push his luck; he couldn't help it.

Kaitlinel growled again and sunk her clawed hand into Andreas's backside as they walked on.

"Ow."

"What do you want, exactly?" Kalon ignored their childish play.

"Chief Investigator of Sullavale Port. I want my own office—big one, cigars, coffee, secretary." The gunslinger chuckled. "Oh, and a machine that does all my paperwork. Daroni can make one, right?"

"I will speak with the right people for you, once the time is right. Again, as long as you do your part."

"I'm in, then!" Andreas gave a low whistle. "A new chair, and no smelly shack of an office!"

The trio left the alley and made their way back to the *Ori*, which looked magnificent on the pad as they approached.

"Do you need to inform your superiors that you are leaving with me?" Kalon questioned Andreas.

"Yeah, just let me do that." The gunslinger looked over the port guard and walked over to one. "Malcom," he said with a tip of his head. "So, here's the deal. I'm off to the Holy City on that ship, there, with that man and woman there. I need you to tell the boss that I won't be back for a while. Might not be back at all—might die heroically in the line of duty." He clasped his hands to his heart. "Ok?"

The man shook his head. "Sure, I'll tell her."

"Good. See you."

He ran back to Kalon and the Khnarnate. "Ok, all done. We can go."

Kalon stepped up to the *Ori*, noticing that Silver was nowhere to be seen on the outside of the *Mist Reaver*. He tapped on the hatch, the door slipped open quietly, and he stepped inside. After a moment to look back at the port, both the investigator and Kaitlinel came aboard.

Fate's Hand thought back to Verity. He nearly stepped off the ship's landing platform, but then he turned his back on Sullavale. Now was not the time to involve her, as he previously thought. She needed to be here at the port, and eventually, she would come back to the church of her own free will, once it could be proven that Mallori was the real killer.

Until then, she was still at risk, and it was best for her to be a ghost until he could make his report to the Cardinal and clear her name. Any other man would have felt a deep pang of regret at this, but something about Kalon pulled emotions like this away into a void.

The door to the *Ori* closed behind him as he entered the ship finally. Next port of call: Messania, the Holy City and the Imper Vatica once more.

He was a man of his word: he would honor the deals that he made with both Andreas and Kaitlinel, as long as they proved useful.

CHAPTER 12

WARD OF SORTS

The ship tore across the sky as Kalon and the other passengers gathered in the stateroom, eager to learn what the Inquisitor had up his gold-trimmed sleeve. They had scarcely had enough time to get a bite to eat or drink before they had been called there.

Now, Andreas, Kaitlinel, and Spry stood in the presence of the right hand of the Cardinal, Fate's Hand—his spine straight, hands behind his back, fingers firmly interlinked.

He studied them with an unblinking, flint-edged gaze.

The Kharnate seemed to enjoy being the center of attention. She sprawled cat-like over her chair, one boot hooked over the edge, and she leaned mostly on Andreas's lap. Spry sat a little way from them both. He stole a glance at the Kharnate from time to time—then quickly looked away when Kaitlinel fixed him with her gaze.

"Andreas, Kaitlinel, Spry," Kalon addressed them. "You have been granted a great honor and a privilege to be taken to the Imper Vatica, and on a church prototype airship no less."

"The *Ori* is a fantastic ship, boss." Andreas leaned back in the chair. He laid one hand over Kaitlinel and heard a soft, playful growl in reply. "But me, I'm curious to meet Her Ladyship. Is that the correct form of address?"

"Holiness," Kaitlinel chuckled softly. "I think."

"Correct," Kalon answered. "Holiness. Her Holiness will do." Andreas made a note of this and nodded. Spry remained quiet, a little withdrawn. This was bigger than he could fathom, and he let the people around him do most of the talking. He didn't know what to say.

"Andreas and I discovered a lair of wizards connected to Sullivale Port. During this time, Spry had been kidnapped by an Anshada woman and taken to Terralion. At the Anshada's lair, I found a book that named Spry as the key. It contained notes that made little sense then," Kalon continued.

Spry looked up, suddenly more interested in the conversation. Kaitlinel noticed this, and Andreas would have, had he not been too busy gawking at the room around him. "Yeah, yeah, we killed a thing, and you found a book. First time I ever saw an Inquisitor in action against wizard stuff. It was pretty amazing," the investigator said idly. He was a flighty fellow, and his attention wandered. It always came back to the werewolf, though.

"My name was in a book, and I am a key?" Spry asked.

Kalon nodded, just the once.

"So, this wizard who had me, she said my blood was key to something, and said something about a book that belonged to her, or to the demon king. It's hazy now. I don't remember much."

Kaitlinel's ears pricked, and she rolled back so she sat up straight. "Wait, you mean you got kidnapped by an actual Anshada? One of the real ones?"

"Real ones?" Spry blinked at the dark-haired woman.

"Yeah, not the ones that play at being wizards, but one of the old-blooded ones. Full of power, and mean as a bucket of cats. They talk about demon king this, and return, that." Kaitlinel made a yapping gesture with her right hand.

Kalon turned his impassive gaze on the woman but said nothing. He was content to let her continue—after all, this is exactly what he had planned on. Information, without the need to interrogate anyone for it.

"She said my blood and his return, he'd raise her up and…" Spry sighed softly. "I just wanted to be left in peace."

Kaitlinel frowned and toyed with her hair, looping a dark lock around a finger, and said, "Spry, look. You're on the Anshadas' list now, and they won't stop looking for you. You're safe, though. This is the last place any of them would try anything. But I'm not going to lie, this is pretty fucking intense—for you—and bad for everyone if they do get their claws on your blood."

Kalon raised a brow. "Explain?"

"So, you know my goddess—the sex and blood one, yeah? Kharnate, the angry bitch with the golden eyes and mean streak. The *best* goddess." Kaitlinel grinned slightly, and the tips of pointed teeth peeked out from behind her red lips. "There are legends spoken among some of our lot, the ones who've slept their way around Hestonia, fucked across continents, and banged people of any sex or no sex to learn all the secrets of the world."

"Kharnates, eh? Can't live with them, and wouldn't want to live without 'em!" Andreas laughed a little. "Sorry, carry on."

Kalon continued to listen. He said nothing.

Spry fixed his eyes on the woman and blushed a little. The sex talk made him nervous.

"Long story short, the Anshada have this book. Powerful as fuck, full of bad magic, ages old, thousands of years. Dates back to before the City of Wyrden was anything but a blueprint. They hold it as a return to the good old days—sex, drugs, and human sacrifice for power." The Kharnate licked her lips with a sinuous tongue. "They want it, and they think Spry is the key to get it. Thing is—and get this—you lucked out with me. Fate and all that."

"Explain," Kalon prompted again.

"A friend of a friend fucked a friend who fucked an Anshada, and the wizard stole a look through all his shit. She—the wizard—let slip about a book they were looking for a few weeks ago. Convenient eh?"

Andreas shook his head and blinked. "I lose track of who fucked who."

"I have a little black book," Kaitlinel winked. "Basically, I can help you find this book, because fuck books like that and fuck wizards like them."

"Really?" Andreas smirked.

"Well, not literally fuck them, because no." The Kharnate's nostrils flared. "Even I have standards. I wouldn't do that, not for a lot of silver, or gold, or a title."

Spry sat silently now, mulling all this over. *Key to a book that could release the Demon King Akas—no fucking way!*

Kalon took all of this in and pondered it. He studied the woman's body language and detected no lies. "You can lead me to the *Book of the Anshada*?"

"So, you do know of it?"

"I do."

"Probably written up as the Big Bad Book of Naughty Magic Shit in the church library," Andreas quipped, eliciting a faint chuckle from the Kharnate.

"I ask again," Kalon said. "You can lead me to the book?"

"Yep." Kaitlinel grinned widely and tipped the man a wink. "Thing is, handsome—and you'll like this—it's not going to be easy, and the connections I have are vital to getting the book. I know people, and the one ship that can get you past the barrier just happens to be captained by a guy I slept with, more than once. Well, there were more than just me and him, and I don't think I need to paint you a picture of that week." She paused to take a breath. "Just know, lovely, I'm telling you this because of our deal, and I really want that favor to be HUGE."

"We will tell the Cardinal all of this when we meet with her," Kalon replied. "I am still aware of this big favor."

"We're going to tell her about the favor and the sex thing, too?"

"No, we will not speak of *that*." Kalon eyed the Kharnate narrowly.

"Yeah, got you, no sex in church." Kaitlinel offered a ribald laugh.

"Wait." Kalon latched onto something in her words. "The barrier… so the book is beyond there?"

"That's the rumor: way beyond the barrier, in one of the mountain ranges—where the big demon fell in ages past." Kaitlinel beamed a little now, happy to be even more at the center of everything. "You need the right ship to get through it, and there's only one—not even the *Ori* would make it."

"The barrier interferes with Tech-magis, I know," Kalon replied. "The *Mist Reaver* can?"

"Clever," Kaitlinel said, sounding impressed that he'd guessed the ship so quickly. "She has a lot of surprises under all that gold and feathers. Pretty little bird!"

"That ship is badass," Andreas said, flitting into the conversation again. He absent-mindedly tousled the werewolf's black hair.

"Silver." Kalon said and something tugged at the back of his mind.

"She's the first mate, and not a woman I've managed to sleep with yet, but you know a girl can dream." The Kharnate batted her eyelashes.

"Focus," Andreas added helpfully.

"I am focused." Kaitinel stretched out across the chair, even farther across Andreas. "Are we there yet?"

Spry remained silent, still trying to fathom his connection as "the key," as Kalon turned on his heel and made his way to the door. "I will leave you to talk among yourselves. I am going to prepare for our meeting with the Cardinal. You will be summoned when we arrive."

The door opened, he left, it closed softly—almost with a sigh. Or was that Kaitlinel?

The Imper Vatica docking bays were a hive of activity most days. Many trade ships and personal ships of the Inquisition and its many branches flitted in and out like insects. The *Ori* sailed in on the soft trade winds, aetheric engines barely whispering as the vessel prepared for landing. At this angle it was possible to glimpse the wonder that was Messania—a city held aloft with giant, turbo-fan Tech-magis engines, powered from the thermal energy from the still active volcano it perched above.

The ramp lowered and the group stepped off, Kalon in the lead, the rest following behind. They appeared a rag-tag band to the casual observer, all barring Kalon, who walked with the air of a man who knew exactly where he was headed.

The rest—Andreas, Kaitlinel, and Spry—spent their time following along, observing an inner sanctum that no one beyond the church had seen for centuries.

"It's impressive, this place," Andreas said. "Really, really impressive."

"Yeah," Kaitlinel replied. "So much potential." She eyed the people around her. "Lots of new connections."

Spry was full of wonder. He said nothing and stuck to Kalon's heel like glue.

As they passed into the upper areas of the complex via lifts and corridors, each new place affected the visitors in different ways. Kalon politely returned greetings from others but made no further attempt to engage.

Fate's Hand created waves just by being there. Even his own were nervous around him; such was the power of his moniker, Agent of the Cardinal and her right hand, a man who could turn on any of them and had the power to punish the slightest mistake.

He did not use it, but that did not stop people from being afraid.

After a while they arrived in a smaller meeting room. Kalon had selected this as a good place to wait for the Cardinal to summon them. He walked over to one of the church minions, a young woman with auburn hair whom he did not recognize.

"Excuse me, are you a messenger?" he asked as the others engaged in barely heard, idle chatter.

"I can be. Do you need a runner for a specific message, sir?"

"Yes. Inform the Cardinal that Fate's Hand has returned and, as requested, her guests are here as well," Kalon said.

She did not flinch under his gaze. "At once. Please wait here for any response so I know where to find you." The young woman took off at a run. She nearly bowled over another figure as she left.

"Bloody hell," muttered a soft, nasal-toned voice. A figure from Kalon's past emerged into the room, pale skinned, dressed in a shabby grey coat, and sporting a voluminous wide-brimmed hat under which round-rimmed, blue-tinted glasses reflected the rest of her surroundings. She beamed brightly and took a dog-ended, odd-smelling, stick-like cigarette out of her mouth. "Knock me on my arse next time."

She adjusted her hat and pulled her long, white, waterfall-cascade hair around her shoulders.

Kalon looked at her, and the woman met his gaze with a cloud of white smoke that rolled out from under the hat as she set her cigarette back between her lips and puffed. "Kalon Rhadon, you're a sight for sore eyes. Not as though mine are sore right now, lack of sun and all that."

"Miss Reva Flynn." Kalon offered a bow. "You have not aged a day, and it has been what, over twenty-five years since I saw you last?"

"Hair's a little whiter," she cackled. "I've been here and there. Your training, mostly observations and tech-magis, Daroni, and Sara. All the lovely, wonderful things that happen when you're out and about doing church-y stuff," Reva drawled, then finally appeared to notice the others. "Guests?"

"Yes, of the Cardinal."

"Ooh, and I see a person there I haven't seen for ages!" Reva waved to Kaitinel and offered an impish grin. "Do you mind?"

"No." Kalon cut Reva Flynn slack, because like Sara, she was a brilliant mind and therefore allowed eccentric behavior at the church. "But our meeting with the Cardinal is soon. Please ensure it's quick."

"Don't worry, sweetie, it will be." Reva tipped her hat and sauntered to the group.

"Reva!" Kaitinel shot out of her seat and wrapped her arms around the woman in grey. She pressed her lips to Reva's and kissed her hard.

Reva mumbled something that sounded like "Pleased to see you, too." Only it was hard to tell under the assault from the woman's red lips.

When Kaitinel stepped back. Both women grinned at each other, and Reva smoothed down her coat.

"That's one way to greet an old friend," Reva said, smoothing red off her lips with a finger. She fished her cigarette out of the Kharnate's mouth and put it back in her own. It was only slightly mauled.

"Aw…I do it for all my old friends, new friends, even some enemies." Kaitinel shrugged and then winked. "It's how we all say hello, goodbye, and pleased to meet you."

"Kharnates never change."

"Technically, we do," Kaitinel corrected with a smile. "But that's why we're so amazing. All that sexy, wrapped up in a fuck-you shape—and we can rip your head off at the drop of a hat, too."

"Well, yes." Reva looked down at the two seated. "Reva Flynn, alchemist, mortician, detective, and tech-magis artificer."

"Spry Genris." Andreas pointed at the boy. "I'm Andreas, and you're, in a word, interesting."

"Oh, interesting?" Reva adjusted her hat at a jauntier angle and slipped her glasses up on her nose. Under her hat, her features betrayed the hint of her non-human blood. "I like being interesting. It lends me an air of mystery. Reva Flynn, woman of mystery—I like that."

"I'd like to find out more," Andreas said with a chuckle. "Maybe later?"

"Much later, work to do, lots of people to see, things to build, wounds to make." Reva stepped back almost theatrically. "Kalon, when you have a moment, drop by the lab. Sara would like to see how your firearms are doing, and I think she'd like to show you her new chair!"

Kalon nodded and waited for the messenger's return.

"Ta-ta for now!" Reva breezed out of the room by another door as quickly as she'd entered.

"Flighty, that one," Kaitlinel observed, grinnng. "Still tastes as good as ever though."

Kalon saw Spry shake his head. He detected the youth's unease, but put it down to the boy being in a very different place to the port.

The door opened again, and it was not the messenger who entered, but the Cardinal herself. Though dressed in informal attire, she still made an impression. She wore a full-length gold and red dress, slightly v-necked to show off her pendant, and her hair had been tied back into an impressive whisper of gold curls and braids. Her features had been toned to perfection by the application of subtle make-up and just a hint of kohl around her expressive eyes.

Kalon bowed deeply and heard both doors to the room lock. They were sealed in, and he blinked at this break from protocol.

"Cardinal," he said and bowed again. "I expected we would be meeting in your chamber, a formal place."

"Fate's Hand," she said in soothing reply. "Forgive me. I felt it was more important to put our guests' minds at ease and to present a more informal side of the church. They have all heard the stories of the ice-veined Cardinal and the dogmatic enforcers of the church."

Andreas chuckled and bowed. Kaitlinel nodded from where she stood, thought better of it, then offered a bow and folded her arms. Spry rose very slowly and bowed the best he could. He saw Kalon's expression shift to one of very scant approval.

Terusa flowed across the floor as she stepped across the marble. "Allow me to welcome you to the Imper Vatica and thank you for offering to aid us in such dire times." She stepped up to the gunslinger. "Andreas, I presume?"

"Yeah, I mean—yes, Your Holiness," he corrected himself and blushed.

"Kalon told me how you aided him. Thank you." Terusa smiled softly, her eyes level with the investigator.

"It was my pleasure, Cardinal."

Terusa stepped to Kaitlinel next. Though they were of a height, the Cardinal regarded her with a low gaze. She saw the green wolf-eyes of the Kharnate and nodded. "We are blessed, it seems, to have one of the Goddess Kharnate's own among us," she addressed the other woman. "You are?"

Kalon observed the Cardinal and the Kharnate closely, noting how Terusa enthralled the other woman. He had observed this from a great many people who met the Cardinal.

"Kaitlinel," she said and took a deep sniff of the air, then smiled even more. "Absolutely pleased to meet you, Your Holiness."

Terusa offered the Kharnate a smile that danced like a fire on her lips.

At long last, she alighted before Spry. Her eyes roved across the youth, and she nodded. "Welcome Spry, Kalon's Ward of the Church. I hope you will learn to love us as much as we will you."

Spry stood there. He had never seen a woman so powerful, so radiant, and so utterly captivating before. He did not reply; he looked shyly away, another behavior Kalon noted in others meeting the Cardinal. Terusa smiled at the youth regardless. She bowed her head and whispered, "You will be happy here; I am sure of it."

Spry nodded, and that was all he could do until he finally found his voice and replied, "Thank you, Holiness."

Terusa chuckled softly and sat in one of the chairs. "Come, tell me all there is to know. We will talk formally of the things you have seen. Kalon, I ask you to speak, and everyone else, myself included, will remain silent and attentive, yes?"

Spry nodded and sat again. So did Kaitlinel and Andreas.

"Good. Kalon, begin."

Again, Kalon summarized his adventure with Andreas in the Anshada lair, and spoke of rescuing Spry from the Anshada witch. "I rescued him from that fate," Kalon said as he continued. "Pulled him from the dark, and together we will discover the reason they consider him a key. I brought Andreas here on orders, made Spry a Ward of the Church, and Kaitlinel is vital to our obtaining the book. Her contacts can help find it."

Terusa nodded and pondered this. She sat in silence a while longer and finally broke it. "What say you, Kaitlinel?"

"He's right. I know people, I know Wyrden, I know of the Book of Anshada thanks to our legends, and I can help Kalon here get it." Kaitlinel saw no reason to beat around the bush. "Plus, he owes me a big and juicy favor."

The Cardinal fixed Kalon with her eyes. "Oh?"

Kalon nodded. "A bargain, with both Andreas and Kaitlinel," he explained, not ruffled in the slightest that the werewolf had brought this before the Cardinal before he did—the Inquisitor's mind simply did not work that way. "Andreas desires to be Chief Investigator, and Kaitlinel, as she has said, wants a favor."

"Then we will honor all of this, in due time," Terusa replied with a nod. "I will see to it personally that Andreas gets his wish, and you will be able to call on Fate's Hand once for a favor of your choosing, Kharnate."

Andreas grinned widely. "Thank you, Holy One."

"Oooh, so many choices!" Kaitlinel chuckled softly, and her eyes flickered with desire.

"Back to what you said, however: the book is in Wyrden?" Terusa asked.

"No, but I know where it's supposed to be: Demon Spine mountains, past the barrier, in the old lands—you know, the cursed place. The place where the church ships can't go."

"I know of it," the Cardinal sighed. "Our ships cannot cross the barrier; it devours our energy like a locust does a crop. How do you know of this, and we do not?" She frowned deeply.

"You can't get agents across the barrier, but some of us come from that side. We hear rumors, and we find things out. It's all anyone ever talks about over there, since it's part of their history and shame, really—imagine being associated with a book that nearly doomed the world?" Kaitinel adjusted her posture and wrinkled her nose. "Does it really matter how I know—as long as the book is found and Kalon gets to destroy it? Plus, if anyone tries to stop us—I get to show them my bad-wolf side. I'll enjoy that!"

Kalon nodded. "It is indeed our best place to search for the book— worth that favor from me—and once we have the tome, I will do all in my power to destroy it there and then."

"No," Terusa said forcefully. "Do not even think of destroying that book without me or the church. Such things are dangerous. The Imper Vatica has many means to ensure the safe destruction of the tome—bring it here so we can dispose of it properly."

Kalon noted Terusa's sudden outburst before she calmed herself. He quirked his brow. Her reaction took the others by surprise, until she followed up with her explanation—that eased their minds.

"Makes sense," said Andreas. "Can any of us touch it?"

"Only with gloves, never with your bare hands," Terusa warned them. "It's said the book is deadly to those who dare take it without proper precaution."

"Noted." Kalon nodded. "So, Cardinal, are those your orders?"

Terusa's eyes moved from person to person. She smoothed her dress down as she rose from her seat. "Yes," she said finally. "Bring the book here for destruction, and go with Spry, Kaitlinel, and Andreas to track it down. People are more than tools, Kalon; learn to rely on them as allies."

Kalon nodded, somewhat surprised by the lecture. "You have my word we will find this book, your Holiness."

"Good. Keep me informed as and when you can. I have dispatched Maxis and Winter to investigate Rand's death. I will let you know as soon as they know more." Terusa moved toward the door and her way out. "A pleasure to meet you all."

"A moment if you would, Cardinal," Kalon said quickly.

"Go on?" Terusa paused her departure.

"What of Verity? Any news?"

"None. Our bird is still out there, fluttering her wings—even though I have explicitly pardoned her." That was the news Kalon wanted to hear. "Now if you do not mind, I have many other matters I must attend to."

As Terusa opened the door, the lock on the other side of the room disengaged, and the Cardinal left quietly.

"We prepare to find this book, then," Kalon said as the Cardinal left. "You are all with me?"

"We are." Andreas knew it wasn't a question, but he felt he had to say something. "Right, people?"

"I've got no choice," Spry said solemnly.

"You don't say no to a woman like that lightly," Kaitlinel observed with a chuckle. "Nor do you want to, I mean, damn…the stories do not do her justice. Plus, favor, big favor, SO BIG!"

Kalon did not dignify this with a reply.

"Very big. Massive probably." Andreas grinned.

"Return to the *Ori*. Await me there. I have a place to visit before we discuss our next steps." Kalon looked at Spry. "Your first task: guide the others back to the ship, and do not stray to explore."

"Oh, ok." Spry snapped out of his funk. "I'll do my best."

"Do better," Kalon added.

"Got you. Come on, folks: to the *Ori* on the master's order."

Kalon let that one slide and watched the three of them leave the room. He regarded these allies as a necessary evil, and the Cardinal's words rang in her ears. Allies, not tools…

Odd, since she had always taught him people were a means to an end.

Odd indeed.

He left by the other door, his destination: the depths of the Imper Vatica and the secrets of Vincent Daroni.

Sara had something to show him, a new chair.

The door closed with a click.

CHAPTER 13

MISTRESS AND MASTERS OF ARTIFICE

The Imper Vatica was vast, deep, and full of secrets unknown to the rank-and-file Inquisitors. Kalon was above them as the Cardinal's Right Hand; he was afforded certain perks, which meant he could draw his arsenal and his support from those areas normally left to the high lords, ladies, and agents of the church.

One such place lay at the very depths of the complex, beyond machines both terrifying and fantastical, pulsing with energies the likes of which mortals never saw. Ghostly shapes flitted inside tubes and cylinders; flickers of energy gleamed in stark bursts of white and blue. Huge aetheric engines fought against the power of gravity, pushing against the force that wished the mighty city to fall. Giant turbo-fans roared beyond the toughened glass, and exhaust fumes billowed into the sky.

This energy powered the engines that held the city aloft, and through the one-way windows, Kalon could see the still active volcano below the Holy City of Messania.

Down Kalon went, through secret stairs and dimly lit corridors, into the lair of Vincent Daroni, the Master Artificer of the Church.

The route to the artificer's lair was a maze-like collection of crossways, maintenance walkways, ducts, and vents. A low, sonorous hum echoed around the area, and at long last Kalon came to the door that led to the heart of invention in Messania and the place where he would find Reva, Sara, and Daroni himself.

"Workshop" was perhaps inaccurate a word to describe the plethora of inventions, machines, and workings on the other side of the dark wood and brass doorway. This place was a factory of ideas and a manufacturing plant for vast quantities of equipment used by the Church of Progression in their day-to-day lives.

The smell of metal, oil, fuel, and other strange scents wafted into Kalon's nostrils, and he took a moment to orient himself. Vast vats of molten ore poured their contents into molds, forming arms of other complex machines, ready to cast, finish, and attach to keep the technology running.

"Kalon!" Sara's voice came from somewhere above him. He looked around, and then up, to see the woman suspended in the air, her chair emitting a faint glow followed by a subtle haze around the underside.

"I see you have made some adjustments, Sara." Kalon nodded with approval. "Your skill has grown since we last met. Then again, it has been a long time."

Sara nodded and brought the chair lower. It was an impressive version of her original, a little more ornate, and even more comfortable than before. "I grew, my chair changed, and I cracked a few minor issues with the old version. This is the Mark Three now. What do you think?"

"You have done well." Kalon affirmed. "So, is this what you wanted me to see?"

"Yep!"

The chair came even lower, and the young woman settled it back on the ground beside the Inquisitor. "It's better than the old one, by lots. We're talking suspension, anti-gravity, slow but effective flight. Some countermeasures and a few surprises if I need to get physical." Sara winked and mimed punching someone.

"Always wise to have a good offence, and a good defense." Kalon studied the chair and examined it thoroughly.

"So?"

"I can find no fault with it, and the design shows you thought of comfort as well as function."

Sara beamed brightly. "Yep!"

"I will be leaving soon, on a mission of some import. Dangerous, no doubt." Kalon looked around again. "I need to speak to Master Daroni."

"Ah, Vincent is probably in the quieter area with Reva. As for a mission, I won't pry, but I will say you came at just the right time. The three of us have been cooking something up."

"I am always interested in what you have been doing."

"Invention and iteration and construction—with you in mind," Sara said and blushed a little. "Our favorite Inquisitor."

"I see." Kalon quirked his brow and pondered this.

"Ok, come on, the suspense is killing me. Reva said you might drop by, so we put the finishing touches to them."

"Them?"

"Come on!"

Sara scooted the wheelchair across the lab floor and toward the quieter area where the artificers did their best inventing. Draft tables, pens, drawing machines, and other such devices surrounded them as they entered the research wing of Daroni's lair.

"Speak of the man, and he appears," Reva drawled as she sat on the edge of a bench, one leg crossed neatly over the other, her grey robe scuffing the edge of a stool.

Vincent Daroni was tall—almost as tall as Kalon—though bent slightly by the need to use a walking cane. He leaned on it and studied the Inquisitor. Daroni was old, probably seventy or eighty. Yet he still appeared spry for his age, with intelligent, hazel eyes and a curly mane of silver-white hair.

His beard was neatly trimmed, and atop the tip of his nose he wore a pair of spectacles with variable lenses and small levers attached. He was dressed in his inventor's smock, leather apron, and a toolbelt around his waist.

Daroni's right hand was sheathed in an elaborate wire-frame cage of some kind, which still allowed his fingers freedom to move. Parts of the cage entered the skin and attached directly to the bone, almost as if it were keeping the hand and arm intact.

"Kalon Rhadon," he said with a smile and offered a stilted bow. "Forgive my lack of mobility, but I'm getting older and older with each passing day. As we all are."

"There is nothing to forgive," Kalon answered.

"Hello again, Kalon. Having fun?" Reva grinned under her hat, chewing on a stick-like root that left her tongue stained slightly black.

"Master Daroni, you look well," Kalon said and then frowned at Reva. "Fun? I lack the chance to engage in fun. You know this."

"I know, I know, more's the pity," Reva drawled.

"Has Sara told you of our tinkering?" Vincent waved his right hand to one of the many benches.

"She said something about invention, iteration, and construction," Kalon answered and looked at Daroni's right hand. "You have had an accident?"

Daroni followed his gaze and shook his head, "Oh, this? No, no. Not an accident; this is faulty design of the body. Or rather, the body has developed a fault. My bones are becoming brittle, as I found out the hard way when these broke and almost turned to powder. Fortunately, I have my other right hand." He gestured to Sara.

"Yep, I built that rig to maintain the integrity of Vincent's bones and help keep that arm together while we look for solutions," Sara said proudly. "It's a support rig, lets him do all the things he could before and makes sure his bones stay intact. Do you need it explained?"

"No, I trust your word. Once again, impressive."

Sara blushed; this time it reached her ears.

"Enough of my bones." Daroni crossed over to the workbench and took a case from it. With a swift flick of his hand, he dropped it carefully in Sara's lap. "You do the honors."

"Really?"

"Yes." Daroni's hazel eyes shone mirthfully.

Sara wheeled over to Kalon and winked at Reva. "You think he'll like this?"

"Knowing what I do of Fate's Hand, this is probably better than an engagement ring," Reva answered and chewed on more of her blackroot.

The young artificer presented the case to Kalon and flipped the catches.

"We thought since time has marched on, it was the right point in your career to upgrade those pistols of yours." Sara opened the case; it was red velvet lined and padded.

Kalon looked down, and his eyes fell on two pistols. They were sleeker than his current pair, emblazoned on the grip with the cog and eye of the church, and matte black in color with just the right edge of gold to set them off.

He picked them up as one might holy artifacts and studied them intently.

He felt the weight change as he held them; they adjusted to him.

He pointed them across the room and felt the balance.

"Impressive," Kalon said finally.

"Do you like them?" Sara asked anxiously.

"They are fine work, and I am sure they are better in every way than my previous tech-magis pistols."

"Yeah, but do you *like* them? They're one of a kind, made with the love and care of three people who are here right now."

Kalon mused on this; his emotional attachment to people and things never seemed to be as strong as those of other people around him. He put it down to his rigorous training, dogma, and a brutal upbringing, where every single person he knew at the church pushed him harder than any other.

Logic dictated there must be a response, so he hedged his bets and, after more study of the weapons, finally said, "Yes."

Sara smiled, and Kalon saw her shoulders relax.

"I...am so glad!" There was an undertone of anxiousness in her voice, but it vanished at the end of her sentence.

"They will serve you well—our combined talents brought them to fruition. They are the perfect combination of magic and technology," Daroni breezed with a soft chuckle. "More ammunition per firing cycle, quicker recharge, self-charging, and a host of features you won't find on any other Inquisitor's weapons. They even have a faster scribe rate for the equations, so you won't have to wait as long to fire the rounds at a mage to break through barriers, or at a demon to shred them into mist."

Kalon listened and pondered, "What did Reva add?"

"Oh, you know." Reva grinned from ear to ear, pretended to smoke the blackroot, and said finally, "Sugar, spice, everything that's not nice, and some extra bit of alchemical wizardry—don't shoot me, Kalon—to ensure charging is much quicker."

"Ah."

"We put our talents, hearts, and souls into this," Sara said with a grin that matched Reva's own.

"Why?" Kalon asked. The question poured like a bucket of cold water over the enthusiasm of the others in the room.

"You are Fate's Hand. You needed weapons that match your rank and role," Daroni said with a hint of the practical in his accent. "We cannot have the Right Hand of the Cardinal—or the left—with just any old Inquisitor's firearms."

"Plus, you're always complaining that things are off—so now you have a pair of weapons made especially for you. All that hand shaking, all that measurement, and all those secret readings we took of you..." Reva mimed writing in a little book with the stick of blackroot as a stylus.

Sara sighed softly and then perked up. "I remembered when I first modified your guns. I felt useful then, and it made me happy to do it."

Kalon nodded. "I am not ungrateful, I was curious. I wondered if there was a special reason, but I understand now."

"You and your need to understand this and that," Reva drawled softly and spun the blackroot around her fingers. "It's almost as though you just don't get interactions with people—then again, perhaps that's the upbringing you've had as the church's prime enforcer. No time to learn to be a person, when there's just the dogma of the church and the will of the Cardinal."

"Yes, Reva, I think that's enough of that now," Daroni admonished her.

Reva turned her head slightly and bobbed out her tongue. The tip was black.

Sara stifled a laugh and watched Kalon as he took his old weapons out of their holsters, put them on the bench, and replaced them with the new ones. "I will ensure these are put to good use. Thank you, all."

That was about the most effusive thanks they'd get out of him.

"How were the contacts?" Vincent asked as he watched Kalon intently.

"Excellent," Kalon noted. "Sara's work again?"

"Yes, yes," Daroni replied. "She really is quite brilliant."

The younger artificer blushed again and rolled her chair back to one of the benches, putting the case down on the side.

"How long before I need to change them?"

"You don't." Sara smiled. "They naturally sit on the eye, moisturize it, and avoid the nasty complications that came with prolonged use of the old model. They also stay in place if you get struck aside the head."

"We tested that." Vincent Daroni chuckled softly.

"Poor Brian," Reva interjected.

"Yes, poor Brian." Sara made an "oops" face.

"Excellent. Once again, you continue to provide a valuable service to us all. I will report this to the Cardinal and tell her how pleased I am with your artifice." Kalon smiled; it was more a formal smile than one of enjoyment or comradeship. He felt like he could do more, but that feeling sank and fell away before he could try it.

Reva, Sara, and Vincent Daroni fell silent for a moment, and then it was Sara who broke the silence. "I suppose you have adventures to go on now?"

"A mission, yes."

"Good luck with it!" Reva waved and caught the stick of blackroot as it nearly shot out of her hand.

Vincent Daroni offered a half-smile and retreated to his chair. "Hopefully this new arsenal will be the key to victory."

"It will help." Kalon nodded. "I must go. Once again, thank you for the support and the time."

Sara waved and tapped the right arm of her chair quietly. "Be safe."

"Yes, be safe and well!" Vincent Daroni gestured with his cane. "You don't want to end up like this old shell, eh?"

Reva inclined her head, tipped her hat. "Give them what for, Kalon."

Inquisitor Kalon Rhadon turned on his heel and left the three of them to their own devices, pleased with his new arsenal and impressed at the work he had witnessed. He had no frame of reference for feelings, of course; they were just emotions that floated on the sea of his mind, then sank down, as if pulled by some inexplicable force beneath the waves of thought.

He was soon on his way to the surface and toward the hangar dock. His destination: the *Ori*, for now. Though as he walked, he fixed on something that Kaitlinel had told him, and a flicker of a face burned into his mind. The kelanari woman, with the dagger-drop earrings and long silver hair.

The *Mist Reaver*, and its flamboyant, gregarious captain.

He would need to leverage Kaitlinel's connections, then, and perhaps it would be better if he did not travel on a church ship for this mission. Especially if he needed to go to Wyrden, and then eventually beyond the barrier—toward the Demon's Spine mountains.

These thoughts walked with him as he made his way to the hangar dock through the vaulted corridors of power before him.

Kalon emerged into the hangar and blinked at the gleaming light. It was brighter than he expected, but the contacts he wore cut the glare down quickly, and his vision returned to normal. He looked around to see Spry, Kaitlinel, and Andreas engaged in a discussion.

"Kalon!" Andreas grinned widely. "The man returns!"

"Hello again." Kaitlinel turned to watch the Inquisitor's approach. "All done?"

Spry looked up with a nervous smile, offered a wave, and sat on a box.

"Yes, I have what I need." Kalon paused outside the ship and fixed the Kharnate woman with his gaze. "You said that you could contact the *Mist Reaver*?"

"Yeah, I can. You need it?"

"Wicked ship," Andreas butted in. "Sorry, had to be said."

"I do," Kalon said smoothly, despite the interruption. "It would be wise to charter Talon's ship; a church ship may tip our enemy off. How long before you can have the ship here?"

"As long as it takes me to borrow some comms equipment from that sexy gal over there, and as long as it takes you to inform Captain Imani you won't be flying with the *Ori* any longer." Kaitlinel grinned and raced off to one of the tech operatives, a ginger-haired woman in overalls.

Captain Imani, curious about the commotion outside their ship, chose that very moment to alight on the hangar floor from the ramp. "Someone called my name?"

"I wanted to thank you personally for your aid and inform you that I will be changing vessels. I am not allowed to speak of the mission, only that if you are needed, I will contact you. Please remain on standby if you can," Kalon said formally. He bowed as well. "Your service in my mission to Sullavale and to Terralion ensured that I can count on you."

Imani blushed a little; unlike Kalon, they were capable of that. "Thank you, Inquisitor, this is high praise indeed. I understood that our arrangement was not going to be permanent, and the *Ori* is, after all, a prototype. I should give the flight and operational data to the techs."

Kalon nodded. "That is settled, then. I will see you again."

Imani bowed and walked back inside the ship, no more words spoken.

"Harsh, Inquisitor." Andreas shook his head. "You dropped Imani like a hot rock."

"Imani is surplus to requirements, and I did not *drop them*. Their time aiding us is over for now." Kalon busied himself looking over the rest of the dock.

"Yep, hot rock," Andreas said to Spry, patting the lad on the shoulder. "Cheer up! You got this, kid."

"Really?"

"Yeah, really." The gunslinger winked. "We got your back, man, don't worry."

Spry blinked at Andreas. "I could count on my fingers, and only the first few, the number of times anyone's 'had my back.'"

"It's true."

"I can't help it." The Stealer sighed. "I'm a little thief, not an Inquisitor, or a gunslinger, or a werewolf, or anything—just a thief."

"Our Stealer mate," Andreas said and looked at Kalon, making a "say something" face. "Right, Kalon?"

Fate's Hand nodded once. "An important member of this team. You are the key, and the reason we will find this book."

The corner of Spry's lip tilted up. "Thanks. I feel a little better."

"It's what we're here for, kid." Andreas patted him on the shoulder. "We're going to be like one big—odd maybe—happy family."

Spry laughed a little. "That would be nice."

"Just you wait and see. I'm not going to let anything happen to you!" Andreas gave Spry a brotherly hug and felt the youth sag a little in his arms. "I mean it."

"Thanks," a tiny voice replied from within Andreas's embrace.

Kalon watched impassively. He fixed his eyes on the rest of the hangar, the *Ori*, and waited.

CHAPTER 14

A TOUCH OF SILVER ON WINGS OF GOLD

Hours later, Kaitlinel returned from her conversation with the ginger-haired tech, a big smile on her face. She loped over to the small group and sprawled on a nearby crate with a pleased expression on her lips.

"Did you contact the *Mist Reaver*?" Andreas asked pointedly. "Or did you fool about a bit as well?"

"Both." Kaitlinel chuckled wryly. "Technicians have wonderfully clever tools at their disposal."

"I don't wanna know." Andreas glanced where Kalon stood quietly and pointed. "You best tell the boss."

"I'm going, I'm going." Kaitlinel rolled off the box and sauntered past Spry. She peered up at where Kalon stood at the edge of a gantry stairwell on the west side of the hangar.

He looked down and nodded. "And?"

"All done. Had some free time, and so I decided to see what all the fuss about the church's tech was all about." Kaitlinel's green eyes regarded the man above her mirthfully. "You are a lucky lot here."

"How long before the *Mist Reaver* arrives?"

"Pretty soon. It's been a few hours since I contacted the ship, so she'll be here, and we can get you underway."

"I am eager to begin the search and recovery of this tome. We have the key and a head start. The enemy does not have the boy," Kalon said. His eyes roved the heavens outside of the bay for any sign of the *Mist Reaver*.

"You look like a hungry wolf, Inquisitor." Kaitlinel licked her lips. "I should know; it's my perpetual state of being. But you—you have something about you that just devours the room."

"I do not follow."

"Like I said." The Kharnate shuffled from one foot to another. "I can't quite work it out yet, but you have an animal magnetism about you. I would love to show you the animal side, but you're just not interested, and it's not because you're into men; I see how you look at women. You might not have the emotional training due to the church—but your instincts are there just under that brooding bad-boy surface."

"None of what you are saying matters or makes sense to me. I have no interest in liaisons with anyone," Kalon replied flatly.

"You're missing out."

"To miss out, one would have to want in the first place."

"Ooh, true, true."

"Is there anything else you wanted, or are you here to see if you can tempt me to bed?" Kalon questioned. His eyes never left the sky.

"Oh, lovely, I'll always be here to tempt you," Kaitlinel growled softly and offered a chuckle at the end. "My goddess would be very upset if it were not so."

What the church had done to Kalon over the years had taken him from his parents, powerful people in their own right, and put him on a path. They had pulled him away from any kind of meaningful relationship, drafted and molded him into an Inquisitor, and hardened him to a core of steel when it came to emotional control.

There was more at work here than just rigorous dogma, and Kaitlinel could sense it. Her goddess's gift had afforded the Kharnate a perception beyond that of mortals. Yet she wasn't an idiot; she knew when to push, and when to back down.

Now wasn't the time to push, not when Kalon was in the church and on his home territory.

Then, where the sky had been empty, the clouds parted, and a familiar eagle-shaped vessel came soaring out of the heavens. Down the *Mist Reaver* flew, trailing small flickers and tendrils of vapor from the edges of its wing tips. The vessel, shining a beautiful gold hue in Hestonia's sunlight, became like a flicker of fire in the sky as made its approach.

Kalon watched the ship curve, turn, and soar gracefully into the bay, where it alighted on the bigger landing pad in the front. Landing legs akin to a bird's clawed feet folded down from the underside, and the ship settled, ejected a small whisper of steam, and then lowered slowly.

Captain Talon Mane had arrived.

Leaving his vigil, Kalon made his way down metal stairs, across walkways, and toward the lower hangar bay where the *Mist Reaver* sat. His small band of misfits watched from a railing above as he homed in on the ship.

The ramp lowered as Kalon approached, popping out seamlessly from under the beaked nose of the golden, bird-shaped vessel. It was near silent as it slowly came down, small stairs folding out to form an elegantly lit walkway of ivory and dark yellow. It was as much a work of art as the vessel itself.

Kalon could appreciate the aesthetic. He was impressed by the look, but it did not move him as it did the others.

Silver walked down that ramp, step by step, boot fall by boot fall. She was dressed in the same attire as when they'd first met, and her hair was pulled back into a long, tight tail.

"Kalon Rhadon. I didn't think we'd end up meeting again so soon." The kelanari woman chuckled softly when she saw the man from the dock below her. "Kaitlinel mentioned a tall, handsome stranger from the church, and I must admit—I thought it might be you."

Kalon quirked a brow and bowed formally. "Lady Danae Silvercrest, welcome to the Church of Progression and the Imper Vatica."

"So formal again. Just how I remember you from our first very quick meeting."

"Indeed."

Silver reached the bottom of the ramp and walked over to Kalon and stuck out her hand. "Pleased to meet you again, Inquisitor. Or should I say, Fate's Hand?"

Kalon noticed slight traces of tattoo work on the bare skin just past her wrist: intricate, mandala-like ink-work. He blinked slightly. Of course, she was wearing gloves and working on the ship when they first met.

He shook her hand and felt a slight sensation of pins and needles. "Is everything ok?" Silver's voice, like spun gold, caught him off guard.

"Yes. And a pleasure to meet you." He let her hand go and looked down at his gloved fingers. "Odd," he said under his breath.

The small group above watched them, and Kaitlinel grinned with a sly smile. She whispered something that neither Silver or Kalon could hear into Andreas's ear. The gunslinger laughed very loudly, then looked around sheepishly.

The moment was broken by the arrival of a tall, dark-haired kelanari man dressed in an elegant uniform, long green cape, and an impressive, wide-brimmed buccaneer's hat. A fantastic multi-hued feather peeked out from the hat band. He almost ran down the ramp, the complete opposite of Silver's elegant arrival.

"Kalon Rhadon, Fate's Hand," he said with a laugh. "I have heard all the stories—read a few too, but honestly the penny dreadful writers do not do you justice. You are every inch the look of the man in the tales. But where are the dry wit, the lady-killer smile, and the women on each arm?"

"Are you sure that is Kalon you're talking about, or Maxis Kane?" Silver asked with a low chuckle.

"Ah, wait, perhaps. Sorry. Allow me to introduce myself." The man doffed his hat, spun it in a fluid motion before him, and set it back on his head with a flourish during the bow. "Captain Talon Mane, at your service!"

Kalon bowed silently. He studied the other man with a quick appraisal and concluded that beneath the foppish exterior, there was something else lurking, like a shark in the ocean.

"A pleasure," he said finally. "I am eager to be underway. Did Kaitlinel explain?"

"Not all the juicy details," Talon replied, leaning on Silver nonchalantly. "But you can fill me in once we're in the sky."

Silver looked across and shuffled away from Talon, more out of amusement than a sense of her personal space being violated. "Don't fall, Captain."

"Oh, but I have—for Kalon! He's so handsome and aquiline of nose, just like my ship!" Talon paused a moment. "No offence. It's a gorgeous nose."

Kalon looked at Silver, and for a moment he felt something that he couldn't describe. Many people would call it irritation, and it was a new experience for Fate's Hand.

"Gather your people, then," Talon Mane said and looked at the ramp. "On the double, let's get back in that sky and on the way!"

"Excellent." Kalon felt the odd emotional blip vanish, and he looked up at the gantry. "Join me. We leave now."

Talon followed his gaze and beamed brightly at Kaitlinel, waved at Andreas, and stuck his thumb up at Spry. These three gestures seemed more planned than genuine, as if the man's personality were a painting upon a very different canvas.

The others joined Kalon, Talon, and Silver at the ramp and wordlessly boarded the ship.

As the ramp rose back into the neck of the *Mist Reaver,* the Cardinal stood upon a high balcony overlooking the bay. As she watched the vessel rise and coast silently out of the hangar, she wrapped her hands around the balcony's bronze guardrail.

"Soon the book will be safe." The mind-voice came to her like silk, wrapping around her thoughts gently, lovingly almost. She felt a sense of well-being and comfort. How lucky she was to have the words of her deity soothe her.

"My Lord, he is the best agent we have."

"The Hand of Fate, crafted from the seed of the enemy and trained by the church I helped you create," the One God of the Infinite Machine's voice entered her mind again.

"A fated child indeed," Terusa answered. "His emotional control shows just how much a servant of the Infinite Machine he is."

"Emotion has no place in logic."

"We had to take those steps." Was she reassuring her god, or herself?

"We have no use of a firebrand Inquisitor."

"It is safe as well; it will not hurt him at all." Again, a reassurance for herself.

"I made sure it is safe," the mind-voice replied. *"It will keep him from being ruled by his emotions."*

"Then we do not need to concern ourselves. He will be fine." Terusa watched the *Mist Reaver* vanish into the distance, a bank of thick cloud swallowing the bird-shaped vessel into the sky of Hestonia.

With a soft turn of her red dress, the Cardinal left the balcony and retreated into the depths of the Imper Vatica. The air grew suddenly colder around her, and for a single moment, doubt grew on the edge of her mind.

The *Mist Reaver* left the mighty city of Messania behind, a giant floating edifice in the wake of the vessel's powerful engines. Messania, a marvel of Vincent Daroni's design, and the very heart of Terusa's empire: it was an incredible sight to behold.

Kalon and his party were now in one of the *Mist Reaver's* many comfortable lounges, which resembled those of the finest airship liners and perhaps betrayed more of the captain's flamboyant and extravagant personality than Silver would have liked.

Spry lay on one long chair, head on a pillow, and appeared to be exhausted as he half-listened to the flow of words around him.

Kaitlinel sprawled over Talon as they huddled up on a nearby chair. She had her legs hooked over the arm and her left arm around the kelanari's neck.

Andreas sat back in a smaller chair, amused and smug.

Silver sat on her own and remained straight-backed, formal—even now, on guard.

Kalon was Kalon, and stood at the edge of a vast window, watching the holy city vanish into the distance. He interlocked his fingers behind his back and turned to address the captain.

"We seek to bypass the barrier and make for the Demon's Spine Mountains; we need the *Mist Reaver*, according to the woman on your lap, to do so."

"She's not wrong at all, my friend." Talon planted a kiss on Kaitlinel's lips. "This clever wolf here knew exactly who to call—and, well, favors, favors for favors, friendship, and so much more, if you are cold at night or really at any time!" The captain's eyes gleamed softly, shards of intelligent emerald against his tanned skin.

Kaitlinel kissed him back. "Flatterer."

"How does the ship aid us?" Kalon watched them both.

"Well..." Talon stretched. "I can go where you can't. Wyrden: protected by that nice no-fly order for church vessels and so on. The barrier devours magic and tech-magis energies from ships that try and cross it. So many wrecks in the early days—but I have a way!"

The Inquisitor nodded, ignored the antics of the two on the chair, and turned back to the window. "I see."

Silver watched him intently. She too ignored Talon and his lap partner. The silver-haired kelanari woman's lips pursed thoughtfully. "What then?" she asked Kalon. "When you cross the barrier, the skies over the Demon's Spine are treacherous even for Talon and this ship."

"We go on foot. A longer trip, yes, but safer for the *Mist Reaver* in the end," Kalon answered without turning around. "The church will compensate Talon for his time on standby."

Talon tapped Kaitlinel on the nose and chuckled. "So, that's why you have Kait here. If things go awry, she can rip heads off for you!"

"Partly, yes. She also said she knows the area beyond the barrier," Kalon replied, studying the clouds as the *Mist Reaver* skimmed them gracefully.

Kaitlinel chuckled. "I know someone else who knows that area better than I do."

Kalon turned around slowly and fixed the Kharnate with a stare. "Who?"

Silver sighed softly and leaned forward. "I do."

"Oh, you do?" Kalon switched his gaze to the kelanari woman now, then found himself lingering on her longer than he expected. Silver was like a dangerous wild cat; even at rest, there was something about the woman that pointed to every single muscle and sinew stretched taut. It was like her relaxed state was a smokescreen for barely contained violence.

Andreas turned to watch this. He studied people as a living, and this was the first time he'd seen Kalon even take a second glance at anyone who wasn't an enemy. He smiled a little to himself; honestly, he couldn't blame the Inquisitor one little bit.

Spry spluttered a snore and rolled over. Andeas put his boot up to stop the young man from landing on the floor to a rude awakening.

Silver, on the other hand, returned Kalon's careful regard. After all, he was a dangerous agent of the church, and the stories of Fate's Hand spoke of a man who did not compromise and very quickly judged those who stepped out of line regarding his precious church.

The exchange did not escape Talon and Kaitlinel's notice, but they were too busy with each other's company to bother.

"I spent time there as a young girl," Silver admitted and sat back a little. "My order comes from there, the Amari Sisterhood."

Kalon turned his head slightly and replied, "Assassins."

"We prefer the term equalizers, since assassins are motivated by money."

"Interesting." Kalon filed this away for the future.

"Me or the sisterhood?" Silver sat back further.

"Both." Kalon heard himself say, and wondered why.

"Get a room!" Kaitlinel laughed softly, then shrugged. "Or don't, your choice!"

Kalon ignored this, and so did Silver. The Inquisitor and the equalizer, two sides of the same coin, and both as deadly.

"So, you could act as a guide?" the Inquisitor asked after the moment had passed.

Silver stood and stretched, then crossed the room to stand by the man's shoulder. Her eyes fixed on the clouds before her, and she pondered.

Talon dug his elbow into Kaitlinel's ribs and flicked his gaze to the doorway. Without a word, the pair crept from the room. Talon would argue that it was impossible to fight the animal magnetism of a Kharnate for long. Truth was, the man himself needed no excuse to seek pleasure with any number of people, Kharnate or otherwise.

Andreas poked Spry awake. "Hey kid, hungry?"

"I was asleep," he replied grumpily, "but food sounds good. Are they coming?" He looked at the pair by the window.

"No, I think they have some brooding to do." Andreas chuckled softly. "Seen it before. They're like twins, or something...let's get food, eh?"

"Oh, ok." Spry rolled off the chair and followed Andreas out of the room.

Silver and Kalon heard the door close, and the lounge fell silent.

"It must be interesting to crew on this ship," Kalon said after a while.

"It has its moments. The crew are eclectic, mixed, and diverse as any ship you could think of. We have waifs and strays from all over Hestonia aboard," Silver replied as she continued to study the sky.

"I see."

"Your first time?" she said. "Properly away from the nest, and not surrounded by members of the church?"

Kalon mused on this. He thought hard and nodded. "Yes."

"Are you a different man away from the church, do you think?"

"What do you mean?"

Silver turned to look at him. She studied the Inquisitor, a man in his forties, with her sharpest gaze. He was guarded, emotionally and physically, like her—Kalon appeared to be like a spring ready to snap.

"Am I a different man?" Kalon echoed part of her question.

"Is the church dogma, the doctrine I heard so much about from Verity, so cast iron it forbids human emotion?" Silver asked, revealing a secret connection with Kalon's "friend."

"Ah, you know her." Kalon kept his eyes on the cloud. He watched the formations and the blanket below—they looked solid, like snow.

"Yes. She was going to join the Amari Sisterhood, but the church poached her from us," Silver said, a hint of regret in her voice. "Verity would have made a splendid equalizer."

"She loves her causes, her justice, and her morality." Kalon felt a half-smile form on his lips, a memory, not pulled away this time. "Odd, this is the first time I thought about it."

"Any idea why?" Silver's eyes did not leave Kalon's face, even though she saw it from the side.

"None."

"Perhaps it'll come in time."

"I cannot afford the luxury of such thoughts; the church needs me to be logical," Kalon said and felt a pull in the back of his mind. Something wormed there, like a thick eel in the waters of his psyche. It lurked toward the front and...then shrank back.

The *Mist Reaver* flew on and smashed through the front of a raincloud, which blotted out the sky around them. Gone was the sunlight, and they were left with rivulets of water cascading down the glass before their eyes.

Silver traced one of the small rivers of water with her finger as it made its way down the pane. "See these rain drops? They are like people, Kalon. They move of their own accord, ever toward a goal. Some meander and intersect with others to meld with them before they run together toward that final destination at the bottom. Some barely touch before they move on." She followed one such small trail. "Others form larger groups, and then there are those who never meet another droplet and continue on their own path. All are valid; all reach that final stop at the bottom."

Kalon regarded this and the woman's slender finger as she traced the glass. The nail barely touched the surface. He blinked a couple of times and thought on her words.

"Raindrops as an allegory for people...and their lives. Fascinating."

"It's emotion, Kalon. That's what the rain speaks to me when I see it on glass."

Silver stood closer to him than anyone had ever done. He'd never noticed the distance between himself and others until now. He felt oddly at ease and strangely warm in her presence. The cold feeling that had dogged him all his life faded like a new morning's mist while he was in her proximity.

He also found it odd that he didn't move—nor did he want to.

The dark eel wormed its way around his psyche and tugged on his soul but could not sup on the emotion therein. If Kalon had known the source of the eel, his anger would have consumed him, a fire brighter than the eyes of a woman who waxed lyrically upon the rain and the nature of emotion.

"Do you not feel it at all?"

"I don't know," he replied. He felt his frown; it sat oddly on his features. "I have never confronted these things before. There has been no need."

The kelanari woman began to suspect that Kalon's lack of emotional response was not just training and dogma. She felt her skin tingle in the patterns inked upon it, her mandalas reacting to something in or around the man. She knew the signs: a dark and fearful magic was close, or a creature of some kind.

She was no wizard, nor did she possess sorcery per-se, but her time on the *Mist Reaver* and as one of the Amari Sisterhood had schooled the woman well.

Something in Kalon reacted to Silver's presence, as for the first time in a long time, the Inquisitor observed the rain as something other than a meteorological effect.

He saw the droplets of water, and he felt the words that Silver spoke.

He didn't just hear them.

Slowly, and unknown to them both, something in the Inquisitor began to shift.

As the *Mist Reaver* skimmed on, the pair now stood in silence and watched the storm unfold around them.

A foreshadowing of things to come.

CHAPTER 15

BARRIERS ARE MEANT TO BE BROKEN

The golden vessel was a home away from home for a disparate and diverse group of people, the likes of which Kalon had never seen gathered in one place. In truth, he was a newly flown bird himself, free from the nest of the Imper Vatica and set loose upon a world he knew little about beyond what his peers at the church had told him.

Kalon knew facts; he did not know people.

The church had trained him to see the lies on people's faces, to recognize patterns in expression and in emotional response. However, he was a machine in that regard himself; he lacked the subtle knowledge that could allow him to form a more nuanced opinion.

This meant he couldn't easily be swayed by emotional manipulation or false tears.

He wasn't aware that people were complex creatures, full of emotion, messy, vulnerable, and capable of so much good and evil.

He was trained in black and white—science good, magic bad.

He had that teaching drummed into him over the years and years, from a very young man to the adult he was now.

There were lots of barriers for the Inquisitor, and many he just did not see.

Lady Danae Silvercrest was the chink in whatever armor Kalon had, and neither of them knew just how important she would be to what was to come. If Fate had been playing the long game regarding the Inquisitor, the goddess did not let on. She shuffled the deck in the background and let the dice fall where they would. Fate was in many ways like a cat, and dice were oh-so much-fun to play with.

Kaitlinel did what any good Kharnate would have: she availed herself of any available playmate for the journey, sauntering naked from room to room without a care in the world. Spry managed to find himself a small room with some younger members of the crew. He spent the next few days talking to them about their jobs and work on the ship. Meanwhile, Andreas—as much as he loved to spend time in the werewolf's embrace—really wanted to play cards. He found the engine room of the ship, and its Chief Engineer: Ryssa, a woman of the sylthen, snake-like humanoids with a mix of human-like and serpent features. He swapped stories of Sullavale Port and played several rounds of Hestonian Five.

Ryssa thought he was new to the game, until she realized he could play. Then all bets were off, and her game became more intense. During these matches, they spoke of the three-tiered City of Wyrden and the Countess Arabella, the mysterious potential ruler of the place—and her mansion, home for every Kharnate in the city. Ryssa was quite free with her information, and Andreas was a sponge for any spicy stories—in Wyrden, there were a lot of them.

Kalon passed the door and caught the sound of the pair as they played. He paused to listen. The strange tug of emotion had vanished for now; it disturbed him, and he set about the task of trying to redress the balance.

"I really want to meet this Countess Arabella now." Andreas dropped a card over the engineer's own. "If what you say is true, she sounds a riot."

"She's certainly a character." Ryssa let out a sibilant chuckle and tapped the card with a clawed finger. "Be careful, anyone would think you had a crush on her."

"Never met her, but from what you describe, she sounds amazing."

"Like honeysuckle and dewdrops on a cold morning." Ryssa laughed softly. "That's my round."

"What, no! Oh, I see what you did. Dammit!"

Kalon shook his head and moved on. He rounded the corner deep in thought and collided with Silver coming the other way. They met physically; this was closer than Kalon had ever been to another person in his life.

Silver was as tall as he was, so she was able to look him eye to eye. She did not move, but a half-smile danced on her lips. Her eyes were full of mirth, rather than annoyance.

"Perhaps we need to widen the corridors?" she asked, and the half-smile became full.

"I apologize." Kalon felt a flush of sorts, an emotion, embarrassment for being so close to the woman, and for colliding with her. "I was deep in thought about the other day."

Silver did not move. That skin-crawl foxfire of energy that shot from line to line danced over the circles on her skin and ignited her mandalas. "The rain?"

"Yes." Kalon nodded. "I dreamed about it, I thought about it, and I wondered about it. Something I have never done, because when you're deep inside the halls of the Imper Vatica there's nothing but solace and shadow."

"It sounds lonely...and sad," Silver said, remaining steadfast in her position. "Imagine never experiencing the rain like we did, or seeing how the sun refracts from the drops on the window as the storm breaks."

Kalon stepped back and to the side. "I should let you pass."

The woman studied him for a moment longer, and then pondered, "Do I make you uncomfortable, Inquisitor?"

Kalon blinked at this, and he felt an odd sense of truth to her words. "I cannot say I am comfortable around anyone, for I have never really been in a situation that warrants comfort."

"No friends, lovers, friends with benefits?" Silver couldn't help but tease.

"Nothing of the sort."

"No wonder Kaitlinel looks at you with hungry eyes—you're like a prime steak to her." Silver laughed softly, and her dagger-earrings tinkled. "You'd be one hell of a buffet for that woman, if she ever dined."

Kalon blinked again.

"I am teasing, of course, but perhaps that's out of line, since you really have no frame of reference." The woman turned on her heel. "Where are we going?"

"We?" Kalon looked around. Suddenly, he felt he needed to be elsewhere. Or was that the eel in his soul?

"Yes. I can't leave you like this. Where are you off to?"

Kalon looked for an exit, and then, curiously, as he stepped closer to the woman to pass her, the desire for flight was replaced by a sense of ease. "I thought I would go to the small lounge, with the view of the fore of the ship, and meditate."

"Mind if I come with?" Silver adjusted her posture and noted again the way Kalon's unease faded as she remained close. The same spark flowed through her body art. This just made her more curious as to what was going on with this Inquisitor.

Kalon thought on this and answered, "It's your ship. I am the stranger here. You may go where you will."

"Let me rephrase. Do you want me to come with you?"

Kalon drummed his fingers against each other nervously, and then said, "Yes. For some reason I am not averse to this idea."

Silver smiled, and for a moment she sensed something lash out at her. But it shrank back again, hurt, wounded, and afraid.

"Good," she said and gestured to Kalon to walk ahead. "After you, Kalon. Lead the way."

The Inquisitor, suddenly out of his depth and off guard, nodded and resumed his perambulation toward the front of the ship. The corridor widened eventually, and they both stepped through into a comfortable, cozy room. The decadence of the main lounge suite was there, but a bit attenuated. The window had a marvelous view of the nose of the ship, just under it, showing the oncoming sky framed with scudding cloud tops.

Kalon sat down cross-legged on the floor right before the window, ignoring the chair. His long coat spread about him like dark water.

"Limber Inquisitor, is that the church meditation posture?" Silver studied him a little.

"Yes."

"Do you mind if I join you then, in meditation?"

"I presume that the Amari Sisterhood has something similar?" Kalon closed his eyes.

"Similar, yes, but we do so without the need for clothing," Silver sat next to him, mimicking the man's posture.

"No garments?"

"None." Silver took her hair out of the tail and let it fold freely across her shoulders. It followed the contours of her outfit.

"It is part of the Sisterhood?"

"Energy is a thing that flows like water, and it can be caught— trapped, even—by garments. You, for example, have a lot of energy blocked by the dark colors you wear. It works both ways, blocking the bad from getting in, but also trapping any bad that tries to escape," Silver said and closed her eyes. She took three breaths and shook her head. "It's as alien to me as meditating with clothes on."

Kalon thought on this: naked, the flow of energy around the chakras of the body and the nexus points—a curious concept that the prudish church would never allow. Garments were meant to cover the body, to prevent certain urges in the younger Inquisitors from taking hold. Hence many of them dressed in formal attire, with no room for sensual dress or provocative show.

His logical mind focused on this, but as he thought further, part of him settled on how the Cardinal was dressed at their last meeting. It was more a statement of her womanhood than her power.

Or perhaps it was both.

He thought back to what Silver had told him of the Amari and pursed his lips. Silver's secret was buried deep, part of her past, and only a select few knew of it. Kalon was one of those now, and neither of them knew why she had confided this in him.

It just seemed right.

The tattoos that the Amari Sisters all had were their weapons and their armor, their protection against magic and demons. The order of demon hunters, now unfairly branded assassins, had its roots in the ancient times of Hestonia's history during the rise of the Regent thousands of years before.

"With your permission, I would like to honor my sisters of the order," Silver said without opening her eyes.

Kalon sat there, his breath slowing as he slipped closer to the core of his meditation. He heard her voice clearly, however.

"I will not prevent you from meditating in such a way, if this is central to your order."

"Very."

He heard the whisper of clothing, the shift of garments, the sound of leather and silk. The very slight shuffle of Silver's form as she removed every item of her clothes and laid them on the nearest chair. She pulled her boots off last and ensured her weapons were hidden among the piles of fabric.

Now she sat before the window, as naked as the day she first knelt as a sister of the order, and allowed herself to experience the memory of tattoo needles marking her in a mystical pattern secret to the Scribes of the Amari. Her body was covered in a mix of lines, curves, circles, and small daggers. They flowed over her form, which had been described by some of Talon's friends as a magnificent work of deadly art. Her curves and muscles spoke of a woman who kept herself ready to fight at a moment's notice, and she was lethal.

Her tattoos, Amari inkwork: protection, weapon, armor.

In proximity to Kalon, the mandalas gave off a faint light in the lounge. She took a few breaths and closed her eyes again.

Kalon was troubled. He could feel the energy from the woman, and it disturbed the Warp and Weft of reality itself. Silver was...silver, her psychic light emanating even with his eyes closed, and it affected the dark, eel-like thing that was part of his soul. He could feel it now: something that was not right, something hungry.

It was not happy. It pulled away and tried to pull Kalon with it.

He defied it, he defied *her*, and he defied the creature.

It lashed out, and Kalon felt it, something tugging at his mind—a pain shot through his brain like a hot knife.

He let out a groan, his breathing labored.

"Kalon?" Silver's voice came to him, soft, yet with a core of steel the like of which he had never faced.

"I am fine," he lied.

"No, you are not."

The eel-like beast raged, thrashing violently against the man's psyche. Another stab of pain, and he felt himself almost slip into unconsciousness. His pulse hammered his chest, and the demon snarled in the void. It stuck its eel-like tail into Kalon's soul and pulled.

He felt like being sick.

"Kalon." Silver's voice wasn't a question, but a call.

"Yes?"

"Listen to me, to my voice, and only that."

"I..."

A veil tore away; the demon's eel-like shape roiled and coiled. A tendril of psychic energy snapped out and latched onto the cog and eye. Kalon sensed it—it shocked him. His logical mind, that which could scarcely operate, realized what the demon tried to do. He heard it wail, *"Cardinal, Akas, help me!"*

The cry never made it from the room. Silver's tattoos reacted to the dark entity and shut down the creature's attempt before it could raise the alarm. Through the psychic link provided by Silver's tattoos, Amari and Inquisitor now shared a picture of part of the truth.

The demon attacked Kalon once more. The pain in the man's head was almost unbearable; the unshakable Kalon Rhadon had been shaken to his core this day. Now, the demon eel pushed harder, tried to devour the man's soul to save itself—it needed more psychic energy!

Kalon felt a soft finger reach out and touch his forehead, and a flood of energy burst into his mind. The darkness was cascaded away by a light so bright, he closed his eyes tighter against it.

"Breathe," the kelanari woman said.

He did, once, twice, and three times.

"Again."

He did so. He couldn't speak, but he felt the pain lessen. The agony in his head and upon his chest began to fade. The demon lashed and lashed as it was pushed away and sent smoldering toward the safest place it could find: the darker thoughts of Kalon's mind, the part of the human soul that permitted such things to exist.

The pain slowly died down.

"In through the nose, out through the mouth. Three in, hold three, out three," Silver said, as if she were teaching an Amari Sister for the first time. "You know this. You are trained to do it."

"I know it," Kalon replied as if in a trance, remembering his training with Seeker Winter. "I am trained to do it."

Silver opened her eyes, and she saw the vague shape of the demon as it tried to hide against the touch of her finger on Kalon's third eye—however, it could do little to prevent discovery. Silver studied it, the blind force, the black eel, and saw the truth—or at least some of it.

As Kalon's fear rose, a strong emotion, the eel grew stronger and fatter.

As Kalon's uncertainty danced across his mind, the same.

As Kalon calmed, the demon tried to draw on his emotions again to fight back against the kelanari woman. It failed.

"You are stronger than it," Silver said and held Kalon's head in her hands now. "I see what is going on, and by my oath as Ninth Sister of the Amari, I will free you," she whispered in a soft, beautiful language that Kalon did not understand. "I see you, demon, and it is only a matter of time before I end you."

That was a promise and an oath made.

The demon knew it.

It was terrified.

Silver's skin lit up with the power of the Amari mandalas, the protective circles igniting with a gleam across her hands. Part of that energy transferred to the Inquisitor as she saved him from the demon's wrath and pulled him back from the eel's grip.

With no emotions to draw on, it was scared, furious, and lost. Silver's tattoos worked on Kalon as long as she drew near him.

For the first time in his life, Kalon was flooded with emotions, hit with a sudden deluge like a cascading fall. Everything repressed came to the surface, and the unbreakable rock that was Kalon Rhadon wept until he could cry no more.

He collapsed on the floor and sobbed.

Silver placed her hand on his back and kept it there.

"Hush, now," she said softly. "What the church has done to you, we will undo, and then we will have a reckoning the likes of which this world has not seen in eons."

She did not speak hollow words; she meant every single one.

In the depths of Kalon's mind, in the unbridled morass of his soul, the eel-like demon lashed back and forth. Walls of light came for it, sharp tendrils of energy poked at it. It smoldered, and it cried out in its own tongue for aid from the Demon King.

None came.

Nothing.

Only the light of the kelanari woman greeted it, comforting, deadly, and a weapon of power the world had not seen since the Regent's demise.

The barriers holding Kalon back, which shackled him to the church and kept him on a tight, chain-like leash thanks to the emotion-devouring demon in his soul, were damaged, and the demon along with them.

Can a demon truly die?

Did it feel pain in those final moments, faced with Amari power?

None can truly say, and Kalon could not tell you, for he was like a child again, weeping over the deaths of his parents, caught in a dream where a dark snake throttled the very life out of him. Then, into that dream came a sliver of light, with a sword of conviction that cut and sliced the snake into ribbons of dark energy that drifted off into the shadows beyond the bodies of his parents.

Finally, Kalon stopped sobbing and settled into a dreamless sleep. Restful and, for the first time in his life, free of control—free of the Cardinal's leash.

Fate's Hand, the so-called enforcer of the church, was meant to be the Cardinal's greatest weapon in the war against the Anshada. Yet Fate's Hand was not hers; he had never been hers.

He was Fate's...

He didn't know it, Fate didn't know it, and the irony of such a revelation just made her love the dice even more.

The gods of Hestonia, young or old, always had a hand in mortals affairs. They couldn't help themselves; it was so much more interesting than being indifferent. Fate had a front row seat for all of it, and she was going to have *fun*.

CHAPTER 16

ONCE AN INQUISITOR

Silver was exhausted from her psychic battle with the demon in Kalon's mind. Her training with the Amari Sisterhood had served her well, and her will was stronger than some shackled church demon—which was the only thing that it could have been.

She knew this, due to the church's strict methods to prevent demonic possession and the enchantments carved into the very archways and doors of the Imper Vatica. Verity had told her one day of the measures taken to ensure the safety of the agents. Kalon had trusted the church, he had trusted the Cardinal, and he had been unaware of the thing in his mind.

Silver looked down at the man on the floor, crumpled and breathing softly. She had thought him a typical Inquisitor for the most part, though his strange aura had been cause for concern. After her battle with the eel-like demon, however, she now knew the extent of the church's influence on Kalon was beyond the training they put an Inquisitor through. The Cardinal had done something else—or at least was party to what had happened to Kalon. Silver had seen the connection through his amulet and felt it too.

But that was not her main cause for concern.

With the eel-demon gone, the man would come to know emotions as he never had before. It would be difficult for him, no matter the dogma or the teaching of the church. He would have to be observed carefully, as he might become unstable—even suddenly violent.

His training and control learned in the Imper Vatica would be tested, and she, as both an Amari Sister and the person responsible for his deliverance, would be right there to ensure he came through. As she continued to observe Kalon, she wondered what plan Fate had in store for them. Her actions had sent out ripples across Kalon's life, tiny waves that reached even the Cardinal in the Imper Vatica.

In her private meditation chambers, Terusa had undergone a morning ritual that left her sprawled naked upon a large bed in a state of euphoria. The vague shape of a man's backside vanished through a doorway, and the rustle of clothing from within the antechamber drew her attention.

"Leaving so soon?" the Cardinal asked softly.

"I must," Drako Mallori replied and peered around the door. "As much as it pains me to go, it would be far more dangerous for me to stay. Especially since you put Maxis and Winter on my trail."

"It had to be done. We cannot arouse suspicion." She hadn't done it yet, but he didn't need to know that.

"Really?"

"You handled Rand's death poorly; you made a wealth of mistakes. Think yourself lucky I still find you attractive enough to invest my meditation time with." Terusa rolled onto her back and toyed with the medallion around her neck.

"Verity escaped, yes; Rand pulled a bomb on me. What was I to do?" Mallori sounded hurt. "I had to improvise!"

"Yes, and by using magic, you put yourself in Kalon's sights…" Terusa's irritation flashed in her words.

"I had to protect myself."

"I know, but now you've made it trickier to hide you."

"I can handle Rhadon."

"No, you cannot." Terusa sat up, tapping her pendant. Something was not quite right. "Kalon has been trained beyond a mere assassin, beyond Winter, beyond Maxis, and he is of a singular mind. He doesn't care that you killed his friend; all he cares is that you betrayed the church and murdered an Inquisitor."

"So, I'm dead?" Drako Mallori slung his coat over his shoulders and sat down in the chamber.

"I will square this with Kalon eventually, but for now…keep out of sight, use the secret ways, and visit me when I send for you," Terusa said idly. "You are to serve me when I want, and do not risk visiting me when you think it suits you. Only I know when it's safe."

"Understood."

The Cardinal heard a click from the chamber, and then a swish, the sound of a door closing, marking Mallori's departure.

"Do not fret," the mind-voice whispered softly. *"Rand's death was necessary to put Kalon on the path. He was but a fragment in the greater destiny of the church. His sacrifice honors me, and you. Question if you desire, but remember, I am the One True God of the Infinite Machine."*

"I do not question." Terusa lay back down and let the pendant settle against her skin. "I only ache for knowledge and desire the power to keep my people safe."

"You shall have power," the voice promised. *"And so much more as well."*

The Cardinal closed her eyes and attempted to see through the medallion to where Kalon was. His was the only cog and eye she had placed such an enchantment on. Her investment was important, and the sensory overload of seeing through every cog and eye would have been far too much for her.

She could communicate through others, as she'd done all those years ago with Lin.

Kalon was special, though, and needed a guiding hand.

She opened her third eye.

Nothing…

"Lord?" she said to the air, worry in her voice.

"Yes, Cardinal."

"I cannot see what Kalon sees. I cannot feel him through this symbol."

"Have you forgotten where they are going, my dear Cardinal?"

Terusa sat up again, blinking against the soft light, and splayed her hands behind her. "Beyond the barrier, where tech-magic is disrupted?"

"*Yes. But do not fret: I have ways to find Kalon, and I will do so for you, my Cardinal,*" the voice promised, like honey, with a dash of vinegar in the word: you.

"Thank you, my God." Terusa straightened up and reached over to a bedside table. She took a gold and ivory brush, and, with great care, began to brush her hair.

The voice did not answer. Something disturbed the One God of the Infinite Machine; something had gone silent.

The events of the day had synched up quite dramatically, for the moment that the link had been shattered between the One God and the demon eel was also the moment that the medallion refused to work to allow the Cardinal to observe Kalon's surroundings.

Fortunately for him, Silver was still in close proximity, and she dressed herself while Kalon droused. The final items to go on were her boots, and she pulled the last one on as the door opened.

In breezed Kaitlinel, her dark hair disheveled and her expression languid. She looked at Kalon on the floor and Silver putting her boot on and waggled her brow.

"You didn't just fuck that Inquisitor into unconsciousness, did you? Because if you did...good for you!" Blunt, crude, and to the point—that was the Kharnate way.

Silver rolled her eyes. "No."

"No, as in yes I did, or no, as in I wouldn't even if I had the chance?" Kaitlinel looked at Kalon on the floor and tilted her head. "Because, you know, I would."

"You would, anything."

"True." The Kharnate grinned a little. "So, Little Miss Chastity— what happened, then?"

"Hah!" Silver pulled the boot all the way and let go. "Believe it or not, we were meditating—and you know how the Amari Sisterhood meditates."

"I heard. All naked, right?"

"Yep."

"My kind of religion!"

"It's not a religion," Silver grumbled, flicking her hair to the side. "Long story short, Kalon was host to a demon. He didn't even know the bastard was inside his mind, latched onto his psyche, and burrowed into his soul."

"Well...fuck." Kaitlinel sat on the edge of the chair, close to her friend. "What did you do?"

"What the Amari do." Silver looked at Kalon. She wanted to move him from the floor. "I confronted it, and it tried to hurt Kalon. Badly, which I couldn't allow—so I had to resort to fighting it on the astral plane, or at least part of it. That part connected to Kalon, where I cut the thing down."

"Ouch, that had to have some kind of effect. What was the demon doing?"

"Feasting on his emotions. As far as I could tell it had been there a long time. May be as far back as when he first joined that church." Silver stretched a little. "I saw when I was fighting the demon—as Kalon got angry, scared, or whatever emotion he felt—it got stronger—so I assume that's what it was doing to him. It'd also explain Kalon's coldness and lack of empathy. His emotions would rise, and then the demon would swallow them whole."

"Shit."

"I feel for him. Imagine having your emotions eaten by a demon, so that you can't experience anything like we can?" Silver knelt and waved Kaitlinel over. "Give me a hand. Least we can do is put him in a chair."

Together both women put the unconscious man into the seat and draped his coat over him. "I don't know what I'd do without my surfeit of emotions. It's too horrible to even contemplate," Kaitlinel growled under her breath. "Do you think the Cardinal knows about it?"

"We can assume she does. She knows everything, right?"

"Yeah, though there are some conniving fuckers at that Imper Vatica. Maybe one of them?"

"Perhaps." Silver sat on the arm of Kalon's chair and rubbed her head. "Ye gods, Kait, I'm tired from that one."

Kaitlinel's expression softened, and she looked at both Silver and Kalon. "Why don't you take a nap? I'll keep an eye on him."

Silver considered, but shook her head. "There might still be some residual demonic magic, and while I'm close to him, the tattoos will keep that dampened."

"How close?"

"Closer the better, to be fair."

"Rowr," Kaitlinel said and waggled her brows.

"Did you just say 'rowr?'"

"Maybe."

"Really?"

The Kharnate laughed and winked. "Come on, would you?"

"That's for me to know and you to wonder about," Silver replied coyly and shook her head. "Always with sex; is there nothing else?"

"Goddess, no, come on. Kharnate!" Kaitlinel laughed a little. "Not even one bit?"

"Do you want me to spell it out?"

"No, because you'd spell it S-E-X," Silver retorted and chuckled softly.

Always with the last word, Kaitlinel snorted and shook her head. "F.U.C.K."

Kalon stirred a little in his chair, caught in a dreamless sleep, wrapped in a meditative quiet as his trained mind locked against all that had transpired. Perhaps another would have had their psyche bruised or broken, but Kalon Rhadon without a demon devouring his emotions was perhaps deadlier than before. His training at the hands of Winter had been impressive, and it had granted the man a will stronger than anyone realized.

Stronger than even Kalon knew.

His brush with the demon, Silver's unorthodox methods of removal, and the front-row seat to his own psychic battle could have damaged him.

It did not.

The dreamless state ended, and he walked the halls of his mind. Where there had been a slew of misplaced and chaotic memories, fragments of his ordeal, there was now a mental construct—a kind of lockbox. This, Kalon would call his "Lockbox of Memories," and into it he ordered all the elements that had made up the day so far.

The conversation with Silver, the strange closeness they shared, the flickers of feelings and emotion pulled away by something burrowing into his mind and soul. Something that tried to take control of his body.

He felt anger stir.

He did not lock it away, but mellowed it, toned it down, and brought it to heel like a barking dog.

Kalon paused in his own mind, picked up a box, and put it in the correct place.

He owed Silver a debt, one he was not sure he could repay. He would speak to her when he woke—of that, he was sure. His mission had not changed; he still needed to find the book and bring it to the church for destruction. The Inquisitor still valued the Church of Progression, the likes of Winter, Sara, Reva, and all the others. The book posed a danger to the world, and to them. It was a risky gambit to take it back within the reach of the Cardinal, but perhaps it would also afford him a chance to speak to her. Tendrils of energy flowed to the amulet he wore when the demon tried to reach out to the Cardinal.

He got angry again, but controlled it.

He would speak to the Cardinal regarding the demon. He needed answers. His own rage at the betrayal—even if it came from elsewhere in the church—could not and would not distract him.

It became a simple matter of eliminating a dangerous source of magic, and if the Cardinal spoke truly, destroying the book without proper precautions could be bad. It was a risk he was not willing to take, so to the church the book must go. Sara, Winter, Daroni, and Reva would know what to do. They always seemed to be there for him—he had never known or realized that until now, or truly appreciated it. His mind snapped back to the task at hand: the book. He was nothing if not single-minded in that regard.

Into his mental construct poured the sound of two voices, both women, both recognizable, and both discussing him and a great many other things. He turned his mind outward and took a deep, soft breath. In the real world, Kalon awoke with a slow and steady opening of his eyes.

Two blurred shapes came into focus, and they were indeed Kaitlinel and Silver. The pair sat not far from him, and as they heard him move, both sets of eyes turned on him in a single motion. He felt uncomfortable, but tamped it down.

"Hello, sleepy head," Kaitlinel said softly. "How are you?"

Silver looked at her, then back to Kalon. "How's the head?"

Kalon stretched a little in the chair, unfolded his coat, and blinked a few times. "I feel disorientated, my head is muzzy, and I have a taste akin to iron in the back of my throat. Barring all that, I feel fine."

"Good." Silver nodded, somewhat pleased. "Kaitlinel, do you think you can get Kalon some water?"

The Kharnate nodded. "Yeah, I know. I'll go and get Kalon some water." She grinned and loped out of the room, though not before a suggestive eye-waggle was thrown in the kelanari woman's direction.

Kalon watched her go, studying Kaitlinel with fresh eyes. She walked with no hint of fear or of modesty. Everything about her spoke one word: predator.

"No headaches or nausea then?" Silver questioned.

"Nothing of the sort, only a mild discomfort."

"That's good. And of your ordeal?"

"Ah, that." Kalon mused on the question and ran his thumb under his nose subconsciously. "Thank you. I have never been beholden to anyone before, and never has anyone beyond the church stepped into the fray to save me from a creature I did not even know was in my soul."

The kelanari woman smiled wryly. "Raindrops on windows, Kalon. Remember?"

"Yes, I believe that was the catalyst."

"Kalon, also, you're not beholden to me. I acted as any Amari would have." Silver tapped her fingers against her leg. "Well, I believe I did."

Kalon smiled a little. It was an odd thing to be able to feel that smile too. "I am pleased you did; without your aid I would never have known otherwise."

"I am glad that you approve. I had to act fast, without permission and without restraint." Silver explained and looked away out the window for a moment. "I wasn't sure if you'd be angry."

"Anger is not an emotion I am used to feeling. Then again, with the emotion devourer in me...emotion was not something I was used to," Kalon replied and watched her look out of the window. "More rain?"

"No, we're getting closer to the barrier."

"Ah, soon we will be on the trail of the book." Kalon nodded softly. "Excellent."

"You're still going to go after it, even though you know the Cardinal could be dangerous—corrupted even?"

"Yes." Again, that single-minded nature.

"Why?"

Kalon smiled, and that looked strange for a moment before it vanished. "To protect people from it. I want that book gone, destroyed, and I will take it to the church and seek counsel there from those who might know how to do it—not the Cardinal per-se. But I have questions, and that book is my way to get answers and achieve my goal of destroying the book at the same time."

"It's risky."

"No more so than the Anshada finally regaining it, and another demonic purge," Kalon countered, folding his arms.

"Now that is true." She turned to look at Kalon once more, taking him in beyond the disheveled mess of his hair, and saw traces of his aura through her Amari training. It was mixed; many colors played around the man, and the grey and black, the muddiness, were almost gone.

"Quite an intense look. Does something trouble you?" Kalon caught her scrutiny.

"No. I was just checking something using aura sight," Silver replied nonchalantly. Perhaps she had looked a bit longer at the man—perhaps not.

"All is well?"

"Yes, you're doing well."

"I am relieved to hear that. Nothing must prevent us from obtaining the book for the church," Kalon said steadfastly, reinforcing his resolve to finish that mission.

"We've a way to go yet—on foot I mean." Silver stood, stretched, and yawned softly. "That battle took it out of me."

"Why do you not go to your chamber and rest?"

"Good question, simple answer: my tattoos are anti-magic and have an aura that disrupts demonic energy. I want to make sure that thing is fully gone, and you're safe," she said and sat down again on the other chair. "I will remain close until I'm satisfied that you're out of the woods."

"I understand." Winter had employed such psychic protection sigils in the past, and Kalon understood enough of this to realize how important it was.

"Amari ink work…there is none finer, save for the equations that you know."

"Yes."

"So, you see, I'm staying by you a while longer." Silver chuckled, then tucked her feet up on the chair. "But I might nap here, if that's ok?"

Kalon nodded. "I will keep watch. My own mind is more settled now, and my control is coming back."

"You might want to get a handkerchief, though," Silver said and daubed her cheeks with her fingers.

The Inquisitor took off his gloves and ran his fingers over his cheeks. "I remember. I broke down. So many tears."

"Yes."

"I have only ever cried once, when my parents perished. Not long after, I remember I could never cry, no matter how hard I tried."

Silver felt her breath catch for a moment, and she realized—at that point—Kalon must have been "gifted" with the demon he carried for all those years. "It's likely," she butted in, "that's when you got your mental passenger."

"I concluded as much," Kalon replied logically. "It makes sense based on the memories I have of that day."

Silver closed her eyes and curled up in the chair. Kalon took off his coat, laid it over the woman, and sat down again where he was. It didn't take long for the kelanari to drift off into exhausted sleep; her body couldn't keep up with the energy drain.

Kalon turned his attention to the sunlight, the way it danced off the clouds, and the onrush of moisture as the droplets hit the window when the *Mist Reaver* turned and arced toward the west. The barrier was in reach, and the Demon's Spine mountains lay on the other side. It made him feel, and that was new.

It was like he had just come out from the dark, into the light. As if a veil had been lifted from his eyes. He felt the emotional shift from the patterns in the heavens and a slight twinge of regret that he had never been allowed to witness the beauty of a sunrise beyond the astrological and astronomical mathematics of the whole show.

The door opened, Kaitlinel stepped in, shut it with her right foot, and presented Kalon with a mug of hot sweet tea.

"She said water, but honestly, I thought you might prefer tea." The Kharnate looked at Silver in Kalon's coat. "Nice touch with the coat. That's real gentlemanly."

"Sugar?"

"Kaitlinel, please. You're far too informal." She winked and presented the man with a spoon from a belt pocket.

Kalon offered a wry smile, feeling the humor in this. "Clever. I didn't appreciate it before, but I can see the amusement in what you say."

"Oh, I love to be appreciated." Kaitlinel grinned again and sat down cross-legged on the floor. "I'll be good, promise, as much as I want to be bad."

"It's a Kharnate thing," Kalon surmised and began to stir the tea, twenty-five quick revolutions one way, and twenty-five quick revolutions the other. "I presume?"

"Yep, you catch on quick, Kalon."

"One of my more endearing traits," Kalon said and sipped the tea. It wasn't too hot or cold; the Kharnate had managed to get it just right. "Ah, this is excellent tea."

"Only the best on the *Mist Reaver*."

Kalon drank some more and felt the tea for the first time, felt the emotion it created and the joy that taste brought. He looked at the window again and saw the edge of a dark mist in the cloud before them.

"The barrier?"

"Yeah, we're almost there. Then you'll get to see what this ship is really capable of."

Talon's voice came out of the speakers high on the arches of the ceiling. "To all crew and passengers, any sneaky stowaways, and everyone else: welcome to the final leg of our journey! It's going to get bumpy from here on out, so if you're doing anything that you shouldn't be doing, finish that up and get ready. Ten minutes and we cross the barrier."

Kalon quirked a brow. "This ship is indeed fast."

"Fastest there is—oh, and I'd drink that before we hit the barrier," Kaitlinel warned.

"How bad is it?"

"Bad."

"Understood."

Kalon stood and looked at the oncoming darkness, shot through with whip-like snares of lightning, tinged red in the sun. He drank his tea, passed Kaitinel the mug, and put his hand on the back of the chair.

"I'm ready."

Kaitlinel hoped he was.

CHAPTER 17

INTO THE DARKNESS

A s the *Mist Reaver* soared closer to the barrier, Talon's voice rang out again over the speakers.

"Kalon, Silver, Kaitlinel, Andreas, Spry," he listed with a chuckle, "if you don't want to miss why I gave this ship her name, get yourselves up to the bridge. Unless you're engaged in other activities, in which case—tough, you'll miss out."

Kalon looked at the Kharnate and Silver, then back to the window. "We should attend the bridge, then."

"You go on ahead," Kaitlinel offered. "I'll wake sleepy over there, and we'll join you shortly."

The Inquisitor nodded and swept his coat from Silver's form carefully. He put it on and fastened the buttons. "I'll see you there."

Kalon tracked the location of the bridge quickly and followed the stairs to the front of the ship. He emerged from a set of doors into a brightly lit, oval-shaped area festooned with machines that would have made anyone else's head spin. Talon sat on a raised platform with the best view of the house.

"Kalon, come up!" He waved his hat, the feather wobbling back and forth.

The Inquisitor made his way next to Talon Mane and looked to the fore of the ship. Through a massive, v-shaped, curved window, he witnessed the barrier getting closer and closer.

The barrier was a magical energy field—but also more than that, and Kalon knew the history of its creation. He had read it, heard it spoken of. Hundreds of years ago, before there was a Church of Progression and during the time of the Regent, there was one final battle between Akas's forces and all those desperate to save Hestonia from demon-kind.

It culminated in Akas's victory, snatched from him at the last moment as the very final tier of the City of Wyrden was laid down. The three tiers formed a magical seal and revealed the city to be a weapon. It sundered the lands around it, ensuring the city was trapped on an island for a while—but it also caused a magical upheaval and resonance that ripped across the world.

Part of that was the barrier, perhaps combined of demon and magic energy—a hungry construct ready to devour tech-magis power and suck it dry.

So why, then, was Talon's ship capable of this journey? "The *Reaver* can make it?" he questioned the kelanari captain.

"Oh yes, she'll sail on through as though there's no barrier." Talon grinned.

Kaitlinel, Andreas, Silver, and Spry made their entrance onto the bridge as he spoke, and together they found their way to the two men. Silver took her place by Talon's chair, which put her squarely next to Kalon.

"Honored guests," Talon said and waved his hat again, ever the showman, "today you will bear witness to why I named my ship as I did: the *Mist Reaver*." His smiled widened. "It's why the lands beyond enjoy some modicum of trade. We shuttle cargo for a price, and that price is steep, friends, because until someone else works this out—I'm the only one who can!"

It was true. Silver and Kaitlinel had crossed from the lands beyond the barrier with the aid of Talon's ship. The kelanari undertook regular cargo runs, smuggling certain goods under the eyes of the authorities and transporting people away from the church's eager eyes if he had to.

He pointed at the dark, misty barrier, for effect and drama. "Behold!"

"I thought it was because of the way it cuts the clouds," Spry said. "Is there another reason?"

"Oh, good one, Spry, well spotted that lad!" Talon nodded approvingly and sat back in his chair. "Navigator, bring up the motion stopping thing, or whatever you call it."

The navigator, a woman with ochre-colored skin, flicked slender fingers over the controls.

"And...prepare to cross the barrier."

She moved a few more controls.

The small group collectively held their breath. Even Kalon felt himself experience the smallest hint of trepidation as he looked at the spectacle before him. Tendrils of hungry, dark energy roiled out from the mist before the ship, seeking magic greedily.

"Wicked view," Andreas said as he watched. It was impressive, and he had never seen anything like it. "It's like it's alive."

"It is," Talon said with a laugh. "Hungry, too—it devours magic."

"Really?" Spry asked.

"Yep, and don't worry: we're going to cause it to skip lunch!" Talon promised gleefully.

All eyes turned toward the barrier and its tendrils.

"Ten seconds, Captain." The helmsman adjusted course, his feline and wolf features revealing his jakatra ancestry. "Ready when you are."

"Steady!"

The *Mist Reaver* gained speed and shot toward the barrier. It arced across the sky, tech-magis engines pushing whispers of cloud out of the way.

"Now!"

The navigator flipped a switch on the brass and wood panel, the ship shuddered for a moment, and the soft noise of the engines dropped away. There was a moment when the vessel dropped down, began to glide, and the tendrils of the barrier simply shrank back.

Another control was turned, and the whole bridge was filled with a roar, as if a dozen lions all took voice at once.

Outside, from hidden panels on the hull came engines that did not use magic for power. They did not rely on tech-magis at all; they were scientific, a form of propulsion that caused the *Reaver* to rocket forth on streams of white with wings of gold.

"You see!" Talon shouted over the roar of the engines. "We don't use tech-magis all the time. We have a backup, and this, my friends, is why we can cross that damn barrier."

Kalon understood, and he was inwardly impressed as he watched that mist get closer. Talon Mane had an edge, as no other ship on Hestonia had engines like these. Other forms of technology had never been developed before tech-magis had fully taken over the world. This was something new, something a poker player would call an ace. The moment people like Daroni and his forebearers discovered aetheric energy manipulation and so on, chemical propulsion was dropped in favor of this clean source.

"Tech-magis is the norm," Talon continued, obviously happy to preen a little. "The church and Daroni saw to that. But my ship is the ONLY ship that doesn't solely rely on it, and thanks to my talented engineers and so forth—the *Mist Reaver* is a ONE of a KIND!" He paused for effect, then breezed on. "Oh, and before you ask about corrupting the skies with big trails of burned fuel, the ship takes care of that. Engine scrubbers pull the pollutants out of the stream. It's all very technical. Most of the time I just say: FINE, get on with it!"

Andreas let out a low whistle. Spry stood open-mouthed, and Kaitlinel dropped her right hand on his left shoulder to steady him.

Silver had seen it before, but it never failed to make her smile.

"Why don't we fall over?" Spry said after a moment.

"Oh, some science thing. Very complicated. It just works, ok?" Talon waved a hand nonchalantly and added, "Enjoy the show; it's spectacular."

In a matter of seconds, the *Mist Reaver* slammed into the hungry barrier, which raised nary a single tendril. The science aboard the ship hid its magic, and the engines that poured out trails of fire and streams of white were nothing but a chemical reaction creating a lot of force, enough to propel the aerodynamic vessel through the skin of that lurking mist.

Beyond the barrier, it was as dark as Kaitlinel's hair. Flashes of red illuminated the bridge, and what was only sixty seconds seemed like a whole year had passed by.

The barrier was comprised of barely contained demonic energy, brought about by ancient forces, the result of the final battle between people and monsters. It affected each person in a different way. Andreas felt cold, Kaitlinel ignored the sense of unease, and Spry closed his eyes and whispered a lullaby. Silver had experienced this before, but still she repeated a few mantras from the Amari teachings.

Kalon studied it with the impartial eyes of an observer, his scientific mind in control, his irrational mind shut away by years and years of training at the hands of Seeker Winter.

Then out of the dark they shot, thundering across the sky with the barrier behind and the land of the West Reach laid out like a tapestry before them. The helmsman adjusted the ship again, and the roar faded as the engines slunk back into their hidden chambers. The *Mist Reaver* once more became almost silent in the sky.

"That's how you cross into the west!" Talon took a bow from his chair. "Nav, give us a place to land. Helm, bring us down. We're not going all the way to the Demon's Spine. That would be far too dangerous!"

The ship arced and swept in a wide circle, lost altitude, and came down in a field not far from an old, muddy road. The gear folded out from her, and the vessel touched down with a single soft *bump*.

"All ashore that's going ashore!" Talon said, mimicking the ship captains of old.

"I'm going with Kalon," Silver said with narrowed eyes. "Amari business. You know what I mean, Talon?"

"Of course, of course." He knew better than to argue, and he wasn't going to stop Silver regardless—she was her own woman. "You are my first mate, but you are also you."

Silver smiled wryly and looked at Kalon. "No objections?"

"None."

"Good." She bowed and made for the bridge door. "I'll get my things and meet you on the ramp."

"That was something else, eh kid?" Andreas looked at Spry. "Yeah?"

"It was." Spry mimed the ship hitting the barrier. "Though I shut my eyes, I imagined it was something else."

Kaitlinel patted his shoulder and chuckled. "It's ok, Spry, it was pretty scary inside."

"Ahem," Talon jumped in. "Off my bridge now, go, go! Silver will be waiting!"

Kalon and the rest turned to leave the bridge. The Inquisitor bowed to the kelanari captain and said, "You will wait here, yes?"

"Yep, we'll be here, nowhere else. Not going to the Demon's Spine, at all."

"Thank you, then."

"You're welcome. Bye now!" Talon waved them off.

The afternoon air was chilly in the West Reach. A biting wind caught the remains of the wheat and tugged at it. The weather was odd here; it changed with no rhyme, no reason. Chaotic changes were the hallmark of the region, the area where the last great confrontation between ancient foes and gods took place.

Kalon and the others emerged into this wind from the warmth of the ship, and they felt it.

Silver was not far behind; she looped her cloak around her shoulders and stood for a moment to take a breath. "Welcome to what was once my home, or at least where my order spent much of its time. Between me and Kait here, we'll be able to guide you to the Demon's Spine proper through the safer ways." She looked in the direction of the jagged spine-line of dark mountains in the west.

"Not as though you can miss them." Kaitlinel laughed a little. "They literally stand up like an erection in the morning, just pointing the way to paradise."

Spry blinked, Andreas laughed, Silver shook her head, and Kalon— he remained silent, though Silver noticed the very slight upturn of his lips that betrayed some primal amusement at the werewolf's ribald humour.

After a while the Inquisitor finally broke the silence. "Lead on then, Silver."

Kaitlinel grinned and fell in step with Silver and Kalon as the small group moved away from the sanctuary of the *Mist Reaver* and toward the western road. A stone marker, pitted with age and broken in two, lay not far off the edge.

"MOORHAVEN 20 miles," Kalon read as he walked past, just behind Silver; Kaitlinel was now out a way from them in the lead. Her head held high, she sniffed the air. Silver kept her eyes on the journey ahead, but she also scanned the horizon for potential trouble.

Spry and Andreas brought up the rear. They talked casually, and the gunslinger engaged the Stealer with lighthearted banter. Spry, well, he couldn't help but take a shine to the man.

"It will take us the better part of a day to get to Moorhaven, or at least what I remember of it. It's been a long time," Silver noted as they made their way down the road, the mud slicking onto their boots. "It's probably worse than it was, so I wouldn't stray too far from each other."

Andreas and Spry only half-heard this. Kaitlinel, still in earshot, quipped, "They best not get in my way, or you know what'll happen."

"More fool them," Kalon replied sincerely. "I pity any who get in your way."

"Now you're getting it!" Kaitlinel nodded, pleased with Kalon's reply.

"Don't you need the moon or something?" Spry asked, clueless about the whole Kharnate thing.

Kaitlinel chuckled. "No, kiddo, just the will to change. Long story short, we're gifted by the goddess—not cursed. We can shift into wolves, and a couple of other forms which I'll leave as a surprise— just remember I'm still me, even when I look like a monster." She winked at the lad.

He hugged himself, still not quite sure.

The West Reach stretched out before them in a cornucopia of broken land. It bore the scars of the battles of old, and great rents had been torn into the beautiful, fertile ground where demonic claws of giant beasts had furrowed it.

Hills and dales had been cleft in two, and lakes of fire had sprung up in the wake of cataclysmic powers. Borders had shifted, and whole villages were swallowed by sinkholes as massive demons burst out of the rock and soil.

Old and ancient curses seemed to linger like mist. Some of the ground had turned black with the darker magic mixed with demon blood. What crawled there barely lived, but existed nonetheless.

Silver kept them clear of those dangers, and they followed the track ever west as the sun arced slowly across the sky. Traces of storms played to the north and south, punctuated by a reverse rumble of thunder.

It was a disturbing and unsettling place for certain.

Moorhaven appeared in the distance as the land dipped into an unnatural valley. The city was old and crooked, a shattered ruin of its former self. Once, it had been a place of culture, learning, and the seat of the Anshada in the time before the Church of Progression. Now, thanks to the descendants of the original population, it was a gathering place for mercenaries, low-lives, vagabonds, and those who sought chaos rather than order—there was still money to be made for the right kind of person. Petty lords and their jealousies made for good coin purses, and there was always a market for a war or two if you wanted it.

As the sun turned from gold to red and sank below the horizon, lights shone as night fell. The place was barely a few miles away now.

The rest of the journey passed in small talk and idle banter until they drew close to a gap in a tall, broken stone wall. Towers, some straight, some crooked, peeked through like bones showing through tattered and ruined skin.

"Moorhaven," Silver said and shook her head. "Or what's left of it. Be wary."

"Fun." Kaitlinel grinned widely.

"I've heard the stories from the few people who have claimed to be from here, and I presume they're all true." Andreas turned to look this way and that as they stepped closer. "It already stinks of trouble, and I'm not even past the wall."

"Well, they either came over via Talon's ship, or they're lying." Kaitlinel laughed. "Either way, what you've heard is probably nothing compared to what you get."

"That's Moorhaven for you." Silver nodded at the werewolf.

Kalon remained silent, wary and watchful.

Spry was also silent, but awed nonetheless. His eyes could have been on stalks as he took in the shabby grandeur of the place. Like some old spinster, the buildings here attempted to be more than they were and catch the eye.

"I never thought I'd ever see a place like this," the Stealer finally said softly. "It's magnificent, if a little intimidating."

"That's the first time I've heard you say something longer than a few words, young man." Andreas grinned at the youth. "Keep it up! We'll bring you out of your shell yet!"

Kaitlinel rolled her eyes and slapped Andreas on the back. "Don't you start, or he'll never speak again. Kid, don't listen to him, he's not a good role model when it comes to talking." She made yap-yap-yap motions with her right hand.

Spry laughed. He felt the weight of the day lift slightly, and he was thankful for the strange crowd he now found himself alongside. It helped with the hurt in his heart for his lost companion, Charlie. The ferret hadn't been just an animal to the Stealer—he had been a friend.

Kalon observed him as they paused just outside the gap in the wall, watching the boy's face change through a few emotions. For the first time in what seemed like forever, he was able to read between the lines and fathom beyond his cold, binary view.

"Charlie was special," Kalon said finally. "I never saw it until now, just how much you cared for that friend of yours."

This hit Spry in the soul even more, to hear the Inquisitor speak of his lost partner and actually sense concern. Was that...genuine warmth in the man's voice? This confused him, and he turned a half-step to regard Kalon inquisitively.

Kaitlinel stopped and did the same, Andreas offered a nervous chuckle, and Silver smiled a little. It was a sign that the demon's influence in Kalon's psyche wasn't permanent and his soul had not been tarnished by the eel-like force.

He was painting outside of the lines, finally. He had broken beyond the box the Cardinal had constructed for him, and while he might not have been able to fully understand or process the emotions in the way that they all could, he actually felt them for the first time in over thirty or so years.

Progress.

"We should get inside, get off the street, and maybe rest up before we head out tomorrow." Silver looked at the sky; the sun was almost gone. "The night crowd here is troublesome, and the creatures outside the walls would make heavy going through the evening if we travel on."

Spry stepped closer to Kaitlinel and Andreas. "I think Silver's right. This place feels off."

The Inquisitor switched his view from Spry to the surrounding area, becoming aware of eyes upon them, and nodded. "Silver is correct. As much as I dislike delay, I can understand my allies require rest—and we require more of a plan."

Silver offered the man a nod and moved through the gap. "Exactly," she said and wrapped her cloak about her body. "Come on, I know of an old Amari safehouse not far from here."

The small group passed through the gap in the wall into Moorhaven proper. Among the tightly packed streets, with many overhanging buildings, there were plenty of places for would-be assailants to hide. Fortunately for those assailants, they didn't show themselves.

Kalon and his allies were being watched, however, and the Inquisitor stood out like a sore thumb with his regalia and that tell-tale cog and eye. The watcher, a man, handsome of face, with a short-trimmed beard and a well-groomed moustache, adjusted his posture to lean on a wall. He was dressed in casual attire, but that clothing spoke of a faded elegance, the kind of outfit that one loves too much to throw away after years of love and care. Stitched together again and again, preserved and looked-after.

Kalon spotted him, and his training told him everything he needed to know. His Daroni lenses picked the man out in the darkness easily. Wizard.

"We're being watched," he said as he walked up to Silver. "A man, a wizard, casually observing by the crumbled old tavern wall."

"You have good eyes—or some good tech," Silver replied softly. "I know he's there; he's been on us since we crossed into Hygan Street and over Moorland Row. Not sure what his game is, but I'd hazard a guess if a wizard is observing us—we're drawing attention from your clothing and the Inquisitorial amulet you wear."

Kalon looked down at the cog and eye. "I do not hide my office."

"I know. We'll see what happens."

Kaitlinel, Spry, and Andreas caught wind of their conversation and exchanged a quick glance, with the werewolf sniffing the air subtly.

"Wizard," she confirmed. "Smells sexy, too. That's some nice cologne he's wearing. Seriously, that's hitting all the right notes."

Andreas rolled his eyes. "Really, Kait?"

"Yeah, don't get jealous. I'm all yours if you want me." The Kharnate offered the gunslinger a suggestive look. "I get bored easily, and you're traveling with me, and...well, I always wondered what you'd be like."

"I...damn, you know how to derail a talk, don't you?"

"Every time." Kaitlinel coupled another suggestive look with a wink.

Spry joined in with the eye rolling. It seemed to him like adults were obsessed with sex. Well, except for Silver and Kalon. So maybe only Kaitlinel was obsessed with it, which made sense, after all, since she was a Kharnate and their goddess's forte was pretty much anything that involved war or carnal delight.

They were about to cross into the final leg of their night's journey when the wizard stepped out before them as bold as brass.

"Hello!" a bright-and-breezy greeting rang out from a voice tinged with a tiny fragment of amusement.

One by one the group halted and observed the man, the air tense.

"Hello?" said Spry, breaking the silence with a reply.

CHAPTER 18

THE WIZARD OF MOORHAVEN

Slowly, like melted butter, the man's face lit with a brighter smile, and he offered a flamboyant bow. "Wen," he intoned with a chuckle. "Pleased to meet you, lad."

Spry was wary of strangers, and his cultural programming warned him this man was trouble. He was right: this man was trouble spelled *wizard*. Spry could feel it, for while the dapper clothing and that faded swagger didn't scream magic—something else did.

Kaitlinel appraised Wen again. Such a handsome person drew her desire, her lust. This was part of the Kharnate's blood—to say they had a sex drive would be to say that the *Mist Reaver* was only a fine ship. The goddess's gift came with a lack of inhibitions and a vulgar forthrightness.

Andreas was like Spry: wary of new people, but not outright hostile to anyone unless they gave him good reason to be.

Kalon remained quiet, impassive, and watchful. He recognized the trappings of sorcery, as years of being the church's enforcer gave him that perception. This was Moorhaven, outside of the church's jurisdiction, and while he might've been Fate's Hand, confrontation at this point felt inefficient to their aims.

Silver relaxed when she saw who it was and nodded gently. "Wen, glad you're still around. Haven't seen you since you were a kid." The kelanari were long-lived—not immortal, but long enough for it to make a difference. Many lived over five hundred years, or thousands if they were truly lucky.

Wen whistled slowly, a soft intake of breath as he caught sight of Kalon's regalia. He transferred his gaze to Silver and bowed again. "Yep, really good to see you too, Danae. What brings you to our humble city?"

"Our?"

"Well, it's not mine. I'd not want it. Running a city?" Wen shook his head and laughed. "I'd have to deal with politics, stuffy nobles, and all that guff—that's not me!"

"No, it's not." Silver glanced at Kalon, seeing the tense lines on the Inquisitor's jaw. He was holding himself back. "So, Wen, how's being a church-sponsored sorcerer out here in the wilds treating you?"

"Same as being a church-sponsored anything, honestly: better than being shackled or shipped off to somewhere to be quietly put down." Wen grinned a little impishly, but that barbed reply was meant—every word of it.

Kalon pondered this and replied with no hint of malice. "An unshackled sorcerer can cause incredible chaos, but I did not know you were church-sponsored, Master Wen."

Wen nodded at the reply. Flattery, he loved it. "Master, eh? Who is this handsome, silver-tongued devil?"

"Introductions, then." Kalon took over. "Fate's Hand, Kalon Rhadon, right hand and enforcer of the Cardinal." He said this and then felt odd for a moment, as if he didn't quite feel the same about that title. "Silver, you know." He pointed to the others. "This is Andreas, an investigator from Sullavale Port, and Spry, a young man of considerable skill with other people's property."

"Oho, a Stealer, nice." The wizard's lips twitched once more into a flicker-smile.

"Kaitlinel, a Kharnate from Sullavale." Kalon paused, then added, "She would be delighted to make your personal acquaintance."

Kaitlinel blinked. Was that *humor*?

Silver's gaze tracked from person to person, and she relaxed. Kalon's response to church-sponsored mages was expected. She wasn't one hundred percent sure that Wen had been recruited by the Church of Progression, but it was a good bet to make, knowing her friend's penchant for quickly running with any ruse.

Just like the old days.

"So, now that we're all friends, what say we go somewhere and get drunk?" Wen offered and flashed a money pouch. "My stand?" Silver shook her head. "Love to, Wen, but we've got to get some rest. Long trip, bad place, typical Amari business just like I used to do." Wen's face fell into a mock pout for a moment, until he winked. "Another time, maybe, unless you need a church-sponsored sorcerer to keep you company? I make an excellent breakfast, lunch, dinner, and supper if I'm a traveling companion."

"Kalon?" Silver looked at the man. He had his eyes fixed on Wen. "Thoughts?"

Kalon's thoughts were odd, and he felt tinges of amusement from Wen's banter. It did not upset him, he did not find it counter to the mission at hand, and he was actually pleased by the flow of words which came easily from the wizard's lips.

Fish out of water was a good description for Kalon at this moment.

"Kalon?" Silver asked again.

"Sorry," Kalon blinked a couple of times. "That has never happened before. Yes, I would welcome a church-sponsored wizard's skill on this mission. Where we're going, we might need a sorcerer to tip the odds in our favor."

Kaitlinel sidled up to Silver and whispered in her ear, "Are you sure you didn't fuck some sense into him?"

The kelanari woman stifled a laugh as she folded her arms.

Kalon raised a brow and offered his hand to the wizard. "Welcome, Wen."

Wen enthusiastically shook the man's hand, and measured his grip. He also did a quick magical poke to see what sorcery surrounded the fellow: nothing invasive, nothing that Kalon could hopefully detect.

Kalon shook the man's hand firmly, then let go.

"Say, Kalon," Wen ventured and rubbed the bridge of his nose, "I don't want to alarm you, but I think someone's been messing with your symbol of office."

Kalon looked at him, hawk-like, and simply said, "Go on?"

"Wen, not here!" Silver snapped suddenly. "Others might observe. How about we go to the old Amari safehouse and then pry into your new friend's amulet, eh?"

Wen frowned but stepped back. "Until the safehouse, then. But yeah, we need to talk."

Kalon did not refute this. Since his brush with the eel-like entity, he had begun to think that the church had enemies within its walls, and someone had orchestrated his involvement.

"Come then, Silver, lead on," Kalon said.

Andreas and Spry were content to keep out of this one. They kept silent and observed the new companion from afar. He was a wizard, and they'd been taught that wizards were nothing but trouble. Kaitlinel saw them both and elected to sidle up to Andreas. She said something which made the man blush beet-red.

"Really?" he replied.

"Yeah, sound fun?"

"I think it strains the relationship of investigator and informant."

"Exactly, that's why it's fun!" Kaitlinel chuckled and moved ahead. She kept in pace with Kalon and Silver at the front. Spry shrugged and muttered under his breath.

"*Wizards.*"

The people of the city watched this group move through the streets, and no one thought of preventing them from reaching their goal. They passed a small row of old shops, flanked by taller warehouses, and a very elegant, run-down coaching inn. The faded sign proclaimed it to have once been "The Moorhaven Inn."

Silver made her way between two stable blocks and descended the cellar steps, the rest of the group following in silence. She touched a stone in the far corner of the room and watched as part of the wall shifted silently to reveal a strange door. The paintwork, a faded shabby red color, was etched with similar patterns to her tattoos.

She put her palm against the middle of it, and the door swung open.

Andreas smirked. "Secret doors—got to love them!"

With a flick of her wrist to beckon the others to follow, Silver vanished into the space beyond the doorway. They followed a neat little corridor. Lit with faintly glowing crystals, it opened out into a large chamber. Functional, nothing too comfortable, but with plenty of tables and seats for ten occupants.

Wen sat down in a chair and stretched out his feet. "I'm glad for the seat, to be honest. Been doing a lot of walking today. You know how it is?"

Silver nodded. "Twenty miles alone from the edge of the barrier to Moorhaven, along muddy, uneven ground."

Spry and Andreas joined Kaitlinel at one of the tables, and they spoke quietly among themselves for a little, though the Kharnate's laugh soon filled the chamber with life. Kalon stood apart and studied the room. He observed the layout and noted other exits.

The safehouse was filled with life again after so long a time, and gradually the atmosphere seemed to come alive. Silver smiled a little sadly, then gestured to the far doors at the north of the room. "Through there are more chambers. Pick one, do what you want, but I suggest resting up as much as you can, for tomorrow we're heading toward the Demon's Spine."

Wen's ears perked, and he sniffed the air slightly. "That's a way off still, and the only open road is through Tapper's Folly."

"I know," Silver replied. "I don't like that place one bit, but then again, since the upheavals here—I don't much care for the western part of this land either."

"You and me both, sister, you and me both." Wen nodded enthusiastically in agreement.

Kaitlinel grabbed Andreas's hand and pulled him to his feet. "Come on, I promised you how I'd show you how to play Three-Fingered Annie."

Andreas dug out his card deck, wrapped in a leather case. "It's a good thing I have this deck then."

"You always carry a deck; you're known for it."

"I guess you have me there." He followed the woman to the door. "What are the stakes?"

"Winner takes all." The Kharnate chuckled softly.

"And the loser?"

"Still wins."

They opened the door, then closed it again once they were through, leaving Silver, Kalon, and Spry together.

Wen observed this exchange and shook his head. "Hope that man knows what he's in for."

"Andreas can handle her," Silver replied.

"You sure?" Wen snickered softly and added, "I guess you are."

Spry drummed his fingers on the table's surface. "Hey, can I have a room as well, a smaller one? Nowhere near, er, those two? I want to get some sleep."

"Go through the same door, but turn right, and then down the long passage." Silver's eyes glittered in the soft light of the safehouse. "We have a small room just for quiet times."

"Thanks, Silver. Guess I'll see you in the morning, all." The Stealer stood, gave a curt nod to Wen, and then followed the kelanari woman's instructions to the letter.

Wen looked to Silver, then to Kalon. "You don't talk much, do you, Fate's Hand?"

"I never had the chance," Kalon offered and finally sat down. He came out of his thought processes swiftly and adjusted the stool. "There was little room in the church for such things."

"For everyone?" Now Wen was interested; it wasn't often he got the inside gossip.

"No, just for me."

"What makes you so special?"

Silver sat next to Kalon and inclined her head to them both. "I'm very curious about this, too. Sorry."

The Inquisitor fell silent. He thought on the question, then answered, "My parents."

"Again, how so?" Wen shrugged. "Everyone has some kind of parental influence, some way in which they enter the world. Even if, like me, they come in one door and get changed in another."

Silver knew what Wen meant and smiled. She'd seen her friend's transition personally; it had been part of both of their lives.

Kalon's guard was usually up. After all, he had no need to offer anyone the hand of friendship or explain his background. Yet around Silver, he was at ease. He struggled to explain, let alone process, the effect the woman had on him. After some minutes silence he finally said, "My mother and father were Anshada of the Old Blood—not trained, born."

Wen and Silver looked at each other. Wen shook his head as if to clear it. "That's some childhood."

"I was little when the church killed them and took me from my home. I was fifteen when I shot my first wizard for the Cardinal. Ryan Seaborne." Kalon thought back to that moment, and he closed his eyes. "I was a blind follower, emotionally stunted, and indoctrinated by rote and rite."

Reflexively Silver covered Kalon's hand with her own and leaned a little into the man's personal space. "We know why you felt no emotion, and Wen is the right person to ask about that, too."

"Back up a second, you killed Ryan Seaborne?" Wen said with a look of shock on his face.

"I did." Kalon nodded. He did not move Silver's hand. "My first test."

"Man was a danger to everyone. He was trafficking with demons, and he only played the innocent to hide." Wen offered this information freely. "He burned down Vicker's orphanage to summon the Unmaker."

Even Silver was shocked at this revelation, and she rubbed her head for a moment. "Wen, what?"

"Yeah, and he got a good woman executed for his crime. She went to the firing squad for his sake, to protect him." The wizard's voice was tinged briefly with anger. "He left here under a dark cloud, accusations and more. Rumor is he disguised himself and bartered passage on your boss's vessel."

"Oh fuck." Silver narrowed her eyes and sighed.

"It's ok. He fooled a lot of people, Danae. At least he got his in the end." Wen smiled slightly.

"I see," said Kalon after a moment. "I am sorry for your loss." Sorry—did he really understand the breadth of such an emotion?

Was this displaced grief for another person he felt? How much of his life had been leashed by the church? These were dangerous thoughts for a man of Kalon's resolve and rank to have.

Wen shook his head. "Old water, lots of bridges gone. Back to you. So, you were saying?"

Kalon refocused and, caught in the moment, continued with the revelations. "I was taken to meet the Cardinal, given a grand design. From that day I was trained to be the right hand of the church—Fate's Hand—and nothing more." He sighed again. Odd.

Silver kept her hand where it was and nodded. "Someone at the church, the Cardinal or another close to her, bound a demon to Kalon not long after he was taken from his parents."

"A demon? What kind?"

"Eel-like, blind, nasty thing—devoured emotions," Silver answered.

Kalon observed Wen's reaction to this, watching the man's lips tighten. He did not seem happy at all.

"Well, that would do it. Those kinds of demons are used by the Old Blood Anshada to ensure you comply with a sacrifice or anything else. They eat the fear and the emotions, they make you into a puppet more or less, and the longer they're attached to your soul, the stronger they become," Wen said, ticking off the features on his fingers one by one. "Kalon had one for that long, it would take an Amari to kill it."

"I did," Silver said with a twinge of pride.

"I am thankful you did," Kalon offered, his thumb moving to give Silver's hand a slight squeeze of acknowledgment. "I have a fresh perspective on so much now, and no longer do I feel as though I am viewing the world through a black and white lens."

"So many shades of grey, Kalon, so many." Wen offered with a wink. "I walk them all too!"

"I can only wonder," Fate's Hand replied, a slight undertone of melancholy in his voice.

Wen leaned forward and peered at Kalon openly. A faint glint danced across his eyes, a spark of crimson. "I said we had to talk, but this was far more interesting than I'd hoped."

"You did. Speak to me of what you know regarding..." Kalon tapped the cog and eye symbol around his neck. "This."

Silver looked at it, and she saw the inky darkness at the center of the eye itself. "Oh."

Wen nodded, "Yeah, 'oh' is about right."

Kalon inclined his head. "Go on?"

The wizard gave a nod, closed his eyes, and pulled at the Tapestry. He aligned the threads, just as Kalon had seen Crimson do on the *Ori*. Only Wen's mastery of the art, of the Warp and Weft of magic, left the sorceress in the dust. He gathered the threads nimbly, reality dancing on the tips of his fingers, and the spell was done in a matter of seconds.

Kalon's amulet shone brightly, then flickered in the dim light as a spark snapped from Wen's fingers and transformed into a tiny, ever-changing shape. A whisper of a long-dead language filled the room, and then all the lights went out.

"Don't worry," the wizard offered softly. "All perfectly normal, trust me."

The Inquisitor was on guard. Wen's offer of trust sat oddly in his brain. Trust—another thing he did not understand, beyond loyalty to a church that had leashed him like a dog. An attack dog, on *her* orders.

I am a dog no more. That thought upset him, and he narrowed his eyes before he pulled the reaction back.

The spirit hovered for a moment, danced back and forth over Wen's right shoulder, and a voice they could understand whispered into the room: *"Wen of Moorhaven, seeker of truth, pretty Wen, changed Wen, you summon me from beyond, and here I appear."*

"Once I welcome you, oh spirit, to our gathering," Wen intoned and winked to the others. "Twice I welcome, and thrice welcome you be."

"What is it Wen that was, and he who is?" the spirit's voice danced in the air, soft, ethereal, with the hint of a candle flame behind it. *"What knowledge do you seek from once such as I?"*

"Spirit of knowledge, I ask for a simple boon, easy for one such as you to accomplish." Wen replied and bowed his head, his dark hair dropping around his shoulders at the neck. "My friend, the Inquisitor, wishes to know who fouled the regalia of his office he wears around his neck?"

"Is he ready for the answer?" the spirit hovered near Kalon.

"I do not know. Kalon? Are you prepared for the answer, even if it flies in the face of what you know?" Wen opened his eyes and looked directly at Fate's Hand.

Kalon thought on this, long and hard. "I am unsure. I am trained to serve the church, and to consider one of the church's own betrayed it and me by doing this…is troublesome."

Silver remained quiet, almost invisible in the near dark.

"I ask again, is he ready for the answer?"

"I am," Kalon said finally, making up his mind.

"Very well." The spirit form danced over the table and began to scribe a picture against the wood top. Kalon had seen this done before, on the *Ori*, only this was different. This was clearer, and it wasn't long before three pairs of eyes lingered on a portrait drawn on the dusty surface, burned into the grain.

Cardinal Terusa, the heart of the Church of Progression.

Kalon's world shattered. A wellspring, a torrent, a waterfall of emotion hit him all at once. He had heard Silver's words, seen the truth, but his attachment to the woman who had been part of his life for so many years had made him hold out hope she might be innocent in all this.

But logic requires evidence, and the evidence here was damning.

His anger rolled like a tidal wave. He tensed, his jaw tightened, and he quickly recalled the teachings of Seeker Winter. He controlled his breath and locked down his rage.

"Fuck," Wen said and put his hand down on the image. "The Cardinal did this?"

"She is caught in a web of her own making. Her understanding is limited. Her mind is too easily led," the spirit's soft voice answered the wizard.

Kalon tensed, but he kept his emotions in check once again— Winter's lessons proved more armor than any long coat wrapped with equations. There was no eel-demon to draw his emotions, so he needed to focus down and dissect the scene before him—logically.

The spirit—was it lying?

Possibly, yet in his recall of past meetings with Terusa, he could, with perfect clarity, remember every single expression the woman wore. Every twitch of her lips, intonation in her voice, and slight quirk of body language. An eidetic or photographic memory was Kalon's boon and greatest strength.

"Kalon?" Silver's voice betrayed her worry at his reaction. Such news had to be hard.

"Spirit," Kalon questioned. "By the law of the Infinite Machine, the equation of truth, I request the answer again under the sacred number and square." He opened his coat, drew out his book, and produced the very sacred equations that were just as binding as Wen's spell.

"Oh my." Wen took a breath. "Did not see that coming. Now that's a professional."

The spirit pulsed an angry red, which turned back to blue. *"So requested, so I acquiesce to such a demand."*

Silver looked at Kalon with a newfound respect—and perhaps admiration. These were Amari teachings as well, the nine sacred numbers that unbound the spirit and demon world and brought order from their chaos.

"Nine, by Nine, by Nine it is," the spirit answered regretfully. *"Ask as many times as the sacred number allows, and the answer will not change. The Cardinal is the root of your ills, but also the world's pain. It was she who allowed the binding of your soul, it is she who looks through the cog and eye of your office. Spy, voyeur, temptress, Demon King's consort."*

Demon King's consort. Those words hit Kalon like a slap across the face, and under the power of the sacred numbers—the mathematics behind the very universe itself—the Cardinal's role was unveiled. If Kalon had been the cups and saucers on a magician's tablecloth trick, the whole dinner set would have been on the floor by now.

Wen's words died on his lips. Silver took Kalon's hand in her own and held it. She felt the man's whole body tense. Kalon Rhadon, Fate's Hand, right hand of the church…he was a lie…a falsehood, a tool to be used to serve a church that consorted with the very enemy that had almost shattered Hestonia thousands of years ago. Akas had risen again a second time; his fall had only come about thanks to a weapon known as Wyrden a few hundred years ago.

Akas: The Bloodless—The Demon King of Hestonia and his Queen Jaziel, consort and second to him. The Inquisitor knew their names, he knew the histories, and he knew the accounts written in the books in the dark spaces of the church library. Kalon learned several emotional responses as the spirit light flickered softly. He knew betrayal, shame, regret, and finally, with a fire that eclipsed the very volcano that burned below Messania—fury...

Out of all his cavalcade of emotions, fury was the most dangerous, and the most unpredictable. Fear took men to flight; fury brought ruin on all.

CHAPTER 19

KALON UNBOUND

Silver and Wen saw the change in the Inquisitor, the anger in his eyes and tightness in his jaw. Yet, it was not anger that engulfed Kalon and drove him to rash action. Oddly, it seemed to set him free, to unbind him from a mind that had been broken and remade by the church.

Seeker Winter's training—and something else, as if Winter had left a gift in his psyche for such an occasion. One designed to prevent his mind from breaking, to allow him to bring himself back from fury and into cold, calculated action.

Kalon could almost hear her voice. It calmed him.

"Kalon, you ok there? For a moment it looked like you were ready to murder," Wen said nervously. "If you are, let me know, and I'll be over there—several landmasses away."

The kelanari woman kept her hand on Kalon's, as slowly their fingers curled around each other. Subconsciously, gently.

The spirit flickered and suddenly shot into the amulet around Kalon's neck. This action startled the three of them, and Kalon fell backward off the stool to land with an ungainly thump against the stone floor. He felt pain and irritation at the sudden event.

Silver looked at her empty hand but moved quickly to assist the fallen man. Wen rubbed his nose with his thumb and forefinger. "What the bloody hells?"

Kalon, with Silver's assistance, managed to right himself and look down at the amulet. It shone with a soft white gleam, small sparks emerging as the spirit spoke from within.

"*Mark of the man, Anshada born, cog and eye. Churchman, puppet, killer, and child,*" the spirit said from within the depths of the artifact. "*A boon I grant thee, a gift of sanctity, safe from the eyes within eyes of she and he.*"

"Oh, right." Wen nodded. "I get you, protective magic on the amulet. She can't see you or us any longer Kalon, nor I grant communicate in any way?"

"*Yes.*" The spirit emerged from the relic and whispered into the air. "*Back I go. Our talk is done; knowledge has been given.*"

With that the spirit vanished with a gentle sound of falling rain. Slowly the light crystals came up and illuminated the room once more.

"That was something else," Wen said after a while. "Sorry Kalon, it must sting to know all this."

"I said I was ready," Kalon replied as he sat back down. "I made my bed, and now I must lie in it."

"The Cardinal made that bed, and not the comfortable kind—the kind that has spikes and blades," Silver grumbled softly as she sat on the stool next to Kalon once more. "I'm sorry, Kalon. We've turned your world upside down."

"No." Fate's Hand stood and moved toward the northern door. "You opened my eyes. Excuse me, I need to meditate on this. I have much to replay, and much to think on. Our mission has not changed either."

"We're still going after the book?" Silver looked up.

"More so now than before. We can still return it to the church, and still destroy it," Kalon said with a flat tone. "She was right, the Imper Vatica could contain the energy if something went wrong."

"She wants the book." Silver looked at Wen. "*That* book."

"Oh, that book?" Wen had no clue. "What book?" he said in quieter tones.

Kalon heard him perfectly. "The *Book of the Anshada*."

"Shit, that book!" The wizard chuckled. "You'll need me then; I know how to break the spell on the Demon's Spine to get you where you'll need to go."

Kalon paused, looking to Silver, and then Wen. "Thank you both." Silver smiled wryly and Wen flicked his head in Kalon's direction, with a sort of *go after him* kind of nod.

"Kalon?" Silver's voice filtered in. "If you're off to meditate, perhaps I can come with you. It is my old order, and this place is conducive to Amari meditation techniques."

The last time he'd meditated with Silver, she saved his life and sanity from the demon. Kalon nodded; he even caught himself smiling, and the vague thought that having her around to talk to was oddly comforting.

Kalon opened the door and heard noises—the kind you heard in Bell Alley on a moonlit night. Kaitlinel, not quiet or shy about her activities in any way.

"Perhaps there is another place?" The Inquisitor closed the door with a sigh; he noticed that reaction immediately.

Silver nodded. "Actually, yes. My old room is where the Amari Nine had their chambers, off here to the west." She headed that direction. "Night, Wen, or what's left of it."

"Night, you two."

"Goodnight, Wen." Kalon bowed to the wizard, which frankly Wen wasn't expecting at all.

"Don't meditate too loud." Wen chuckled as the pair left the room. He closed his eyes, sought inner peace, and put himself into a slight trance to block out the noise from the demon world that clawed at his every waking moment.

Silver led Kalon to another room, this one just as frugal as the rest of the Amari safehouse. It had a bed, a table, a few chairs, and some chests to store goods in. There was a bareness that reminded Kalon of the church's more barren rooms.

"Here we are." Silver sat on the edge of the bed and pulled off her boots. "I am really sorry you had to learn all this, but perhaps it's better than learning it after the Cardinal gets the book?"

Kalon sat cross-legged on the floor to face Silver and offered a nod. "Like tearing a binding off a sticky wound."

"I suppose." The kelanari woman laughed a little. "It's not a bad way to describe it."

She paused in her boot removal, looked at Kalon, and wrinkled her nose. "We smell," she concluded. "Not overly bad, but our travels from now on will leave little room for bathing save in rivers and streams."

Kalon did the same and nodded. "I took advantage of the *Ori*'s shower before we disembarked, but yes, you're correct."

"My chamber has a shower as well, tech-magis water crystal system. Should still work, even after all this time."

"Shower if you wish, and then when you are done, I will shower as well." The Inquisitor closed his eyes.

Silver nodded, though she considered inviting the man to shower with her. Not a sexual gesture—at least that's what she told herself.

"I'll be back shortly." The kelanari woman stripped off her clothes, no hint of modesty, and left them piled neatly at the foot of the bed. She looked at herself in the long mirror; her tattoos were no longer gleaming brightly. A good sign, it meant that nothing eldritch hung about Kalon like a demonic cloak.

Kalon heard her walk past and felt her hand brush his shoulder, then whisper through his hair. Silver's fingers sent tiny sparks along his skin, even through several layers of clothes.

After a while he heard a sound like a small rainstorm had sprung up behind him. He sought inner peace, as Winter trained him to do, though his body ached from the day.

In the world beyond the worlds, at the edge of all things and none, where the stars came to fear. The demon realm glowered, like an angry eye. Energies both lethal and chaotic swirled around this dimension, and clashed in violent storms. Akas' palace hung there like an impossible inverted black iron chandelier, full of sin, misery and torment.

Once an Old God, the Demon King was far more suited to this role. Yet, he despised the New Gods, the Young Gods, Kharnate, the Shroud, and the others who dared to think they were worthy of power.

Jealous, bitter, and angry—the old demon stood at the edge of a grand balcony and looked down into the vortex below.

He wore the shape of a feeble old man, barely able to see, barely able to stand, and he hated it. This was what he had been reduced to, beaten, knocked back by the heroes of old.

Fucking pathetic.

Not even allowed to die, because demons always come back to the other world. That was the law. Fucking gods, fucking laws.

Fuck them all.

He drew his attention to a twisted mirror held by a nude man, phallus removed, iron bindings across his body. His hands meshed into the mirror, and his head attached at the back of the relic.

He saw the Cardinal's chamber and her dalliances—every one of them, even that foul-stank of a man, Arch-Inquisitor Roland. How true he was, and the most real of all those strutting religious fuckers in the Imper Vatica.

"Fuck that place," he spat at the mirror. "I will break it, and you." He poked the mirror with a jagged fingernail, right at the Cardinal. "Your Puppet-Churchman best fetch that book soon. I miss my old body, my power, and my position."

He stalked slowly back and forth. "Things don't even work properly. Fucking bullshit."

He knew that time did not flow the same in this realm. In fact, time was often so distorted in the demon world that it could take hundreds of years to reflect events elsewhere, or it might happen in a few seconds. Not so for the mirror—that was the only gods-forsaken piece of crap in the Demon King's possession that worked properly.

It clouded over, and Akas focused on it, hungry for news.

"Well?" he snapped at the visage in the darkness.

A pair of luminous, wicked eyes illuminated the darkened silver, and the vague shape of a thin naked woman appeared before him. Her dark hair looped around her body, almost like black snakes, both revealing and hiding the waiting joys, pain, and torment.

"King of nothing, but soon to be king of all," Jaziel intoned with a soft half-chuckle. "I bring you grave tidings, and… I'm sorry, I can't, I really just can't talk like that any longer."

"Oh, for fuck's sake. Get on with it then."

"Thousands of years, Akas. We have to move with the times."

"Report?"

"Someone broke the demon's hold on little Miss Golden Britch's Puppet-Churchman." Jaziel pouted and licked a finger. "No details, but we think it might be an Amari sister who survived our purge of their order hundreds of years ago." She yawned and flicked a lock of hair across her shoulder.

"What the fuck?" Akas coughed several times; his rage just caused the old shell to stumble. "I can't even get angry properly in this vessel. Screw the Amari." The palace shook for a few seconds; that was all the Demon King could muster. "I'll mention it, next time I'm in her head," Akas said of the Cardinal. "She thinks I'm her One God of the Infinite blah-blah-blah." He laughed softly. "One God of the True Bullshit, more like."

The Anshada-demoness laughed gently. "Oh, I want to be there when you take her world and royally fuck it up."

"You will be. Everyone will be, when I get my old form back. I'm going to rip Hestonia asunder and burn it to the bloody ground this time," Akas promised, a fragment of power in his eyes once more; it faded quickly.

Before Jaziel could speak again, the palace shuddered and the lights dimmed; time shifted, vomiting out seconds and minutes to run on again three times as fast.

"I hate that," she snorted.

"So do I."

In the mortal world, a light spirit tore the demonic magic asunder in Kalon's cog and eye. Akas felt it. Jaziel felt it.

"The fuck was that my Lord?" The demoness doubled over. "Feels like someone just kicked me hard in my gut."

Akas touched the mirror again, putting Jaziel onto a smaller pane of glass and focusing on the Cardinal. She was dressed and seated at her desk, looking worried.

He read her thoughts. She'd felt Kalon's mind-link vanish. The dark realization gripped him—someone or something had snapped the connection to the Puppet-Churchman's amulet.

"Oh wonderful," he said to the demon woman. "We lost our little show with the Cardinal's lackey."

"Oh shit, that's not good."

"No, it's not."

"What do we do?"

"Well, for starters, we...and by we, I mean, you...get off your pretty arse and send some demons to follow the broken link. Find the fucker that did it and end them!" Akas coughed three times, and the body almost forced him to pass out. "Before I die in this place, GO!"

Jaziel's image vanished, and it left the Demon King alone with his mirror.

He narrowed his eyes and wiped blood off the back of his hand. "Fuck today."

Barely a few minutes had passed since Silver stepped into the shower chamber. She washed the day away, washed her hair, and cleansed herself properly, just like she would for an Amari meditation, a day-to-day occurrence back when the Order was at its height.

She was aware of Kalon in the other room; he moved now.

Fate's Hand came out of his meditation, mind clearer, more focused, and calmer than he had been. A wealth of mixed emotions ran rampant through him until he brought them, like good dogs, to heel in his mind. *His* will, the master, not the hound.

He divested himself of everything. His weapon holsters were placed in the chamber on a hook, and he hung his cog and eye there as well. Knowing that Terusa could have observed him at any moment made him feel violated, even ashamed. Not as though he had anything to be ashamed of.

He was a well-toned man, scarred from his years of battling demons, but they were thin and white against his skin. The church and Reva's potions, her oils, and ointments had done wonders to regenerate the skin. Church sorcery had done the rest to ensure nothing was ever permanent, but even their shackled wizards could not fully remove the signs of battles won.

Silver emerged, and they could not help but observe each other. The kelanari woman was toned as well, her curves athletic, and her body revealed she was perfectly suited wielding weapons. The sight of her Amari ink took Kalon's breath away, and her hair clung to her wet skin like cooling argent waves.

She moved gracefully, side-stepping the naked Kalon Rhadon as he made his way to the chamber beyond.

He didn't get far.

Darkness exploded into the room, through the walls. The ancient protections of the Amari had been strong long ago, but now, with no sisters to ensure they remained so, they were as weak as a new born kitten.

Demons, three of them—a sudden whirl of claws and sharp teeth turned the room into a would-be charnel house. They were long-limbed, four-armed, and sphere-headed with dozens of eyes and plenty of fangs.

A regular pair of occupants would have been dead in seconds.

Not Silver, nor Kalon.

They acted as they were trained to. As the demon's claws sought purchase in soft flesh, both people twisted out of the way. They were like a pair of hunting cats, lithe, deadly, and rather than prey—pure predators.

Silver's tattoos brightened the room, blowing the darkness aside like a wind scatter of leaves. The demons snarled away from the light, crashed into the walls, and hissed before they renewed their assault. Both mortals were nicked and cut by the talons, an inevitability in such a tight space.

Their blood became one on the floor.

The kelanari woman reached Kalon's pistol and yanked it from the holster. She knew the tech-magis system would not allow her to fire it. So, she hurled it to the Inquisitor, then ran her hand over her right ear, tugging the earring that still dangled there.

Kalon caught the weapon perfectly, ducked a blow that would have removed his head from his shoulders, and fired three times into the mouth of the creature. It was loud—loud enough to wake the dead—and in such a confined room, it hurt both their ears. The demon was worse for wear, the tech-magis rounds singing with a mix of sorcery and equations that tore the demon's jaw right off and sent the gangly monstrosity back to the pits that spawned it.

The tiny earring melted away, and Silver brandished a gleaming dagger, bringing it to bear on the second demon in seconds. She turned the lethal storm of whirling claws into a mewling mess of black oily blood at her feet, demon gore across her skin from where the dagger had disembowelled the enemy.

The Inquisitor saw the woman's next movement, read it, and ducked as she leapt across the room, vaulted his shoulder and kicked the oncoming final creature in the throat. It howled in frustration until she rammed the dagger into its many eyes and black smoke poured forth.

The monster melted into mist, and the room fell silent.

Both of them breathed heavy and hard. Silver wrung dark blood out her hair. "No one's coming to see if we're ok; the room is sound dead, as all of the chambers of my sisters were. It allows for better meditation, and no one can listen in."

Kalon huffed softly, sliding his gun back in his holster. "I see." Then he said, "The dagger earring, nice touch."

Silver smiled and flipped the dagger over and over. "I've always got a trick up my sleeve, or in my ear."

Kalon smiled—perhaps it was the flush of battle, or the near-death experience that he felt for the first time. Before, he'd only ever entered combat with cold and calculating precision, but this was something else. He felt euphoria; he felt success and the rush of chemicals that came with it.

Silver looked down at herself, and then the demon blood. "Wonderful. I only just washed my body and hair. Fucking demons."

Kalon's lips upturned into a wry smile. "I never got chance to bathe, and now our blood is one, with ourselves and the demons."

"Like raindrops on windows," Silver said absent-mindedly. "We should bathe again. But I don't recommend leaving that gunk on you while I modestly go and shower again. No buts—get in that chamber with me and get this vileness off."

Kalon quirked a brow, but she had a point. He swallowed a fresh breath of air and did as she suggested.

Into the shower chamber they went, and both felt the sting of the water and soap as they rinsed themselves off. They removed every trace of the demons' vile stink, which clung to the skin like tar. It was easier to see they both had a few fresh cuts and nicks. Kalon felt where the claws had gone into his shoulder, a hard place to reach by yourself. Silver looked up from her own examinations, and he noticed as she did so that not a single mark had damaged the Amari ink.

The naked kelanari woman leaned over, turned him round and slapped a cloth onto the wound before he could protest.

"Got anything in your coat for deep wounds?" she asked softly.

"Left pocket, wound cleanser, and Reva's own mix. Take some for yourself."

"Perfect. Be back in a moment. Don't bleed out," Silver quipped and left the chamber.

Kalon put his hands against the wall of the chamber, felt the water and soap sting his skin again, and mused on the feelings that brought out of him. He also considered his feelings regarding the naked kelenari, who was determined to play nurse rather than become his lover–not as though he'd known that joy.

Silver stepped back in a few moments later, and he felt her hands on his back again. She cleansed the claw marks and daubed the cloth over them. Then with a swift motion she applied the wound cleanser, which made Kalon growl softly. She ignored this, busied herself with the wound site, and then poured Reva's mix on it.

The skin turned whitish, and in a few moments Kalon had another nice scar or two to add to the white lines. "Damn," she said. "Effective stuff."

"Reva," groaned Kalon through the pain, "makes some excellent medicinal products."

"She does." Silver nodded and turned around, mimicking Kalon's posture. "Now me please."

He took the cloth from her, and the pouch, plus the half bottle of cleanser. He approached this with a clinical professionalism, even though anyone else—especially Kaitlinel—would be using the shower for things other than showering right now, bleeding to death be damned.

He was surprisingly thorough, the same as Silver, and perhaps even more gentle, trained in first aid, surgery, and setting of bones. The Inquisitors had a varied role in the church, and they could heal as well as kill.

Silver closed her eyes, felt the water, his hands, and expected far more of a botched job.

He cleaned her wounds, applied the cleanser, and then the mixture.

She turned to face him; the water ran down her skin, like raindrops on a window pane. Kalon looked at her, for the first time in a long time, and felt that neither of them was ready yet for a step that might not be correct or prudent. Silver judged his expression, saw his eyes, and thought the same. She smiled and flitted out of the shower chamber to find a towel before he could.

"First one to the towel gets to dry off!"

Kalon stepped back against the cold stone wall, felt the water touch his skin, sensed the emotions around him, and calmed his mind. Once again, Winter's training paid off, and the man's heartbeat slowed to a more casual rate: a man at rest, still tormented by the knowledge he had been given by Wen.

A man surrounded by those who he might later call "friend."

With a kelanari woman, an Amari Sister, who perhaps might become one of those raindrops she spoke of.

The ones that join each other, and run right down to the bottom of the window at the final destination.

Only time would hold that answer.

CHAPTER 20

FALSE TRAILS

Many miles away, across the almost endless sea and rolling waves, the great and holy city of Messania continued to defy the downward pull of gravity, held up by the gigantic aetheric engines that prevented it from crashing into the fire-spewing volcano below. It floated, a beacon of hope for many, a promised utopia for all. This was the last bastion of the Church against the darkness presented by magic and wizards. Or at least, that's what the Cardinal wanted her people to believe—her message spread far and wide on wings of fear and loathing.

The population was whipped into a frenzy by the thought of chaotic sorcery, a danger to them, their children, and their future. Anshada wizards had nearly broken the world thousands of years ago, and the church had risen from the ashes. They were perfect foil, a perfect catalyst for the people, and a wonderful placebo for them to swallow.

Was it all a lie? Like the lies the Cardinal told Kalon about investigating Rand's death and who she put on the trail?

Only the Cardinal knew or cared, but in her lavish office this morning, she had two visitors. One man, one woman. Both of them served her—served the church—and they were an excellent pair. Terusa knew when she allowed romance to flourish and her servants to engage in affairs of the heart and body, they would be more likely to protect each other in the field and fight harder to save that which they loved.

Just watch a cat family and their kittens if they come under duress; she often used this as a reason to justify such relationships. Plus, it made it easier for her to engage in her string of lovers, sometimes more than one at a time.

Now she faced Vass Drae, a highly decorated, clever Inquisitor with a penchant for puzzles and enigmas. Her partner Maxis Kane, the Justicar, was a man who held a position higher than any save for that of Kalon Rhadon. Vass's mahogany skin was in stark contrast to the tanned olive tones of her husband, her hair dreadlocked, his cut sharp, short and tight.

Vass preferred red for her coat and clothing, with a smattering of black. Maxis chose black shot through with silver. She was stunning, he was handsome, and the Cardinal enjoyed the aesthetic they presented, as well as their bond. Terusa, of course, centered herself in this matter, safe in the knowledge that ultimately, they were brought together by her.

Two of the most powerful people in her church, and they answered to her.

Now that was what the Cardinal loved.

She stood beside her highly polished, darkwood desk, dressed in the formal robes of the day. Gold, red, slightly v-necked, and with a near-scandalous slit up the left to her hip. Flirting with the eye was one of Terusa's penchants, and she had a whole wardrobe of garments designed to do just that. With her makeup perfect, her cheeks slightly flushed, her body seemed to glow.

"Vass, Maxis," she addressed them both, smiling as they bowed. She inclined her head everso carefully in response.

"Cardinal." Vass's smooth and velvet-like voice caressed the air. "You asked for us?"

Maxis smiled a little wryly; he was not as awed by Terusa as many in the church. This was due to his Justicar training and his desire for simpler, straight to the point things. He had eyes for Vass only, and while he might have spent time bouncing from man to woman in his youth, ultimately, he married the person he fell in love with.

Her. Sepia-skinned and deadly, her voice always sent shivers down his spine in a good way.

"Cardinal, I understand this is a matter of some importance?" Maxis queried.

Terusa flashed a smile and adjusted her pendant as she trailed from the left to the right side of her desk. "What do you know of Drako Mallori?"

"A church-sponsored assassin, not part of our order per-se, but still effective nonetheless. Only in my humble opinion, my Cardinal, the man is more hammer than scalpel," Vass answered with surety, grinning at Maxis as she compared Mallori to a blunt tool.

"I concur," Maxis replied. "If you send him to deal with our enemies, prepare for collateral damage and chaos."

Terusa's smiled faded, then returned. "You are correct, but a tool is still useful."

"Oh, of course," Vass replied with a nod. "What about Mallori?"

"Well." The Cardinal stepped closer to the pair. "What I tell you must not leave this office, or be spoken of to anyone else beyond this room."

Vass and Maxis exchanged glances, then each offered a single, "Understood." Almost in unison.

"Drako Mallori is a danger to us all. He killed Inquisitor Rand, and he's out there hunting Verity."

"He did what?" Maxis's expression went dark, and the lines around his eyes tightened. His beard crinkled in a manner that meant more to Vass than to Terusa.

She had seen that expression before, and it was a dangerous one.

"How do we know this?" Vass was calmer in these situations; she went for the direct route.

"Kalon Rhadon investigated the incident. You know how meticulous, thorough, and emotionless he is." Terusa inwardly chuckled at her pet enforcer.

Vass nodded, and Maxis rubbed his chin for a moment.

"Yes, Kalon would leave no stone unturned, and if he calls doubt on Mallori, I have to respect his judgment," Vass replied and looked to her husband.

"If Kalon points the gun at someone, there's a reason."

"It gets worse." The Cardinal's ace in the hole. "Mallori used magic—unlicensed magic. He lied and concealed his art from us."

A subtle gaze from husband to wife told Terusa all she needed to know. Maxis's lips went thin. Vass's expression remained unchanged as she folded her arms across her chest, the leather of her outfit crinkling.

"Kalon is on a mission elsewhere, secret, important. So, I need you to track down Drako and bring him in alive. He must not be killed, since I need to know his reasons for ending Rand's life and hunting our sweet Verity."

"Another church-sponsored assassin," Maxis said dryly.

"More effective than Mallori, and more likeable too," Vass replied.

"True, true."

The Cardinal looked from one to the other. "Do I have your support on this? Will you engage in this request?"

They both knew they could not refuse, but by making it appear like a friend was asking, it softened the fact that it was a solid-stone order.

"Of course, my Cardinal. Have you any leads?" Vass asked, eager to hunt down Mallori. She'd never liked him, but Rand was a good man.

Maxis waited to see what Terusa had to say, pondering thoughtfully.

"Wyrden, the city. Last we heard, he was attempting to hunt down Verity there."

"We have no authority in that place," Maxis pointed out softly. "But we're not prevented from travel. No church vessels can get into the city airspace, but it doesn't mean we can't ask Captain Parr for a lift."

"Symon?" Vass quirked her brow. "That old war dog?"

"Yes!"

The Cardinal grew bored with the exchange, then reminded herself to remain engaged. She chuckled. It sounded so false. "Whatever method you use, please go to the city as quickly as possible and track down Mallori."

"On it." Maxis waited, though; he wanted to hear his wife's final thoughts. He knew they were coming. "Vass?"

"It will be done, and if Mallori gives us no choice, are we to harm him to make him see reason?"

There it was!

Terusa thought long and hard about this, then nodded. "Nothing excessive. He must be able to answer for what he has done."

"It shall be so," Vass replied again, poker-faced.

"You both may go, then. May the One God go with you."

"Let His wisdom guide you," Vass replied. Maxis nodded as she spoke the words, but in reality, he didn't quite buy into the whole One God of the Infinite Machine—but he kept his own counsel on this.

They left the chamber and moved off into a side corridor. The Cardinal watched them go and breathed softly—a little sigh of relief. Mallori was not in Wyrden at all. In fact, she had changed her mind on a whim when she'd lain with him the other day.

Where was he?

Sated in the other room, left breathless by their love-making half an hour before Vass and Maxis arrived at her office.

They would not think to look for the assassin right under their own noses, and she got to keep all the power to herself in this game.

Perfect.

Vass was thoughtful as she walked by Maxis's side down the corridor. There were too many people around to openly discuss this new mission, mostly servants and the guards who kept them all safe. Nods were exchanged, pleasantries offered, and silence gripped the pair.

Seeker Winter moved into view. The white hair was a dead give-away, and her slim frame, wrapped in soft shades, always set the mind at ease. She came from a side door, swiftly and with great purpose. Her direction altered, and she cautiously intercepted the pair.

"Come," she said. "If you don't mind, I have something of importance to tell you."

Both Maxis and Vass flicked a quick glance to each other. Maxis shrugged but offered, "Lead the way."

Winter gestured to the pair and put her finger to her lips. She walked to the next room, then ducked swiftly into a sealed meditation chamber, the kind she had trained Kalon in, all those years ago. Husband and wife followed, curious, silent, and on guard.

When the three were inside, Winter closed the door and activated the sealing stone. Then she fished out a key and locked the door. She looked around and took a soft breath. "I trust you, and I know you both are not given to rash decisions."

Maxis frowned a little. Vass elbowed him in the ribs and shook her head. "Go on, Seeker?"

Winter nodded and steeled herself. "I know the Cardinal is sending you after Mallori, and to Wyrden."

Again, the pair looked at one another. If their mission was so secret, how did Winter know?

"For a secret mission, that's at least one more person who knows who isn't us," Maxis quipped.

"Winter is a Seeker; do you expect her not to know?" Vass liked this puzzle. It was quick, simple. "Visions?"

"How'd you guess?" Winter asked.

"As a Seeker, psychic visions come as part of your occupation," the mahogany-skinned Inquisitor answered with a foxlike smile.

"Then you ease my mind somewhat," Winter replied, and her expression softened. "I am not telling you not to go, but I will tell you, something does not feel right in the church. I sense a darkness, a thing, watchful and manipulative. But where I sense it…is most troubling."

"Go on?" Vass put a hand on the woman's shoulder. "We lend you our strength, sister."

An empath like Winter lived for this kind of contact, and she nodded gratefully. "I had a vision—a dream—during today's meditation. I saw the Cardinal, a book, a mirror, Kalon, fire. When she turned to me and smiled—it was not the smile of a benefactor."

"That's some vision," Maxis blew out a soft whistle-like breath and rubbed his forehead. "Complicates things."

"And?" Vass gestured Winter should carry on.

"Kalon in shackles, and the Cardinal with eyes, within eyes, within eyes." Winter shuddered a little; she knew just what that omen meant.

"Akas." Vass knew as well. She was extremely knowledgeable,

having read many books in the vast library of the church. She knew the history of Hestonia from past to present, and the Demon King's mark was just that—maddening eyes whirling with eyes within bloodshot eyes.

"Are you saying what I think you're saying?" Maxis's olive-hued face went pale.

"I am," Winter said steadfastly.

Vass removed took Winter's hand in hers, gave the woman's fingers a little squeeze, and pulled her into a warm hug. "It took courage to say this, and to trust us—you do not know how others will react, even with your psychic knowledge."

Winter sighed on the woman's shoulder. "I am trained so well, yet I fear."

"Fear is our strength. It shows us when to run, and when we must withdraw," Vass whispered softly. "We have your back, sister. Do we not, husband?"

"Oh yeah, treason, heresy, and all that. Just what a Justicar is supposed to support," Maxis said with a dour note in his voice. "Wife, if you support his, then I have your back as well."

"Thank you, husband."

Maxis quipped, "Don't mention it."

Winter looked from one to the other, stepped back, and adjusted her robes. "I am worried for Kalon, for our church, and I fear the Cardinal does not know the danger she's in."

"Or she does, and she's very good at hiding it," Vass, ever the blunt one, pointed out.

"Layers, wonderful. Why isn't anything ever simple?" Maxis shook his head. "See bad wizard, shoot bad wizard, job done."

"Because, husband, life is not like that."

"I know."

Winter felt the emotion from the pair; it eased her mind, and she relaxed. "Please, do not let on about what you know. It could be a false sending; I could be wrong."

Vass fixed the woman with an amber-eyed stare. She sighed. "Seeker Winter, have you ever given anyone here a wrong sending or led them to an incorrect conclusion?"

The white-haired psychic thought about this, long, hard, and concluded, "No, I haven't."

"Then do not doubt now!"

"Thanks, Vass."

"Tough love, Winter. I get it all the time." Maxis chuckled softly.

"Are you a man or a mouse?" Vass turned to face him.

"I am a Justicar," he replied.

"Evasive."

"I do that well."

"I know you do."

"You love it, really." Maxis hedged his bets. "Right?"

"No." Vass frowned and narrowed her eyes further. "I love you."

Winter felt her troubles begin to evaporate and drew on this energy. She closed her eyes. "Thanks to you both."

"So what's the plan, Inquisitor?" Maxis returned them to the here and now.

"We go to Wyrden, and we look for Mallori still," Vass concluded.

"Just like that?"

"Yes."

Winter thought on this, and she nodded. "This seems to be the best for now."

"But…" Vass smiled thinly. "Be ready, Maxis, Winter, and be careful. If the Cardinal has been corrupted by Akas, then he will be insidious, and he will bide his time. What is Kalon's mission? Do you know?"

Winter bit her bottom lip partially in thought. "He was investigating the death of Inquisitor Rand."

"The Cardinal said something similar, but that was then. What about now?" Vass queried.

"He went on the *Mist Reaver* to cross the barrier." Winter considered, then added. "This is as much as I know. Terusa keeps me in the dark."

Vass nodded, and to her it made sense. "I think I know why, but I will not hazard a guess just yet. I need more information first."

"So, Wyrden then?" Maxis looked at the door.

"Yes. As soon as we can, but as I said: be ready. We may have to choose where we stand," Vass replied, setting her jaw. Her expression brooked no argument. "Akas divides to conquer."

"I already know where I stand." Maxis moved closer to his wife. "We might not see eye to eye on everything, but I trust you on this one, love."

"Good."

"I think I would like to stand with you both," Winter admitted and shrugged her shoulders. "I could not support a Cardinal who lies in bed with the Demon King, so to speak."

"No honorable person, no good-hearted soul, would." Vass nodded. "We go to Wyrden. We have spent too long in this room."

"Oh, yes, you're right." Winter unlocked the door and slipped the key back in her pocket. "Be safe, both."

"You be safe as well."

Vass and Maxis left the room, closed the door, and headed off toward the outer ring of the Imper Vatica, the single long path that would lead them from the bosom of relative safety to the outer sections of the complex, and finally into the thronging streets of Messania itself.

The holy city was a vibrant place, colorful, beautiful, and almost perfect. A triumph of geometric design, the math involved echoed the sacred numbers of the church in every way. The Imper Vatica sat at its heart, and the long path that led both husband and wife from the complex stretched for miles until it reached the very heart of the city.

Cardinal's Way was a famous landmark paved with red and gold stone. From this long walkway, there were branches of roads that led to streets, which in turn curved back around and joined each other.

It could take hours to get from one place to the next, and the city had hover carts, anti-gravity gondolas, and air-carts for such a reason. They orbited like planets on an orrery or insects in a hive. The interplay of brass, gold, silver, wood, and tech-magis gave the whole scene a fairy tale aspect, with gleams of magical light that danced in multi-colored fields over the underside of the contraptions. Add to this the near constant trade and commercial flights from wind ships and more, and it could very easily take your breath away.

Now all Maxis and Vass had to do was to find Captain Parr, charter the *Orca* to Wyrden, and play the Cardinal's little game.

Easy…or so they thought.

The people of the Holy City of Messania were a diverse lot, drawn from the various cultures and species of the planet. Kelanari, with their pointed ears, walked alongside jakarta, the panther-jackal people of the hotter climes. Couples dotted the many parks, benches, and shade-spots in the city as the pair wove their way to their destination. They passed dozens of inhabitants, each with their own lives, stories, struggles, and triumphs.

At long last the pair arrived at a pleasant but heavily populated spot, one of the busier places to frequent in the city. As luck would have it—or perhaps fate?—the *Orca*, the large, iron-clad, wind-borne vessel of Symon Parr, sat tethered to the dock, held steadfast against the high winds above. The bulky ship was a hive of activity, and its captain stood watching his crew proudly. He heard Maxis and Vass approach and turned, laughing when he recognized them.

"Blow me hard," Symon said. "Vass and Maxis, haven't seen you since ever—well, the wedding at least!"

Vass and Maxis smiled together and looked at Symon. He was a bit older than when they'd last seen him, stood shorter than the tall couple, and wore the outfit of a typical merchant captain. He sported a bushy beard, which he had let grow out, and dark short hair. His grey-blue eyes settled with a friendly gaze on the two church agents.

He adjusted his waistcoat, beamed again, and asked, "What brings you to my door?"

"We need the *Orca*," Vass said. "A charter. We'll pay. We need to fly to Wyrden."

"Wyrden, eh?" Symon smoothed out his beard and grinned. "Now, I won't pry, but I bet it's a juicy thing that takes you to that place?"

"No comment." Maxis nodded, even though he said the opposite.

A well-dressed Justicar, with the outfit to match, regal and powerful; an Inquisitor with blood red clothing, modestly dressed as was proper, and battle-ready—what merchant captain could say no to them? The fact they were old friends meant that the next words out of the man's mouth were…

"When do we put to sky?" Symon Parr was loyal, dependable, slightly drunk now and then, and full of good cheer, the perfect person to ferry them from Messania, where they were the law, to Wyrden, where the lawless cavorted like the free always wanted to.

"Mind if I join you sweeties?" The nasal-toned voice of a familiar soul cut across the three's reunion, and a familiar-if-shabby figure in a battered, old, grey hat stood at the dock. "I have urgent business with Agatha Black, and Winter told me that I would find you off to Wyrden."

"Reva Flynn, as I live and breathe—and drink. Who could say no to you, darling lady?" Symon said.

"Not many, true," Reva quipped sardonically. "No idea why, too. I'm nothing special."

Symon turned to the pair of agents. "So, happy to have her with ye?"

"We are," Maxis said and looked at Vass. "At least I reckon so?"

"Reva's charter is her own, not our affair." Vass winked. Something passed between both women, and then the Inquisitor set her face back to its poker expression.

"Settled, then. We'll be off. Wyrden awaits!"

Reva grabbed her bag and put it on her shoulder. She looked for a moment at the Imper Vatica at the heart of the city. Her smile faded and she turned to the rest.

All four boarded the *Orca* via the dock lift, and it wasn't long before the crew did the same. The chunky vessel took to the sky, even though it looked for all the worlds like it'd never make it.

Tech-magis at its finest.

Or at least, most effective.

CHAPTER 21

WEST OF MOORHAVEN

West of where the *Orca* took flight, the barrier snarled and thrashed, as if it sensed something from ages past lurking just under the surface. The sun on the other side of the darkness bathed Moorhaven in a hazy light before it was blotted out minutes later by a howling gale, then a snowstorm, and finally more sun.

Magic unleashed; chaos unshackled.

Silver was still naked, but dry, when she opened her eyes. She lay under Kalon's coat on the bed, with a vague memory of the man placing it there after she had left the shower. He had taken a lot longer to come out; he must have spent at least another hour in that chamber.

So, she'd fallen asleep. But not before she'd spent the rest of that night making sure no more demons could just appear out of thin air. Three demons were enough of a problem, let alone an army. With deft fingers, she chalked Amari mandalas and a few tricks of her own around the room.

Kalon was dressed in his clothing, sans coat, and his tunic was tightly buttoned. He did not wear the symbol of his office; he looked at it hanging from his gloved hand as if it were a snake ready to strike.

The kelanari sat up, coat draped around her front not for modesty but for warmth. She crossed her arms over it and blinked a few times to clear her vision from sleep.

"Good morning," Kalon said. "Did you manage sleep?"

"Some. You?" She ruffled her frizzed hair, then gave up.

"I meditated; I was able to reach a state not unlike sleep."

"You could have said yes. But then you wouldn't be you."

"Correct."

The kelanari woman stretched, the coat fell, and Kalon observed her. He watched the lines, the flow, the form and tautness of her muscles moving under the skin. She grinned at him and shook her head. "I'd be scolding another man, but since I've seen you naked, and you've seen me, modesty—who cares?"

Kalon pondered this. He flicked the amulet back and forth, as if he were a cat toying with it. "Modesty is a construct created by old men to shackle women's bodies into some form of taboo mindset."

"Or by women to police their own," Silver added.

"A good addition," Kalon replied, and his eyes met hers. "You fight well."

"You said so before."

"I reiterate it now." He smiled, a genuine one. He tried it on for size, and it felt oddly right. "Seeing you combat demons brought to life the stories of the Amari Sisterhood, of which I read every single one. The archives of the church are vast."

Silver blinked, and she quirked a brow.

"Powerful women, warriors from the ancient times—fascinating and deadly."

"Aw, that's a kind way to describe me," Silver teased and tried again to straighten her hair.

"I am not sure I could describe you like that; it would be somehow ill-fitting?"

"Hmm, in what way?"

Kalon thought on this. He didn't quite know how to phrase it. "Elegant, deadly grace, and lethal speed," he concluded. "No, still not enough."

"Don't try, then, but thank you all the same." Silver blushed and gave up on her hair again.

Kalon changed the subject. His newfound state of mind confused him still. "Do you think the others will be up?"

"Spry, probably. Wen, most likely. Andreas and Kaitlinel? Depends on the definition of up." Silver couldn't help herself. Sure, it was ribald and rude, but Kalon would have to deal with this, especially if Reva found out he'd been freed from his shackles.

The joke slipped by Kalon. He might come back to it later, on one of his many reveries, replaying the day's events. "We should be moving soon, and I feel the need for food."

"We can get some in Moorhaven. Small, dependable tavern. My treat." Silver tossed Kalon his coat and slid off the bed. Perhaps she took a little longer to move than normal. Part pain, part tease, and it amused her in a way she hadn't experienced for a long time.

He caught the coat, laid it on the side of the chair, and watched the kelanari woman before he went back to the amulet.

"Worried that she can still see through?"

"No, I trust the spirit to have broken the spell," Kalon said, shaking his head. "Trust. That word again."

"Yeah, it's a funny one." Silver began to put her garments back on. Again, the last thing she added were her boots. One by one, with the two daggers as the final touch, one in each sheath at the top.

"You carry many weapons, but you don't really need them, do you?"

"Do any of us who are properly trained?"

When they were dressed, they sought the rest of their companions and found the whole group, sans Wen, gathered in the main meeting chamber. Spry looked up and frowned a little, but then he smiled when he saw both Silver and Kalon smile back.

On Kalon's face it looked odd, since Spry had only ever seen the man with a flat expression, barring the odd breakthrough reaction.

"Enjoy your night of passion?" Kaitlinel said hopefully and grinned at the gunslinger. "We did."

"Yep." Silver nodded. "Kalon is wonderful as a lover. You're missing out, dear Kaitlinel," she teased. "Actually, we talked for most of it, then killed demons sent to end us."

"I bet you…" Kaitlinel trailed off and narrowed her eyes. "What did you just fucking say?"

"Three hunter demons. Assassins sent to kill us." Kalon backed the kelanari woman's words up, and he didn't joke about it.

Wen stepped in from outside and caught the edge of the conversation. "Demons, what?"

"Demons, three, sent to kill us, Wen," Silver said. "I think someone knows what happened regarding Kalon's mind and his amulet."

"If demons are popping up out of the blue, that's got to be it." The wizard's face turned sour, and he looked to the door. "Means we should get out of here before more turn up. Why didn't more come?"

Silver pulled out her chalk and waved it at the wizard. "I made sure of that. They caught us by surprise before I could do the first of the wards. I won't make that mistake again."

Wen nodded.

Spry listened open-mouthed, then thought, *But what if Wen brought them—he's a wizard. He can't be trusted.*

Andreas looked with concern at the pair. "You're ok, right though? Not badly hurt? Hurt at all?"

"We took some minor wounds; nothing that our supplies couldn't sort out," Silver answered the investigator. "We're good, right, Kalon?"

The Inquisitor nodded, though Andreas got the feeling he could be half dead and he would still consider that minor. Kalon followed Wen's gaze to the door and added, "Silver has suggested we move to a tavern she knows, get our breakfast, and be gone from this place."

"Yep, that's good thinking." Wen nodded enthusiastically. "I'm bloody ravenous, I could eat a horse!"

"I agree," Kaitlinel got up and grabbed Andreas by the hand. "Let's set an example, show these lazy sods how it's done."

Andreas muttered under his breath, allowing Kaitlinel to drag him to his feet, and followed her out the door. "Looks like I'm going, people. Bye!"

Spry glanced nervously at Wen, but pulled back his hatred and distrust of wizards. Kalon would have killed Wen by now, Spry was sure of it, if the man had wanted to cause them harm. He could do this; he could learn to work with a wizard.

"Hey, Wen, so…would you tell me more about the kind of magic you do as a church-sponsored sorcerer?"

Wen beamed brightly in reply, nodded several times, and walked on toward the doorway as well. "Come on, let me tell you outside." He gestured for the young lad to follow him. Spry did so.

"So, we're really off?" Silver asked as she looked around the old safehouse one last time. "It feels strange being back here."

"Old memories."

"Old memories, older ghosts," Silver said, a hint of melancholy in her voice.

Kalon stepped closer, looking her in the eyes. "Older ghosts are meant to be left in the past. They shy away from the sunrise, and they fear the future," he said, which took Silver's breath away.

"Damn." She looked back. "That was almost human."

Kalon leaned closer, and Silver almost wanted their lips to touch. He kissed her on the forehead and turned to the door. "The book awaits—and a reckoning."

Silver touched the tip of her finger to that gesture and followed. "It does." She was lost for further words.

Early morning Moorhaven greeted the group as they emerged from the secret safehouse, blinking at the now-sunlight, observing a layer of softly melting snow upon the ground. They moved as one, following Silver to a small tavern with a garden outside. Breakfast spread before them: freshly made bread, cheese, thick cuts of meat, and a helping of a drink made from the fruits of an orchard just a stone's throw away.

"Not bad!" Andreas sat back, sated from the repast. "Wild night, great company, good food, wicked sex, and an adventure to go on too." He burped a little. "That stuff is a bit gassy."

Kaitlinel devoured hers. She nodded through mouthfuls of meat— for her, there was always meat involved. "Keep your grass and flowers," she growled. "This is my kind of morning."

Kalon ate quietly; Silver did too, and Spry chatted to Wen over their smaller meal.

"I never thought I'd ever talk to a wizard, let alone even start to like one, but you seem ok." The Stealer had made progress. His mind clearer now, he was even happier.

"It's nice to be sort of liked; makes you feel good in here." Wen tapped his chest over his heart. "Still can't get used to this, but it feels right."

"Huh?" Spry chewed some bread.

"Oh, old life. Don't worry about it. I prefer this one; it's so much more me!"

"Ok!" Spry was satisfied.

The rest of the meal passed quickly, and it wasn't long before the group turned their attention to the western gate of the city—one that actually functioned and wasn't a big gaping hole. They moved through and were soon out in the wild again. There, in the distance, stood the Demon's Spine mountains and the location of the *Book of the Anshada*.

Miles of terrain lay before them: uncertain roads, places less traveled, and dangers beyond the unpredictable magical upheavals, such as monsters and bandits. They worked well as a group, however. This disparate array of individuals from all walks of life traveled as one, to the west.

The sky darkened; lightning split it with whip-like strikes as thunder roared. The wind followed, then died down. The sun returned, and the rain flowed upward. All in the space of a few miles and half an hour.

"Spry, what do you think of our weather?" Wen asked as they crossed a barren section of ground before a few miles of lush terrain greeted them. "Odd, eh?"

"Scary. Never seen so many weather things in one place at one time."

"Yes, chaotic. Do you know they call this place Missiva's Playground?"

"No. After her?" Spry looked up at the wizard expectantly.

"Yes, the Goddess of Chaos herself." Wen patted the lad's shoulder in a companionable fashion. "Worry not, she won't cause us harm."

Other whispers of conversation followed as the group chatted over some miles, fell silent for others. Finally, they entered the lush grassland beyond the barren rocks, turned across a field, and made their way to a longer track. It curved north, then shot sharply west as the terrain started to resemble foothills and rocky inclines.

"Tapper's Folly is close," Silver said, breaking the silence as they crossed an old stone bridge. "A few miles to the northwest, a gateway to the Demon's Spine."

"I know of it," Kalon replied and tugged his coat away from bracken and brambles that sought to claw at it. "A mining town, correct?"

"If you can call it a town. It's more a settlement, if they still work it," Wen replied and wove a quick casting with his hands. He wrapped the threads over the others, though they slipped off Kalon due to the equations sewn inside his coat. The spell was a simple one; it ensorcelled their clothing so that bracken, or brambles, or even thorn bushes would slide away.

The tugging undergrowth stopped trying to impede them as Wen's sorcery did its trick, and Spry was kind of impressed. "Was that a spell?"

"Yep," Wen said with a chuckle. "I was going to incinerate the lot, but I thought, why not prevent it from cutting and snagging instead. Prove that wizards aren't always about destruction. So, I wrapped your clothing with it. Should help."

Spry smiled a little at this. "Nice."

Kalon pulled his coat free again and sighed. "For once I wish my coat allowed this magic to work, but I'll manage."

Wen smiled impishly.

"Rumor was there was an accident at Tapper's Folly years ago," Silver said. She sniffed the air. "Anything, Kait?"

The werewolf had been discussing less-than-polite things with Andreas, but she caught Silver's question. "Nothing. Smells like old stone and boring nighttime." Then she added, "I wish I could have fucked those demons up with you two."

"Sad you missed out, killer?" Andreas chuckled and caught an elbow to the ribs from his Kharnate friend. "Ow!"

Kaitlinel grumbled. "I am always sad when I don't get to rip something into bits."

"Touchy."

"Sorry, grumpy. That time of the moon," the werewolf lied.

For a few more miles, the weather remained stable, but the wind grew colder. The mountain loomed, and the dark, jagged peaks formed the spine of the range's name. Soon, they saw the old stone marker that proclaimed, "Five miles to Tapper's Folly."

The sun was ready once more to die on the horizon, swallowed by the peaks of the Demon's Spine, and it bathed the sky in a crimson tint as it descended slowly.

The road climbed ever higher and went ever on.

Until finally, in the dark, about half an hour past sundown, they came to the outskirts of a ramshackle settlement nestled just in the cleft of the early foothills of the mountain.

"Tapper's Folly," said the sign.

Kalon concluded it indeed was folly to have constructed such a place here—so bleak, so devoid of anything but function. It was ironic that a few days ago he would have only categorized this collection of huts, broken wood, and shattered beams with the same emotionally dead perception as the place itself.

Kaitlinel looked at it, shook her head, and kicked a stone. "Now you see why I hate places like this: nothing, no life. Hells, imagine trying to get a fight or a fuck here?"

Andreas offered, "I am pretty sure you'd find a way." Then he stepped out of range of another possible elbow.

Kaitlinel grinned at him. "Too damn right."

Silver picked up a small rock, turned it over and over, studied it, and set it back down. Wen watched her, then his eyes fixed on a building at the back. He enhanced his vision to allow him to see better, a simple casting, nothing more. No need for complex threads.

A person watched them, nervously.

"We are not alone," Wen said and pointed. "Anyone who can see in the dark, take note."

Kaitlinel turned her attention to where the wizard indicated, as did Kalon. Silver followed suit, narrowing her eyes. Spry was as clueless as could be, so he put himself by Wen and Kalon. Andreas flicked his fingers to his hip, resting them there, ready to shoot if need be.

It was the Inquisitor who moved first. He stalked forward in an authoritative manner, his dark leather coat flapping against the rocks underfoot, and he gestured for the rest of them to follow. Silver moved to his right and Kaitlinel to his left. Wen kept to the back, with Spry, and Andreas fanned out a little to give himself a good sight line.

The shabby person looking at them lit a lantern. A few more lanterns came on across the settlement, and Kalon's group observed the people. They were thin, dusty, but otherwise seemed perfectly fine, dressed in work clothes, simple shirts, breeches, heavy boots, and gloves.

"We thought you were bandits," a gangly man addressed Kalon. He had a month's growth of beard and a scar on his right cheek. "Name's Eamon, Eamon Tapper, one of the Tappers of Albr who founded this place."

"Kalon Rhadon, traveler." He tucked his amulet out of sight into his shirt before he presented himself into the light. "This is Silver, Kaitlinel, Spry, Andreas, and Wen." In the past, Kalon would have blazed in and declared who he was. Now, something warned him to keep his cards close to his chest, just like his cog and eye.

This exchange was observed by workers and miners, all armed with lanterns and tools. Andreas knew from personal experience that a farmer's tined fork could make one hell of a scar on the buttocks if someone had a mind to shove it there. He'd deserved that, though, considering whose daughter he was rolling with in the hay that time.

"What're you doing here?" Eamon said cautiously.

"We pass through on the way to elsewhere," Silver replied. "We don't want to trouble or scare you, so we'll walk away and camp the night beyond here."

"Oh no," Eamon shook his head and tutted. "I can see you are fine folks—nice folks too, I bet. It'd be rum of me to deny you our hospitality. We're simple people out here, but we've got a few spare rooms if you want to keep safe from the monsters out this night."

"Monsters?" Kaitlinel grinned, then turned her eyes from the lantern light. They almost gave the game away. "I'm sacred! Protect me, strong, handsome stranger!" She leapt at Andreas's arms, and he almost dropped her.

"Kait, I can't shoot like that," he grumbled with a laugh.

The werewolf grinned at him. "I bet you could, if you tried and I wiggled in just the right way?"

He rolled his eyes; she really could turn anything into an innuendo.

"Oh, that's lovely. It's settled, then. Come on, come one and all, come to my table and we'll get you properly fed. Got some lovely grub just on the boil: stew, thick and meaty." Eamon smiled. "You look famished, and I know we are—hard day's work, nothing like eating a good meal to set you up for the rest of the day."

"My kind of thinking exactly." Kaitlinel slipped out of Andreas's arms, murmuring to him, "Don't go far. If I get frisky, I am not frisking any of these miners—I'll keep it to a friend with benefits tonight."

Andreas blinked. "I, er, thanks."

The group followed Eamon Tapper to a communal hut, and Spry kept close to Kalon for once. He wasn't sure he liked Tapper's Folly, and the people here seemed awfully friendly for a first acquaintance. He also saw no children.

Unless they were in hiding.

He looked at his companions, in which case, yes—he couldn't blame them.

CHAPTER 22

TAPPER'S FOLLY

The hut was old; it had seen better days, and the interior was serviceable at best. The building sat on stilts, and parts of the floor had rotted away, repaired the best the miners could out in the wild with little access to abundant materials. A few tables and chairs provided a decent place to converse and eat meals.

A small kitchen with a stove lay at the back of the hut, and Kaitlinel could smell a strongly spiced stew. Her stomach answered with a low and grumble-like growl.

"I'm famished," she admitted. "It's been a long time since breakfast."

"You're always hungry." Andreas chuckled and found himself a seat. He tipped the stool out for the werewolf and grinned. "Not always for food."

"It's part of our charm." She sat next to him.

Eamon went to the back and busied himself in the kitchen. He talked in a low mumble to a man and woman there, and the sound of iron pots and pans rattled from the small room. Meanwhile, Kalon and the others moved to the tables. Wen joined Spry and Kaitlinel at the bigger table. Silver sat opposite the Inquisitor; she had a good view of the back. Kalon kept an eye on the door.

"This is a bit dour, but the only comfort we'll see for a while I reckon," the wizard noted. "You ok there, Spry?"

"Yeah." Spry shuffled on his chair. "I'm just not used to places like this, or having a lot of people around me who seem to give a damn." He fiddled in his pocket and then sighed. He fished out a small packet containing hard, biscuit-like crackers. They had gone stale, but they were Charlie's favorite treat.

"Yep, it's odd, all right." Wen nodded. "I can see you've got some good people backing you up, even if you can't."

Spry sniffed a little. "I was kidnapped by an Anshada witch. She threatened to sacrifice me, and Kalon got me out. But he didn't get me out because he was my friend—he needed me, and that's it."

Kalon overheard this and thought about it; he frowned a little, but *Spry was correct.* At first, the young man was a means to an end. But now, he wasn't sure. So much had happened in a short timeframe, and he wasn't certain how to put things right with the lad. "A lot has changed. Believe me, Spry."

"I know," Spry said softly. "Charlie's gone." He flicked a cracker and broke it up into his hand. He nearly tossed the lot—then he stopped, thought better of it, and put them back in his pocket.

"Charlie was Spry's trusted friend and companion, a ferret," Kalon explained. Suddenly the feeling of Spry's loss hit him, and he understood. "A dear friend, even though I didn't understand that concept at the time."

"Small comfort, but thanks all the same." Spry brushed crumbs off his hands.

Silver smiled wryly to Kalon. "Give him time; he'll come round. It's hard to accept a sudden change in someone, especially when you meet them at their very worst and logical best."

"Logical worst, and very best perhaps?" Kalon smiled thinly.

Wren smiled warmly and shrugged. "The way I see it—and don't take my word for it one hundred percent—Kalon was different, due to the church. They did things to him that I can't explain, but I know the effect," he continued. "Magic like that, it's bad. Only the most arrogant of my people did it back in the day, and that's why things are like they are now."

"Yeah?" Spry queried.

"Oh yeah, not every wizard of the Anshada blood is an arrogant arse, lad. Some are much worse." He winked. "In all seriousness though, binding demons to mortals is what caused us to fracture as a people as well as a cabal."

"Not every wizard did it, then?" Spry worried his bottom lip nervously. Talking to Wen wasn't easy, but Wen made it easier by being, well—Wen.

"Only the worst of us," Wen sighed and shook his head sadly. "That's something you can probably empathize with. Being a Stealer, not everyone loves you for what you are."

"Yep, especially if you nick their things." Spry couldn't help but grin. Then he grew sad again as he remembered Charlie.

Kaitlinel and Andreas kept quiet and just talked between themselves, much like Kalon and Silver. In their case, as was Kaitlinel's whim, it devolved into smut pretty quickly.

"Imagine, though," Wen said, "being born with all those emotions, and then at an early age, they're sucked out of you by a demon you don't even know you have. The church takes you; they make you into a flesh and blood machine—no better than an actual automaton, really."

Spry blinked and then nodded. "I get you."

The clatter of bowls interrupted everyone as Eamon returned. He laid one down before each of the companions, smiling. "Stew's a'comin!"

This cut all conversation short.

A dowdy woman, thin as a rake—malnourished almost—and just shy of thirty summers came in. She ladled a thick, spicy stew into the bowls and steam rose. Kaitlinel watched hers hungrily, like the wolf she was, and her nose twitched as she caught scent of some familiar smells beyond the spice.

It was time to eat, and they did so. Not a word was spoken through mouthfuls of the thick meal. When they were done, every bowl was empty, and Kaitlinel had several more.

Eamon Tapper returned not long after the last spoon was laid down. He looked pleased. "Glad to see you were ready for that. Greta makes a very nice meal. As for rest, we've got a few spare huts where the families moved out on the west side of the settlement. Use them for the night if you like; we're going to turn in ourselves soon."

"Thank you," Silver said and looked at Kalon. "We'll let this settle and be off to those huts. West side, you said?"

The miner nodded and pointed in the vague direction. "Yep, you won't be able to miss them. We left a few lanterns on for you."

"That is kind of you," Kalon said, following the man's pointing finger. Through the dirty glass, he was just able to see the gleam of lights where the huts lay.

While Greta took away the bowls, Eamon returned to the kitchen to help her clean up. Kalon and the others made their way across the camp to the west side, where they found the buildings with the lanterns lit. They were frugal, old, and held together by luck and rope.

"We should double up, right?" Andreas said as he observed the buildings and looked back at the communal hut. "Not as though I don't trust the people here, but I just think it'd be better if we had someone to watch our backs."

"I agree," Kaitlinel nodded and grinned suddenly. "You can sleep in that one with Spry, and me and Wen will go to this one."

Andreas blinked. Wen laughed. Spry looked confused for a moment, then shook his head. "If it's all the same, I'd rather have Wen in with me. I want to talk more about magic."

Kalon furrowed his brow and pondered this. Spry's interest in magic was troubling, but Wen was a church-sponsored wizard and probably one of the best to warn the boy away from it.

"I agree, lad." Wen winked at Kaitlinel. "You go and keep Andreas warm, eh?"

"Spoilsport." Kaitlinel's pout appeared to be put on, and she chuckled softly. "I was just teasing anyways; I am happy to share with Andreas. He's a pretty decent pillow."

"That leaves just us." Kalon looked at Silver and opened the door to the nearest hut. "After you?"

"Ever the gentleman." Silver crossed the threshold and whispered to the others, "Be watchful."

The Inquisitor followed her. The door closed, and once again they were alone. They heard creaks from the other huts as they took on their night's occupants. The interior was the same as the communal hut, not lived in and certainly not welcoming. There was a fireplace, which hadn't been cleaned in a while, a table, and some chairs. Two old and dusty beds completed the picture of neglect.

"Rustic," Kalon observed as he paced around the room to check it, prodding things with his gloved hands. "To me…this appears as if no one's slept in here for a long time."

The kelanari woman lifted a spoon on the table and peered at it. It was badly tarnished and covered with rust. "Longer than that."

"Something does not add up here."

"I'm glad you're on the same page as I am," Silver said with a yawned. "Something is definitely off."

The air was thick and heavy, almost warm, and a sound like a low-beating drum passed through it. They exchanged glances, and Kalon's kneels buckled. Silver reached to catch him, and they hit the floor together. Their eyes felt heavy, their breath became labored, and they glimpsed a single rune above their heads that gleamed in the dark. Something in their stomachs rumbled, resonating with the runic symbol as it shimmered.

Old magic…

Silver's tattoos could not protect her, not if the magic were already inside her body, and Kalon was the same—his coat did little to save him from the full effect of the rune.

Light faded, and they plunged together into the depths of unconsciousness, without sleep or dream.

Kalon heard a voice that called to him in the dark and felt a presence, cold yet oddly reassuring. Into the black miasma of his unconscious state, he sensed a pinprick of light, which formed into a tiny ball of white fire. It flooded his mind, pulling his attention, and he heard a familiar voice—Wen—call him awake.

"Hey, you need to wake up NOW!"

The Inquisitor opened his eyes and saw a creature. It was perhaps once human, but misshapen now, with a bulbous head, distended belly, and long, spindly limbs. The jaw was elongated and full of rock-like, jagged teeth.

It drew the still unconscious Silver into its maw, like a boa constrictor might. Right up to her middle.

Glassy eyes observed the Inquisitor's awakened state, and both Kalon and the creature reacted.

Silver's eyes shot open at the same time, and she kicked out with her feet in the thing's throat. Kalon whipped one of his pistols from its holster and judged the section of the beast where the kelanari woman's legs or torso were not.

The sound of gunfire broke the night with a thunderous roar as the pistol discharged a rune-inscribed round directly into the monster's mass. It had the desired effect. The creature bellowed in pain, rocketed back, and left Silver behind on the floor—covered in mud, but otherwise unharmed.

From elsewhere came a full-throated growl. It was followed by a howl that meant only one thing. Chaos exploded within the camp as the Kharnate woman blasted through the wooden wall of the hut. Kaitlinel was revealed in all her Kharnate wolfish glory, dark furred, green eyed, angry, and supported on digitigrade legs. She clawed, bit, slashed, and crashed her way through any obstacles, holding part of the thing in her powerful jaws and tossing it aside before she pounced off and took the rest of the beast with her.

Part woman, part wolf, all rage.

Andreas's gunfire joined the melee, and flashes of pistol reports lit in the dark.

Kalon pulled Silver back with his free hand and righted the woman. She shook the viscous, mud-like ooze from her boots, pulled them apart, and brought both hands up to her ears. When they came back down, she brandished a pair of daggers akin to those Kalon had seen earlier.

"Are you injured?" he asked the woman.

"No, just my pride. Where are Spry and Wen?"

Kalon looked past the broken wall to the camp, finding more of these gangly-thin earthen monstrosities. "I'll go and see. You back

Andreas and Kaitlinel up." He paused. "Not as though she'll need much in the way of backup."

He fired at their own creature once more, and a second pistol joined the first in the duet. Now Kalon blasted the monster back out of the hole into the night air and swiftly followed through the gap, Silver on his heels. She broke away from the Inquisitor as he sprinted toward where Spry and Wen were last seen. Her daggers glinted in the moonlight as she went into action.

The Inquisitor found Wen covered in the same goop Silver was plastered in. He put down his pistols and tore the stuff free from the wizard as quickly as possible. Wen snarled awake and said something in the old language that sounded incredibly rude.

"*Bazkat!*" he growled. "Honestly, that was unfair. They have Spry—took him into the mine. I tried to go after him, but the Tapper just gunked me before I could get a cast off."

He pointed at the entry. It was blocked by three of the monsters Wen called Tappers.

"I cannot believe I am about to say this." Kalon retrieved his guns and shook his head. "Unleash what magic you can and carve me a path to the lad."

"Say no more." Wen got up, ran toward the mine entrance, and beckoned Kalon to follow. "On three."

He didn't know what Wen was about to do, but that was the tried and tested method of counting down to an event. He was not disappointed.

The wizard wove a spell as he moved, pulling the threads around him as his eyes picked out the magical lines that crisscrossed and tried to avoid his motions. Reality fought back, trying to make him miss or lose contact with the forces of sorcery.

Reality failed.

Wen caught the threads of fire, of motion, of change, and of protection both in body and spirit. He wove the transformation lines, the kinetic lines, and wrapped it all in a single ball of mystic force before he tugged on the thread that split the whole spell apart.

He burned brightly, like a star, becoming a ball of fire that roared from where he ran toward the Tappers and struck them with explosive force. They were sundered, immolated, and scorched all at once, their fleshly and earthen corpses torn to pieces by the wizard's spell.

Bits of rock, mud, blood, and flesh rained down around the mouth of the mine.

Kalon followed closely behind, sprinting through the gap in the flames. He barely felt the heat thanks to his long coat. Anger and worry burst up through him as he hit the mine running; he pushed those emotions back down—he had a task to do and Spry to rescue.

Outside he heard the Kharnate, Andreas, Silver, and now Wen battling to keep the other Tappers at bay.

The monster that was Eamon Tapper dragged the unconscious Spry deeper into the mine, to the lair he called home. He slowly tugged the youth past rock walls and through a maze-like warren of similar looking passages.

So intent was he on his job, he didn't notice that Spry was in fact awake and very slowly crumbling cracker-like biscuits—carefully, so as not to be seen by the creature. He hoped they could act as a trail for anyone who might come and get him.

If anyone did.

If anyone was still alive.

The Tapper hummed a ditty as it reached the final stop on their journey, a cave where human skulls lay among partially digested bodies wrapped in the dark grey-green ooze the creatures spat forth.

Spry took a deep breath and felt the slime hit him in the face as Eamon vomited gunk all over the Stealer's body.

Kalon followed into the darkness. There was only one way down into the mine and it took the Inquisitor deep below the camp. A sloped passage crept ever on, and the air became thinner, a faint smell of gas tainting it.

Down Kalon went, then stopped as the passage split in several directions, his contact lenses picking out details in the dark. Once more he silently thanked Daroni for his work. He saw the tiny crumbs of biscuit and lifted one to his nose, recognizing the crackers that Spry had been holding during their meal. They were stale. Kalon could use this.

Spry, he thought, *well done, lad—you gave me a trail to track.*

The creature that had Spry took no pains to hide where it had taken him, seeming to trust to the confusing layout of the passages and corridors of the old mine to conceal its path. Kalon followed the crumb trail, creeping forward slowly and carefully.

He listened in the dark, and the dark answered back.

Ahead, there were sounds like a faucet being opened or a sluice disgorging foul liquid out of a sewer.

He wasn't far wrong.

The Inquisitor caught sight of the partially digested, buried, and entombed bodies decaying slowly in the cave. The Tapper's larder, it looked like, and a faint glow suffused many of the cocoon-like structures. Tendrils of energy leaked and flowed into the large Tapper that stood at the center, slowly burying the Stealer up to his waist in rock and mud. The foul chamber was lit by small lanterns that shone in the dark.

Once his work was done, the Tapper stepped out of the way, drank in the life essence from the room, and then started to feast on the youth's. It was tinged with sparks of gold and red, colors unlike the others in the lair.

Kalon took aim with both guns and then cocked his head. He heard a sound back in the mouth of the mine; it was fast, it was on four legs, and it came with a growl. Perhaps Kaitlinel had finished with the upper Tappers and now sought the one who had their companion. It sounded like her, powerful nose tracking the scent of the lad.

He was barely able to get out of the way in time as the werewolf shot out of the tunnel behind him and into the Tapper's lair. Her furred body moved like liquid velvet as she careened toward the Tapper, jaws extended and green eyes lit with raw fury.

The creature turned to meet her, and they crashed together, claws, teeth, and limbs flying.

Kalon holstered his firearms and ran to Spry. He began to rip the glue-like goo from the lad's body, head first. He cracked chunks off with the heel of his palm, and soon he had the Stealer's head free from the mess.

He wasn't breathing.

Amidst the chaos of the battle between two creatures, Kalon shattered the rest of Spry's prison and lay the youth on the ground. He checked his heart and then his pulse, which was very slow and very low. So, he administered first aid, following the guidelines to work on the boy as the battle turned the lair into a gladiatorial arena. Spry's pulse was weak, his heart was weak, but Kalon was careful and persistent as he breathed life into the boy again, compressed his chest correctly, and did everything the church healers had taught him.

Meanwhile, the fight between werewolf and Tapper was not going Eamon's way.

Just as Kaitinel was about to strike a blow that would tear off his right arm, the Tapper's form shifted, and he shrank to become the weak-looking old man they'd met earlier. He looked up at the rage-fueled werewolf with pleading eyes.

"Please, we're so hungry. We haven't eaten for months."

Kaitlinel's maw dripped with the fluids from the other monsters she had chewed to pieces. Her eyes narrowed, and she said, in a low, and brutal voice, "I should care, why?"

"Just leave us the boy. He would sate us for hundreds of years. You can go. We're sorry," Eamon whined.

The werewolf's nose sniffed the air, then she snorted one breath. "Is that so?"

"Yes, he's full of so much energy, so much magic, so much tainted blood."

"You promise to leave us all alone if we give you Spry?"

"I do." Eamon nodded furiously.

"Beg."

"I beg of you." He dropped to his knees, wringing his hands. "I implore you."

Kaitlinel looked at Kalon, saw Spry's unconscious form give a tiny, hitched breath, and turned back to Eamon Tapper. "Fuck you." Her right arm swung with claws the size of daggers and tore the monster's head clean off his shoulders in a shower of mud, blood, and fleshy gore. "Fuck you forever."

She caught the monster's head with her other hand, and her body began to shift, melting back to the Kaitlinel that Kalon knew—albeit naked, covered in a mix of fluids, and slathered in mud. She kissed the corpse's head, her eyes lit red within the green, and there was a curl of smoke from Eamon's black eyes.

She dusted the ash from her fingers and ran over to the Inquisitor.

"Move," she snarled and bent over Spry. "Sorry lad." She winked. "Or perhaps I shouldn't be sorry."

Kalon rocked back on his heels as the naked werewolf woman pressed her lips to Spry, letting the energy from the Tapper flow into him. Then she lifted her head and bit down on her bottom lip. A small sliver of blood flowed into the Stealer's mouth, and he coughed several times.

"That did the trick," she said and stood up. "Naked werewolf kisses always win, Kalon."

"I see." The Inquisitor remained alert.

"You should try one sometime."

"I do not need to," Kalon offered and finally stood as Spry blinked a few times, threw up, and then coughed loudly again.

"I hope that wasn't you, Kalon. No offense, but I'm not into older guys."

"It was her," Kalon replied.

Spry opened his eyes properly. He looked at his friends, looked again, and blinked once more. "Hey Kait, er, thank you."

"Don't mention it. Kiss of life to the rescue."

"I think that was more than the kiss of life." The Stealer rubbed his mouth where she'd bruised his lips. "Whatever it was, it worked."

"We thought we had lost you," Kalon said and offered the youth his hand. "Wen put me on your trail."

"I was able to fight their sleep off just enough to crumble some of Charlie's old treats up," Spry said and coughed a few more times. "That stuff is terrifying."

"Monsters, kid. Wen would know more, since he's pretty clued up on those things," Kaitlinel snarled softly and tugged mud out of her hair.

The Inquisitor nodded and let out a breath; it was one of relief. "I am glad you're safe, Spry, but we should leave this place and check on the others."

"Good idea. It stinks down here, and I don't want to be here any longer than I have to," Spry replied and looked around. He couldn't see a thing outside of this cavern. "Someone lead me?"

Kaitlinel took his hand and squeezed his fingers. "Don't let go. I can see perfectly beyond the cave."

The three left the chamber, each of them deep in thought, and made their way through the dark to the outside world. It was easier for Kalon to lead; he retraced his steps with perfect memory, reversing the way he'd come into the mine.

He could also have followed the trail of cracker crumbs.

CHAPTER 23

A MOMENT TO REFLECT

K alon was the first to step out of the mine, followed closely by Spry, and finally Kaitlinel brought up the rear. The settlement of Tapper's Folly reflected the werewolf's furious battle with the monsters. The moon had barely moved on.

Silver sat on a ruined porch step. It was barely holding together, and it creaked a little as she put her weight onto it. She cleaned off her daggers, wiping them down with a cloth.

Andreas stood close by, both guns still out of their holsters and resting in his hands.

Wen busied himself with a quick patrol of the camp, immolating any Tapper bodies that he came across in the wake of Kaitlinel's trail of destruction. He looked up as the Kharnate stepped out of the shadow of the mine head. "They're back!" he called to Silver.

She tucked the daggers away, and they shifted back to earrings again. Then she stood up and walked over to the others. "How is Spry?"

"He's alive, Sil," Kaitlinel replied and began to slowly brush the mud and goo off her skin. "Took me and Kalon to save him."

"Anyone hurt?" Wen asked as he casually burned the last Tapper to cinders.

"No. Spry might need a healer's eye to see if he's got injuries we can't see." Kaitlinel took him to Wen, then sat down on a broken step, tugged more mud off her hair, and growled softly. "I hate bloody things that get stuck in every single place."

The wizard quirked a brow and chuckled. "Stand up, Kaitlinel, I've got the cure for that mud."

"Oh?" the werewolf huffed. "Brought a shower stone with you?"

"Sort of."

Wen pulled the threads again and wove a quick spell, dragging the lines of water and certain elements out of the air. Before she could say another word, the werewolf was drenched to the bone and soaked through. She spun around and eagerly washed off the grime and blood from the fight.

She didn't care that people saw her naked, either. Not one bit.

After the deluge, Wen shifted the threads and brought with the next spell a warm wind that helped dry her off.

"Tickles!" she laughed.

Once Kaitlinel was sorted, Wen turned his attention to Spry and checked him over. He formed another spell, one designed to flag up any illness or shift in the lad's health. These cantrips were Wen's bread and butter, and to the wizard they were as simple and natural as taking a breath.

Spry watched this and concluded it was no wonder magic was regulated.

Kalon's lips twitched at this. So much magic at all once! Like Spry, he was glad magic had been regulated by the church in his homeland.

The werewolf stretched lithely and shook her hair out. Wen wasn't the only one with magic; this came as a gift from the shifters. Her clothing melted back onto her body like black wax until she was once again dressed—or at least had more clothes on than previously.

Andreas watched, smiling wryly. "Nice trick, though the reverse is more fun."

"Yep!" She nodded at that. "Totally agree, and the Tappers put a stop to tonight's demonstration, but still, they provided more fun—in a different way. Haven't had a battle like that for ages!"

When Spry was deemed uninjured, Wen checked everyone else

over, tending to minor wounds on Silver where some of the monster's teeth had caught her skin.

"So, how did we get caught?" Spry was the first to raise the question that had been troubling both Silver and Kalon.

"I think I can answer that one," Wen said, sitting down by the werewolf. "We got fed that stew, probably made from previous occupants, nice and spicy—which also hid the secret ingredient inside the broth. It was some kind of sleep agent, activated by the runes carved on the ceilings of the huts. That's why they wanted us to go in there."

All eyes turned to the wizard; no one spoke, so he took that as a great sign and continued. "The rune touched off the liquid, and we all fell asleep. Not even Kalon or Silver could resist that, because it was already past coat or ink. As much as you're the tattooed lady, Silver, and Kalon's coat is protecting him—you both have a chink in your armor."

"Oh?" Kalon quirked a brow. The thought of eating food made from other people didn't sit well with him, but he kept his composure.

Silver perched lightly on a broken step. "Damn, you're right. That's a dirty trick, Wen." Though this made the Amari Sister angry, she too remained composed.

"Clever, though." Wen was mildly impressed at the Tappers' gall to feed previous victims to travelers, but wasn't fazed in the slightest. "You eat the food, the food coats your throat. Kalon's coat doesn't cover his head, and your tattoos don't yet cover your head—see the gap, straight down from your scalp?"

"Yeah," Silver snorted. "I might have to get more ink."

"I see." Kalon nodded. "A flaw in our protection, but usually the coat prevents exterior magical effects from harming me. The food we ate, laced with a reactive to amplify the rune, would probably be enough to tip the odds in their favor by accident."

"Exactly." Wen nodded once more. "That's pretty much it."

"Look where it got them, though—we won." Andreas rubbed his hand through Kaitlinel's hair, and she growled softly. "Our ace in the hole, our wonderful ragewolf." Inwardly he felt somewhat sick at the thought of eating other people, so he deflected with humor.

"Hah, I like it. Ragewolves, sounds like a bad title for a book."

The werewolf snorted softly. "The sleep didn't last long with me; one chomp of those Tapper teeth woke me up. Didn't take me long to see Andreas here being deep-throated by that Greta woman Tapper. Had him three quarters of the way down her gullet, and not in a good way."

The gunslinger made a sour face.

"Yes, they pull you in to that bulbous belly and use it to transport you to where they leave you to digest, only they don't use digestive fluids, they suck your life force very slowly as you die over a period of months and months," Wen added, helpfully. "They move slowly then, and they're an easier target—probably why they just pulled Spry by hand until they could get him to where they wanted him."

"I'm special," Spry said dourly. He wanted to be sick, throw that food up, and most of all just forget the whole thing. His mind was too scattered from the Tappers' kidnapping to truly focus on the fact that their meal had been made from other people.

"What about you, Silver? Kalon?"

"I believe Wen was able to reach me via the astral and snap me awake." Kalon looked at the wizard. "You have my thanks."

"Welcome." Wen winked. "Sorry I had to barge in, but I didn't want you devoured."

"I woke and saw Silver had been almost swallowed by the beast." Kalon brought the memory back perfectly. He deconstructed the scene.

"He saved me from being stored and gunked," Silver replied, a genuine smile directed to Kalon.

He smiled back.

"I was able to get her loose, we fought the monster off, and I found Wen outside." Kalon continued. "He carved me a path to Spry, and I was able to—with Kaitlinel's help—save him."

Spry smiled a little. "You came for me. Didn't know if you would."

"I did," Kalon replied. He sat down on a thin bench and interlocked his fingers, then rested his hands on his lap for a moment. "You are a companion of ours, and a member of this group. You aren't just a means to an end."

Spry blushed slightly. "You heard that."

Wen grinned. "See? Told you."

Kalon nodded. "You were right."

Silver got up, moved next to the Inquisitor, and sat down. "That porch step was too broken."

Kaitlinel grinned a little and yawned. "Sun will be up in a few hours, but I don't know if I want to stay here tonight."

"It feels worse than it did when we arrived," Silver admitted and looked over at Kalon. "We're a few days off the main Demon Spine yet, but we're well into the foothills."

Wen thought on this, tapped his fingers on his leg, and hmm'd at the back of his throat. "If we all piled into that structure there, I could circle it with a ward, and we could at least get some kind of rest." He pointed at a still-intact building.

They followed the wizard's gesture, and Kalon nodded. "We'll do that. At least then we can get some rest and be ready for the next leg of our travels."

They entered one of the intact huts, made sleeping spots as best they could, and settled down for the night. Wen wove the Tapestry outside and walked a full circle around the hut. Where his feet wandered, the ground burned with runic patterns and silvered over with a gleam of energy.

He stepped through the door to find Kaitlinel and Andreas curled up together and Spry in a corner on his own, but not far from Andreas's back. Kalon and Silver were seated together, and the kelanari woman had fallen asleep with her head in the Inquisitor's lap.

"From Fate's Hand to pillow, in one fell step!" Wen chuckled as he walked into the hut. "Safest pillow this night, I wager."

Kalon thought on this. "Honestly, my friend," he began, testing that word, "it feels strange. This is something that's beyond my knowledge."

"The church really did do a number on you, friend."

"They acted out of their own self-interest." Kalon replied. His eyes narrowed almost imperceptibly, but Wen caught it. "The feeling of her on my lap is…comforting?"

"That's a start."

Kalon thought back to the day he'd spent looking at raindrops, not long ago, and it seemed that things moved quickly here. "Is connection to another person always this rapid?"

Wen sat down, crossed his legs, and brushed his mouth with his hand to stifle a yawn. "Connection with another person, rapid..." He blinked, oh, and it dawned on him. "You mean love, or the first tiny ember?"

"I suppose so."

"Oh boy," Wen chuckled softly again, and his eyes gleamed. "Honestly, it can take months, sometimes years, and sometimes a single hour of a single day. It's really...mutable, just like people. Confusing, odd, maddening, and when it strikes...it makes you lose all rhyme and reason. You can't get them out of your head, and they you."

"I see. And they, you," Kalon echoed those words, and he absent-mindedly stroked Silver's hair. She gave a little contented sigh and settled once more.

"Don't take this the wrong way." The wizard smiled warmly. "I envy you, Kalon Rhadon, not for the woman, but for the experience you can have of getting to know this for the first time. Might sound trite, and I can imagine some in the peanut gallery out there thinking that right now."

"What?"

"Oh, sorry, used to be an actor, so I always think in terms of the performance," Wen replied and swept his hand to encompass the rest of the room. "Plus, the audience in their galleries viewing on as we strutted our stuff on stage."

"I see." Again, Kalon stroked Silver's hair. This time, he left his hand there, gently.

"You get to feel it for the first time. Like never having known it, or been taught it, or remember it." As Wen listed these off, he ticked them off on his fingers. "You may remember your family's love, but that's parental love. This kind of love is dangerous, powerful, and might just be the key to victory when all appears lost."

"Cryptic."

"I often am—and whimsical, and handsome, and very modest." The wizard winked a little.

"It appears," Kalon said after he'd thought on this a while, "that I have much to learn and a great deal to understand."

"That's life, only you're coming at it from a long time in the dark," Wen soothed.

"Yes."

"My advice: Silver is tough, dependable, strong, all those things that you can use to describe her role as an Amari Sister and First Mate of the *Mist Reaver*. She likes her own space, her own place, but she's drawn you into that circle, Kalon. You're in a position of trust now, and you will have to choose between her and the church—can you do it?"

Kalon looked Wen in the eyes, then down to the woman in his lap. "Choose between the woman who freed my soul from a demon or the Cardinal that placed it in chains."

"Yep, that's the conundrum."

"Logic dictates that the church is the power I serve."

"It does."

"The Cardinal betrayed that trust, betrayed me. I am more likely to trust others at the church than her now."

"Probably, but can you really trust them?" Wen said carefully. He watched Kalon intently. "These others."

The Inquisitor pondered this. He thought carefully, and he came back to the raindrops on the windowpane once more. Two droplets ran down in a river, then combined halfway and ran to the bottom of that glass pane. Together. Far from the church, far from the Cardinal.

Cardinal Terusa, who was responsible for the demon in his soul, who voyeuristically observed him through his amulet. The same woman who wanted the book. Kalon looked at Wen.

Trust her? No. Trust the church itself under her? No. Trust Winter, Sara, Reva, Daroni, and certain others in that organization—potentially yes. But he would be wary from now on.

He looked down at Silver again.

This question put a great weight on him. He felt it, and that emotion that played with the heart and often bypassed the head. The longer he looked at her, the more that the church seemed like a tarnished vision of what he'd believed.

"The Cardinal shackled me," he repeated. "Silver pulled those chains free and risked her life to save me, even though I was no one to her."

"Odd, eh?"

"I cannot fathom why."

Wen nibbled at his lip and yawned. "Well." He settled back and closed his eyes. "That's the most human response to all of this. It's confusing, but the answer lies in your heart—and hers. Silver is a kelanari; she's not human, she burns with a fire that's more intense than any of us. So, her people have a different approach to those they find attractive—or even fall for. It can happen fast with the kelanari, and when they see something they like, they want to experience it without the dilly-dallying that humans often spend so much time on."

"Ah."

"She's decided you are a potential love, good sir, and honestly, you're lucky to have garnered her eye. I can think of no better match for an Inquisitor like you than an Amari Sister."

Kalon thought on this and closed his eyes. He would think on it even more. "To answer your question, I serve the church, but it has broken my trust. If it came down to her or them, I would stand by her—and this might get me branded as Arch Heretic, but I would stand by all here in this room if it came to it."

"Chains broken, then." Wen grinned and then said, "Rest, my friend, we've got miles to go and more to do before we cross that bridge to the Imper Vatica. Or at least you do, because I am not setting foot in that building if I can help it."

"You're church-sponsored," Kalon said and then he too took that moment to drop into a restful state of mind—one of the tools given to him by Seeker Winter. The sun would rise in a few hours, and they would be off to the west once more.

Wen's reply was a soft snore, it didn't take long for the exhausted wizard to fall asleep.

Across the ocean, the *Orca* flew on, slow, ponderous, but dependable. The ship was headed in a direction similar to the trajectory of Kalon and his companions, only it would stop before it reached Moorhaven and land at the neutral port city, the City of Wyrden.

Maxis and Vass slept in the same room, together, and had no idea of the trials faced by Fate's Hand in the west.

Nor did the Cardinal, who sat awake on her silken sheets, troubled, angry, and furious that she could not contact Kalon. She could not see through his amulet, and she didn't even sense a single thought. Her broken connection to Fate's Hand weighed like a millstone on her mind.

Not even Drako Mallori's body could soothe her.

Nor could the idea that Maxis and Vass were on a wild goose chase in Wyrden, to keep the assassin safe and to allow her to hide him in plain sight.

When the time came, she would pardon him, and Kalon would accept it—he was a loyal hound of the church.

He was *her* hound.

The demon realm rocked with Akas's anger, the walls of the palace shook, and the old man kicked over braziers in his fury. He collapsed on the floor and smashed his head against it until there was black blood everywhere.

He healed—slower than usual, but he healed nonetheless.

"Fuck this," he snarled. "I can't die, and I can't live. My body is shit, my palace is crumbling around me, and now this."

Jaziel watched with a hint of amusement on her thin, dark lips, today's shade the ash of the condemned. "My lord, I'm sorry, but the demons were no match for both Kalon and this Amari Sister."

"Bollocks," Akas snarled. "Amari this, Amari that. They always fuck up my life."

"Might I suggest less cursing?"

"Did you become a prude like the rest of those bleach-souled motherfuckers out there beyond the realm? Become human, have we? We're demons! We're not the same as those shits."

"Still, it's easier to talk to you when you're not swearing every five seconds." Jaziel swept her long dress up, ready to leave. "I tried, and then I thought, 'no, I'm not sending another bunch of hunters to the Inquisitor.'"

The old man stopped in his rage. "What did you say?"

"I said I am not sacrificing any more of our brethren for your whims."

"I thought so. No, no, you're right." Akas's eyes lit up for a moment. "Perhaps I was too angry. I mean, that's part of what I am. Perhaps you are right."

"Go on." the demoness purred softly. If she'd had a tail, it would've curled right into a little curve.

"We let them get the book and take it to my puppet Cardinal. And then we fuck them up." The Demon King's eyes whirled with eyes-within-eyes, and he laughed. "All of them, including that Amari Sister."

"Now you see, my lord," Jaziel soothed softly. "Once you stop cursing, you can think straight."

"Yes, yes." Akas laughed again. "All I have to do is convince Terusa—somehow—that her pet is a danger to her, and I get her...get the book...get revenge, and get a body back."

Jaziel slipped an arm around the old demon's shoulder. "Dear lord, if you wanted a body, why not slip into something more comfortable? Why not think outside the box? Why not use the woman who thinks she's the one in charge as the vessel for your energy?"

Akas's jaw opened slightly; he showed many teeth. "You sneaky bitch."

"I am."

"It'd be easy. She already believes I'm her One God. So why can't I get her to lower her defenses and let me in? She would love to be one with her god after all, wouldn't she?"

"She craves it."

Akas nodded. "Like you crave debauchery."

"Exactly."

He waved Jaziel off and turned toward the mirror that sat in the corner of his throne room. He snarled softly and licked his pointed teeth. "Old I might be, but I can still use this mirror to do what needs to be done."

The demoness turned, wiggled her hips a little, and left the throne chamber with a triumphant swish.

It was good being wicked. Especially on days like today. Soon, they would be back.

The world would burn.

Starting with the Imper Vatica.

CHAPTER 24

SKY ON FIRE

A s events unfolded elsewhere across the realms, Winter moved through the Imper Vatica on her own business. Her conversation with Maxis and Vass had inspired her to find Reva Flynn and set her on the path to Wyrden with them. Today she would make another countermove against the woman she'd once sworn to serve loyally.

The Seeker had to move people out of the Cardinal's reach and protect them from what was coming—her visions had shown her so.

Roland was too much a pawn to trust. He had fallen for Terusa's honeyed words—and her body. She used him, as she did Drako Mallori. Winter hated this; this was not her church.

Imani was a possibility, but Winter would have to be careful; the wrong approach would see Winter's plan fail before it even had chance to blossom.

Vincent and Sara could be trusted. So she wended her way deep into the bowels of Daroni's lair to find the master of artifice himself.

She was thorough, double-checking that she wasn't followed, moving like a ghost in the vast complex that was the heart of the church. Down she went through secret ways known to only a few select members of the Cardinal's inner circle. While the church went about its morning rituals, she whispered in silk and satin through the corridors and passages below.

At length Seeker Winter emerged into the hot and noisy mechanic's foundry, made her way up two flights of metal stairs, and entered the small but comfortable office chamber atop the main gantry. There she found Vincent Daroni and Sara discussing some new invention, as per usual.

"Hello, Winter." Sara beamed at the woman and flicked her wheelchair around. "What brings you down here to our little gossip corner?"

Vincent Daroni finished his preserve-covered toast and waved a finger; the tip was still covered in butter. He wiped it off. "Seeker, to what do we owe the pleasure?" he asked softly.

A woman of action rather than mere words, Winter crossed the floor to them and offered her hands. "There is something I want you to see, something you must tell no other soul of."

They exchanged worried glances and nodded. Sara spoke first. "Of course, you know we listen to you whenever you speak, Seeker Winter. Your visions have kept us all safe in the past."

Daroni nodded. "Yes, yes, don't be afraid to tell us."

Winter took their hands and knelt. She showed them the same thing she had revealed to Maxis and Vass: the Cardinal with her eyes-within-eyes and the sky on fire.

Sara shuddered, her small frame shaking with tiny tremors of fear. Daroni was worse; he felt sick and covered his mouth as he let go of Seeker Winter's hand.

"Terrible," he said at long last and took a deep breath, followed by a stiff drink from his hip flask, the rig on his arm and hand tinkling against the metal container. "Will this come to pass?"

"Yes." Seeker Winter nodded.

Sara let go of the woman's hand and folded her own across her lap, her expression transformed from scared to resolute. "What do we do?"

"Maxis and Vass are in Wyrden with Reva. We will regroup there; what's coming is something we cannot stop from the Imper Vatica. I have been shown visions of what I—what we—must do. Our path must take us to the Three-Tiered City for now," the Seeker said solemnly, her eyes almost tinged with tears. "I only ask that you trust me, and in time I will explain more. How you get there is up to you, but do it quickly. I pray that we can leave in time."

Vincent Daroni muttered softly, "I think I can get us there. Leave it to me and Sara."

"We'll figure something out." The young artificer smiled ever-so slightly. "We got this."

"Good." Winter sounded relieved. "I am glad you can see the importance of this."

"Yes, you'd best be off before someone gets suspicious. You're not at your usual teaching post already," Sara pointed out and swung her wheelchair around. She began to collect a few things off a nearby table. "See you in Wyrden, later."

"Fortune go with you, my friends." Seeker Winter turned, troubled, but set her shoulders straight and made her way back to the core buildings of the Imper Vatica. Once more she took the secret ways and kept out of sight until she was back in her familiar chamber.

That was enough work for one morning. Slowly, she'd have to find others to join her cause—and hopefully they could act before all hell broke loose.

Before *he* escaped. Before *they* returned.

Far to the west, another sky was on fire. This time it was the first red rays of light across the mountains and the sun's radiance that fell across the bedraggled settlement that had once been Tapper's Folly.

The group emerged from their broken night's sleep, still tired, but at least they'd managed some rest. They ate a frugal breakfast, consisting mostly of what they had in their bags.

Silver offered Kalon a warm smile as she stretched in the ruby light of the morning. After a moment to collect themselves and make idle chatter, they turned as one and headed to the opposite side of the camp, leaving via the west gate.

Soon they were once more treading on stones as they moved away from the now silent place.

"At least they're gone now," Spry said and spat on the ground. "They can't catch any more travelers and eat them."

Kaitlinel nodded. "They won't be eating anyone, but for the record, they tasted bad. Not fun at all."

"I imagine not." Andreas offered her some of his jerky. She took it, winked at him, and ate it suggestively.

Wen, Kalon, and Silver led the way through the winding trail that climbed ever higher to the upper regions of the foothills. As the miles passed, they noticed the ground changing and the sky overhead crackling with bolts of barely contained mystic energy.

"This is why Talon couldn't bring our ship right to the doorstep," Silver explained as the roar of discharged energy made a crack-bang sound over their heads. "It would rip the *Reaver* apart. She'd be torn in two by that."

"I see!" Kalon shouted over the din. "A wise choice to remain far from this chaos."

"Yes."

The cacophony from the ever-present magical storm overhead drowned out any further talk, and they spent the rest of the morning's journey in silence punctuated by occasional chatter.

Kaitlinel spied a couple of mountain goats, and her stomach commanded her. Before anyone could stop the Kharnate, she ran forward, transformed mid-leap into a black wolf, and shot after the two creatures. She was an excellent hunter, and soon the woman emerged from the rocky incline with the two dead goats in her hands.

"Lunch, and dinner," she said proudly.

"Hell yes!" Andreas grinned. "Goat is good."

Wen and Silver chuckled as Spry licked his lips. "Not had goat in ages," the Stealer noted. "You're going to share, right?"

"Oh yes." Kaitlinel winked at the young man. "Pack is pack, and right now, you're my pack. I always look after you."

Spry blushed a little.

"We'll find somewhere better to dine, then," Wen said, indicating a nearby cave. "It'll prevent unwanted, accidental lightning strikes for a start."

They moved out of the open air and took shelter in the small cave, spreading their blankets and other belongings on the ground. Wen made a fire pit and wove a few threads to bring flames from nothing into a cooking blaze.

Kaitinel grinned. "I'll clean and gut yours. Then, if you don't mind, I'll go and eat mine."

This bonding moment came as a surprise to Kalon. He wasn't used to the feelings it evoked or the interplay between the people around him. He observed them and watched the various reactions almost scientifically.

Good as her word, Kaitlinel prepared the one goat for the others and then slunk off once more in wolf form to go and enjoy the whole of her meal in relative peace outside the cave mouth. The wizard took the duties of cook seriously and suspended the meat in the fire with more sorcery.

"She's private like that," Andreas said between mouthfuls of well-cooked goat. "This is so good."

They shared the meal together and sat back, sated for now.

"How long until we reach the lair of the book?" Kalon questioned the wizard.

"One day and a half, I reckon." Wen licked his fingers as the juices from the meat ran down them. "It's almost a straight shot from here, and honestly, the Tappers didn't delay us for too long."

"They almost stopped us dead," Spry said. "Well, me, dead."

"They didn't, and that's what matters." Silver smiled at the youth. "We got you out. You're with us. All's good."

Spry wanted to feel reassured, but the back of his mind replayed that encounter with Bala Mora and the fact his blood was a key.

"Yeah," he said, chewing some of his goat meat thoughtfully. "You did."

They took one hour out of their journey to rest, eat, converse, and drink. Then they were off once more out across the rocky trails, moving ever closer to the book.

The sun traveled with them. From the east it made a curve across the ever-changing sky. The area's weather remained chaotic and dangerous. Part of a nearby peak was split by a massive bolt of aether-born energy, which ricocheted around before it burst into the heavens with a bang.

"Shit." Andreas blew out a harsh breath. "That was a big one."

They moved on, and night came. Now the mountain was lit with the fires of red, gold, blue, and green above their heads as chaotic forces raged against each other, the result of magic unleashed thousands of years before, when the greatest of all demons fell.

Despite the perilous terrain, Wen was sure-footed and led them through the places he remembered as a child. Silver had similar memories of when the Amari used to travel these roads. With both kelanari and wizard, they made great time across the pass and into the mountain range proper. They camped that night in a small cave on the leeward side of the range, and then once more in the morning they continued.

As they walked, their conversations were varied, and the trek was uneventful. Even the out-of-control weather seemed to back down, and their travels brought them to the edge of one of the smaller peaks of the Demon's Spine—a peak that resembled the mouth of a large creature. Inset into the rock was a small cave. The stalagmites and stalactites within were like teeth.

They ate the last of the goat as the firelight crafted shadows on the rock wall of their next camp. Spry's gaze lingered on the visage of the mountain. From that angle, he could see it resembled part of the back of a giant monster, with the spines the smaller peaks.

"You know it's called the Demon's Spine for a reason, right?" Wen followed the youth's gaze and poked the fire with a dry stick. "Long ago—thousands of years, in fact—the biggest demon fell here, and the mountain formed around the body."

The Stealer blinked and stopped, half-chewing his goat. "Really?"

"Yes." Kalon took up the explanation. "Wen is correct. That is what our archives say at the church."

"The Amari have old scrolls on that battle," Silver chimed in. "Many of them were there the moment the Demon King's champion broke the ground."

Kaitlinel chuckled. "The bigger they are."

Andreas pondered this, bit his tongue on a smutty retort, and finished off the last of his meal.

"Imagine the size of that thing's—" Kaitlinel waggled her finger and looked at Andreas.

"Don't say it."

"Co—"

"Don't!"

The werewolf raised her brows and laughed softly. She dropped the last of the goat into her mouth and licked her fingers one by one. She took her time, too, and stared Andreas down as she ran her tongue over every single one.

"So, the demon fell, and the ground opened," Wen continued, ignoring the pair. "The body was pulled below, and only the spine stuck up. The spines of its back are the smaller peaks, and the tunnels that run inside that whole range once thundered with demon blood." The wizard steepled his fingers to mimic the event.

"I hope we don't have to come out of the back." Spry shuddered at that thought and wrapped his arms around himself.

"So do I, lad. So do I." Wen grinned.

Wen added wood to the fire and tended to the flames. He kept the fire alive with some magic, but held most of that sorcery in reserve. He'd need it for tomorrow.

"What are demons?" Spry asked.

"Oh...shit, lad," Wen laughed softly and poked the flames once more. "The easy answer: they were once gods that fell out of favor with their worshippers and devolved. The Old Gods became demons, and the New Gods usurped them. That's what the lore teaches us."

"Old Gods?"

"Yeah, you know, the Taker was once the god of death, and he was replaced by the Shroud. The Taker devolved into a demon."

The rest of them listened as Wen continued to speak. Even Silver and Kalon, who were among the learned ones, kept silent.

Spry thought on this and rubbed his nose; the tip was cold. "So, the Demon King was a god?"

"Yep."

"Now he's a demon. A devolved god."

"Yep."

"Who are the New Gods then?"

Kaitlinel yawned and butted in with a soft laugh. "Kharnate, my goddess, who fucks you and you turn into a werewolf."

"Sign me up." Andreas chuckled a little.

"Be careful what you wish for, trust me," Silver warned him. She caught the look in her friend's eye and shook her head.

"Missiva, goddess of chaos." Wen looked at the sky. "The Shroud, God of Death. Fortune, Goddess of Luck, and Fate, Goddess of, well, Fate." He daubed a stick he'd found on the ground into a patch of earth to tick them off. "That's not the whole list. There are more, and they're all capable of meddling in our affairs without a thought for us."

"Really?" Spry said with a frown. "Kind of like the church?"

Wen looked at Kalon. He made an "uh" face at the Inquisitor and then looked back at the Stealer.

"A harsh condemnation of the church, since the order does care for its charges," Kalon replied, narrowing his eyes in a moment's flicker of irritation at Spry's words. But the lad spoke true. "However, it seems that some of my peers use their position to lord their power over others."

Silver patted the man on the shoulder and said, "Don't worry, Kalon, we still love you."

The Inquisitor blinked a little at this and looked at Wen, their talk in the Tapper's hut still fresh in his mind.

"I'm grateful," he replied.

The kelanari woman's face lit up a little—or was it the fire, the flames made her ears take on a little pink glow at the tips? "We don't expect you to understand all of this at once, Kalon. It's got to be hard to come out of that demon's thrall and be hit with all these strong feelings."

The Inquisitor nodded and pondered Wen's words again. "Some feelings can be backed down with mental mantras that Winter taught us; others are not meant to be controlled so." He looked at her, and she looked back at him, a tiny flicker of realization dawning in the woman's eyes.

Wen hid his smile behind an expertly crafted poker face. "In any case you need me to shatter the protection on the maw that lurks out there in the dark. Beyond that, whatever happens, Kalon, know this: no matter where you are and what transpires—"

"That sounds ominous, Wen," Silver butted in.

"Wizards are like that," Wen reminded her. "I will find you, remember that."

The wizard did not elaborate further, but perhaps he had seen something in a vision, like Seeker Winter could. Or perhaps Wen just knew all too well the lengths to which Terusa would go to secure power.

Kalon Rhadon felt the warmth of friendship, the glow that came from having companions by his side, for the first time ever. People were not tools or a means to an end. They did not form a stepping-stone to the next leg of a journey.

When you needed them, when all was bleak and mired in doubt, they came to your side, regardless.

Kalon looked once more at Silver. She sidled over to where he sat. "What Wen said: if you ever need us, we'll be there," she said after a short moment. "Trust us."

"It is not easy, but I will try."

Spry felt warm too, thinking this company was better than the waifs and strays of the port, and much better than being bullied by the bigger kids.

The cold of the night came upon them swiftly. As if foreshadowing things to come, a wicked chill ran through their bones as they all settled down to rest. Tomorrow, the maw would lead them to the next step on their travels.

No one knew what waited for them in the tunnels below the Demon's Spine.

The book was close now, and as the companions slept, the rest of Hestonia moved on. A complex chess game played out. There was no turn order, no clock to mark off seconds in this complex series of events.

The Cardinal stood before her mirror, observing herself, connected to her god. The One God felt stronger than ever, and she opened her mind to him joyously.

It was her biggest mistake.

The Demon King sent his will through that link, and it struck Terusa full-force—hard enough to knock her backward onto the floor and leave her gasping for breath.

Her eyes whirled, lit by the swirling of eyes-within-eyes-within-eyes.

The Cardinal looked at herself in the mirror once more, shed her clothing, and slipped into a red robe. She tied a blindfold around her face to obscure her mark. It was a black band, set with the cog and eye of her church.

Perfect.

Somewhere in the back of her head, Terusa screamed as the Demon King's force locked her in a cage inside her mind. Her fate mirrored that of Kalon's recruitment to the church.

Ironic.

The *Orca* was slow, but eventually it crested the skies above the grand, dusky, three-tiered City of Wyrden. A place of villainy, friendship, lust, and crime. A true neutral haven in the sea that surrounded it, and when viewed from the air, a powerful symbol to ward off demonic influence.

Maxis and his wife knew the history. Wyrden, the city that had been constructed and finished in the last days of the demon war. When the final tier activated, the city shone, and the demons were blasted to ashes—along with most of the land around it, to leave the city as a lonely watch upon a pinnacle of rock in the middle of a sea that once held a continent.

Far to the west, the energy-hungry barrier marked the edge of Wyrden's power, and the Demon's Spine where the champion fell as the city burned with eldritch sorcery. The city that saved the people of the past almost killed everyone around it.

Now the Justicar and his Inquisitor spouse were here, a place where the church did not find favor. They were accompanied by the woman in grey, Reva Flynn, and their mission was simple: find Verity and warn her of the things Winter had told them.

Something was coming, and it would be here soon.

As the *Orca* touched down on the windship platform, Maxis turned to the captain, nodded, and then looked to his wife.

"Ready husband?"

"Always."

They left the ship. The three gigantic circular tiers of buildings, walkways, and more awaited them in gusts of wind.

Wyrden, at long last.

CHAPTER 25

MAW AND MIRROR

The board was set and the pieces were moving, the mortals were gathered in their groups, and once again the world spun with plots and plans aplenty. This was the playground of the New Gods, and with mirthful eyes they watched the game play out.

They were not omnipresent, or omnipotent, just powerful beings who had unlocked a door to another world. One where they were capable of great things when they set foot in it.

It was like being a three-dimensional entity in a two-dimensional world.

Or demonstrating the power to make fire to those who had never seen it.

Magic.

Fire.

Gods.

Fate, of course, was a master of this game, and she tipped her hat to Kalon Rhadon.

Fate's Hand.

The dawn broke rudely with a rumble of thunder that brought no rain, just a shower of rocks that cascaded upward from the north, flew into the sky, and came crashing down at the base of the Demon's Spine.

The group had been up for an hour before sunrise, breaking camp and preparing to head down to the maw that held many secrets of ages past in its depths.

"That's our cue." Wen doused the remains of the fire with a quick spell. He put down the last of his breakfast and looked up. "If one of those comes down on us, we're in trouble. If one of those happens by us, we're all skyward."

"Agreed." Kalon moved first, and the rest fell in with him. He could see the jagged teeth of the dead demon's mouth clearly now as the sun rose.

Half an hour of travel with no talk led them to the maw.

There it was, clear and massive, a giant cave-like throat yawning off into the dark, crackles of magic blocking the way and spitting forth chaotic energies from tooth to tooth.

"Allow me." Wen stood before the barrier. "Haven't done this in a while, so if I explode—it's been fun."

Kalon looked at Silver, and she nodded. Spry looked on nervously; he never thought he'd see a place like this in all his life. The werewolf and the gunslinger found a place to perch, and Kaitlinel sat back on her leather-clad backside to observe.

The wizard cracked his knuckles and opened his vision to the magic energies around him. He smiled a little at the various threads as they dangled and thrashed. The demonic power here did its very best to keep the maw sealed, but Wen could find a way through.

He pulled the threads quickly. Finding the most powerful, he connected them to a siphon construct he wove with his right hand. His left hand wove a second spell, the fingers grabbing threads with an expert touch.

Now he sent his left-hand thread into the barrier. It pulled the demonic energy forth and let it flow out through the right.

To mortal eyes, Wen's right hand hoovered up the energy of the barrier, and the left hand spat it out in magical force harmlessly into the air.

The whole operation took just under ten minutes, and by the

end of the show Wen's face was streaked with sweat. "Worth it," he chuckled softly. "Totally worth it." He sat down hard. "I'm ok, going to need a minute. Or a day."

Kalon looked on. For the first time, concern showed on his face. "Will you be all right?"

"Yeah, I'm good. Won't be going into that place with you, though. I'm spent. That took way more out of me than I expected. Weak as a kitten now." The wizard waved his left hand, smoke rising from the fingertips.

"How about this?" Andreas offered. "I'm no good in dark places, can't see properly. But I'm pretty good at looking after people when they're down but not out."

"I know what you're going to say, and if that's the case, I'm going to have to stop here and make sure you both don't get eaten." Kaitinel said from her rocky perch. "It makes more sense that Kalon, Spry, and Silver go in. Kalon is the guy who wanted to be here, Spry is the important one, and Silver is Amari, which means demons are fucked."

Wen couldn't argue with this, Andreas didn't want to, and Kalon saw the sense in it.

"Settled, then," Spry said and moved to the mouth of the cave. "I can do this; we can do this. Kalon?"

Wen smiled softly; he used the last tiny fragment of his energy to summon a small orb of blue-tinged light. It bobbed and weaved over to the Stealer. "Ok, I really am done now. Good day-night!" He thudded over and lay there, breathing gently.

Kalon and Silver moved to stand with the youth. "Guard Wen well. I will see you soon." With those words, the man who did not care for long goodbyes, or even short ones, turned and vanished into the dark of the Demon's Maw.

Spry took the orb of light, and followed.

Silver looked at the other three, then she joined Spry and Kalon in the shadows.

The air within the tunnels of the Demon's Spine was old and

smelled foul. The charred stink of the immolated demonic entity clung to the air, seeming to emanate from every porous wall. The way down was obvious. Kalon could see perfectly in the dark thanks to Daroni's marvelous lenses, and Silver was as much at home in the dark as she was in the light. Spry's orb helped him keep up with the pair. Hundreds of feet of arterial walls spread through the whole body of the demon, turned over the years into a temple for the Anshada who once worshipped here. Here they had brought the book and sealed it away from the eyes of all, even demons and gods.

Silver knew the history of the place well, just like Wen.

"It is not hard to believe that the Anshada would turn this demon's body into a temple," Kalon said after a while. "You can feel the foulness in every breath you take."

"Old places like this still linger with enough power for all kinds of rituals," Silver replied and continued deeper, Spry at her heels.

Kalon fell silent once more and concentrated on the descent.

After a few hundred more feet, they turned out of the curved and curled corridor into a long chamber, the center of which was even deeper below. Their eyes just picked out what appeared to be a shriveled heart in the dark mass. They followed a spiral of calcified flesh down; someone had cut crude steps into it.

Deeper and deeper they went.

One wrong move, one perilous footfall, and they would tumble down to die in the shadowy depths.

They kept going.

What seemed like hours passed on this deep descent, the orb casting its soft light to keep Spry from falling in. Kalon kept his own counsel, and Silver peered around, worried that the floor might be gone any second due to the age of the burned foundation.

Nothing like that happened, and eventually they came to the center of the demon. The heart of the champion, who once roared and slew thousands with pure delight.

Only one walkway was intact, a thick strip of barbequed muscle that snaked out to an opening in the demon's stone-like heart. Long dead, long since stopped and long gone. They paused at the edge of the walkway.

"This must be it," Kalon said and looked at Spry. "Take courage, young man, and whatever happens…we are here."

Spry nodded. Again, he couldn't shake the feeling that destiny was laughing at him, and that he was one of those stupid child-prophecy characters who took up the sword and saved the world at the last moment. Happy endings only happened in stories, and even then, very rarely in the ones he'd been told.

"What Kalon said, Spry: we are here for you." Silver walked over, put her hand on his right shoulder, and squeezed a little. He didn't throw it off.

"Thanks, both."

Wen had two reasons for the orb cast: one, so that he could light Spry's way, and two, so he could view their progress in the dark. He might have even been able to assist through the little sprite; it wouldn't be powerful magic, but he could at least try.

A lot was riding on this now, and he knew it.

The book had to be destroyed, but only the church had the means to do so. He knew that too. He felt it was the only—to use Kalon's words—logical way.

It was a gamble to take it so close to Terusa, but it had to be done. In the past the book had been notoriously resilient to any form of destruction, but Vincent Daroni and the Church of Progression were a wild card in this age—one card the wizard was prepared to gamble on. There was the possibility that Terusa would take the book and betray Kalon, but he'd cross that bridge later.

Silver had helped free Kalon. He hadn't figured on the kelanari falling for the Inquisitor when he'd met them, but that spark would light the fire to burn Terusa to the ground. If the Church of Progression was freed from her grasp, it might just lead to a harmony for wizards, and he'd be free to walk around without fear.

Or at least, that's what he hoped.

So, in his mind's eye, he floated with the trio as they came to the demon's heart. He kept another eye on Kaitlinel and Andreas, who now sat by a flat rock playing dice and cards.

Some guardians they'd turned out to be. He chuckled inwardly and turned his attention to the events unfolding before him.

Spry made up his mind. He sighed softly, put one foot on the walkway, and moved with slow, steady steps over it. He walked inch by inch, yard by yard, to the opening. Kalon and Silver followed, and the Stealer was glad the Inquisitor and the Amari Sister stood by his side.

The walkway held their weight, and it was wide enough so that they could walk three abreast if they wanted.

Eventually they entered the demon's heart chamber and saw it had been furnished, lavishly and decadently. A massive four-post bed lay at the center, skeletons all over it and around it. Old stains that appeared to be blood daubed the floor.

The skeletons were frozen in time, in lewd and loving acts.

Whatever happened here had killed the participants, leaving their bones blackened and fused in their final moments.

"Goddess," Silver said softly. "In Amari's name, what happened to these people?"

Kalon observed this, taking in every detail. His investigator's mind flicked over the scene as if it were a crime. "A ritual, perhaps an orgy, but whatever was unleashed here burned all to blackened bone—yet touched no inorganic material."

He was right: neither the bed, nor the rest of the furnishings were harmed.

Then they saw it.

As if it had been hiding in plain sight, all along.

The mirror. A tall, free-standing oval of silver-black glass with a border that depicted demonic creatures coupling, their oiled bodies writhing around each other, caught in that moment of pure pleasure and disturbing pain.

Gold shone with a temptress's gleam.

Ancient writings that followed the curve, traced upon the surface in red-tinged fire. Silver read them out loud. "Some doors lead to fame, some doors lead to power, some doors lead to riches, and some doors should never be opened."

"The book lies beyond." Kalon took out the tome from the Anshada lair and leafed through it. "I do not read this script," he said and showed the page to the kelanari woman. "It is alien to me. One part of the book that I could not decipher with all my knowledge gained at the church." His eyes had passed over it at Sullavale, though he did not know why. The text tried to elude him even now, appearing to slither away from the page.

It was disconcerting, and he felt it.

Silver looked at the text. "It is old, a mix of Anshada and demonic letters, used by the wizards as a kind of code I suppose."

Spry joined the pair, then walked past to stare at the mirror. His eyes fixed on it. It was beautiful, seductive, and elegant all at once.

"You can read it?" Kalon stood close to her, taking in her scent.

"Amari training." She began to look it over. To her eyes the words remained still and easily readable.

"Ah." Kalon nodded. "The weapon of my enemy?"

"Pretty much," she replied. "The book is beyond the black-silver glass. We placed it there. We put it in the one place the demons cannot go, the one place he will never find it. It will give us power over him. We will rise again," she read and sighed. "Always with power. Always with bloody power."

"What else?"

"The key has been found; we take steps to secure it. Soon the blood will open that door we covet, and the crown to rule as the Demon King will be free to take."

"Is there more?" Kalon pointed at the last part of the text, intent now.

They did not see the young Stealer approach the mirror. However, Wen did.

He tried to call out. The orb shot forth and zipped over to Spry.

The Stealer was mesmerized; the sound of sex sang in his ears, the moans of the mirror called to his soul. One step, two steps, he grew lustful. He looked at the black-silver glass. His reflection stared back at him.

Wen's orb winked out; its power suddenly sucked dry.

The figures around the mirror began to move, back and forth, their bodies to show the way.

Spry stood now, his nose almost on the glass.

He did not see his face. He saw someone else, an unknown woman of utter beauty and grace with features of a feline cast—yet her face was still human, with pouting lips. He wanted to kiss them, kiss them so badly.

He did, just as Wen's orb popped back into being. The wizard saw all, and his heart felt heavy.

Wen of Moorhaven suddenly understood the word "key."

Power flooded Spry, and then flooded the room, and the mirror screamed with pleasure. Black-silver arms wrapped around him, pulled him toward the mirror, and then legs from the lower part of the glass did the same.

Sharp lips pressed against his; he tasted blood, and the demon of the looking glass smiled thinly, razor sharp.

Fire licked across his skin, and he screamed.

The youth's strangled cry changed to a deep moan. His lower half was now meshed with the mirror. He didn't try to pull free. Kalon dropped the tome and sprinted over toward the youth. For the first time in his life, fear gripped him—and he too understood how Spry was the key.

Silver reacted as well. She followed the Inquisitor and skidded to a halt just before the glass. "Spry!" she called out.

Before the pair could prevent it, the mirror rippled and the Stealer vanished into the dark surface, only to appear again by the side of the demon lover within the glass. She caressed his cheek. Blood followed down the skin in the path of her fingernails.

"The key at last," she mouthed in glass-like tones, crystal whispers, the mirror vibrating. "Sacrifice accepted, master and mistress of old."

Spry looked at Kalon and Silver from beyond the mirror, immense pain and pleasure two-fold. He mouthed the words, "I'm sorry" over and over. The demon woman kissed him again, and the mirror cracked. Light burst forth, and both the Stealer and the demon vanished from sight.

Replaced by a whorl of magical energy.

Kalon snarled and smashed his gloved hand against the surface.

Silver saw him vanish, and without a thought for her safety, she followed the man into the dimension beyond the oval glass.

The room behind them fell silent, the mirror deadened, and the orb that Wen had conjured winked out of its own accord, but not before it saw one last image.

The mirror reflected a world long gone, dead. With the ruin of a golden, bird-shaped vessel plunged part way into the ground. A world where the horizon was lit with two glowing, coal-like eyes above a ravenous maw which opened to devour the souls of the dead.

The glass shimmered, and the mirror became a mirror once more, a one-way door to the Shroud's domain—and the hiding place of the *Book of the Anshada*.

Wen swore loudly, causing Kaitlinel and Andreas to send cards and dice flying. They stared at the wizard, and then Andreas questioned him first.

"Bad dream?"

"No, fuck, fuck, fuck, and once more FUCK!" the wizard's face was a mix of anger, sorrow, and fear. "The bastards hid the book behind Jaziel's mirror."

"Slow down, sexy, and tell me what's up?" Kaitlinel said and rolled off her rock seat. "Who or what is a Jaziel's mirror?"

"Demon Queen, Akas's consort, and his right hand." Wen snorted. "Spry was the key, he was the catalyst to open the door. He must have been the child of one of our people, Anshada. Only Anshada were sacrificed to her mirror in the past. Bastards!"

"Wait," Kaitlinel growled, her shape starting to alter. "What killed him? Where can I find it and fuck it up?"

"Back it down, wolfy!" Wen said crossly. "There's nothing to kill, only a mirror that's far too powerful for any of us to break. The Demon Queen saw to that when she made it."

She snarled again. "I can try. Just point me to it—and her."

"No! I'm not losing you as well!" Wen shouted. "Look, I barely know you all, but we've grown close over the last few days through this trip. The Tappers bonded us in battle, and our laughs and companionship did the same in travel. Jaziel is too powerful for any of us—trust me—and Akas eclipsed her in his prime. We have to be patient, clever, and not rush in like an angry bitch in heat!"

The werewolf backed her anger down. Her face returned to normal, and her eyes calmed a little. "That's me, Wen, all the time."

"I saw Spry die, I saw Kalon try to smash the mirror and vanish, and I saw Silver follow him." Wen fought back tears of frustration and clenched his fists. "Fuck!"

"Fuck!" Andreas matched Wen's curse and picked up the dice. "We should go after them."

"No!"

"Why the fuck not?" the gunslinger said with a grumble.

"We can't follow. No one can. Kalon and Silver are on their own." The wizard shook his head and stood up to pace back and forth. "I saw them through the spell I cast. They passed within the mirror and into the realm beyond. The Shroud's realm. You don't go there unless you're dead."

"Then what do we do?" Kaitlinel growled in frustration. "I am not dying to go meet them. Fuck that."

"We wait. It's all we can do, Kait. It's up to the inquisitor and the Amari Sister now," Wen explained. He stopped pacing. "The best I can do is find a full length, silver mirror, one that's the opposite of the demon mirror in there." He looked at the maw in the mountain. "I've a few ideas what I'd do with it, but nothing solid yet—that part is still rattling around in my jumbled mind!"

Andreas was still processing the news that Spry was gone. He racked his brain for a moment. "Talon's ship! It has mirrors, especially in the cabins. Me and Kait looked so good in ours."

Kaitlinel snorted, but had to nod in agreement.

"Then we return to Talon Mane. Where did he leave the *Mist*

Reaver?" Wen said, dusting his jacket off. "Once I get a mirror like that, I can figure out what I can do with it."

"East of Moorhaven," Kaitlinel answered. She was still angry. Spry's death had not hit her in the same way as the others. For Kharnate followers, it never did.

"Now that is some good news in all the bad," Wen replied and looked to the east, beyond the horizon. "I couldn't get us here magically, because the mountains interfere with spells in such a way you could arrive inside a rock."

"Not good." Andreas made an "ow" face.

"Can you magic us to Talon?" Kaitlinel quirked a brow, her breathing slowed.

"East of Moorhaven, it's easier. I know the place like the back of my hand." Wen sighed. "Not today, though. Remember, I'm spent, and I need to get my focus and concentration back. Tomorrow morning, we go. A night's rest should see me recovered enough to pull the threads."

"We'll keep watch, then," Kaitlinel snarled, catching the flash of something at the edge of her vision. "Food, that'll do. I need to fuck something, or fuck something up."

With another snarl she was off, fast.

She left Wen and Andreas in silence, both men affected by the news of the Stealer's demise—and the role he had to play in the whole game.

Elsewhere, Fate just shrugged. She took a drink and moved another piece on the board—her favorite one. Her Hand.

CHAPTER 26

THE BOOK AND THE DEAD

kas knew the exact moment that the mirror devoured Spry. He felt the boy's soul cry out as the Anshada artifact, a gift from him in the thousands of years before the world almost burned to cinders, consumed the Stealer to open the door to his precious book.

He smiled and signed a few documents on the Cardinal's desk. He did not cause chaos; he did not stray from the path. That would come as a perk when Kalon brought him the tome.

He gave Terusa back control and soothed her troubled mind.

Her body was an odd one, unique in many ways, powerful and possessing so much untapped potential. He busied himself with allowing her to believe she had full control and voyeuristically watched events unfold like a fly on the wall.

Akas let the Cardinal believe that she held all the cards and that she was orchestrating everything.

"My lord?" she asked.

"Yes?" the One God spoke to Terusa as though he were in her soul.

"Of the book—do you think Kalon has found it?" Her eyes sparkled.

"Yes, he is close," Akas-One-God replied. "Very close. Patience my child."

"Yes, my lord." She went back to her documents, signed a pardon for Drako Mallori, and tucked it away in her drawer. "Soon, my Mallori, soon you will be exonerated, and we will have so much more fun."

She was almost as devious as Akas-One-God, he thought. Perhaps there was a way to leverage this — a union of souls when the time came.

He would see.

Winter remained watchful. She could sense a powerful energy in the Imper Vatica, close to the Cardinal, so she kept her distance. It was difficult, as the Cardinal could summon her at any moment to hand out a mission or request an augury.

It was old though, this force, and she knew who it was. It scared her, but she remained steadfast. She could not falter now, not if she could save Kalon or at least tip the odds in his favor. She'd also caught Mallori spying on her and wondered if the Cardinal knew he was so dangerously close to being discovered at the heart of her empire.

Winter always made sure the assassin saw her doing the right things, and with such a child's mind, he was no match for the mental coercion she leveraged on him when he got too close. He always found his way back to Terusa with nothing to report.

But for how long?

Imani was next, and she needed to make sure that she approached them very carefully.

The land of the dead was a place of howling psychic winds, tormented spirits, and bleak surroundings. Silver knew the lore: that it was the time at the end of all, where the Shroud sat with his monstrous wolf, Fathriir.

She looked around, but saw nothing she recognized in terms of landmarks. Until a broken, beautiful, dark ship appeared at the edge of her vision, stuck in the ground like a shattered toy. The *Ori*, the vessel she'd seen Kalon board at the port dock.

There he was!

The Amari Sister found Kalon quickly. He had not moved far from his point of arrival on this side of the mirror, and he stood with the ghosts of the past grabbing and clawing at his coat, their spectral fingers akin to a breeze playing with the hem.

He was watching the monster wolf as it towered hundreds of feet above the skyline.

"Kalon?" She walked up to him and threw her arms around the man.

He turned into her embrace and held her for a moment, felt the woman's heart beat against his chest, and laid his head on her shoulder. She felt the cool sting of tears run down her skin there and remembered the first time he'd cried in her presence.

This time it was not emotion unbottled, out of control. It was Kalon; he allowed himself to lower his barriers and let the woman in. She saw him at his most human, unshackled and grieving. In the short time he'd known the Stealer, outside of his conditioned response and demonic guest, the Inquisitor had come to count the boy as a new friend.

He hadn't even been given time to get to know him beyond their working relationship.

That hurt.

Silver saw the man behind the human machine, and she melted close to him. "I know you are in pain, Kalon, but now is not the time to lose focus. Your emotional control is what we need, otherwise one mistake may doom us both. I would hate for that to happen. Spry gave more than anyone should to bring us here, so let us honor that action and make him proud."

Kalon heard her. He focused, and all the fear, all the uncertainty, and all the pain melted as he once more relied on his lessons from Winter.

Breathe, Kalon. Slow your heart, let your head control it. Winter's words came back to him. The woman had been a rock in his time at the Imper Vatica—her teaching had honed his mind to its current razor edge.

He held the kelanari woman for a moment longer, then let her go and took a breath to center himself. "One day we'll embrace when we're not in the middle of some kind of hell," he quipped.

"Was that humor?" Silver teased.

"Dark humor, for a bleak time," Kalon replied and then moved quickly. He ducked down behind a stone wall, dragging the woman with him. She made a small "oof" noise and followed.

The wolf's amber gaze lit the sky of the dead like balefire.

Fathriir was hungry; the wolf was on the prowl, and Kalon was certain he was not going to be on the menu. A quick glance around the ruined streets told him they were in the shattered heart of Messania, the metropolis that they called the Holy City.

"We're home, not far from the Imper Vatica," he said and then shook his head. "Oh, the irony of such a place."

"What?" Silver whispered.

"Where better to hide the book than in the ruin of your enemy's greatest stronghold?"

"Oh, no way!"

"We're in the courtyard. I recognize the statuary and the structures, shattered as they are." The Inquisitor could remember every detail from when these buildings thronged with life.

"Sneaky, bloody Anshada."

"The mirror is now closed, I presume? We could leave the tome here." Kalon hunkered down to avoid Fathriir's vision. "It would be safe."

"Until another Spry comes along." Silver frowned. "I don't trust the key to be just one poor soul. Wen would know properly, but I don't think a mirror that powerful would be limited to a single key. Any Anshada child could do it."

Kalon came to a realization. His parents had been Anshada—or that's what he had been told. He didn't voice it. *I could be a key,* he thought, and that chilled him to the bone. He made his mind up: the safest course of action would be to pull the book from this realm and see it destroyed. Spry had brought them this far, and to do anything else would dishonor the lad's sacrifice.

"Come, I can get us past the wolf's watchful glare." Kalon took the woman's hand and began to pick his way through the rubble. He moved slowly, deliberately, and used the abundance of cover to avoid the black wolf's vision. Silver kept pace with him.

The monster mewled in the distance, so hungry.

What seemed like an eternity passed as the pair slipped through the ornamental gardens, ever closer to the central complex of the city, the Imper Vatica's heart, the Cardinal's stronghold. Small motes of dust flicked up as bored ghosts toyed with it. They sensed the living, and like wild dogs they howled off into the distance. Afraid.

Kalon found the hatch he was searching for. Letting go of Silver's hand, he pulled at the rusted square, and then with her help he pried it open and climbed down a bent ladder into the tunnel below.

"Secrets upon secrets." Silver smiled. "I'm glad you know them."

"I never forgot a single one, even as a child when I found myself in here for days on end," Kalon replied.

They moved through the old ways, the passages that Winter had once trod on the other side of the mirror, the ones that Kalon knew by heart. By some kind of miracle, they had survived Messania's fall mostly intact.

He led the woman he'd come to look upon as his equal through the dark and into the open corridors of a place that he once thought to be the most powerful upon the planet. It was a ruin now, broken, tattered, and shabby.

Time had not been kind to the grand halls that led to the Cardinal's chamber; time had been ruthless. It had torn down everything that Kalon knew, and he had to remind himself that he was at the end of all things, in the domain of the God of Death, the Shroud, just so he could keep his sanity.

"It must have been incredible once," Silver said as they crept through the shadow, past broken doors, and fallen statues.

"With luck, I will walk down here with you when we escape and return the book for destruction," Kalon said, steadfastly.

"I'll hold you to that." Silver didn't have time to grieve for Spry. Her mind was locked on this place, getting out, and getting back. Then she'd light candles and say the rites of the dead for the youth.

Finally, they found the chamber they were looking for.

The Cardinal's office.

"Do you really think they put it in here?" she asked.

"I am sure of it." Kalon nodded. "I can feel something beyond the door." It was true: he sensed power. It lurked like a spider just behind the cracked, red and gold ironwood.

Silver pushed one of the double doors aside. The other fell in with a crash. Inside, the room was ruined, all its glory faded. Terusa's skeleton sat in her chair, draped with the red and gold robes of her office, now also old and faded.

It was a miracle they had not rotted away—or perhaps there was something else at work here.

There she sat in her still intact chair. The dark, leather-bound tome in her hands flickered with a light both disturbing and mesmerizing.

"The book," Kalon breathed. "Spry, we found it."

"He would be happy he was able to get us here, I'm sure of that," Silver said. "He gave so much for people he barely even knew—but did he have a choice?"

"Do any of us?" Kalon mused from before the desk. He leaned over. "It's now or never."

Silver nodded. "Take it. Be careful, though." She leaned over his shoulder.

"I always am."

Famous last words—they could have been engraved on many a traveler's headstone. They were the catalyst of so many misadventures and demises. But not Kalon's; he was not destined to die here, as much as the Shroud wanted that to be true.

As the God of Death and his faithful wolf reached the door to the Cardinal's study, the Shroud stopped.

This was going to be interesting.

Kalon pulled the *Book of the Anshada* free, and in that moment, he understood why the book had been sealed away. Power touched every corner of his being, raw, untapped power bathed in the tinge of demon fire. The self-same blaze tore up from the book and gripped him like a vice. He shoved Silver back out of harm's way.

She was caught in the arms of the Shroud, who politely turned her around and set her aside. He put a chalk-white finger up under his hood, where a pair of glowing eyes sparked.

"Shhh," he spoke.

Fathriir whined.

"No, she's not for eating."

The wolf whined again.

Kalon's will met the Demon King's untapped, stolen power. Anyone else might have been destroyed—but Fate had orchestrated many things upon the path to winning her game, to getting her own champion.

Fate's Hand. His mother and father met and fell in love. Two wizards, one child. Marked by the blood in his veins. Fated, you might say.

It was not Spry who was a child of prophecy. In fact, there was no prophesy to be found.

Kalon was a child of Fate, literally.

That Fate-bound blood lit on fire. It pulled the energy from the book and devoured it, sucking it dry and leaving only a tome of useless words and scribbles behind. Just as the goddess had planned, all those years ago.

Only one other was privy to her secret, and he wore the cowl of death itself. The Shroud knew. He'd always known. This was the game his sister had played perfectly. He didn't care about being part of it, not really, because he always won the bigger game in the end.

All things come to an end—even gods.

"Well played, sister, well played," the Shroud whispered, nodding in the shadow of the office as he watched.

Silver looked on in concern. Fury and worry marched across her face in equal measure. "What do you know, God of Death?"

"Kalon will survive. The book would kill anyone else, but as Fate would have it, Silver...he's not the child of any ordinary parents." There was no discernible smile, or any sign of one.

"What do you mean?"

Kalon stood, bathed in the demonic fire as it tried to tear him asunder. But his blood fought it, and it was winning.

"He's Fate's child, lass. Fate's Hand. My sister's champion in the war against the demons. You should understand. I mean, Amari and all."

"What?" Silver blinked.

"Amari, your goddess. Demon hunter, you know. Or have you forgotten?" the Shroud chuckled thinly.

Silver looked from him, to Kalon, and back. "Amari."

"Fate likes to hedge her bets. It's why she wins. So, she made sure your order could fight demons, and Kalon's parents were wizards." The Shroud moved his hands as though he were pulling strings. "It's what we do. Mortals are so much fun to orchestrate."

"But free will?" Silver growled.

Fathriir did the same.

"We move the pieces on the board, but you do all the work. We just set up the game table."

"I hate this."

The face under the cowl regarded Silver with glowing eyes. "You always have, all of you. But it keeps us coming back for more. We were just like you once. We hated being pawns of the Old Gods, so we took power for ourselves. Now we do the same they did."

"I still don't understand."

"Kalon's mother and father were brought together by Fate, only Fate was the mother. Got it now?"

"He's a child of the gods?" Silver blinked and shook her head. "That's not possible."

"Oh, it is, if the goddess or being in question is mortal during that time. We can do that, but our power lingers. The children aren't as strong as, say, Fate or I, but it's there, dormant. Just needs a spark." The Shroud snapped his fingers with a flicker of light between them.

Kalon was oblivious to this. As he took the book's power, his Anshada blood coupled with the demonic energy and transformed it. The divine spark in his body prevented his death and gave him back his life from all those years before.

Fully.

Silver wanted to hold him, to soothe that pain. "Will it harm him?"

"No, he's won. He's turned that book into a candle flame rather than an inferno." The Shroud laughed softly; it sounded like old leaves against the wind. "Your Inquisitor is pretty impressive, and that's coming from a god."

"I don't care."

"You should."

"Why?"

"Well, I can get you gone from this place. But I need you to do me a favor, if you will." The Shroud leaned against the door. "I want someone from your world that should have been mine a while ago, but he avoided his doom by being a dirty, magic-using trickster."

Silver wrenched her gaze from the man she'd come to care for, even love, and fixed the god with the full fury of her eyes. "Who?"

"Drako Mallori," the Shroud whispered. "Kill him, let me collect the soul, and we're square."

Kalon gasped for breath and let the book fall to the floor. He collapsed and propped himself up on the chair. The skeleton of the Cardinal watched him, seeming to judge him.

"Deal," Silver replied and smiled thinly.

"I thought you might say yes."

"Good bet."

"I learned from my sister." The God of Death laughed. It rang hollow, as did most of his words.

Silver moved to the Inquisitor and knelt. She looked him in the eyes and waved her finger before his gaze. His eyes tracked her movement, and the pupils dilated. She breathed a sigh of relief.

"What happened?" Kalon asked. Seeing the Shroud, his jaw tightened. "You."

"Me." The Shroud nodded. "Guilty as charged, Kalon Rhadon. I guess that makes us related."

"What do you want?"

"Been there, done that, deal made. Drako Mallori for your escape from my realm." The God of Death snapped his fingers. "Silver said yes."

A dark smile tugged Kalon's lips at Mallori's name. He nodded. "I find that acceptable."

"Good, but immaterial—as you might have said once. The deal was made with Silver, not you." The Shroud's tone flirted with amusement.

Silver put her head on Kalon's shoulder. "Where to start? I thought I'd lost you. Then you defeated the book; you fought the Demon King's malice and won against it. Now the energy of the book is lesser. According to the Shroud, it can no longer serve Akas properly."

Again, that smile, which looked strange on the face of a man who was not used to such emotional reactions.

"I see. You can tell me later. I think I'd like to be gone from here, wouldn't you?" The Inquisitor allowed himself to be helped to his feet, holding onto Silver. She supported him under his arm, tucked it around her neck, and hauled him up.

"I really would," she replied.

"I want you both gone! The living here in the land of the dead? My reputation would be in tatters if the other gods found out." The Shroud's glowing eyes narrowed under the cowl. "So, be on your way."

He picked up the book from the floor and threw it to Kalon, who caught it.

Then, with the arrogance common to many of the New Gods, the Shroud reached out his will and expunged both people from his realm with a single flick of his wrist. They vanished without pomp or circumstance.

Fathriir looked up with a whine.

"I know, they would have been tasty, but you can't fight Fate. My sister would see to it that you ended up neutered, old friend, and that would change the timbre of your bark."

Fathriir whined again, his ears flattened, and he growled.

"I thought that would change your mind."

The wolf sat back on his haunches, licked his lips, and looked up expectantly.

The Shroud chuckled ever-so softly. "Drako?"

Fathriir nodded just the once.

"Oh yeah, he's my treat to you, since I spoil you rotten."

Fathriir's tail swished back and forth.

The God of Death put his hand on the wolf's neck, and they vanished from sight, just as the Cardinal's head fell off her skeletal body.

CHAPTER 27

PULLING THE THREADS

Time ran differently in the land of the dead. It was mutable. Not even the Shroud could predict which part of his realm would shift chronologically. From hours and days to minutes and seconds, the future Hestonia could rocket forward or slow to a crawl.

Kalon and Silver's trip followed suit. A few hours to them was a full day to Wen and the others outside the Demon's Spine. The night came and went. Kaitlinel kept them supplied with what food she could hunt in the cold upper slopes. They took turns keeping watch, Andreas first, and then Wen. Lastly, the werewolf took over to allow the others to rest.

Each of them processed the news of Spry's death differently.

It angered Kaitlinel more than saddened her, the way that he had been torn from them.

Andreas hadn't known the youth for long. He'd liked him, and he hated the idea of sacrifice to progress. He just hoped Spry didn't die in vain, and that Kalon and Silver actually got that damn book.

Wen was perhaps the most affected, since he'd gotten to witness Spry's final moments through the light orb. The wizard was disturbed by what he'd seen, but too tired to do anything but collapse into a sleep that allowed him to get back his energy. He wandered the astral while he was sleeping, and on this plane of existence, connected by his soul cord, he kept vigil for any sign of his two missing companions. He knew morning would bring change, and once he was back to his full power, he could spirit the three of them to Moorhaven and Talon Mane's ship.

The night sky moved on.

Dawn crept carefully over the horizon, as if the sun sensed the change in the air. The first few tenuous fingers of light poked up to the east, and the sun slunk out from its slumber like a lazy cat. The moment the light touched Wen's cheek, his eyes snapped open, and he sat up.

"That's so much better!" he said, taking a deep breath. "For us, not for Spry, poor lad."

A pair of mumbles echoed from his side, where werewolf and gunslinger had curled together for warmth. The fire had died down to nothing but a few smoky embers.

"Is it morning already?" Andreas peered out from the armfuls of Kaitlinel in which he was wrapped.

"It is, and we need to be off." Wen kicked dust over the fire. "Breakfast on the *Mist Reaver* if we're lucky."

Kaitlinel's eyes opened, and she propped herself up on her elbow. "I heard breakfast, and now you have my full attention." She paused and glared at the maw of the mountain. "Fuck you, mirror! Fuck you!"

"Wen?" Andreas got to his feet, dusted his clothing off. "Do you think Kalon and Silver are ok?"

"Honestly?" Wen yawned and stretched his arms in the sun. "No idea, but if I were to bet on it—yes."

"Ok, good. So what's the plan?"

"Break that fucking mirror, avenge Spry, kill the Cardinal, avenge Spry, and slaughter anyone who stops us?" the werewolf growled hopefully.

"No, not yet—or at least not until we have the full knowledge of what the hell happened." Wen shook his head. "To do that, we need to get back to Talon's ship. He'll want to know what's transpired." He paused for a moment. "Especially to Silver."

"What are we waiting for then?" The werewolf stood, shaking out her hair and snarling softly. "I hate mornings."

Wen ignored this outburst. He focused his mind on the far-off place he knew so well. He pictured the land, the walls, every single detail. Then, with a slow breath, he stepped outside of himself. Once more in the astral, the wizard traversed the land back to Moorhaven—or rather, he used a single thought to bring it to him.

Movement on the astral plane did not obey the laws of reality. Why should it?

Once he'd arrived at the chosen spot, he began to connect with the threads of magic and weave the Tapestry from there. He created a circle of magic energy at the arrival point on the astral and then wove the real-world lines around it.

Meanwhile, back at the mountain, Kaitlinel and Andreas watched the wizard at work.

"Creepy," she said. "He' s all stiff and glassy eyed."

"Magic," Andreas offered with a snort. "Not the little stuff either."

"What do you think he's doing?"

"I'm working," Wen said and opened his eyes, back in his body and ready for part two of his casting. "I have woven an arrival circle; now I need to do the departure." He pulled the threads at the camp together, weaving the same kind of spell he'd constructed on the astral. "Then I connect the two, and the real magic happens."

"Right…" the pair said in near unison.

The wizard did just that, and in seconds the air was alight with the corralled forces of magic, a shimmering disc that showed them their point of arrival.

"Portals like this burn out fast, so step lively now," Wen directed.

That was all it took for the werewolf and the investigator to run through. Wen walked after them, took the thread that held the whole thing in place, and pulled on it casually. The door closed behind him as the three of them stood blinking in the bright sun outside of Moorhaven.

The golden, bird-shaped ship of Talon Mane wasn't too far off. They could see it reflecting the light of the day as it sat there proudly.

Without another word, they ran in the direction of Talon's vessel, hoping the captain was in a good mood.

He usually was.

Akas sensed he was close to the endgame; the book would soon be in the Cardinal's grasp, and all he had to do then was divert that energy into his own. He'd burn her out, emerge reborn, and lay waste to the damn church and city once and for all.

His confidence grew as he listened to the Cardinal's plan for the book. Honestly, he was proud of Terusa; it would be a shame to end her. He still thought about a possible alliance, but she was mortal and he was a demon—and once a god.

"The One-God informs me that the thing I desire will be in my reach sooner than I thought," Terusa informed Drako Mallori as he sat with her in the chamber. "I have written your pardon, and all will be well."

"Kalon won't like it." Drako smiled thinly. "But who cares what he thinks? He'll go back to doing his job, and you'll have everything."

"Yes."

"Be wary, though: I don't think he'll capitulate as easily as you think. He's stubborn. You made him so. His lack of emotion is a detriment. That cold logic has one outcome out of a series that can be manipulated if you have an ounce of feeling," Drako warned, his tones soft, but he flirted with insubordination.

"I can control him."

"You can?"

"Don't think for a moment I cannot bring Kalon to his knees if I have to," the Cardinal said, and her lips curved into a smile.

"That's good, then, but why the blindfold?"

"I told you already, but I will repeat myself. It's a focus, and it allows me to more easily bend the book to my will," she lied. "It also adds to the mystique. I can see perfectly with it."

It also covered her mark, Akas's whirling eyes.

"All's good, then. Just got to wait and see."

Akas smiled at the back of her mind—or at least it was some kind of smile. Drako was right; Akas liked him, the murderous little shit. He could do things with that one.

Now that was an idea. Leave Terusa's body, possess Drako, and go on a murder spree with his hands. They looked very skilled at robbing people of their lives.

Tempting.

Winter stopped for a moment on her way to speak to Imani. She felt a sudden pull at her soul as a great power lashed through the psychic planes and something tore reality into splinters. She leaned on the wall and waved off a nervous acolyte passing nearby.

She sensed the force in the outer courtyard of the Cardinal's ornamental garden.

Then, with a sigh, she felt a familiar mind once more in the Imper Vatica.

She took off at a run.

The Seeker positively flew into the garden to see the figure of Kalon Rhadon and a kelanari woman next to him. From the brief description she'd been told via her eyes and ears in the world, this was Talon Mane's first mate, Lady Danae Silvercrest, once an Amari Sister of the ancient order.

A good ally, Winter concluded.

The dust of an old, dead world covered Kalon's coat, his hair unkempt and his expression grim. He held in his right hand a dark book—*that* book. But it did not seethe with power as she'd expected it to.

The Cardinal's guard moved as one to intercept this sudden intrusion. Winter shook her head and waved them off.

"Guards, you're dismissed! Kalon, welcome back. An unorthodox return, but a very welcome one indeed," her voice rang out, drawing the Inquisitor's attention.

It also caught the shadow of another, the rotund Arch-Inquisitor Roland, who had been crossing the garden to the west wing when he caught sight of a ripple in the air and heard Winter's voice.

He watched.

Kalon turned a half-step and offered the Seeker a bow. Silver bowed too and looked around her. So this was the Imper Vatica as it should have been; she'd only seen the interior of the hangar bay and hadn't been privy to any other parts of the place when she'd stepped off the *Mist Reaver* a few days before.

"I wish to speak to the Cardinal," Kalon said, turning his wrist out to present the book. "I have what she desired."

Winter caught a flicker in the man's eyes. Something had changed; something in him had shifted. She couldn't help herself, so she focused her mind and found a part of the man missing—a part she'd always suspected was there without his knowledge.

"Who is this?"

"Silver," Kalon said with a smile. "She helped me take the book."

"Spry?" Winter quirked a brow.

"Dead, I'm sorry to say," Silver replied, her eyes turning to Kalon.

"Oh," the Seeker frowned. "Terrible news, but you can tell me later. For now, that book needs to be dealt with."

Roland heard the words, and his heart raced. Was it that book? he wondered. Had Kalon gotten sent to find the Anshada book Terusa had babbled about during their trysts?

"I agree, and there is a lot to speak on," Kalon said with a nod.

"Silver will not be allowed to enter, but I am sure she understands the protocol of the situation." Winter looked at the kelanari woman. They mirrored each other in many ways, barring the ears. "Don't you?"

Silver smiled thinly and replied with a nod, then she warmed a little and added, "I do, I understand. Perhaps you can keep me company, er...?"

"Seeker Winter."

"Seeker Winter." Silver bowed and smiled. "A pleasure."

Winter nodded, partially relieved that Kalon had found someone to help him who was Amari. Her mind eased a little. "Follow me, then." She also noted, but only to herself, that the man had smiled. Something had definitely changed, and her mental probing couldn't reveal what–yet.

Imani would have to wait, but that was fine. Kalon would want to give the book to Terusa, and as much as Winter didn't want her to have it, she felt this was the only and right course of action—again the Seeker's psychic powers were a blessing and a curse. She saw the litany of actions and reactions; the correct course had the most risk. By giving the book to the Cardinal, Kalon would be set on a path that changed the Church of Progression. Her visions and dreams all pointed to this like a compass.

She stepped across the courtyard toward the corridors that would lead to the Cardinal's office.

Silver and Kalon followed silently.

The closer she got to the Cardinal's office, the stronger emanation of the dark thoughts became. Winter's mind flashed, a series of images where she observed Kalon being bundled into a cylinder and a fragmented series of flicker-frame shots of the *Ori* chasing down a bulky church merchant ship.

Portents of things to come. She needed to act soon.

Winter paused not far from the Cardinal's office, and smiled before she continued her stride. "Kalon, you go on ahead. I will take Lady Danae—Silver—to the antechamber. Come find us when you're done."

Fate's Hand stopped in his tracks. He considered, concluding that he had to follow protocol and be better than the Cardinal. He needed to remain calm, collected, and prepare himself for whatever awaited him in Terusa's office.

He did not wish to cause a ruckus in the church, as much as his anger wanted to. He knew that there were many loyal to Terusa, and they would come to her aid if he appeared to oppose her. Best to play along and get what he wanted carefully. "I will see you soon, Winter, Silver. Be wary, though." With those words he strode toward the Cardinal's office.

When he reached it, he straightened his shoulders and stepped quickly to the door. He had questions and wanted answers.

"Come. Let us chat a while, Amari Sister." Winter used Silver's title and inclined her head. "What rank are you?"

"How do you know what I am?"

"Your name, and the tattoos I can just see on your skin." The Seeker chuckled a little.

"I am the Ninth Sister, or I was." Silver said with a tinge of regret.

"Impressive."

Winter took Silver to a private room, one of the nearest antechambers to the Cardinal's wing. There she sat down and invited the kelanari to do the same.

"Stay alert," Winter warned the other woman. "I saw Kalon trapped and the Cardinal with the book. I saw in her eyes the Demon King's own." The Seeker put her cards on the table. "I want to help, and I am doing my best to ensure that things fall into place. It's a dangerous game of cat and mouse."

Silver looked around and nodded. "I thought so. Kalon has spoken kindly of you."

Winter sighed. "He is my best student, and I have no idea of the lengths to which the Cardinal went to make him so."

"Too far." Silver frowned darkly. "What she did, or what the church did, was terrible."

"Go on?"

"An emotion eater, a demon in his soul, sucked his love, compassion, as well as all other emotions from him," Silver said bluntly.

"In Amari's name..." Winter's eyes widened. "I had no idea of the full extent of this."

"Yes, it was pretty well hidden," Silver replied. "Not to an Amari, though, so I freed him from the creature."

"Poor Kalon." Winter shook her head softly, her earrings tinkling with crystal vibrations. "He must be a whirl of emotion."

"He is. I've been trying to help him understand."

"Thank you. I almost feel like his mother." The Seeker laughed a little. "Now, we need to discuss what to do next."

"We do."

"I was going to speak to Imani, a captain of a ship that could help us. My plan was to go to Wyrden, to regroup there and gather allies to fight this force that lurks in the heart of the church. Now that Kalon is back, though, things have changed."

"Go on?"

"Kalon is in danger here, and we can't do much while he's in the church. I saw a vision, and I think I know what needs to be done. But can you wait to do it?" Winter fixed Silver with a long look.

"I care for him, but if it means a chance to prevent a dark outcome, I will bide my time." Silver bit down on more words.

"Good. I promise you, we will save him."

"What's to happen?"

"I only saw flashes, but I can't delay. I need to get Imani with us before we can move to save our Kalon."

Silver nodded, worried about what would happen to the Inquisitor. "You best go, then; I will remain here until the time is right."

The Seeker rose from her chair, offered another bow and a half-smile, then moved quickly in the direction of the door.

Silver did as she was asked; she waited. After all, she had a quarry here.

Drako Mallori. Only he didn't know it.

Kalon knocked on the door and then waited, book transferred to his coat. There was a commotion inside that sounded as though someone scrambled to move very quickly, and a door slammed.

"Come in." Terusa sounded irked, as if disturbed from a secret meeting.

Fate's Hand made his way into the room with a poker face. He hid his emotions and portrayed himself as he once was: cold, logical, and her right hand.

Akas-One-God saw through her eyes, and he salivated at the sight of the man. He couldn't see the book, but he could feel its eldritch power. It was so tempting to reach through the Cardinal and take it all.

No, he had to be patient. It would tip his hand too soon, and he needed to time this perfectly. There would be a moment where he could leverage the situation and claim a pair of souls for his own rather than just one.

"Fate's Hand." Cardinal Terusa wore her casual attire, and she blinked. "No one told me you had returned; no ships have come in."

"A guest and I came back with the aid of the Shroud," Kalon

explained. As much as he wanted answers, he was determined to trip the Cardinal in her web of lies. He needed to grant her a wealth of confidence that he was still that lapdog of the church—of her especially.

"Who is this guest?"

"Silver, the First Mate of the *Mist Reaver*. She was helpful in obtaining that which you wanted."

"Oh? Is she here right now?"

"No. I believe she is in the nearest antechamber to the office." Again, Kalon told the truth.

"The others?"

"We were split up when I was focused on retrieving the book," Kalon replied. He remained by the door, closing it carefully. "Spry was the key. His life opened a door to the land of the Shroud, and eventually we took the book from the God of Death." He delivered this news deadpan, factually.

"Fascinating." Terusa's eyes roved across the man—where was the tome? "Do you have the book now? I presume you do."

"Yes."

"Did you touch it?"

"I had to."

The Cardinal's smile faded a little. Akas knew the rules of the book, and through her, he worried. Had the man stolen the power of the book? He needed to see. He needed to hasten this meeting to the conclusion.

"I see, I see." Terusa kept control for now. "May I have it?"

Kalon nodded. He produced the tome and judged the Cardinal's expression. It was akin to that of Kaitlinel when she saw Andreas: want, lust, need.

He put it down on her desk, red fire flickering around his fingers.

The Cardinal gingerly picked up the book, and she felt nothing. Akas sensed only the tiniest candle-flame of power from it as the woman looked it over. "Is it damaged?"

"The Shroud observed that my contact with the tome may have done something, yes." Kalon wanted to smile, but he kept his expression flat.

Terusa moved catlike around the desk. She laid a hand on Kalon's arm and felt for the power. It was there, in him. This did not please the woman nor the Demon King bound to her. Terusa's connection to Fate's Hand bridged a gap, but it did not have the effect the Demon King expected.

Terusa became aware of the truth of the being in her body. The thing was also wrapped around her soul, just like the demon-eel on Kalon's. She was horrified, and she focused her will to mount a defense. With the aid of the energy from the man before her, she drew on power that she had never tasted until now.

Kalon did not see what happened next; the battle transpired in the astral plane. The Cardinal and the Demon King faced off across the space between him and her soul. Her anger fueled her psyche, and her desire to taste more of this untapped power—this Anshada energy—became an addiction. Kalon was akin to a drug in this regard.

She finally understood what the wizards of old, the Old Blood sorcerers, felt when they cast magic.

She wanted it, and to get it, she wanted the Demon King gone. How dare he!

She was no plaything of demons; she was the Cardinal, Terusa Ekarta, of the bloodline of Ezian Ekarta, the First Inquisitor. Akas the Bloodless was nothing compared to her!

Now she gathered her mental might, honed by Winter's teaching. She borrowed liberally from her new connection with Fate's Hand, creating psychic armor and a sword of piercing psychic energy. Akas did the same, clad now in the darkness of his power.

Only it was nothing compared to the Cardinal and Kalon aligned — Kalon a pawn once more within her grasp.

The battle in raged for what felt like hours, but in reality, it was over in under one minute.

Akas flew at Terusa with all his final power, and the Cardinal used her knowledge of the sword gained at Kalon's hands. She thrust that psychic blade into the Demon King's dark essence, and it lit like wild fire.

In the real world, Kalon's body jolted, his eyes went wide, and he convulsed as Terusa held on. She used this energy, pulled from it, and cast Akas the Bloodless back into his own realm.

He flew from her soul like an arrow shot from a bow, careening across the planes. His demonic presence was hurled back through the mirror in his palace, to slam back into his frail old form.

"Cardinal?" Kalon said through harsh breaths. "What...?"

"Sleep, Kalon." Terusa caught his body as it folded like cloth and set him in a chair. "You have done well, my enforcer. Not the outcome I expected, but I will rectify this to suit me even if you do not survive." She was serious; she meant those words. Kalon's life meant nothing compared to the power of the book and what it would allow her to do.

From the shadows, Mallori watched, terrified. Yet also, impressed.

Akas arrived back in the demon realm with a snap, his old man's body cast from the mirror and hurled across the room. His skin smoked, and every bone in his body was broken, almost turned to dust by the backlash of energy.

Jaziel watched from her observation point just at the edge of the throne. She smiled and shook her head. "Oh my Lord," she soothed.

"Fucking help me."

"No." She walked over to the writhing body and put her foot on the old man's chest. "I've had enough of your abuse, your typical male force. You think you can control us, control our bodies, control our minds. Not any longer. I've been waiting for you to screw this up, and now you have."

She stamped down hard until she heard his breastbone crack. "You're weak, and I know just what to do with you."

She knelt, kissed the old man on the lips, and left nothing but ashes on the floor, a tiny tendril of demonic energy whispering past her and away into nothing. She ignored it.

"Demon King?" Jaziel spun around. "Demon Queen, my lord." Her laughter shook the very foundations of the Bloodless's palace. "It's time I took over. Did things my way and took what was his."

Jaziel grinned in what was once Akas's palace. She drew in the energy that made up the realm and focused her will quickly, her eyes fixed on the décor around her. "This utter hellhole has got to change into something more fitting."

She saw what she wanted in her mind's eye, and the architecture shifted easily to match it.

"So much better."

Akas's dour and torturous palace morphed around the demon woman. When she was done, it reflected the subtle and seductive nature of the creature who now owned it. Decked out in dark, luscious colors, with fittings and fixtures to match the most expensive mansions on Hestonia, it was part manor and part bordello.

And all Jaziel.

"Demon King." She snorted once more. "Just a title, all useless really. Now as a Demon Queen, as I should have been all along...I can do things. Gather an army again. Have fun. Toy with mortals... and I think I know where to start."

She smiled—it wasn't pleasant—but it might just be fun.

CHAPTER 28

A CAGE OF SOULS

N ot even the gods, as powerful as they were, could predict the events that transpired as the book once more made its way into the world: Akas's demise, Jaziel's ascension to the throne, and Kalon's betrayal at the hands of the woman who made him who he was.

Or had she? Terusa was only the direction that Kalon had followed; the true crafters of the man he had become were Silver and the others he had encountered in his time beyond the Imper Vatica.

Verity, Reva Flynn, Kaitlinel, Andreas, and Spry.

Yet Kalon's life hung by a thread, his soul in peril, not from demons or demonic force, but from the very woman he had sworn to serve: Cardinal Terusa, who at that glorious moment felt very much like she had just been given a second birthday. If she celebrated such things. Kalon had returned, he had the book, and he had drawn out the power of the tome. His Anshada blood had reacted to the dark magical force and trapped it. Now all she needed to do was find a way to get that power for herself.

Harness it.

Use it.

Kalon's released energy had also made her wise to the lurking Akas and the lie of the One-God of the Infinite. She didn't care, though;

the church had consolidated its power on the lies Akas had told her. He'd served a hidden purpose in her rise, and honestly, for all his manipulation—in the end he had been thrown out like so much trash. She would keep to the ruse of the One-God and use it to further spread her might.

Someone knocked on the door to her chamber. Drako emerged from the other room at the same time and immediately began to retreat.

"Stay," Terusa commanded and looked to the door. "I have need of you."

Mallori felt the power in her command, and he obeyed. He stood by her right hand as she said sharply. "Come in, don't stand there lurking."

Arch-Inquisitor Roland stepped smartly through, closed the door, and turned round to see the tableaux before him. "What happened?" he asked, all mock concern.

"Oh, don't fake your worry, Archie Roland." Mallori snorted softly. "We both know you can't stand that man."

Roland looked at the Cardinal, then back at Mallori. "So, you're not dead then?"

"Pardoned, by my lovely Cardinal."

Roland fumed inwardly: *Your lovely, you little...*

"What happened was that Kalon could not control the power he so unwittingly stole when he foolishly touched the book without proper precaution." Terusa smiled sadly at the man. "He could have gone about his life, but now, I need to find some way to wrestle the book's energy from his soul."

Roland put his finger up as if he were at school. "I might have a way you can do that."

Tersusa took off her blindfold, her eyes back to normal, gleaming with an inner fire. "Speak." Then she furrowed her brow. "Wait, one moment. Drako, my faithful servant?"

"Yes, my Cardinal?" Drako Mallori sneered at Roland as he was addressed so.

"Go to the antechamber closest to my office. You'll find a kelanari woman there, Silver. Lead her through the secret ways to the depths, then kill her. Dump the body over the rail so she's never found. She is an Amari Sister, according to my information. She could be a problem in the future, and I want that problem dealt with now."

Mallori grinned from ear to ear. "Whatever you say, Terusa. I'll do it quickly and dump her into the volcano mouth, right from the lower walk. She won't know what's hit her."

"Be careful. She's dangerous," the Cardinal warned.

"Not my first assassination. Don't worry."

"Go."

He bowed to her, ignored Roland, and left by a secret path in the back of the chamber. Terusa heard the hidden door click softly.

With Drako gone, the woman in red and gold turned her gaze on Roland. She opened her robe a little and shook her hair loose. "How can I persuade you to tell me what I can do with Kalon?"

"No need," Roland grinned wickedly. "He is someone I cannot abide; I will happily tell you all you want to know about our little secret project. It was to be a surprise, something I had Daroni cook up with his assistant to allow us to extract power from defeated demonic beings."

The Cardinal's eyes shone softly. "Continue?"

"Soulcage, a way to rip a demon's soul from its form and store it for later use. Like a power core," Roland boasted. "The prototype hasn't been tested, since we were going to get Kalon to trap us a demon. However, it sounds like he has been snared by demonic energy, and for his own safety—and ours—we should transfer him to Skyborne Penitentiary and test out this new equipment soon."

Terusa paced as Roland outlined the plan. She stopped by him, kissed him softly, and nodded. "Kalon could wake, and with the power of that book at his command, he could stop us."

"No, see, there's another part to this: a new tech-magis, one that works even on our anti-magic equations. We found a chink in our own armor. It's a pod, a cylinder—you put a demon in there and it cannot escape. It can't wake. Put a man in there and he'll sleep without dreams for eternity."

The Cardinal laid her arms about the man's shoulders. "I will summon my guard, and they will help you take Kalon to this cylinder.

Put him in, put him on a ship to Skyborne, and return to me when all is done."

Arch-Inquisitor Roland grinned again and nodded. "Yes, yes, and we can finally be free of that abomination once and for all."

"We can."

Terusa drifted away from him and called for two of her red-and-gold-armored guards. It wasn't long before they manhandled Kalon out of her office, Roland strutting alongside like a cross between a peacock and a hog.

Alone at last, Terusa let her smile fade and narrowed her eyes. She had been lied to by the One-God and manipulated by Akas the Bloodless. First she'd use the book to consolidate her power; she would bring Hestonia to heel one way or another. No longer the plaything of gods and demons, it would be her way or nothing.

Magic first, demons second, and burn all those who stood against her.

If you allied with the Church of Progression, she would love you, mage or no. If you stood apart from it, she would hunt you down and make you suffer.

She did not need Fate's Hand, only her own.

Not even Wen could sense Kalon in the depths of the Imper Vatica, and he certainly didn't see the man being dragged down through secret tunnels into the artificer's secret lab at the back of his workshop and manufacturing complex. Arch-Inquisitor Roland led the way with a wicked smile.

He was not the only one in those tunnels. Drako Mallori, as good as his word, had found Silver and told her that Kalon was waiting for her at the main hangar. He was a good liar, and Silver went along with it because she had a task. It was as if Drako was offering himself on a platter by taking her through the dark tunnels to the very bottom of Messania where the wind threatened to pull both of them off into the hungry lava below.

Mallori put her out in front. The assassin liked to do things like this. He kept his distance, though, and prepared a small spell with his free hand: lines of force, lines of motion, and lines that would allow him to dart forward like a striking cobra and stick his dagger in her flesh.

Silver was an Amari Sister. She didn't trust the assassin one bit, and unknown to him—or most—the Amari had a few tricks of their own. They, however, did not use the Warp or the Weft. Sorcery was not their forte.

As they moved on over the long walkway which led to the underside of the city, toward the hangar, the assassin tensed and prepared to pull the thread that would cast the spell.

Silver had said nothing. Her body almost moved automatically. Her reason? She stood behind the man, in her astral body. The Amari fought demons both on the physical and astral plane. They could destroy both at once, and they were like a scalpel compared to a mallet.

Mallori felt the thread in his hand drop, and he moved. Only the knife didn't obey him—it fell from his fingers.

What?

He looked down and saw a strange thing transpire. He could see his hands, but above them were another pair. White tinged with red, they glowed with an inner light, dimly. Then he felt pulled, and when he turned, he found himself staring at a silver-white, fire-rimmed ghost with blazing eyes.

Silver's astral form was terrifying and beautiful, like a demented angelic being from the old stories. She stood balanced in the other world as though it belonged to her.

He tried to speak, but all his words were mumbled, slurred, his light wan and pale.

She burned like the core of the planet.

He wasn't able to control himself; she had pulled his astral body out of the physical and caught it by his cord. He saw his own body on the floor, lying as if waxen, stiff and asleep.

The Amari Sister smiled and flicked out a sword made of white fire. With a single snap of her wrist, she severed that which bound him to his body and caught the other end, the one that tethered him to his vessel.

Drako didn't understand.

The psychic wind howled, the howl wavering into the mournful cry of a wolf on the hunt.

The Shroud stepped into the astral as if it were child's play, followed by the hungry Fathriir. Silver's task done, he smiled at her. It barely showed under the cowl.

Death needed no words, nor did the kelanari woman. She let the end of the cord go and stepped back from the God of Death and his wolf.

The Shroud nodded, satisfied.

Drako Mallori's spirit tried to scream as the wolf pounced. Silver walked on in the real world, her astral form slipping back into her body as if it were a glove.

Behind her, Drako Mallori's body rocked once and then became still, his eyes dead.

The giant engines of the city snarled with force, and at the edge of the woman's hearing she heard a second howl.

She opened the door, stepped inside, and made her way to the hangar.

Time moved swiftly, and as the rest of Hestonia continued, many of the people who played a part in Kalon's tale still moved to one single place: Wyrden. Kalon, on the other hand, had been brought into the secret place of Daroni's workshop.

Vincent Daroni was not there. He had left to seek a way to leave the church in secret. But Sara was, and the woman in the magnificent chair had been tinkering when she heard the door to the workshop open and observed Arch-Inquisitor Roland and the two Cardinal's Guard step in.

They had a prisoner.

To her horror, it was Kalon. Where were they taking him?

She tapped a button on the chair, dropped it into hover mode, and snatched a slim, clockwork-style box off the table. With a muffled sneeze from the dust, she took off into the high dark of the cavernous workshop and watched.

The three men took Kalon to the back of the lab. Roland pulled a sheet off the cylinder waiting there.

Sara took a soft breath, knowing now what was going on. She angled the contraption in her chair and then pressed the small lever. The device began to rotate a small circle of crystal, and slowly, it recorded everything that happened via the lens at the front.

Roland was not going to get away with this.

"You two, put him in. We need this to work. I have watched Daroni fiddle with the machine enough to know how to operate it," the man ordered with a sneer. "The Cardinal wants him alive and shipped to Skyborne as soon as possible. Don't fuck this up."

The unconscious, dreamless Kalon was dumped into the chamber and sealed inside.

"I hope this works. If the energy inside is as powerful as she says, it'll take our Soulcage to remove it. If it kills him, she doesn't care. She only needs him alive long enough to make the trip to Skyborne Penitentiary."

Sara listened intently, her face darkening. She was furious, but she knew better than to blow her shot at capturing evidence for others to witness.

Roland closed the circuits, manipulated the controls, and carefully set wheels, dials, and valves. The cylinder pulsed and throbbed, the energy around it gleaming as the crystals and contraptions came to life.

The men watched with impassive expressions, but it was obvious they were disturbed by what they saw.

After a moment Roland checked the dials, sniffed, and grinned. "It works. He's not dead. Perfect! Let's go, let's go! Cardinal wants this done quick."

The first guard asked, "What ship?"

Come on, say it. Sara looked at Roland and willed the man to spill the destination.

"The merchant hangar, Captain Collins's ship, the *Aurus Machina*," the Arch-Inquisitor said with a chuckle. "Slow but dependable, with enough defenses to deter sky pirates—and very inconspicuous. Tell him to set course for Skyborne and explain it's on the Cardinal's orders. He knows better than to pry."

The man nodded and looked at his compatriot. "You go and inform the captain, and I will see to securing tech-magis means of shifting this bottle."

The second returned that nod and left wordlessly.

Satisfied things were panning out and trusting of the competence of the Cardinal's Guard, Arch Inquisitor Roland smiled triumphantly. "Grand! I will inform the Cardinal all is well and handled. Good day."

He turned on his heel and bumbled out, leaving the first man in the room with Sara.

She turned off the recorder, stored it in her chair, and swiftly made her exit from the workshop's upper floor to the back chambers of Daroni's lab. She needed to find someone who she knew she could trust, like Winter, and quickly. If she moved fast enough, thanks to her flying chair, she could probably prevent a tragic event from happening.

Hang on, Kalon, she thought, *I've got you!*

Wen and the others had bolted across the ground and arrived near-breathless at Talon's grand ship. As luck would have it, or perhaps fate, they found the man himself at the bottom of the ramp, drinking an iced tea and casting his gaze in the direction of Moorhaven.

He looked extremely pleased to see Kaitlinel and Andreas, and then concerned when he saw that the others were missing.

"Who's this?" he asked with a tip of his hat when Wen appeared. "Handsome and lovely looking fella."

When the wizard got closer, he took a deep breath and answered. "Wen."

Kaitlinel and the gunslinger skidded to a halt next to him.

"Oh, hello, Wen. I'm Captain Talon Mane."

"I know."

"You do?"

"Yep, ship, hat, ears, handsome." Wen took more breaths. "Problem."

"Problem?"

Blunt as ever, Kaitlinel took over. "Silver and Kalon are missing, Spry is dead, and fuck-knows what's going on."

Talon frowned but remained pragmatic as always. "Well, Kalon and Silver are capable. I am terribly sorry about Spry. Seemed a nice lad, if a bit out of his depth. Plan B, then."

"Plan B?" Andreas asked and put his hands on his knees. "Oof, I'm so out of shape."

"In the event that we can't meet up, Silver knows that I will take the *Mist Reaver* and chart a course to our favorite home away from home: Wyrden." The kelanari smiled gently. "She'll keep Kalon safe, and I am sure he'll enjoy her company, from what I've been told about his change of mind."

"Oh, I reckon so," Kaitlinel chuckled lewdly. "So, to Wyrden then?"

"Yes, and don't spare the horses!" Talon tipped the last of his cup out, turned, and sprinted up the ramp.

"There are horses?" The werewolf's grin was wide, hungry.

"Figure of speech," the kelanari quipped as he vanished inside. "Come on!"

"Is he always like this?" Wen asked with a cough. "So...energetic?"

"Yeah, seems to be. We should get aboard, before he takes off without us." Andreas put his foot on the ramp.

The three boarded the *Mist Reaver*, and soon, the golden bird took flight, turned her back to the city, and roared across the sky in a plume of fire and smoke—ready to cross the barrier again and blaze her way to the City of Wyrden.

She was like a flash of gold against the coming storm.

Wyrden had become a focal point, by design or by accident. Then again, in history, it always had that kind of pull. There was a simple saying among the sky pirates: "All heavens lead to Wyrden."

Where it sat, there were no roads and only one sea.

It had drawn Maxis Kane and Vass Drae, Reva Flynn, and Verity, and soon it would bring many others to its free streets, far from the church's tight grip, their oppressive ways, and hatred of any magic not shackled to their will.

Wyrden was the core of self-expression, the focus of the power that defied demons, and the home of people who had not yet stepped on the board of Fate's game.

After Reva Flynn left Maxis and Vass to find her old friend Agatha Black, the Inquisitor and the Justicar sat in an open-air tavern garden to drink and ponder what on earth to do next.

Vass sipped her iced tea, with just a hint of spices, and looked across at her husband. Maxis was deep in thought, and he tapped his thumbs together idly around his own glass.

"A sovereign for your thoughts, my love?" she asked.

"Oh, just wondering where to go now. Winter put us here, but what do we do? Finding Verity will be like trying to get Kalon to laugh."

"Easier, I feel."

"Well, yes." Maxis grinned.

A slim woman with short hair approached their table. She laid down a clean napkin and freshened their water.

"Thank you." Maxis looked up, ever polite.

"Hello, Max." Verity looked down. Her other hand had a hidden knife, just under the sleeve of her waitress's blouse. "Vass, I think we need to talk. Meet me at the Old Copper Theatre in the Middle Ring, sundown, and please try not to think like the church for this one."

Vass stiffened but understood the other woman's caution. "No worry, Verity my dear. Winter sent us to find you. You are being hunted by Mallori; he's still very much alive and very much after you."

"We've got you, Ver," Maxis said with a whisper. "No need for the knife. We'll chat and tell you what's happened." He paused. "Ok?"

The assassin adjusted her hand, flicked the knife back in, and nodded. "I'll trust you for now, but don't make me regret it, Justicar."

"Promise," Maxis replied. "On our honor."

"Good enough." Verity smiled sweetly. "Enjoy, sir, miss." She walked off to attend to another table.

"Ok, so now we know what we're doing," the Justicar said with a cheeky grin. "Amazing, really. The needle came to us."

Vass took another sip. "Indeed."

All heavens, it seemed, did lead to Wyrden.

CHAPTER 29

SILVER ARROW

Tick tock went the grandest clock in the hall as Roland made his way back to Terusa. He did not yet know Mallori's fate, but he was about to discover it. As he took the longest path, he encountered a lifeless corpse being pecked by crows under the shadows of the holy city.

Roland shooed the birds away.

He stopped and looked down. Mallori, the church's best assassin, lay unmarked on the tenuous walkway. Roland blinked, experimentally kicked the body, poked him, and then slapped him hard across the face.

Only after that did Roland actually check for a pulse.

Dead?

D e a d?

D E A D?

He laughed. It wasn't uncommon for rivalry to spark at the church, but this was more than he'd ever hoped for. Obviously, Mallori had been killed, and honestly…Roland didn't care who was responsible. So, with a flick of his boot, he pushed the man's body to the edge of the walkway.

Just a bit more.

A little more.

He stopped to rifle through Mallori's pockets, taking the dead man's money and sundries.

One last push, and Drako Mallori's corpse went sailing off into the sky below, toward the lava that waited to devour it.

"Sorry, old boy," Arch-Inquisitor Roland rubbed his hands together. With a spring in his step and a little cheerful whistle, he carried on.

With Kalon imprisoned and Mallori dead, the Cardinal would be his alone—what a day!

Elsewhere, with the aid of tech-magis lifters and many hands, the guard bought Kalon's capsule to the merchant hangar. His compatriot had already been there, and he found Collins, the rough and ready sky captain, more than willing to prove his worth to the Cardinal.

It was easy. No papers to sign. The crew took over from there.

Collins was an umber-skinned man of dubious morals. He asked no questions of certain cargo. Not the human kind, especially since Roland often used him to shuttle prisoners to the destination he knew so well.

Skyborne: a lofty prison with little hope of escape, or parole.

A place where the Cardinal put her most villainous enemies.

He exchanged nods with the techs, allowing them to put the cylinder in the hold, secure it, and go about their business. He even let a ginger-haired woman remain aboard to monitor the occupant's state. It would do him no good if his passenger arrived dead. The first guard had made this abundantly clear when he chartered the *Aurus Machina*.

As for the ship, it was serviceable, not pretty by any means, but crewed with the kind of people who served a man like Collins. Lethal, dangerous, mercenary, and totally without mercy for anyone who wasn't part of the ship.

"All done, sir," he said to the guard and looked at the blocky hull of his ship, which resembled a box attached to other boxes, plated with armor and festooned with four big guns. Six massive aetheric engines poked out around the back in a circle and provided the motive force for the grey and gold vessel. A tarnished gold ship, for a tarnished soul.

He nodded to the Cardinal's man, boarded his ship, and in moments the hatch closed and the ramp pulled back. The *Aurus Machina* put out to sky and thundered away at speed across the heavens in the wrong direction.

All a ruse. He'd get out of sight, and range, then change course to the Cardinal's jail.

That should ensure no one followed him.

After several dead ends, Silver found her way onto the upper floor of the Imper Vatica, and with a few more false trails managed to locate the hangar deck where she'd first met the man who was at this moment—or so she thought—deep in his meeting with Cardinal Terusa.

She looked around. Kalon had not yet arrived, but she couldn't trust a word that Mallori had said.

Silver walked over to the edge of the dock and saw the trail of a bulky, six-engine merchant cruiser as it soared away from Messania. The angle put it on course to Sullavale. The vessel seemed somewhat familiar to her, but she couldn't place it.

A familiar face greeted the kelanari woman as she searched the hangar. Seeker Winter stood apart from a beautiful person, dressed in a sari-like uniform and sporting a scowl. Silver changed her direction and went directly over to catch the end of their conversation.

"I'm sorry, Winter, but what you're saying seems like it's flirting with heresy, let alone treason." Imani sighed and frowned. "Visions can be distorted, and if what you say is true, we know that demons can alter them."

Winter sighed as well, but Imani had a point. She hadn't thought of that.

Silver stopped a respectful distance away and let the pair talk.

Imani glanced at the ship, back to Winter, and then answered flatly. "No, I can't do it."

"I understand. What now?"

"I should arrest you."

"That would be awkward."

"Excuse me?" Silver said softly. "Hello, I'm Silver, First Mate of the *Mist Reaver*, and I'm looking for Kalon."

"Kalon?" Imani quirked a brow.

"Yes."

"You know him? Why are you here without your ship?"

Winter rolled her eyes; now was not the time. "Imani," she soothed, "Silver has been assisting us on a mission—the one Kalon was on for our Cardinal."

The captain of the *Ori* stopped, and their face took on a moment of "ah." Then they stiffened slightly. "I haven't seen him; didn't know he was back."

"It's a long story," Silver said and smiled a little.

"Winter!" Sara's voice sounded frantic as the young woman rolled her chair across the hangar deck, vaulting a few cables and at least one toolbox.

Winter looked in newcomer's direction. "Hello, Sara, what's the rush?"

Imani began to move off. "Excuse me, I have a ship to attend to."

"Wait!" Sara flicked her chair into hover mode and shot over the rest of the way. "I need to speak to all of you."

Silver pointed to herself. "Even me?"

"Who're you?"

"Silver. And you?"

"Sara."

"Pleased to meet you. I love the chair."

"Oh, thanks. I love your hair!"

"Sara, what is it?" Winter brought the woman back on track. "Captain Imani is a busy person, and so are we all."

"I know, but you need to see this." The inventor pushed a box into Winter's hands. "It's a recording box, one of Vincent's inventions. It concerns Kalon."

Imani stopped dead, half-turned, and then walked to peer over

Winter's shoulder. They were joined by Silver, who was curious the moment her friend's name was mentioned.

The four of them watched the image, perfectly captured, and heard the whole conversation. Imani could not believe what they heard, and saw, as the evidence pointed at the Cardinal sickened the captain to their stomach. They shook with anger.

"When was this?" Imani said sharply.

"About an hour or so ago?" Sara checked her chronometer; it wasn't one hundred percent accurate.

"Kalon in a tube, taken to Skyborne?" Imani said slowly.

Silver's face flushed with anger, fear, and frustration. "I knew we couldn't trust that woman," she snarled. "If she's harmed Kalon at all, then I'm going to end her like she tried to have done to me."

"Wait, what?" Winter, Sara, and Imani said at the same time.

"Drako Mallori came after me when he was sent to 'escort' me to the hangar to meet Kalon. He had to have been there on the Cardinal's orders." Silver growled softly. "He was alive."

"Was?" Imani repeated, still reeling from the images and sounds of Sara's recorder.

"He isn't any longer, and that was the Cardinal's order originally, so I did her a favor." Silver snorted.

"Good," Winter said softly. "One less thing to worry about. I never liked or trusted that man."

Imani nodded. "We have a ship name," the *Ori*'s captain offered, and their eyes drifted to the vessel that sat quietly on the deck. "I have a loyal crew, and we have the evidence."

Sara looked from one to the other. "We do: *Aurus Machina*."

"Oh fuck," Silver suddenly remembered where she'd seen that departing vessel from. "That's Collins's ship."

"Yes, it is." Imani nodded.

"It left recently, took to the sky when I came here. I saw her go." Silver's shoulders slumped a little.

The sound of a cane tapped on the metal deck, and the figure of a man they all knew wandered into view. He walked slowly, but surely, and he smiled under his wide hat.

"I heard it all as you talked," Vincent Daroni said, tapping his right ear with a finger. "Sara, good use of that box, excellent work. Kalon in that chamber, their first mistake."

"How?" Imani asked what they all thought.

"I don't like my things being stolen, so I make sure I can track them. I have the device that does so. All I need is a ship."

"So, what are we waiting for?" Imani turned to the *Ori*. "If we're going to commit treason, we should do it for one of our own."

"Change of heart?" Winter inclined her head.

"No time," the captain snapped, walking smartly to the ship. "Come on!"

Silver fell into step, Sara flitted after them on her chair, and Vincent followed, his cane tapping a staccato beat on the metal decking.

Soon, Imani took control of the ship. They logged that they were departing on a routine test flight, put Vincent Daroni down as the chief tester, and sent the request for launch.

"That should keep them off us for a bit."

Green light, test flight approved.

Once more the *Ori* took flight. This time, it was to pluck Kalon Rhadon from the hold of the *Aurus Machina* and dent the Cardinal's schemes.

From this moment on, Imani, their crew, Winter, and the two inventors would turn their back on the Cardinal and the church, chart their own course, and join the rest of the pieces on Fate's giant game board.

One man who never turned his back on the Cardinal—barring that one time she taught him what it felt like to be taken in a way he'd never experienced before and made him understand the power he held as a man during sex—was Arch-Inquisitor Roland, the most loyal of her servants. Or was he loyal to her power and body?

It didn't really matter; he got things done, and he served Terusa faithfully.

He knocked on the door to her office and heard her golden tones proclaim, "Enter."

Roland stepped in. He was greeted by a smile and Terusa in the full glow of victory.

"Is it done?" she whispered.

"Yes, all of it. Kalon is on route to Skyborne, and Drako Mallori has dealt with our other problem. In fact, he told me he was going to oversee Kalon's arrival at the prison personally, and not to contact him on the *Aurus Machina* due to the secret nature of that run," Roland lied. It really did come easily to him. What he'd said was technically true—except the Mallori bit.

Terusa walked over, draped her arms around his shoulders, and kissed him. "A reward for my faithful. Do you love me?"

"I do."

"Do you serve me?"

"Oh yes," he beamed at her with a bright smile. "In every way."

"Good," she replied and kissed him again. "You are my very faithful. You are my hand, my right hand now while Drako is away. I will need you to do my bidding."

He was weak for her. "I shall."

"I will ask you to do me many things, and of course, obedience is its own reward." She led him to the bedchamber. "Isn't that right?"

"Yes, yes, it is," he said gleefully.

She pulled him inside and closed the door with her foot.

Its own reward.

The *Aurus Machina* was not a fast ship, but she was fast enough, and left a trail of engine wake to follow if you had the right equipment. The *Ori* was a fast ship, a prototype enforcement vessel capable of using a shimmer cloak to hide from everyone. That cloak made her graceful shape match the clouds, and only a slight whisper against the sky gave the *Ori's* position away.

Unless you were trained to spot it, you'd have no clue.

No one on the *Machina* was trained in that regard.

Also, the captain had no idea that Vincent Daroni helped Imani navigate the vessel to where Kalon's chamber was located, deep in the hold.

His tracker pinged away, and the inventor called out headings while Sara worked to refine something on her chair. She was adjusting the weight-to-lift ratio and had been able to squeeze a lot more force out of the newer model.

It was tech-magis at its finest, and her pride and joy.

Silver perched on the bridge like a hawk. She was angry, but she collected herself. She needed all her wits and all her Amari training at hand to get the man she loved back.

Fuck it, she'd tear that ship apart to get him.

Winter stood next to her, resting her hand on the woman's shoulder, and said, "Silver, I have an idea. Why don't you use our communication facilities to contact Talon and set his mind at ease?"

"Oh shit, Talon! He'll be wondering where the hell I am."

"I thought so."

"Imani, may we get a contact to the *Mist Reaver* at this point in time?" Winter asked and pulled her hand back.

Imani turned from their station and nodded. "I can do that, but it'll have to be quick. We're almost on our quarry."

"I would like that, and I can be quick," Silver replied.

The communications panel lit up, and Silver moved to the controls. The device spun and formed a cloud of mist. It wasn't long before a familiar and much-relieved captain appeared in the image vapor before her eyes.

"Silver, you're alive!" Talon grinned widely. "Where are you?"

"Is that her?" Wen's voice, followed by a yell. "Hey, Silver, put Kalon on."

"They're probably busy fucking!" Kaitlinel yelled and stifled a laugh.

"Kalon has been captured by the church." Silver said. "Long story. We're going to get him back. I cannot talk for long, but we'll meet in Wyrden at the usual place, right?"

"Ok, won't press for details." Talon's face turned and he relayed the news. "I'll see you then."

The connection cut, and the mist vanished. Silver stepped back and turned her head to the others. "We will get him back."

"Yes, we will." Imani, who had been stand-offish before, nodded. "If I have to blast the guns off that thing to do it."

Sara looked up and shook her head. "That would probably damage the ship, and we don't want to ditch it in the ocean until Kalon's safe."

"Good point." Silver nodded. "What are you thinking?"

"Oh, I think you'll like this." Sara's eyes gleamed, and she popped out a small ball from inside the chair. "So, the *Aurus Machina's* guns are coil based. They use vast amounts of electrical energy to fire the same. This little beauty disrupts that, and it's a radial field, so it won't cause harm to the actual workings of the ship. It'll just limp-dick the weapons."

Imani and Winter chuckled, and Silver smiled, catlike. Daroni harumphed, then chuckled too. "Got them! One mile that way. Fly, my friends!"

Imani took the helm, and the *Ori* shot forth quietly, invisibly, on the hunt.

The *Ori* barreled down on the *Aurus Machina*, the sleek vessel like an arrow in the sky. In the bottom bay, where the ship's ramp was, two figures affixed masks to their faces.

"They're designed to make sure you can breathe at this height, and you don't get your lungs sucked dry," Sara said through hers, though it was connected to her wondrous chair.

"Ingenious." Silver fixed hers in place. "So, are you ready?"

"Not really, but Kalon is a good friend, and I kind of like you already." The young woman felt her heart race. "I'm scared, but he needs us."

"So am I." Silver winked.

Imani's voice echoed through the speaker in the bay. "It's time."

Then, with a sound like clockwork, the door to the *Ori* opened and the wind rushed over both Sara and Silver. Below them was the vast deck of the *Aurus Machina*, with its only weapons well within the range of the inventor's ace up her sleeve—or in her chair.

"If they fight, Sara, don't care who they are—put them down and do it hard," Silver said as she narrowed her gaze onto the ship.

"Ok."

Time seemed to stand still, then Silver took hold of the chair. Two small platforms swung out at the back, and the kelanari placed her feet upon them. Sara hit the controls and steadied herself.

"Now!"

They flew from the bay. The inventor matched the speed of the *Aurus Machina* perfectly; her chair could more than keep up with that old thing. Aether thrusters designed by her, built by her, and tweaked by her took their weight as the wondrous contraption flew the skies like a bird.

She couldn't help but smile beneath her breathing mask.

Silver did too. Her heart pounded, and her blood sang in her ears.

"Once I have Kalon," the kelanari woman communicated through the mask, "bring the *Ori* in and rake the deck. We'll get him back on board and then ditch the *Aurus* in the ocean to stop them in their flight."

"Understood," she heard Imani reply. "Fate be with you."

"Yeah, I think she might be."

Down went the chair; Sara put them onto the deck with a skid of anti-gravity engines. "Honey," she chuckled, "we're home!"

Captain Collins had no idea he'd been boarded until it was too late, because immediately after Sara's quip, she dropped the sphere and let it blast out. A flicker of energy burst from around her wheelchair and crackled with barely visible sparks. When it hit the *Aurus's* guns, however, they burst into flame, their circuitry and electrical conductors fried by the mix of technology and magic.

Silver sprinted away to the nearest hatch and met an emerging tech with the full force of her elbow. The human woman crumpled like paper and rolled to a stop down the stairs. Silver ignored her, sprinted on, and sought the lower hold.

CHAPTER 30

AURUS MACHINA

Klaxons sounded across the ship. Collins grabbed his cutlass and pistol with a scowl. "What the blazes? Are we under attack?"

"No idea, sir. The guns are offline. They're fried."

"How the fuck?"

"Again, sir, no clue. There was some kind of explosion on the upper deck."

"Did you think to send some people to GO see what the FUCK it was?"

"Doing it now, sir," the tawny-skinned crewman answered while punching buttons. Alarms sounded again.

"It has to be the cargo hold. Sky pirates maybe, or someone has friends." Collins growled. He headed out of the bridge and descended to the lower part of the ship. If they were after the cylinder, he'd wait for them to come to him.

Easy.

Meanwhile, as Silver made her way down, Sara flipped a few more switches on her chair. Right on cue, the doors burst open and several of *Aurus's* crewmen flooded out to engage the would-be sky pirate army.

They saw a young woman with a mask, in a wheelchair.

They stopped, approached slowly, and then inevitably someone started to laugh.

Sara smiled under the mask and opened fire; the shredders built into the chair's front spewed out shards of super-heated razor-sharp metal. The tech-magis system was a refinement of Sara's original fix to Kalon's guns all those years ago.

The shredders lived up to their name as the crew took hundreds of lethal shards to their knees and legs, as well as the upper torso and some to the head. Sara spun the chair to face each one, fury in her eyes. They had her friend, and she was going to prove she was a force to be reckoned with.

She wasn't wrong, either.

As the weapons cooled, there was a mewling mass of people on the upper deck who had lost all their fight—and unless tended to by a medic, they'd lose their lives as well.

It was ruthless, but so were they.

No mercy.

They'd have given her none.

Silver was careful as she moved into the depths of the ship, slipping unseen past many of the crew to conserve her energy. The kelanari's natural grace, athletic skill, and lithe form used the structure of the *Aurus*'s interior against everyone. Ships like this had a lot of empty space, they were full of platforms, handholds, and pipes.

A spiderweb of metal and rods went deeper. Silver was able to drop onto small rectangular plates, jump onto girders, and shimmy across beams. She took each movement without stopping, a form of free running that helped her get to her target.

She dropped straight down and caught the pipe that jutted out from a redundant steam overflow, flipping around it a few times and launching off again into the dark to land catlike on a lower gantry. She waited, ducked a moving giant cog wheel, and leapt again.

She repeated this, and before long, she had made it to the hold.

It appeared empty, all except a lone cylinder chained to the deck at the back.

Kalon!

"Uh-uh, girly," a voice cautioned as she stepped from the shadows.

"Collins," she spat. "Captain Edward Collins, slaver and merchant prince."

"I prefer the latter, compared to the former." He waved his pistol at her. "I can shoot quicker than you can move, girl."

Silver narrowed her eyes; she was older than he was by more years than he had seen of life. "I'd be flattered to think I'm girlish," she snorted. "But really, give me a chance and I'll open your throat."

"Where's Mane? That's what this is, right, a raid?"

"He's not here."

"You expect me to think you just grew wings and flew here by yourself?" Collins laughed and kept his gun on her.

Silver opened the comm channel in her mask and spoke again. "Having my friend in the hold of your ship was reason enough to come down here. Don't think you've got me at a disadvantage at all."

Silver's sharp ears picked up a sound beyond the others, not part of the *Aurus Machina*. She smiled, just a twitch. It could have been Sara; she hoped it was.

"I have the gun, and I have your friend. I am open to negotiation." Collins knew Talon was rich, and whoever this was to Silver, Collins would make the kelanari pay a lot for him. "What say we adjourn to my cabin and talk?"

"I'd rather talk here, if that's all the same."

"Ok." He nodded. "Not into me, I get that."

"I want the man who is in that chamber." Silver's eyes narrowed slightly. "I will gut you and your whole ship to get him back."

"Worth a lot, then?"

"More than you'd ever know; more than you could ever fathom."

"Pay a lot for him then, like I said?"

Another sound above them. Collins put it down to the rumblings of the ship, but Silver recognized the sound.

The Amari Sister gritted her teeth, but then saw Sara drop down out of the shadows, her chair quiet and deadly. It hovered out of the man's sight. "He's worth more to me than money, and I hope he knows it one day." Silver paused. "Now let him out, before I cut your throat where you stand."

Sara dropped farther down. Before the captain's crew could turn up again, she took a breath, hit another button, and yelled, "Hello! Excuse me, I'm looking for the idiot that runs this dog scow?"

Collins blinked, then turned around and fired at the young woman in the chair. It was a magnificently accurate headshot—which failed as it shattered on the tech-magis field protecting her, converting all the kinetic force to light and sound before it shorted out.

This was all the time Silver needed. She moved like a panther, striking quick and fast. Her knife drew a thin line across the captain's throat in seconds, and he choked on his own blood. "Fuck me," he managed to gurgle before he collapsed. "That was fast."

Sara landed by the kelanari woman and smiled. "I did ok, right?"

"You did more than ok; you're a natural partner. Your chair is wickedly impressive. Didn't expect that shield."

Sara beamed, then checked the panels on the cylinder. "Good, Kalon's all right, and the energy readings are stable. I can bring him out. It'll take a few minutes."

"Do it."

The young woman hovered up and hit all the right buttons, flicked the switches, and turned the wheels. Soon the crystals on the control panel lit up green.

"Now we wait."

During this time Silver poked around the hold. She found a chest that had been stuffed in the shadow. Payment to Collins, no doubt. When she opened it, she found Kalon's things inside: his coat, his guns, and all his tools.

"They took his things," she said to the inventor.

"Bastards," Sara growled. "We made him those guns!"

More time passed, and then some more. Ten agonizing minutes, all told. Then the seals on the chamber whispered, and the front slid open. As the stasis field dissipated, Kalon Rhadon opened his eyes. He saw Silver and Sara as he stepped from the cylinder.

He wore a face that showed anger, not all reined in by his mental training. His expression changed when he saw the two women—oddly, two women who mattered a lot to him.

"Silver," he said and stepped over to the kelanari woman. He put his arms around her and pressed his lips to her mask. Then he stepped back, looked at the hovering Sara, and smiled. "Sara, good to see you too."

"No kiss?" the inventor teased before shaking her head. "Kisses like that are for people who you know are special. Look, as tender as this is, we're on the *Aurus Machina*, and the crew are not happy. We killed a bunch of them, and Silver cut the captain's throat all so we could get you back."

The Amari Sister smiled at the kiss, though she wished it had happened with her mask off. "You'll need these," Silver said, drawing the Inquisitor's attention to the chest. "They took your coat and your weapons."

"Wise." The man nodded. "Give me a moment."

He put his coat back on and stowed his tools, but kept his guns out of their holsters. "Lead on," he said as he looked at them both. "Thank you."

"Save it for later." Sara winked.

The three of them left the hold, Kalon and Silver via the stairwell while Sara just soared into the air. She grinned down at the two people below her, determined they were going to pull this off.

"Captain Imani, we have Kalon," Silver spoke into her mask as they bounded up the stairs. The crew were already on them. "We've got company—come in hot."

"I only do hot," Imani chuckled into the comm. "Hang tight, on our way."

Kalon's guns blazed in close quarters. This crew had captured him, and if they engaged Fate's Hand, they were dead. He did not shoot to disable, he shot to kill. One by one they fell as the Inquisitor helped Silver clear their escape path to the upper deck.

He saw the carnage Sara had left behind and quirked a brow. Again, the dead were responsible for his capture and worked for Collins. He knew the ship's reputation well, as it had been captained by a slaver and murderer.

A fitting end.

The *Ori* came out of the sky, melting like butter from the clouds, and swung around gracefully to lower her ramp. Kalon took off at a sprint with Silver at his heels. Sara flew past them both and gunned her chair to the max.

"Impressive rescue," the Inquisitor yelled as they ran up the ramp. "You'll have to tell me in full detail how you managed it."

"Only if you tell me how the great Fate's Hand ended up being shipped to Skyborne," Silver said as she slammed the hatch control to close it and pull back the ramp.

"Deal."

Sara landed gracefully and checked the charge on her chair's systems. "One more hour, and I'm spent. Gotta improve that, but all in all, wicked field test."

"A very impressive artifice." Kalon smiled and took a breath. "Thank you both, for coming for me."

Sara grinned widely and blushed. "You're my friend, and I think you're more than friends with her."

Silver took off the mask and dropped it into the young woman's lap. She stalked over to Kalon and wrapped him in her arms. Then, like she'd wanted to in the hold, she kissed him fully and properly.

Sara looked away, grinning like a wildcat.

After the kiss broke, Amari Sister and Inquisitor looked at each other. Kalon spoke first. "That was some welcome back."

"If you ever do that again—get caught—I'm going to..." Silver bit her lip. "Come and find you, no matter where you are."

"And I, you," he replied.

Sara hid her amusement. "Maybe save the mushy stuff for later? Maybe go see Imani?"

"Good idea. Come on, they'll be glad to see you're ok." Silver took Kalon by the hand and led him out.

Sara watched them go, chuckled softly, and smiled as the door closed. "I'll be up in a bit, need to tinker first."

As Kalon and Silver walked onto the bridge, Imani turned and said, "Just in time, I'm about to send the *Aurus Machina* into the water."

"A deserved ending." Kalon looked at the rest of the people on the bridge, including Winter and Daroni. He blinked. "I have more friends than I realized."

"Took you long enough, young man," Vincent said with a laugh. "Still, you got there in the end."

Silver let go of Kalon's hand and stood to his righthand side, watchful.

"Fire!" the captain ordered, and the *Ori* blazed with light. Her weapons, designed to fight giant demonic entities and sky pirate ships at the same time, opened up. She wasted no time in blasting the engines and deck of the *Aurus Machina*. Huge holes appeared in the hull; the big ship belched smoke, the engines guttered, and down she went.

"They deserved it," Winter said softly. "Not a single one of the people on that ship had a soul worth anything." She said this with perfect clarity and authority. Those who knew Winter and her power knew she meant it.

The merchant ship smashed into the water below, rocked, and then sank slowly beneath the waves.

The *Ori* flew on, retracted her weapons, and angled in the sky.

"Where to, then?" Imani turned to the rest of the people on their ship. "That's me finished. I just rescued a prisoner of the church and turned my guns on a church-sponsored merchant, stole a prototype, and threw it all away for a man who barely acknowledged me."

"Kalon had his reasons," Winter said quietly. "I will explain everything to you soon, Captain, but I must ask you to put us on course to Wyrden."

"Wyrden? Why there?"

"We'll be safe in that city," Kalon said, almost as if he'd read Winter's mind. "It's a free port. The church has no sway there, and there are very few who do: Captain Talon Mane is one, but the Cardinal could never truly pin down who else in the city held any real power."

"Ah." Imani nodded. "You heard the man," they ordered. "Set us on course to Wyrden."

The *Ori* curved across the sky and flickered out of sight as she headed for her new home.

Men cannot be trusted to do anything right, Jaziel thoughts. *Well... most men.* There were some, like that Kalon fellow and a few others, who were bothersome enough to do the right thing and who then had to be killed, fucked, corrupted, or enslaved. Something.

Akas was an idiot!

The women though, they were another matter, especially the Cardinal. This Terusa Ekarta was a woman who had her eye on the prize and displayed many of the things the demon liked. She was clever, subtle, conniving, and craved power. Like a potter at the wheel, Jaziel could work with that clay.

She stepped before the mirror and bade it view Terusa's chamber. Perfect timing. All hell was about to break loose for that woman.

Cardinal Terusa was having such a good day, and it would have been a good night. It was getting late, and not quite sundown. Roland dozed on her bed, and she paced back and forth, red and gold silk whispering like a voice in her ear.

Only her own thoughts filled her mind now, no other's.

Why did she sleep with that man? He was repulsive, but he knew how to use his tongue in a most interesting manner, and that pleased her.

It was up to her, though. Fuck tradition, and fuck social norms.

If she wanted something now, she could reach out and take it. Even Kalon. Now that might have been fun.

Her door banged again. Roland mumbled, "No, I don't want caviar. Take it away and fetch me the whores."

Terusa looked at him askance, then slid from the room. She paused to belt her robe and don some soft slippers. The door banged again, and she snapped. "What?"

"Cardinal, urgent news."

She didn't like the sound of that. "Enter!"

Inquisitor Avala Vara made her way into the chamber. She was shorter than the Cardinal by a foot, and her skin was as black as the night sky. She wore the silver-and-white of the information branch of the church. Her amber eyes were rimmed with dark eyeshadow, and tiny golden markings peppered the skin of her face. Her body, trim and muscular, showed that she'd honed her physique.

Terusa drank her in, echoing what she'd thought earlier on. She knew Avala only had eyes for women with power.

"Report?"

"I bring grave tidings." Avala's soft voice soothed the blow. "Our scouts intercepted a message from the *Aurus Machina*. It appears sky pirates attacked the ship and blew her out of the sky. We're not sure if there are any survivors, or if the cargo is intact."

The Cardinal sat down in her chair hard. No, it couldn't be. Kalon was on that ship, and so was Mallori. "No survivors, and the cargo lost?"

"Until we send a salvage crew, the outcome is unknown."

"You, go." The Cardinal's eyes flashed. She barely contained her anger. "Find out what happened if you can, and send for Imani."

"Imani has not reported back from her test flight."

"What flight?"

"The one she took with Vincent Daroni," Avala Vara answered, watching the Cardinal's expression.

Terusa controlled her rage and smiled thinly. "Oh yes, that one. Good, well, you get someone to send them to me when they return. In the meantime, please find out what happened to the *Aurus Machina*. Take what ships you need and get me some answers."

Avala Vara bowed, turned on her heel, and swept from the room.

Cardinal Terusa snarled and slammed her hand on the desk. "What the hell happened?" she asked the air.

"I don't know," it said back to her, in tones that spoke of velvet hiding a viper's fangs. "But I could guess."

"Who? What? Guards!" Terusa made to hit her alarm at the console on her desk, but her wrist was wrapped in an electric-warm embrace.

Jaziel, Demon Queen of Hestonia, purred softly in the woman's ear. "Just a friend, my dear—a lover if you want. Much better than a One-God. Much better than a Demon King."

Cardinal Terusa sniffed the air. It smelled like roses and wickedness. "Tell me more." She paused. "But be warned, I threw Akas from my soul, and I will end you if you cross me."

"Fire! I like it!" Jaziel nodded. She could definitely work with the Cardinal. This was the kind of mortal she liked. "You have what I want, and I want you. Carnally too. Sorry, it's kind of what I do."

With that said, the demon appeared from the air in all her glory and took form—a form which mortals found hard to resist, all the pleasures and sin rolled into one package that oozed power and sensuality.

"We will talk terms, and mine will be strict." Terusa appraised her. Jaziel was stunning, and her power was unlike Akas's.

"Who needs a Demon King as their patron when you can have a Demon Queen as yours, in your ear, in your life, in your bed...or wherever you wish?" Jaziel whispered. Her tone promised a thousand pleasures and a hundred lusts. "I will give you the world."

"What do I need to do?" Cardinal Terusa savored that smell and felt that power as the woman did not let go. She drank in the demon before her, and she looked so, so tasty. Her body was perfect, just how the Cardinal liked her women, a little on the softer side, and with just a hint of snake-like muscle beneath the skin.

The Demon Queen was robed in a material that was scandalously, wickedly diaphanous; it hid every curve and pleasure as much as it showed it to the viewer.

The trap was sprung, the snare worked perfectly, and the finale?

"Just let me grant you power," the Demon Queen whispered, tracing the Cardinal's breasts with a fingertip. "We will make everyone love us."

"Yes." Terusa wanted this and more. It was a seductive power, stronger than Akas's, for the Demon King had been at the ebb of his strength. Jaziel was in the full bloom of hers.

Game, set, match.

Who needs a Demon King when you're a Queen of Demons?

Jaziel had bigger plans for Hestonia than destruction, and Cardinal Terusa was the very tip of that beautiful iceberg.

"Come, then, and let us show Roland what we can do."

The dark-eyed temptress led the Cardinal from the room and back to the bedchamber, closed the door, and chuckled softly.

"Roland, wake up. It's time to taste real power."

He screamed, but all that followed was laughter.

Both Terusa's and Jaziel's. Wicked, seductive, and strong.

CHAPTER 31

WYRDEN

The world around Kalon and Silver had changed so much in so short a time. So many things had transpired on their relatively short journey together. Lesser people might have been overwhelmed, but Kalon, with his mental training, could at least fall back on mantras and psychic control. His emotions had been caged for so long; they were now free, and it took all the Inquisitor's skill to keep many of the darker ones in check.

He was not used to any of them, even the positive ones.

The *Ori* was a fast ship, and she was a home away from home for a few days as the vessel whispered across the heavens, her course set for Wyrden. It afforded Kalon time to get to know the people around him in various ways, and that was perhaps one of the greatest gifts offered to such a man, one who had been forged as a weapon by the very order he swore to serve, and by the very woman he had trusted with his immortal soul.

Sara, Vincent Daroni, Imani, and their crew were all now firmly pulled away from the Cardinal and her machinations. Winter, who had helped Kalon overcome his early trials, was there with them. She had been, in many ways, the secret catalyst that had driven a singular wedge between Terusa and those who were once loyal to her.

Sara, the young inventor, was the hero of the hour. Her recording in Daroni's lab and her actions on the *Aurus Machina* had tipped the balance.

Mirroring Kalon's journey was another vessel, as the *Mist Reaver* flew on her way to the city.

So many lives, all converging, so many stories yet to be told. Captain Talon Mane was without his First Mate, though he wasn't overly bothered since Silver had her own path to walk and he felt she always had.

Wen, Kaitlinel, and Andreas interested him—especially the wizard. Talon pondered asking the man if he'd like to join him on the ship, as his magical ace in the hole. That would be fun, and he thought Wen might enjoy action and adventure.

Time would tell.

Then there were the others in the Three-Tiered City of Wyrden itself, already there, placed on the path by Winter. The alchemist, lady in grey, Reva Flynn. Vass Drae and her husband, the Justicar, Maxis Kane.

Verity, once a church-sponsored assassin, now lived one day at a time, fearful that the Cardinal's hired killers and agents like Maxis would find her and end her life.

The Cardinal's world had altered, and her plans had unraveled, only to present her with a new chance to gain power via a seductive and tempting new sponsor. Gone was the One-God of the Infinite Machine, now known to her as Akas the Bloodless. She had become the confidant, plaything, and favorite pawn of a new player in the game.

Or perhaps that player was just on her side until the right moment presented itself.

Jaziel had shown Terusa a new world, and it was one that she utterly embraced—one that left Arch-Inquisitor Roland butt-naked, bound, and gagged, with his backside in the air on the bed after the last night's events.

"So now you see what I offer. Domination over men like him, power over the world." The Demon Queen rolled over a little. "Control over your own destiny—oh, and over time, you'll come to wield magic as we demons do. Fuck the Warp and the Weft, the Tapestry. We make reality our slave. We command the rules. Mortals have to make magic like this, but demons, we don't play by those bullshit rules. We're not going to wave our hands around like we're swatting flies or trying to wash a window. With my help, you will be the first true Anshada wizard this world has ever seen." She stood up and paced the room, bored.

The Cardinal grinned wickedly for a moment, a smile that matched Jaziel's own.

When one door closed, another opened, and in this case near the end of the *Ori's* journey on the very last day of their flight from the church, Cardinal Terusa sat at her desk. Her gown was a formal one, and she signed paper after paper.

New laws, new edicts. Bolstered by all the promises—sweet, sweet promises.

Jaziel now sat to the side of her, lazy, catlike in the shade of the room. Her eyes glittered in the half-light, and she toyed with an orb of crystal, one of the Cardinal's many paperweights.

"Tell me again of this Soulcage?" The Demon Queen's smile lingered too long. She was plotting something.

"It was meant to pull demonic energy from people, to suck out demons in cases of possession and turn the energy into a useful power core." The Cardinal scribbled once more on the parchment.

"Well then, why settle for just one Kalon when you could have hundreds—if not thousands—of Kalons? Put that machine to work, dear." The Demon Queen's smile turned into a wicked grin. "Get those brain-cases of yours to make it suck the energy from wizards and harvest that. Then, when you have enough, drink it all in like we demons suck the life force out of mortals after fucking them."

Terusa sat open-mouthed for a moment. "No wonder I felt tired more than usual."

"Oh dear, it was only a little nibble," Jaziel snickered.

"I will see what can be done. You're right." The Cardinal's smile appeared once more, this time ruthless and without light. "We will take those wizards who do not join us, capture them, and feed them to the Soulcage."

"Now you're thinking!"

"You are wicked."

"Guilty as charged." The Demon Queen tapped her nose with a languid motion of her finger. "You're not so bad yourself. You have promise, lover, and I can take you to places you only dream of."

Cardinal Terusa nodded, and she looked down at the parchments she had signed. She gathered them in her hands and crumpled the lot before she placed them in a bin. Then, with fresh insight and a newfound plan, she began to draw up new documents.

Ones that would change the fate of wizards in Hestonia—and not for the better.

Jaziel grinned once more. Perfect.

"Oh, and if Kalon tries to stop us, we'll suck him so dry he'll be a withered husk."

"You think he will present a problem?"

"Oh yes, men like him never stop. You fucked him without asking first or taking him for a meal. Lady, he's going to want revenge—even through all that iron-codpiece, ball-shaking will."

"Then we'll deal with him as well. Why bother to give him time?"

"Ooh, see, now that's the Cardinal I lust for!" Jaziel gave her a kiss and smiled. "Let's send some Shadow Knives out then, eh?"

"Good idea."

Terusa reached for a sheaf of papers and began to select the contracts slowly. To each one she signed the names of a target and an assassin. Silver, Kalon, Verity, and more were inked onto that parchment.

"Beautiful," said the Demon Queen as she began to undress the Cardinal. "Time to play again!"

Terusa smiled. Honestly, she could not resist.

Sundown came upon the City of Wyrden. The lamps dotting her streets whispered to life, touched by the same hand that wandered from pole to pole, bringing radiance from the crystals within. Such had been the ritual every night for as long as the city had stood—which had been a good few hundred years.

No mortal hand touched the lamps—or rather, no living hand, as the shade of Old Samuel continued his work long past his death.

Wyrden was like that. The dead lingered there for some inexplicable reason, out of the grasp of the Shroud, and they almost lived in another world. Free from bodily pain, but not the torment of the soul.

The Old Copper Theatre, the scene of many a play when it was the focal point of all the entertainment in the Middle Ring of the city, was another ghost. A shadow of its former glory with faded bricks and broken tiles, the theater had gaping holes that allowed the moon's wan light to strut the decaying stage alongside the ghosts of long-dead actors.

When the living—in this case, Verity—entered stage right, the ghosts of so many long-ago performances took their cue and bowed out in whispers of wind. They tugged at the ruined curtains and flitted out of sight.

The former assassin sat on an old, battered chair, looked down at the floorboards, and sighed.

Maxis and Vass came in not long after. They were not overly cautious, and did not appear to operate as the church's agents might. Just like Verity had asked, they did not approach this like agents of the Cardinal.

"Verity." Vass Drae brushed a cobweb off her shoulder as she spoke. "You look hunted, dear."

"Haunted, I'd have said." Maxis picked his way over the broken furniture. "You pick your spots, lass."

Verity ruffled her auburn hair, the latest wig, short and with a pixie-style cut. "Safer that way. So where's Mallori now?"

"No idea. Winter told us he was on your trail, just as we were on his. He's supposedly here in Wyrden, so she sent us to find you and stop the man from ending your life," Maxis said as he stopped when he reached even footing.

"I'd like to believe that, but you're a Justicar."

"He's also my husband," Vass pointed out. "A good man, and one who does not lie."

"Not in my nature. Justicar's code. I *can* lie, but I choose not to. It's complicated." The Justicar spread his hands wide. "Look, believe it or not, we're here to help. Whatever Winter has planned, she has her reasons, and after what we saw in her vision—I'm not sure we can do much."

The sky above them lit as dozens of small lights reflected off a giant, golden, bird-shaped vessel. The *Mist Reaver* soared overhead, home at last. She was faster than the *Ori,* and had begun her journey closer to Wyrden than Imani's vessel.

"Damn, is that who I think it is?" Maxis ignored Verity for a moment. "What a beaut!"

"The *Mist Reaver,* yes. Talon Mane's ship." Vass followed her husband's gawking stare. "The sky pirate comes home to roost now and then."

"What happens now?" Verity called their attention back to her.

"Nothing. Well, we don't do anything to you. You don't try and fight us, and we live relatively happy ever after?" Maxis joked, grinning sheepishly as he caught a dour stare from his wife.

"What he means is that we protect you, and you trust us."

"Hard to do, but you seem genuine." The former assassin put her head in her hands. "I'm tired, Rand's dead, and Kalon is out there wherever. What happens if they send him after me? You know what he's capable of."

"It would be bad, yes." Vass could not argue with this.

The sound of scrunching stone and wood caught their attention. A few cats scattered as another figure made her way into the moon's natural spotlight. Dusty beams shone through the gaps in the stone.

"Hello lovelies, sorry to interrupt."

Verity relaxed; it wasn't Drako. That voice, like nasal nails down glass, and that familiar shabby coat under which a pair of glasses that glinted in the ambient light told her who it was. Maxis and Vass relaxed as well.

"Miss Flynn," Vass greeted the woman in grey. "You turn up like an old penny all the time."

"A beautiful habit of mine." She puffed on her favorite kind of cigarette. It helped with the chronic pain she always felt. "I've been sent to find you, and by a very important, busy, and influential lady."

The three others exchanged glances. They weren't sure how Reva had tracked them down, or who this mysterious invitation was from.

"Who sent you, Reva?" Verity was the first to ask.

"The Countess Arabella. You are in her city, and, well, she'd like you to come and say hello. She's throwing a party, part art show and part performance art. Don't come if you don't like to see naked people, though. You know her parties are quite the talk of the city."

"My kind of party," Maxis said and sidestepped a dig from his wife's elbow, aimed for his ribs.

"Really?" Vass narrowed her eyes.

"No, I'm kidding," he soothed.

Verity shook her head, then changed her mind. "It would be a good place to blend in. Maybe I can get some work. Or maybe I can get her to hunt Drako down for me," she mused. "Arabella has a whole menagerie of Kharnates, right?"

"She does." Reva's eyes twinkled. "You had to have seen the golden birdy, right?"

"I did." Verity nodded. "We all did."

"Talon will be there, and his crew, his new friends." The alchemist puffed on her cigarette until the tip glowed like a beacon. It lit her pale face ever so slightly.

"Quite a gathering," Vass noted.

"All heavens, dearie, lead to Wyrden," Reva replied with a grin. Her lips caressed the cigarette like it was a lover.

Maxis pondered and then asked, "Is Kalon aboard?"

Reva took the slim white smoking stick out of her mouth. She sniffed the pungent herbal aroma and flicked ash on the floor. "He's not on the *Mist Reaver*, love, but he will be coming too."

"How do you know all this?" Verity narrowed her eyes; Reva was always good at secrets.

"Sweetie, I'm Reva Flynn, alchemist and inventor. Ok, I also spoke to a little bird who spoke to another, and the game of Wyrden Whispers began—only these don't change over the telling."

Verity sighed. Reva was not going to tell. "Fair enough."

"So, are you all coming?" The alchemist popped her cigarette back in her mouth and made her way to the stage right exit. "Arabella awaits." Verity got up. "Nothing to lose, save for my life." She was in.

"Lead on." Maxis grinned, and then checked his wife's expression. "That's if it's ok with you, Vass my love?"

"For now." The sepia-skinned Inquisitor fixed her husband with a frown, but mirth sparked in her eyes.

One by one, the figures left the stage. As was proper, they used the stage-right door and melted into the night.

The *Ori* was on track to the city, slower than the *Mist Reaver*, and delayed by a storm bank that forced Imani to skirt out to the edges. They did not want their ship caught in the thick black clouds. Some storms on Hestonia seethed with magic—and worse. So rather than lightning, it was only rain that pelted the slim ship as it cruised through the sky.

Winter slept soundly, finally; her dreams were still tormented, but she saw a destination. A street magician in a top hat, with an elegant cane, performed at an elegant mansion, surrounded by wolves. There she met, kissed, and made a long dalliance with a red-haired beauty with lupine eyes who was gone by morning.

Sara tinkered in her makeshift cabin, dozing off as the storm played outside the windows. Vicent Daroni was already asleep. The old man was in his own chamber aboard the *Ori*, and he had been soothed by the rain.

Imani sat on the bridge, pondering all that Secker Winter had told them regarding Kalon. A demon in the soul, which ate his feelings and emotions—they shuddered softly and shook their head. What right did the church have to do that to him, or anyone? It made sense now, his actions, his mannerisms, and his lack of praise when they'd helped him originally. They half-dozed in their chair, fearful of the future, but also excited in many ways—free, like Kalon, of the Church of Progression.

As for Kalon and Silver, they had retired to Kalon's assigned cabin. Now, at long last, as the sky cracked with white fire and the rain plastered across the cabin's toughened glass, they stood and faced each other. Silver drank from a phial she always kept and offered it to Kalon. He took it wordlessly, thinking that it might be some part of a ritual. It was; it prevented children, simple as that. Now, they stripped away their armaments, their weapons and armor gone, nothing but their skin to show to the storm. Her, muscled, scarred, just as he remembered in the Amari safehouse. Him, the same, with a few more new nicks and scratches from the demon attack. Silver's body was aglow with the storm, and her ink mesmerized the eye.

They moved closer. The rain lashed against the window as the wind tore at the *Ori* futilely. Their lips met, their skin touched, and like the storm outside, something jolted between them. Like two drops of rain on a pane of glass, Kalon and Silver came together that night and melted as one, a tangle of limbs, as the rain formed a river, and that river slipped down to the bottom. Two people, now on the same course.

Kalon learned then what it truly was to be human, and to have someone who trusted him enough to share her all. It was beyond anything he'd ever thought possible.

The storm mirrored their togetherness: gentle at times, fierce at others, and breathless at the end.

On the grandest Upper Tier of the city of Wyrden, past the clockwork lifts and steam-driven tech-magis horses and carts, stood the mansions of the city's elite. These people had helped make the city what it was—and they knew crime like the backs of their hands.

Countess Arabella was one such person, and her manor was the grandest of them all. Set back in acres of cultivated forest and gardens, with four large, circular windship landing pads, she was like a glorious spider at the center of a very elegant web.

The *Mist Reaver* touched down on the pad marked with an effigy of the ship. This was Talon's Plan B. As he disembarked from the ship with Wen, Kaitlinel, and Andreas in tow, Talon stopped to take a breath of fresh air and stretch his legs.

"Welcome to the most glorious place on Hestonia."

"Fuck me, this is one hell of a home." Kaitlinel looked around, picking out the wolf-motifs and all the naked statues. "My kind of place, goddess be fucking praised!"

"The stories I've heard of this manor..." The wizard's eyes lit up. "All the rumors, are they true?"

"All of them, and the ones you haven't heard about, especially those." Talon laughed softly.

Wen grinned. He was going to love it here, then.

Spry's death had not been forgotten, but hearts and minds are odd things. They replay at the strangest moments—when you least expect it—and they can be distracted by the right stimuli. Arabella's manse was one such distraction.

The gunslinger blew a soft whistle-breath from between his teeth and shook his head. "I'm a simple man. Look at this place! Who has so much cash they can make this a reality?"

"The Countess, duh." Kaitlinel rolled her eyes and thumped him on the shoulder.

"Ow."

A tall, tousle-haired man approached them from the direction of the house, ascending a flight of metal steps to the pad. He wore a tunic, breeches, and huntsman's boots, and his lupine eyes told everyone what they needed to know. He was a Kharnate, and Kaitlinel and Talon both were in lust.

"Welcome!" The man's northern accent rolled out, with a hint of feral about him. "My name is Martin. I am the Countess's righthand man. Captain, as you know, you're always welcome here, but let's have some introductions. Who are your other friends?"

"Kaitlinel!" the werewolf said, rather too quickly. "Come find me later, ok?"

"Right." The man sniffed the air and grinned. "One of us. Welcome, sister of the pack."

"Andreas, friend of the lusty one." The gunslinger nodded at the other man, still awed by the pomp and grandeur around him.

"Wen," said the wizard. "Just Wen. And you are gorgeous, sir? Just the right hint of dandy danger." He winked at the man. "Kharnates always are, and I do so love a man in those boots."

Martin gave another grin and swept his arm in a gesture to the house. "Well, that's out of the way. Let me take you to see Arabella."

Talon stepped up, took the man's arm, and his smile broadened. "On to all kinds of naughty adventures! Come, my friends, you have a treat in store for you!"

They followed the right hand of the countess, and as they got closer to the mansion, they heard music, beheld people engaged in raw sex, and witnessed acts of debauchery that would shock most normal folk. The goddess's gifts on display.

Kharnates, humans, and non-humans coupled fiercely in the mansion grounds, an orgy of flesh and sound. Kaitinel grinned from ear to ear at this. "Oh, I'm going to *love* it here." The gardens were more for hosting pleasure than they were for looking at.

Among the largest collection of sweating limbs and howling was a woman, tall and red of hair, her skin tanned gold. She mounted a man and writhed with him, her eyes on fire, her fingernails raking his flesh. The new arrivals couldn't look away. Something stirred in their blood, something primal in their souls. It resonated most with Kaitinel, who stopped to cheer on the red-haired woman and howl at the height of her lungs. Without a pause in her frenzied passion, the red-headed figure locked eyes with the werewolf and something unspoken passed in their gaze.

"That's how you make new Kharnates." Kaitinel laughed a little. "The Kharnate likes you, she brings you into the family, into the pack, and fucks you senseless. You get her gift, and you become one of us. Best way to become a werewolf if you ask me. Fuck that whole bullshit story about lacerations and full moons."

"Come on, show's always on!" Martin turned to the house. "The Countess awaits!"

The red-haired Kharnate howled. The woman looked at Kaitlinel and licked her lips, bloody against the smile. Then she went back to her partner and continued the primal dance.

Martin's entourage entered the Countess's home.

CHAPTER 32

FATE'S HAND

The interior of Countess Arabella's mansion was lavish, decadent, and full of artful and tasteful statues that depicted nudity in all its forms and body types. There was no specific gender nor frame on display.

They were met by the woman herself, alone in the hall and dressed in a black, full-length evening dress. It was festooned with tiny diamonds that made it appear as if she were a dark sky alight with stars. Her neckline was not modest; though her curves were hidden, her necklace drew the eye to where she wanted it: an obsidian wolf pendant with tiny green eyes that matched her own. Her olive skin faded slightly to ochre. Her face, framed by devil-red lips and long waterfalls of pitch-black hair, drew all eyes, and she knew it.

"Talon, my dear, you have been away for so long. What brings your lovely bird to nest at my home?"

Talon kept hold of Martin's arm and offered a bow, with the man still held. "Arabella! Lovely, sweet, delectable, and delicious Countess." He grinned. "The winds of fate have blown me back across your skies, and you know me: I'm always eager to roost in you—I mean, in your lovely home."

The countess stifled a laugh and shook her head. "The same old kelanari. Never change. And you have brought new friends?"

"Wen, Andreas, and the werewolf, Kaitlinel," Martin said with a chuckle. "Not sure why they're here, but you know Mane and his penchant for unexpected arrivals."

"I do, and I care not." Arabella stepped down the stairs. Her bare feet poked out from the hem of the dress, and her toenails were painted black. "Welcome, Wen. Welcome, Andreas. And doubly-welcome, unknown wolf-sister, Kaitinel of—?"

"Sullavale Port, but fuck that. Got a place in Wyrden needs a charmer like me?"

The woman's green eyes fixed on the werewolf, and Arabella allowed a very faint smile to peek on her lips. "Oh, something can probably be arranged. I like collecting Kharnates, and they seem to like it here."

Andreas chuckled a little. "Can't possibly see why." He drank the Countess in, of course. It was hard not to.

"Judging by the garden activity and the sounds all around...I presume you are throwing a party?" Talon asked as the conversation drifted away from him.

"Sort of." Arabella shook her head. "It's a favor for a friend, and let's just say a gathering of like-minded souls. Any other guests?"

"Yep," the kelanari man nodded. "My first mate and her lot should be here in a day or so. They're coming on a church ship, so you know, don't get all antsy."

The door opened and in walked Reva Flynn, Verity, Maxis Kane, and Vass. Reva beamed at the countess, took a drag from her cigarette, and said, "As asked, here they are. Ooh, hello Andreas, Kait." She pointed the others out. "Maxis, his wife Vass, and the very tired Verity."

"Hey Reva!" Kaitlinel laughed softly. "You really are everywhere."

"Lovely, I always am." The alchemist grinned.

Arabella looked from one to the other, and then in the direction of a room up the stairs. "Thank you, Miss Flynn."

"Reva," the woman in the grey hat grumbled.

"Miss Flynn," Andreas said with a wink, "we meet again."

"Oh yes, that happens," Reva assured him.

"Martin, there's lots to do," Countess Arabella said softly. "Show these people to their chambers and let them have the run of the fun. Meanwhile, I must speak to Maxis, Vass, and Verity." The woman looked at her office door. "Come, ascend the stairs with me, and we shall chat."

Martin nodded. He showed the others out and left Reva in the hall. The woman in grey stood, smiled at one of the statues which looked a lot like her, grinned again, and said, "They never get my breasts just right."

With that, she was off into the garden. The night air was perfect to soothe her pain, and she needed more smoke-stick heaven — it was always the way. People thought her drugs were just recreational, that she loved to smoke herbs and imbibe concoctions. This was true in many ways, but in others *Reva Flynn required these smoke-sticks to* soothe the chronic aches she hid well.

The trio of Maxis, Vass, and Verity followed the dark-haired woman into her office, where she offered them drinks and a seat each. Then she stood by a beautiful marble fireplace. Her office was incredible, a history of the world, covered in priceless things and paneled in ancient woods.

"What brings church agents to my door?" she said directly.

"Well, can I just say first?" Verity sighed. "I'm a former church-sponsored assassin."

"Noted," the woman replied. "Care to elaborate?"

"Not really. Not being rude, but I'm just rundown, the man I love is dead, and another who killed him is hunting me."

Maxis and Vass gave Verity their best sympathetic looks, and the sepia-skinned Inquisitor wanted to hug her.

"That is a lot," the countess acknowledged. "Don't worry, Verity. You are safe here. My Kharnates are protective of our guests." Arabella meant that too.

"We were sent here by Seeker Winter, and hopefully she'll turn up and explain just what in the Warp and Weft is going on," Maxis said. He was irked about being left too far out of the loop. "Because, honestly, my lady…we're in the dark about much of this."

"What my husband says is correct." Vass nodded. "We know only some, but would rather you hear it from our benefactor and friend? We came hunting Drako Mallori, and to protect Verity on Winter's orders."

"Very well, that's good, then. That I can allow, and honestly, I would love to talk to you about your church—it fascinates me. So does the Cardinal, especially all the things people in my inner circle say about her."

Vass and Maxis exchanged glances, and then nodded.

"I could tell you some things," Vass offered. Her loyalty had been tested after she saw Winter's visions. "My perspective has changed."

"And you, Justicar?"

"I'm with her. Not sure what's going on, but where Vass goes, I'm not far behind. Love is funny like that," Maxis replied.

"It can be blind, yes," Vass noted.

Verity yawned and looked longingly at the chez lounge in the corner. It was so inviting. "Excuse me, but could I have a room?"

"Of course." Arabella followed her stare at the long velvet seat, covered in cushions. "Or you can stretch out there. My home is your home."

Verity was suspicious; this stranger was too nice, but she was a good friend of Talon Mane, and he never once struck her as someone who could be wholly bad.

She stood and flopped into the embrace of the other seat, stretched out, and buried herself in the pillows.

"Now," Arabella said with a smile as she spread her dress around her knees and smoothed it down, "tell me more."

So, they did. It all came out, every vision they knew of, and the Cardinal's treachery with Kalon and the demons.

As the three talked, time moved on, and eventually all the new arrivals in Arabella's mansion took to chambers and beds—some together, with their husband or wife, some with more than one, and others with brand-new, first-time, gregarious partners who were fire-haired and made Kaitlinel seem like a rank amateur.

Andreas had his mind blown that night, and many times.

Night gave way to day, and the *Ori* came down over the city, her wings curled back and her form hidden from prying eyes. Not even Wyrden Port authorities knew she had arrived, and that was the beauty of the vessel—one of the reasons that the captain had stolen her. If you were going to defang a viper like the church, take its newest weapon away.

Silver entered the bridge in the morning, her hair loose and tousled. She looked a world away from the tired warrior she had been last time Imani saw her. She was dressed in her usual attire; it had been brushed and cleaned a little.

"Sleep well?" the captain asked with a smirk. "You and he make quite a pair."

The kelanari blushed. "Slept well for the first time since this began. He makes a good pillow."

"I'll say no more." Imani smiled.

Silver grinned. "Nor will I."

"Good." The captain looked at the city. "So, this Wyrden? What a marvel."

Silver nodded; she'd seen the city many times from the *Mist Reaver*. "Talon's favorite place to return to."

"Do we know where we're going?"

"Indeed, just angle her to the Upper Tier and aim for the mansion with the four landing pads." Silver pointed out the small house in the distance, sitting atop the city. Now, from the air, they both could clearly see another feature of the city that made it truly unique: a giant clocktower that stretched hundreds of feet from the Lower Tier ring to the Upper Tier and pierced the clouds above it.

The *Ori* whispered on, curving down to the mansion that Silver pointed out. As the vessel passed overhead, it threaded the skies like a needle and hovered gently above the pad like a ghost.

"Might want to drop that invisibility thing you do." The Amari Sister chuckled. "Or Arabella won't know we're here."

The door opened again, and in stepped Kalon Rhadon. He regarded both people, and upon seeing Silver he smiled — a smile that, for once, looked like it belonged on his face.

"Kalon—" Imani paused. "Are you still Fate's Hand?"

"Is it a title granted to me by the church," he replied. He took a moment to observe the landscape of Arabella's mansion, the grand house and its three wings, and added, "Good morning, Silver."

"Sleep well?" She chuckled.

"Yes." He turned to look at her. "Eventually." She blushed.

The *Ori* dropped her cloak and glided down amidst a scatter of birds until she landed gracefully upon the pad.

"Here we are." Imani stood up from the chair. "Do you need us for this?"

Kalon quirked a brow and nodded. "You are part of this, so yes, you should come."

"Arabella's mansion. Kalon, you know her?" Silver wrinkled her nose for a moment.

"I know of her, yes. We had information on her in the record wing." The Inquisitor stepped to the side and allowed Imani to pass.

"She is unique, and very friendly. So, just be warned. You might want to be on your guard with her guests," Silver replied chuckled softly.

"Oh?"

"Kharnates."

"Ah."

With the talk out of the way, the trio left the bridge, gathered Sara, Vincent Daroni, and Seeker Winter, and then left the ship in the gleam of sunlight on a cool day in Wyrden. It was not Martin that met them at the bottom of the *Ori*'s landing ramp, but the countess herself.

She smiled in the morning light and turned her gaze upward.

What a group.

Winter, with her snowfall of locks, slim frame, and piercing eyes.

Vincent Daroni, old, but strong, with limber limbs and a spark in his glance.

Sara, wheeling down the ramp with her eyes agog at the splendor of the place. Captain Imani, with their straight back, clean-cut uniform, and elegant posture.

Silver she knew, and she always loved the look of the Amari Sister. Well turned-out, sensibly armored, and deadly.

Finally, her eyes fell on the tall man who walked alongside Silver. She saw his cog and eye and traced the lines of his coat and its trim.

"Kalon Rhadon," she said before anyone else could speak. "My spies do not do you justice; you are so handsome and so perfectly elegant."

The Inquisitor raised a brow and chuckled softly—a new thing for him. "Countess Arabella. Then your spies do me a great honor, and I am pleased to meet you at long last. Our spies have painted a picture of you that pales in comparison."

Smooth, thought Silver. *He's getting it.*

The countess clapped her hands together. "And who else do we have?"

"Seeker Winter." The woman bowed. "A true honor."

Sara, somewhat ill-at-ease in such a big social occasion, pushed her anxiety aside. "Sara, inventor and genius."

"Did you design the wheelchair?" Arabella regarded it; it was magnificent.

"I did, and I built it too."

"Then you are indeed more than you say you are." Arabella smiled warmly. "Welcome! I think we will be great friends. I love inventions and science—and what is it you call some of these?" She pointed to a random thing on the chair.

"Doohickeys?" Sara grinned.

The young woman's mentor stepped forward and bowed, tipping his floppy hat. "Vincent Daroni, Belladonna." The old man said, eyes sparkling. "When I paint a picture of you, I will have to find a priceless canvas upon which to put it."

Arabella put her left hand over her heart, mock-fanned herself, and smiled. "Oh, you rogue, I love that."

Imani halted in their stride and then bowed. "Captain Imani of the *Ori*."

Arabella looked at the captain, then at the ship, and then back to Imani. "You and your ship are both so beautiful."

Imani coughed, blushed, and for the first time was lost for words.

"Come, come, we have much to talk about, and you all need rooms. Here you will stay while we plan what's to transpire next. You are safe, and you are sound. All your companions have come to Wyrden, as if Fate herself willed it." The countess whirled and made for the house. "We shall not delay a moment longer. Captain, later you can speak to the crew and find them lodgings here—I imagine they are going to take some time to get used to not being at the Imper Vatica."

This was true. The people here were going to have to take some time to adjust, all save Silver.

They passed Reva Flynn admiring a naked woman who sunned herself at the edge of the garden. She waved but didn't talk any further. Her answer was a steady cloud of smoke, this time from an old, lacquered wooden pipe.

Inside, they were taken to a grand room, one of the many solars of the place. A wide window offered a panoramic view of the hedge maze and other features of the manor. Inside, Kalon saw nearly everyone who had touched his life in some way.

Wen smiled, and it set off a chain reaction. Kaitlinel, Andreas, and Captain Talon Mane stood and crowded around the others. They exchanged greetings, questions flew like arrows, and Kalon was wholly overwhelmed. Then he saw someone who sat aside from the rest, someone who reminded him of a lost companion.

He shook his head, stepped away from the others, and approached Verity.

"Hello, my old friend," Kalon said with a warmth to his voice that he had never shown before. "It's been too long."

Verity looked up, lost in thought, and her eyes widened.

"Kalon?"

"I would hope so." A soft laugh escaped his lips. "At least, I think it is, though I have been through a lot."

The change in the man was stark, like a bright day that had become a dark, stormy night. Verity stood up and threw her arms around him. The others stopped talking and stared for a moment before the bubble of banter continued once more around them.

Arabella looked on, and Winter came to stand to her right side. "We need to speak, Countess," the Seeker said.

The dark-haired woman nodded and flicked her eyes to the nearby door. "My private room, just us. Is it bad?"

"Very."

"Then speak we shall." While the rest of them talked, Seeker Winter and Arabella slipped out.

Kalon bathed in a warm hug, and Verity could not believe it. All she'd ever wanted was for her, Rand, and Kalon to be good friends. She loved Rand romantically, but Kalon...he was her tall, dark, and forthright brother who could have kept her safe.

"What happened?"

"It is a long story. Silver and I will tell it soon," he replied.

"I'm not sure I have a soon. Drako Mallori is on my tail." Verity turned her head away, bit her lip, and fought back tears. "He never paid for Rand's death."

Silver, upon hearing her name, joined them, and she set her lips into a grim smile. "Mallori is no longer your problem, Verity." The kelanari put her hand on the other woman's shoulder. "He's dead."

"What? How?" Verity's heart skipped a beat.

"Mallori is dead. I killed him. He deserved the fate he got," Silver promised. "So, you're safe. Safer here than anywhere else in Hestonia, I'd wager, considering how you were branded a traitor and so forth."

For the first time in a long time, Verity's hard shell dropped, and she collapsed into Silver's arms. She sobbed and sobbed. All the thoughts of Rand's death flooded back, along with Drako's smirking face.

"Did he suffer?"

"Oh, very much." The Amari Sister smiled.

"Good."

Kalon kept his distance, observed the exchange, and made mental notes. He was still coming to terms with his own emotions and social interactions. These were uncharted waters, and he was only just learning to swim in them. He was getting there, slowly but surely.

Talon wasn't worried about interrupting the moment. He dropped his hat on Kalon's head and spun the man into a massive hug. The Inquisitor had no clue what to do, so he just eased into it.

"Right, there are things happening. We need to talk, but let's take a bit to relax, shall we?" Wen clapped his hands together, drawing on a few subtle threads for a moment with his fingers to make the sound was louder "Gather round, friends. There's one thing I have to say before we lose ourselves in good company and stories."

All eyes fixed on the wizard. He smiled, happy to be the center of attention. "Spry Genris did not like wizards, and honestly thanks to Kalon's former church, not many people who don't know the truth do. But Spry gave his all, his life, and his soul to bring us to where we are now. That damn kid was a hero, and hopefully his sacrifice won't be in vain."

A murmur ran around the room, and the companions nodded in agreement. Sara listened in, and she said a little thank you to Spry.

"So, let us enjoy this day, for him and our group reborn."

Maxis nodded, Vass drank from her long glass of wine, and everyone gave a small clap. Then, one by one, they formed friendly social groups. Eventually each moved among the others, like rain down the window—some of them barely touching, others melting together as only friends can.

The solar came alive in Spry's honor. Two people stood apart from this, by the long window to the garden. One with her silver hair and soul on fire, the other, Kalon Rhadon, Fate's Hand, cast adrift from his church and now amidst a sea of new and old faces.

A future uncertain, and a path before him, where once he trod it on his own—one with her, the woman who had managed to take Fate's Hand in her own and never let go.

Even when he was imprisoned in the hold of the Cardinal's ship.

So, against the backdrop of good cheer, grand new friends, and partners all, Silver and Kalon kissed once more. With the sunlight in her hair and his hand on the back of her head, the world melted from chaos to order.

For now.

CHAPTER 33

EPILOGUE

As the manor hosted Arabella's guests, she and Winter spoke again of a great many things: of visions that the Seeker had witnessed, of the Cardinal, her eyes whirling with Akas's power. The manor was a place of joy, sorrow, lust, and more in such a short time.

Then again, that could've described Wyrden in a nutshell. The city was so many things to so many people.

It was also Reva's city, more than anywhere. She had her lab, her lovers, her friends, clients, and customers. Her art, alchemy, and her passion, artifice.

So, she left the manor, worked her way into the city proper, and chanced upon a colorful market day. There was every kind of person here, engaged in their lives. Men with men, men with women, women hand in hand, and so many lovely partnerships under the giant clock tower. Some were married, not by church, but by ancient ritual that adhered to no strict backside-on-seat dogma. Nothing was forced; these were partners by consent and bound by love. Some people walked with many others, their lives too grand and their passion too great to be constrained into one single relationship.

Reva knew it all, she had seen it all, and she had helped bring some of these into the world. The woman in grey, mysterious, cocky, and sure of herself. Skilled at the art of potions, with a knowledge of the body across many different heritages that allowed her to function as a mortician and even a healer. Reva, though, was modest—or at least she'd tell you that.

Her travels took her closer to the market stalls that sold sweet-meats, and she chanced upon a person she knew—only they looked different. Gone were their colorful dresses, their curves, and their feminine features. The woman in grey stopped, and the person approached them shyly.

"Hello Reva," they said with a soft tone. "I don't know if you remember me, but…"

Reva Flynn smiled warmly. "I'm sorry, have we met?" She took out a cigarette, lit it, and popped it in her mouth. "Herbal. Keeps the pain away, and makes sure I can function."

"Oh." The man turned to step away. "I am sorry, I thought we knew each other."

"Oh well, you remind me of someone I once knew, but really, I think this is the first time I've met *you*?"

The handsome man turned again, nervous and worried all at once. "Peter." He bowed a little. "My name is Peter, and I'm out for the first time."

Reva Flynn offered a single nod, took a drag of her stick, and smiled. "Lovely to meet you, Peter. You look marvelous. I do love meeting new people."

Peter smiled at her. He realized what the canny alchemist had done, and it made him feel better.

"Thank you. It's good to be me."

"Good, hold on to that," she replied and tipped her hat. "Well Peter, sorry, but I'm on a river of sorts today and have work to do!"

She was off to her lab.

"Drop by if you need anything." She passed him a card with her address on it. "I'm in the city for a while longer."

Peter took it and melted into the crowd, watched by the alchemist as she sighed softly, smiled, and wandered on.

At length she came to a sign and a stage. Upon this stage was a woman. She was, as Reva would have said, darkly attractive and as hot as lava coffee. She wore a tight leather corset, a top hat, and carried a cane that reminded Reva of something.

The sign said: *Nox Arcana, mistress of magic and fate.*

She had drawn quite a crowd, old young, various genders and peoples. Her magic was impressive, card tricks mostly, and sleight of hand. No rabbits from a hat, but she did pull one startled woman's lacy underwear out from her coat. That got a round of applause.

Then she came closer to Reva Flynn. She picked her out from a sea of faces and tapped the stage with her cane.

Reva pointed, mouthing, "Me?"

Nox nodded and smiled once. "Yes, you."

Up Reva went on stage, to the chuckles of the gathered people. She stood and looked at the tall woman.

"Now what?"

"Pick a card, my dear," Nox said, and the pack rose in the air before the startled alchemist, moving on invisible magical threads.

Reva took a moment, chewed on her herbal stick, and then selected one.

"Keep hold of that card," the magician said. "Now pick four more, for a total of five."

The alchemist wondered what the trick was as she took more cards, one by one. She looked at them. It was interesting: they were all blank.

"What do you see?" Nox chuckled softly.

"Not a lot."

"Look again, Miss Flynn."

Each card had a face on it; each one depicted someone she knew. The ace, of course, was Kalon.

Nox Arcana tipped her hat and watched. Reva held up the card to put it in line with the magician's own face. She saw the resemblance between Kalon and the street mage.

"Bugger me," she whispered. "So alike."

The woman chuckled softly and tipped her hat once more. Then, with a wink and a snap of her fingers, she was gone. So were most of the cards; only one remained in the alchemist's hand. The crowd broke out in applause and cheered.

Kalon was the card she'd been left with. How odd.

In the distance, a man screamed, calling for the guard. The sound of booted feet followed, and people dressed in armor rattled up the street. They were followed by an angry-looking woman who had recently left her port for a new job in a bigger city.

Anna Kora, newly minted sergeant of the Wyrden city guard, was on her first day on the job as she ran past the alchemist.

"Excuse me!" Reva called. "I am a bit of a healer; will you need me?"

With a wave of her hand Anna simply signaled the woman to follow. She'd talk when they got to the scene. From that scream, it sounded like they might need someone who could help put people back together.

So, Reva ran after the other woman.

The screaming man's location was just outside a small alley off the main street. Frightened, he pointed into the alley, and Reva passed him one of her sticks. "Smoke this, it'll help."

He took it, lit it, and did as she said.

The alley was a charnel house, covered in blood, with a single body: a nobleman with two distinct puncture wounds where his eyes once were.

Anna Kora waited for the alchemist. "Anna Kora," she said. "Sergeant of the Wyrden guard."

Reva passed her a card and knelt in a cloud of smoke. "Reva Flynn, all on the card."

"Cause of death?" Anna said, noting the eyes.

"Massive trauma to the back of the head. The eyes were taken post death, and the body was moved here from the murder site in another alley." Reva noted the trail of blood that led off to the shadows beyond the tight street.

Smoke trailed up from under her hat.

"Are you available to perform the autopsy?" the sergeant asked, hopefully. She'd rather have someone good look into this. This Reva seemed just the ticket.

"For you, lovely, yes."

"I, er, thank you."

"Don't mention it. Move the body carefully." Reva noted the pool of blood that was close to the edge of the street. "One moment."

She got up, went to it, looked down, and made a note of the color. Then, she froze.

The blood reflected, for a brief moment.

Eyes-within-eyes-within-eyes.

"Bugger," she said. "Rain check on that thing."

"What?"

"Got to go see a man about a demon!"

With that, the alchemist took off at a run. Her feet would carry her back to Arabella's mansion, back to the man they still called Fate's Hand. She didn't notice the card she had dropped on her flight.

Anna Kora sighed, and then picked up the playing card. A man's face she knew: Kalon Rhadon.

Her life turned full circle.

Fate tipped her hat.

It was not over.

She never lost the game.

ABOUT

THE AUTHOR

Darren W. Pearce is a British fantasy and sci-fi author, game designer who has worked in the industry since 2000.

He created and wrote the *Set Rising* RPG book for Suzerain, and crafted *Nocturne* for 13th Age. He's also a regular at the UK Games Expo. His work on the *Core Box 11* for the *Doctor Who* RPG won him a Gold Ennie in 2013. He won an Epic E-Book Award 2011 (Best Anthology) for his anthology work on *Bad A$$ Faeries 3*.

He's also worked on *Dragon Kings*, the spiritual successor to *Dark Sun* by Tim Brian Brown. Taking on the role of *13th Age* lead writer, and working on the core book. He was the lead writer on *Judge Dredd And the Worlds of 2000AD*, the RPG developed and published by En Publishing, including the *Strontium Dog* setting book - Darren has worked on numerous other IPs over the years, including the likes of *Doctor Who*, *Warhammer 40K*, *Carbon 2185*, and *Shadow of the Demon Lord* for Robert Schwalb.

Darren's other work includes various short stories, and published books outside of the RPG space.